LAUNCH SOMETHING!

BAE MYUNG-HOON

Translated by Stella Kim

Honford
Star

This translation first published by Honford Star 2022

Honford Star Ltd.
Profolk, Bank Chambers
Market Place
Stockport
SK1 1AR
honfordstar.com

ISBN (paperback): 978-1-7398225-4-5
ISBN (ebook): 978-1-7398225-5-2
A catalogue record for this book is available from the
British Library.

Printed and bound by Short Run Press Ltd.
Cover illustration by Jisu Choi
Typeset by Honford Star

This book is published with the support of the
Literature Translation Institute of Korea (LTI Korea).

3 5 7 9 10 8 6 4 2

CONTENTS ·

Characters		5
1.	Launch Something!	11
2.	Trash Talk	49
3.	Space Force Honor Guard	89
4.	Romantic Relationship Occurrence Report	123
5.	Strict but Flexible	163
6.	Throwing Away a Stuffed Bear	201
7.	Peace-Preserving Design	239
8.	The Logic of the Jungle and the Logic of Civilization	283
9.	The Front Line of Humanity	317
Author's Note		361

Characters

Master Sergeant Han Summin, Launch Base Operations Division
Han Summin is an ace remote pilot. She dreamed of becoming a
Space Force pilot as a child but mistakenly enrolled at the Aerospace High School, the training school for future non-commissioned officers, instead of the Space Force Academy. However,
recognized for her outstanding skills in high school, she received
exceptional support from the then principal, Gu Yemin. Summin
has a soft spot for mint chocolate and is a fan of Oste.

Gu Yemin, Chief of Staff, ROK Space Force
The highest-ranking officer of the Space Force, Gu Yemin pos-
sesses intellectual dexterity, cool-headed decisiveness, and
natural charisma. Determined to make the launch base the Space
Force's de facto headquarters to escape the interference of the
Ministry of Defense, she regularly dispatches spacenauts from
the Space Force headquarters to the launch base. Formerly, she
served as the principal of the Aerospace High School.

Captain Um Jonghyun, Intelligence Department

Um Jonghyun is a special appointee and officer in charge of origami interpretation (analysis) with a degree from a prominent university abroad. He salutes air conditioners on hot days. His duties involve reverse engineering the shape of satellites in the orbits of Earth and Mars. Putting his academic major to practical use, he makes a significant contribution to resolving the case of who transmitted firearm data to the interplanetary shuttle.

Weather Specialist Suh Ga-ul, Weather Agency

There are numerous strange tasks you are assigned to do when you work for the ROK Space Force's Weather Agency. One example is forecasting the weather on the day of a rocket launch a month in advance. But that's nothing to Suh Ga-ul—she says the weather will be good and, when the day comes, announces that she'll make an effort to get a southeasterly wind going. A wiz at giving people nicknames, she is the life of the party at the Space Force.

Major Park Soojin, Acting Inspector General

Park Soojin is the launch base's Inspector General and joined the ROK Space Force's Internal Review Department to learn the necessary skills for space accident investigations. Unfortunately, until now she had only been playing detective as there were no spacecrafts, and therefore, no accidents. She is considered kind, for the most part. She befriends Kim Eunkyung through their frequent encounters on the rooftop of the launch base main building, and she is also the first to learn about Eunkyung's teddy bear.

Captain Park Kugyong, Public Relations Corps

There is no sound in space, like a silent movie, but Kugyong readily assumes the role of a silent film narrator in order to promote the Space Force. With an outgoing, cheery personality, he gets along with everyone.

Secretary Kim Eunkyung, Planet Management Corps
Mars completes one rotation every 24 hours and 30 minutes or so in Earth time. As a result, Eunkyung's work hours as the officer in charge of communication with the Martian settlement are delayed by half an hour every day. She occasionally suffers from hallucinations featuring a teddy bear her ex-boyfriend gave her. She frequently runs into Park Soojin on the rooftop of the launch base main building.

Private Lee Ja-un (Oste), Public Relations Corps
Lee Ja-un is a member of K-pop boyband B Density and is currently doing his mandatory military service. Having dreamed of serving in the Space Force, he voluntarily enlisted despite a longer service period than other military branches. He hosts the Space Force radio show *Let's Raise the Density!*

Major General Lee Jongro, Vice-Minister of Mars
AKA Mars Governor-General. Lee Jongro has had great success as an officer, suppressing the Mars Rebellion. Cold, cruel, and full of ambition, he is a one-of-a-kind in the Space Force. He chooses to return to Earth for reasons no one can fathom, creating a stir in the otherwise peaceful Space Force.

LAUNCH SOMETHING!

Chapter One

Launch Something!

There cannot be two suns in the sky, but there were two suns in the sky that summer. One of them was shaped like Pac-Man.

As there were too many people who had no idea what Pac-Man was, the government and the media outlets often used the analogy of a pizza pie. A whole pizza with a slice missing. A circle with a missing wedge. But since no pizza glowed with soft yellow light, many people still preferred to allude to the old arcade game character Pac-Man—the yellow circle with a piece cut out for a mouth that went around chomping and gobbling up yellow dots. In the government organizations and policy-making groups in which people in their fifties were considered young, Pac-Man was a better metaphor for the second sun than a pizza. In any event, it seemed unnecessary to choose one analogy over the other, as both the sales of a remake of the Pac-Man game and pizza consumption grew all throughout the summer.

The problem was not whether it was Pac-Man or pizza. The more significant issue was that this second sun snatched an extremely tiny portion of the original sun's rays that scattered into the universe and reflected it to Earth. There were probably many more problems resulting from the second sun, but one of them was this: on October 23, when people would typically be wearing long sleeves in nippy weather, the temperature in Seoul reached a high of thirty-two degrees Celsius.

On top of that, the second sun was growing bigger. The summer was going to be even longer than usual.

As soon as he stepped out of the car, Um Jonghyun, an intelligence analyst from the Intelligence Department of the Republic of Korea Space Force, began to sweat like a pig. Wearing a white shirt and a black jacket of the Space Force uniform, he seemed to be dressed for a funeral. The black tie certainly added to the mournful look. Had it not been for the badges, medals, the nameplate, and insignia that indicated that this was the official Space Force service uniform, he might have given off a solemn and somber vibe.

He tried to flap his unbuttoned jacket to fan himself a bit. It didn't help at all. The jacket's fabric was thick and unbreathable, and underneath, his sweat-sodden shirt stuck to his skin. He held up a folder to shield his face from the sun—the Republic of Korea Space Force logo on the front sparkled in the sunlight. It sparkled twice. Just as it was impossible to cover the sky with your hands, it was impossible to escape from the rays of two suns with just a single folder.

Jonghyun cut diagonally across the plaza. The ground was paved, so it wasn't a training field. However, it wasn't quite right to call it a plaza since civilians were restricted from using the area. The purpose of this place was a mystery, but the sound of footsteps resounded throughout the expanse. It was part of the Space Force headquarters, so perhaps it was meant to convey the emptiness of outer space. The small planets and constellations etched in the corners of the plaza seemed to support this notion. So he was crossing a plaza that encapsulated the universe, so to speak. The plaza was enclosed by roofed corridors like a European cloister. Stone roofs supported by stone pillars. Jonghyun glanced at the shade in the roofed corridors with envy but kept his eyes focused on his destination. Sweat poured down his face. On his shiny, polished shoes, two suns sparkled in turn. The tiny specks of sparkles embedded on his black jacket glimmered like distant stars.

Jonghyun stepped into the building and faced a pitch-dark lobby. It was the effect of having walked in from a very bright place, but for those who walked across an open plaza and into the building, such dark shade was a welcome relief. Jonghyun's face visibly relaxed.

On one side of the lobby, the chief of staff's aide-de-camp stood waiting, clad in the same uniform as Jonghyun. Recognizing Jonghyun, he quietly saluted. Instead of saluting him back, Jonghyun exhaled the breath he'd been holding and greeted the aide with his eyes. Then he looked to the ceiling where the air conditioner was installed and saluted it with the Space Force motto, "Ascension!"

The air conditioner mounted on the ceiling moved its flap in response. The spacenauts standing at the information desk let out a chortle. Jonghyun lowered his arm down by his side with control.

"They are waiting for you, sir," said the aide, rushing Jonghyun to join the meeting.

"I would love nothing more than to have three minutes to myself," Jonghyun grumbled.

"You are already very late, sir."

"It's because of this uniform. I took it out for the first time since being commissioned, and there were no badges or ribbons on it."

"You should not say that to them inside, sir."

"It's the main conference room, right? Third floor?"

"Follow me, sir."

The aide headed toward the elevator before hurriedly turning around and rushing over to the information desk. He held out his hand to one of the spacenauts standing on the other side of the desk. The spacenaut quickly took out a service cap and handed it to the aide. It was an officer's cap with a red band around the edge. With the cap in his hand, the aide strode over to the elevator.

He said to Jonghyun, "There is such a thing as a service cap in dress uniform, sir."

"Do I have to wear it?" asked Jonghyun as he buttoned up his jacket.

"Hold it by your side, sir."

"Do I have to walk in and salute? Should I say 'Ascension' too?"

"They are in the middle of a meeting, so just go in quietly. And when you make eye contact, salute without saying anything. And don't salute as you're walking either. Stop and salute. Just … you know, what seems appropriate."

"Is the conference room air-conditioned?"

"No, sir. It's the government policy. There's someone here from the Blue House."

Jonghyun frowned.

When he opened the door and walked inside, there were a lot of empty seats. He strode into the room without making eye contact, and when he reached a point within a reasonable distance from the chief of staff, he raised his head and met her eyes. Holding the folder and his cap under his left arm, he stopped short and gave a salute. Chief of Staff Gu Yemin waved her left hand in the air in response.

Blackout curtains were draped over the windows in the main conference room. A portion of the windows was left uncurtained to let the light in, and only the sky and the woods could be seen outside. There were three people in the meeting: the chief of staff, who was clad in the field uniform of a Space Force t-shirt with insignia; a middle-aged man in a suit; and a male colonel in dress Air Force uniform.

The voices of the three people filled the entire room. Jonghyun felt cooled sweat beading on his forehead again. It did seem that the room wasn't being air-conditioned. When the conversation came to a short lull, Gu Yemin pulled Jonghyun into the discussion.

"This is an intelligence analyst in our intelligence service." She introduced Jonghyun to the two other men in the room. "Captain Um, this is the secretary of security at the Blue House."

The introduction went smoothly without a single wasted second, almost as though Jonghyun was being led to hop into a long, rhythmically swinging jump rope. Jonghyun felt like he needed to jump otherwise he'd trip over the rope, disappointing everyone.

"Tell him about what you briefed me yesterday," Gu Yemin nudged Jonghyun. "Take a seat."

The chief of staff of the Space Force was not someone who needed help explaining what she'd heard the day before. She not only understood everything she'd heard even just once but could also organize and summarize the information she'd heard and explain it with all the necessary details. The fact that she'd waited for Jonghyun to give a briefing suggested that she wanted to show something to the other two people in the meeting. Perhaps even her long silver hair tied in a ponytail was a calculated style.

Jonghyun placed the service cap and the folder on the table and spoke.

"Captain Um Jonghyun, in charge of analysis at the Intelligence Department of the Space Force, sir."

"He is our origami expert," added the chief of staff.

At her words, the secretary of security widened his eyes.

"Origami?"

The chief of staff smiled and answered, "Due to the lack of budget, we fold spaceships out of paper. In the past, the Air Force also used to fold planes and fly them, but now that they have a lot of money, they can make the planes out of metal. Isn't that true?"

The Air Force colonel roared a laugh. It was sharp and short. The secretary of security looked at Jonghyun with eyes devoid of humor. The jump rope had come around full circle, and it was Jonghyun's turn again. Jonghyun studied the face of his superior, whom he admired and almost revered. She didn't meet his eyes, but her face was relaxed. It was a signal that he shouldn't be worried. *I've got this meeting under my thumb, so nothing you do will ruin it,* she seemed to say. Jonghyun exhaled with a hint of a smile.

He said, "Should I continue with the briefing, sir?"

"Go ahead," the secretary answered.

"Thank you, Mr. Secretary, sir. Last Friday night, the Allied Space Force Command's Data and Intelligence Bureau shared the blueprint for Pac-Man with the space forces of all twenty-nine member states. It was Friday morning ASF Command local time. The blueprint was raw data without interpretation, and the ASF Command did not respond to any questions. So each country began to interpret the data on its own. We assume that there are eleven countries that are capable of interpreting the data."

"Fortunately, we are one of them," Gu Yemin interrupted. Her voice sounded indifferent, almost like a footnote.

After a quick nod, Jonghyun continued, "The shared data was thirty-three pages of blueprints, and these three pages of the two-dimensional plan seem to be the most important. They contain the images that show the operating principle of Pac-Man's key components."

Jonghyun opened the folder. Inside was a yellow manila envelope with the flap tied closed by a string.

With a nod from Gu Yemin, Jonghyun untied the string and opened the envelope. He took out its contents and placed them on the table. It was a four-page document, and the ROK Space Force cover was stamped with the word "SECRET" at the top and the bottom. It was also marked with "1/1," meaning that this was the only copy of the document.

Jonghyun flipped open the cover page and showed the secretary of security a portion of the blueprint. It was an image of a trapezoid, made up of three equilateral triangles.

He explained, "It consists of a repeating sequence of this shape. The size of a single triangle is about as big as the palm of your hand. The thickness is, well, it is extremely thin. Like a thin film. It seems that these triangles are unfolded one by one, gradually increasing the overall size of the film. Pole-like structures stretch outward radially from the center of the spacecraft, and these triangles fill the space between the poles. We believe that there is about a five-meter-thick prism made up of thousands of these triangles. And that pile is gradually unfolding, triangle by triangle."

"In that Pac-Man?" the Secretary asked.

"Yes, sir."

"And you've observed this? Using a telescope?"

"No, sir. The things we astronomically observed are the main body of the spacecraft, the first pole-like structure extending from the body, the size of the film that acts like a mirror reflecting the sunlight, and the shape and speed in which the film is expanding its size. We have discovered the rest using reverse engineering."

"You're saying that you've worked out how this thing was made from what's up there now? With just that amount of observational data?"

"Yes, sir," Jonghyun answered. "Astronomy is a field that involves a lot of inferences and deductions from a tiny observed difference, so this is nothing special. On a math test, when you have a multiple-choice question, sometimes it is faster to test out the answer choices than to come up with one from scratch. We have used that specific method. We took all the alternatives of space structure expansion techniques that have been developed by humanity, tested each one by simulating how a structure shaped like that Pac-Man sun would expand and at what speed, and compared the simulation results to the observed data. From that, we found one structure expansion technique that roughly corresponds to what is happening up there, and that is the paper-folding technique. Although it's not paper that is being unfolded or folded. In all, we could call this origami."

At this point, Gu Yemin chimed in again with the same indifferent voice, as if to indicate that she was merely providing relevant extra information rather than taking over the conversation.

She said, "When we launch something into space, we often convert weight into money, don't we? However much per ton, or per kilogram. But volume is also money. If something takes up too much space, we can't take it on the spaceship. So we fold it. If we can fold something extremely small and later unfold it to make it big, that's perfect. They call this origami engineering, and it's one of the key techniques in space engineering. No one likes to share their technologies, but luckily Captain Um Jonghyun here, whom we recruited last year, turned out to be an expert with a doctorate in the field and seven years of research experience. Well, that wasn't just a stroke of luck."

The Air Force colonel asked, "A doctor with seven years of experience? But he's just a captain?"

"Major select," replied Gu Yemin. "Captain Um, continue."

Major select meant that he was about to be promoted and could therefore take on the duties of a major, but this was the first time Jonghyun was hearing about it. Yet his face didn't betray his thoughts as he continued the briefing.

"This image on the next page shows how this triangular prism consisting of triangles is unfolded. The page after that shows how the unfolded parts are joined. These are all hypotheses, but they have been proven to a considerable degree."

The Secretary of Security asked, "Wait, who is doing the unfolding? Is it done through a robotic arm?"

"Oh, it unfolds automatically, sir," answered Jonghyun. Then, carefully removing a thin piece of tinfoil that was tucked inside a pocket on the folder, he said, "This would be helpful as a reference. It is a kind of magic trick that people in our discipline show to others who are unfamiliar with this field of study."

It was a thin piece of tinfoil in the shape of a square, with each side about five centimeters long. What looked like an image of a circuit board was printed on top, but it was inconspicuous unless you looked very closely.

Jonghyun explained, "Some people mistake it for a gum wrapper, but I would get into trouble if I just crumpled it up and threw it out. This is a rather expensive robot."

Holding a corner of the tinfoil between his thumb and forefinger, Jonghyun stood up and walked over toward the window. Then he placed it on the table where the sunlight that came through the gap between the curtains pooled. Jonghyun cracked open a window to have the sunlight shine directly on the tinfoil rather than through the windowpane.

About thirty seconds passed. Suddenly, the tinfoil twitched. The two guests' eyes sparkled simultaneously. There was no look of surprise on Gu Yemin's face—she seemed to have seen it before—but her eyes shone with intrigue.

In the next moment, the tinfoil folded itself, twitching with some kind of power that seemed to have surpassed a critical point. It wasn't a complex shape—with the corners of the square folded down to points like legs, it looked like a simple spider with four legs.

The tinfoil robot began to walk on the table. It didn't have any joints, but it had no trouble walking stiffly since it was made of light material. It certainly walked like a paper robot.

After looking at it for about thirty more seconds, Jonghyun scrunched up the robot. Stuffing what was now nothing more than a gum wrapper into his pocket, he said, "It is expensive but works only once. And it is a secret. As you have just seen, it folds itself. From the folding mechanism to the operating mechanism, generator, basic communication device, and simple artificial intelligence technology, all the necessary data is printed on it. Just now, the sunlight generated micropower to power the circuit, and the robot folded its legs on its own to operate itself as programmed. For the time being, we use this robot for magic tricks, but considering that it can be mass-produced, we could use it in many fields. In any event, the triangles that make up Pac-Man seem to be able to unfold on their own without command. It means that there is no point in performing radio tracking. And as I have explained, the triangles are only about as thick as a thin film, and therefore don't really function as a mirror. The reflectivity of the sunlight would not be very high. I believe that the unfolded triangles only work as a frame, and some kind of chemical is coated over them once they are unfolded."

"Sounds like a complex mechanism," said the secretary of security.

"It is complex and elaborate. It is too sophisticated to say that it was executed on an impulse. It must have been tested dozens of times. Gone through innumerable simulations. It is obvious that large-scale research has been conducted, and it is unlikely that there are a large number of research personnel capable of such activities. It seems that the Allied Space Force is conducting an investigation based on this reasoning. Information on the investigation process is not currently being shared, but there is a high likelihood that this is the case, sir."

"I see," the secretary of security answered. "Well, then, everyone's been curious about this, and I've personally been wondering as well. What is that section that corresponds to the Pac-Man's mouth? The missing slice?"

Jonghyun answered, "It seems to be a malfunction rather than an intentional design. The triangles have not been properly unfolded in that section, and actually, that was how we were able to confirm the analytical results. Because the malfunctioning triangles were not fully unfolded but still coated, it gave us an opportunity to examine the process. An entire block is first unfolded and then coated, and therefore it would have been difficult to learn the mechanism behind Pac-Man had it not stopped in the process."

When Jonghyun finished his last sentence, the chief of staff chimed in again. This time Gu Yemin's voice was full of life, as if she'd decided to stop footnoting his briefing and take over.

"That malfunctioning part is its weakness. Without a complete form, the structure's durability is bound to be weakened. The attack will be carried out in a way where that portion can be effectively targeted."

"Our Space Force is going to attack?" asked the secretary of security in surprise.

Lazily, Gu Yemin looked at the secretary of security and replied in a calm voice, "The United States will probably do it through the Allied Space Force. We don't even have a missile to launch as of yet. As I've said before, we can only fold spaceships with paper, so we won't get that kind of money, no matter how hard I squeeze. We can, however, purchase as much paper as we want."

"I understand your situation. We've seriously discussed the matter at the State Council meeting. I can't guarantee the results, but I believe that you will finally be hearing the first good news about funding at some point."

At the secretary of security's words, Chief of Staff Gu Yemin answered in a sincere voice, "I'm always looking forward to such developments. It's about time it happened. It's been about time for a long while now."

"I know you must have heard this often, but I believe that now is finally the time."

LAUNCH SOMETHING!

"You think so? From my perspective, I don't think it's anything we should be taking too seriously in the Space Force. It'll be another empty promise. It doesn't ring true in regards to the Space Force, at least. I imagine the Air Force would consider a well-funded Space Force to be a looming crisis. Isn't that right, Colonel Kim?"

"Surely not, ma'am," the Air Force colonel who had been listening to the conversation responded without missing a beat. He seemed skilled in jump roping.

The chief of staff quickly turned her attention to the secretary of security and said, "Let's say that's not the case for the Air Force then. Anyway, I agree—I wouldn't want anything to come between our two organizations. But Mr. Secretary, now that you've heard our briefing, to what do I owe this discreet visit? Oh, Captain Um, good work. You're dismissed."

Jonghyun got up and pushed his chair in before gathering the documents he'd laid out on the table. Then he waited for the right time to hop out of the jump rope. Gu Yemin continued her conversation with the two guests without looking at Jonghyun. That was his cue. Jonghyun quickly turned around and headed to the door at the far side of the room.

Murmuring voices filled the main conference room. If the Space Force tried to express its identity in the design of this conference room by imitating outer space, they had indeed failed because sound doesn't travel in space.

The three people were deep in conversation when Jonghyun arrived at the far door and reached for the door handle. So Jonghyun was able to hear them say:

"The time is ripe. However, you would need an opportunity."

The voice belonged to the secretary of security.

The chief of staff then asked, "An opportunity? Do we have

to wait until one comes up, or are you talking about something that can be arranged?"

"I didn't come here to say that you should wait with an open mouth for grapes to fall in. The Blue House is saying, what if you launch something first?"

"Something? Anything? Is this the president's idea?"

"It's the Blue House's position."

"I'm unclear as to what you mean. It can't be something the Blue House building itself thought of. Launch something? With what we have right now, we won't even be able to reach that Pac-Man or pizza or whatever."

"That's not an issue."

"Are you certain?"

Jonghyun slipped out of the conference room and closed the door. The chilly air that permeated the hallway touched the nape of his neck. Relief spread across his face as he turned away from the door. The chief of staff's aide, who had been waiting in the hallway, approached Jonghyun with quiet footsteps.

"How was it, sir?"

Jonghyun held out the service cap toward him and answered, "Hot. And it looks like something interesting is going to happen."

"Something interesting?"

"Obviously, it's confidential," Jonghyun replied. "Oh yeah, and since when have I been a major select?"

One afternoon several days later, Jonghyun drove his car toward the Space Force launch base. Behind the wheel, his face exuded boredom. He had been unable to speed along for several minutes now.

A truck blocked the view ahead of him as it slowly cruised

the road. There were five or six cars behind Jonghyun who were in the same boat as him. A cow was loaded on the back of the truck—its eyes looked sad and resigned.

"It probably just looks like that, no?" Jonghyun asked aloud. "I know nothing about cow faces, but I'm sure it's nothing. It's just probably moving to a different cowshed."

Both of his hands were on the wheel. Instead of the Space Force uniform, he wore a t-shirt that revealed his soft, white arms. He kept on drumming the steering wheel with his right forefinger, unable to hide his impatience. On the winding two-lane mountain road, he'd tried to overtake the truck several times, but every time cars came at him from the other direction. It was the same for all the other cars behind him as well.

"It looks healthy, so it should be OK, right?" said Park Kugyong, who was sitting in the passenger seat. "It looks young, but I honestly can't tell how old it is."

Also clad in t-shirt and shorts, Kugyong looked like someone who was far from ever being in a military uniform.

"Honestly, you're not even that good at telling how old people are either, are you?" asked Jonghyun.

"Is age that important? People are just people."

"That's true, but if you're working in the Public Relations Corps, isn't it good to have the ability to distinguish between human beings at least? There must be some kind of sales involved in your work."

Finally, Jonghyun found an opportunity to pass the truck. As he did, Kugyong glanced at the truck driver's face. The man looked neither apologetic nor brazen. He seemed as though nothing out of the ordinary was happening.

With the cow out of their sight, their conversation ended as well. They drove in silence for a long time until a four-lane road appeared. There wasn't a lot of traffic in this section, so Jonghyun sped up. The road was spotted with occasional military facilities, such as barricades and checkpoints, and it was flanked by guardrails on both sides, but no barrier marked the center of the road. There were signs: NO IDLING, ROAD CLOSED IN EMERGENCY, and MILITARY VEHICLES TAKE ABSOLUTE PRECEDENCE.

Jonghyun asked Kugyong, "That road sign, that means in case of emergency, a military vehicle carrying something huge could take up all four lanes of the road. But does something like that ever happen?"

"I doubt it," Kugyong answered.

"Right?"

"We won't be launching anything from our launch base, and if that ever happens, they'll get it here by ship. The sign means that we'll be transporting something via land if the seaway gets blocked or something goes awry, but we don't even have a propulsion system big enough to launch something that would take up four lanes. It's probably just there to mark the territory."

"Like we're showing people that we *can* do something tremendous?"

"Exactly," Kugyong said. "And having the surrounding roads like this is like a tacit sign that says, 'Up to this part is our territory.' But Captain Um, do you think we'll actually launch something next week?"

The road stretched far in a straight line like a runway. With no need to change lanes or stop for traffic, they only had to stay on and keep going.

Jonghyun answered, "It sounded like they are going to launch something, whatever that may be."

"Is it possible?"

"I don't really know since I'm pretty new here. You'd know. You've been here far longer."

"Yeah, I suppose. I guess it can happen. But launch anything? Launching a rocket is not like getting something from a vending machine."

"Looks like the chief of staff is intent on doing it. And in my opinion there's no harm in doing a launch. Wouldn't this be a good opportunity for the Public Relations Corps? It's good for us to make some kind of a move when the time is ripe."

"It would be an opportunity. If it works out, that is. If it doesn't go well, then it's going to be a real pain. Imagine having all the cameras there to shoot a launch and then, it blows up in the air."

"I wonder if it'd be like broadcasting the Olympics," said Jonghyun. "You know, saying that such and such athlete is bound to win the gold medal, and then when he loses in the semi-finals or something, they switch to some other game even before the athletes shake hands."

Kugyong answered, "We'd be lucky if that happens."

"You mean they'd keep on covering the launch even after it fails?"

"It's like watching a fire. The most interesting things in the world to watch are fights and fires, so why would the reporters not air that? And as a captain in the Public Relations Corps, guess who has to work to death to try and stop such scenario from happening."

"Really?" asked Jonghyun. "I wonder why the chief of staff is trying to go ahead with it then. We're not even prepared."

"She's taking a risk," Kugyong said thoughtfully. "In *On War*, Clausewitz said that a soldier is a risk-taker who likes to gamble. The public opinion looks pretty good about increasing the budget for the Space Force right now. They're saying that this is the first time things are looking this good. You know that the government doesn't take the Space Force seriously as part of the armed forces. We're more like the Korean branch of an international organization to them. Like development assistance payments. We do pay a decent share of the Allied Space Force expenditure, and we couldn't *not* have an organization to deal with the contributions, and so they were forced to create the Space Force—was what it felt like. But when the elections used to roll around, everyone from presidential candidates to provincial assembly candidates used to pledge that they'd cut the size of the Space Force. But now it's the opposite."

"Is it because it's too hot?"

"Of course it's because it's too hot. And you can see the reason why right up there. It looks like it's laughing at us with its mouth open."

"And on top of that, it's getting bigger," Jonghyun added.

Kugyong continued, "It's late October, but we're still wearing short sleeves. People are annoyed. You know, Clausewitz also said that those who are the most barbarously violent are not the soldiers but the public. Right now, everyone's obsessed with killing that thing in the air, and if we fan the flame just right, we might be able to raise the status of the Space Force. You can't see New York from here in Korea, but you can see the moon. So in a way, the moon is closer to us than New York. But, you know that this is the kind of quotable content that you in the Intelligence Department should be giving me, not the other way around, right? Please settle in and carve out your place here, and be a great source for us."

"Oh, is that how it is?"

"It's just my hope," said Kugyong. "Usually, when we try to write up something for the public, the Intelligence Department just scratches everything out with a red pen. But let's turn this relationship into a mutually beneficial one. What would we get out of fighting among ourselves anyway?"

The car was now racing along a bridge that stretched over the sea and onto an island. It was a two-way, four-lane bridge just like the road they'd driven along, but theirs was the only car that was crossing.

The car stopped at the first traffic light upon entering the island. It was by a town. There was a bus stop about ten meters from the crosswalk, and a spacenaut clad in the semi-formal Space Force uniform was standing by the bus stop sign.

"Must be heading back to the base," said Jonghyun. "Should we give him a ride?"

Kugyong shook his head and said, "He'll be fine since the buses are still running. It's already pretty terrible having to return to the base. And it'll be a drag to head back with us."

"That's true."

There was no need to stop at the next intersection, as there was enough time for Jonghyun to cruise through before the light changed. But Kugyong suddenly sat up and started yelling at Jonghyun to stop the car, startling Jonghyun enough for him to swerve into the other lane.

"She's a weather specialist at the Weather Agency, that person over there," said Kugyong. "She still must not have gotten a car. I don't know how she thought to come to this place without a car. We can give her a ride, right?"

When the car stopped, the weather specialist recognized Kugyong. When Kugyong gestured at her to get into the car, she got in and instantly started chatting away.

"Captain Park Cooking! Have you been summoned too? Oh, I don't think I've met the driver. Thank you for giving me a ride."

"Don't call me that," said Kugyong.

"It's an affectionate nickname. Park Kugyong sounds like Park Cooking. Anyway, nice to meet you, sir. My name is SoCal!"

Not quite understanding what she said, Jonghyun hesitated, and Kugyong chimed in, "She means Suh Ga-ul. Now she even says her own name like that. Strange, right? She's a civilian worker for the Weather Agency at the Space Force headquarters. Looks like you two haven't met. And from what she just said, it sounds like she's been summoned to the launch base because of next week's launch. This, here, is Captain Um Jonghyun from the Intelligence Department. He's a specially appointed elite officer who went to school overseas."

"Oh, him!" exclaimed Ga-ul. "The one who got parachuted in without ever having to actually pull the strings of a parachute in basic training! Oh, I mean, I'm sorry, sir. I saw you on the news. Never in person though. At HQ you must not come to the mess hall for meals either. You shouldn't pay too much attention to the rumors."

Kugyong turned to Jonghyun and said, "You can just leave her here. No one will say anything."

"But you won't, right?" Ga-ul asked as she buckled herself into the backseat. "I did get abandoned here. I got a ride from Seoul with Shoojeans, but then she dropped me off here saying that she wasn't going all the way to the base. She told me to grab a cab or the shuttle. Oh, Shoojeans is Park Soojin. She's a funny lady who works at the Internal Review Department. She's nice but oddly not all that nice. People who don't want to live in the dorms on the base live in this town. Oh, this isn't your first trip to the base, is it? Well, we call this a town, but there's nothing around here, as you can see. There's a supermarket at the far back of the town somewhere. But anyway, if you abandon me here too, it'll be a tragedy. I was waiting for the bus for over twenty minutes."

Right then, Kugyong interrupted her, determined to stop her from rambling on. The timing was perfect, as expected of a public relations officer.

"Are you planning to stay in the dorm?"

"I should, shouldn't I? The busiest streets in town are in the base. Plus, the security's great. I'm not much of a country girl."

The car started racing again. After a little while, another bridge appeared before them. It was higher than the previous bridge, making it possible for big ships like cruise or cargo ships to pass under. And it had a great view—the spectacular scenery made even those who regularly traveled the area turn their heads and look out the window.

In the sky, the second sun was casting a soft light toward the Earth. A white half-moon hung farther up in the sky.

"Even until last year, it used to be dark around this time, but now it's too bright," said Kugyong.

For the first time since they picked up Ga-ul, Jonghyun spoke to her.

"I have a question about that second sun. Is it really hot?"

Ga-ul pulled herself closer to Jonghyun. She said, "Well, it's hot but not as hot as you'd think. But then, it did have a bigger impact on the climate than we'd expected. It's getting bigger, so the longer we let it be, the more problems it'll create."

"It's so hot here, but that thing's not as hot as we think?" asked Kugyong.

"The planet was already getting warmer," Ga-ul explained. "Global warming. It's not easy to say how much impact global warming has on climate change or how much impact Pac-Man has. But it's not that the mirrors are reflecting heat from the sun to the Earth's atmosphere, raising the Earth's temperature by that exact amount. What's actually happening is that the high-pressure system from the North Pacific decided to settle here in Korea instead of moving back to where it came from. That's how complicated meteorology is. But people completely forget about that. They're talking as though the Earth suddenly turned hot in early June."

"So we can't say that *that*'s the reason we don't have a fall this year?"

"Correct, sir, Captain Um. It's Captain Um, right? There were twelve days last year that could be called 'autumn' based on the traditional standards. That means we were Pac-Man last year. But you know what the funny thing is? Although people have spoken for decades about stopping global warming, it's been difficult to earmark the budget for it—for us here in Korea or in other powerful countries around the world. Then that Pac-Man appears, and suddenly the government is handing out money like an ATM. Isn't humanity amazing, in many ways?"

"That sounds like you're saying ..."

"That the people who shot that up into the sky are environmentalists? Not exactly, but the result is the same. I think it was a good thing. As long as we don't launch anything next week."

"Why's that?" asked Jonghyun.

Ga-ul answered, "Because of what a weather specialist is expected to do. Figuring out whether the weather will be good or not on the day the higher-ups decide to make a launch. But the weather forecast model has become a mess this year. All the academic papers on meteorology have become ancient meteorology. They're not right anymore. None of them are. Not for the typhoons, not for the rainy season. Well, they were often wrong even before, but anyway. It's like this. They pick a date for the

Space Force HQ sports day three months from now, and then the chief of staff asks the Weather Agency whether it'll rain on that day. But how would we know?"

"So then what do you do?" asked Jonghyun.

Once again, a storm of chatter rushed down on the two men.

"It doesn't rain for eighty percent of the year, so we just tell her that it's not going to rain, and then we wait. It's not like we can make the weather happen. Oh, and me, I majored in astronomy. Planetary meteorology. It's true that it's also meteorology. The Earth is a planet, after all. Though it's much too close for my liking. I can explain the meteorological changes that occur over the course of thirty million years or so, but I'm not confident in forecasting tomorrow's weather, yet here I am."

What followed was silence. A natural yet awkward silence among coworkers who don't have anything to say.

Like the cow truck driver, Kugyong was impassive. Jonghyun's face soon turned the same. Around the time they passed through the barricade at the entrance to the base, darkness had finally fallen outside.

The weekend passed, and Monday morning came. Jonghyun strolled toward the launch base main building, which stood on top of a hill overlooking the ocean. The spot would've been a perfect site for a fortress to defend against pirates in ancient times. Or had it not been the government that took an interest in this spot, a Buddhist temple might have been built there.

The main building wasn't far from the dorm, but many came to work by car. The S-shaped road meandered up the hill. Jonghyun cut across the serpentine road and walked up the stairs that led to the building. He was clad in semi-formal, short-sleeve uniform and loafers befitting an officer, instead of a Space Force field uniform t-shirt. Yet when he reached the top of the stairs, he looked nothing like an intelligence officer.

"Have you gone for a hike this morning, sir?"

People heading into the building from the parking lot recognized Jonghyun and asked him the same question, as though they were reading from a script. And they all responded to his reply the same way—with disinterest.

When he stepped into the entrance of the building, Park Kugyong from the Public Relations Corps came over and greeted him.

"You look tired."

"Tropical nights," said Jonghyun. "And I thought it was going to be cool here because it was by the sea."

"Well, they built the thing without giving any thought about ventilation. Don't you have a fan in your room?"

"Nope. Don't they have air conditioners here?"

"Oh no, air conditioning in the single occupant dormitory near November? Normally they cut it off when September rolls around. They did go easy on us this year since they are still air conditioning the offices. In fact, they might turn the heat on at night in late November. These tropical nights better stop before that happens."

"What? Why would they do that?"

"Because we're supposed to turn the heat on at night in late November. This is the military. What do you expect?"

"Common sense?"

"Ah, yeah, yeah. Are you going to do the exercises? Apparently we have to do the exercises before the morning briefings starting today."

"The Space Force freehand exercises? I don't even remember how to do them."

"What? It's only been a year and a half since you learned them. Well then, just sit back and relax. Now that I look at you, you're sweating like a pig. Have you gone for a hike this morning? Oh, oh, I see, I see. You must have missed the MAIN BUILDING IS FURTHER THAN IT APPEARS sign."

Jonghyun sat in the Operation Briefing Room to cool himself down, and a few moments later people filed in. There were chairs lined up on three sides of the room, while the middle of the room was empty. The side without chairs had a gigantic projection screen. When the beam projector was turned on, people took their seats by the walls. There were about forty people in various clothing, from t-shirts to camouflage field uniforms, maintenance uniforms, civilian blouses, and shirts. It was a meeting for important officers, and consistent with the gender ratio in the Space Force, a little less than half of the people were men.

There were six people in semi-formal uniform. Aside from an Air Force liaison officer who was there dispatched on an assignment and Jonghyun, the other four were from the Weather Agency.

"I heard the Weather Agency pulled an all-nighter."

Jonghyun heard someone whisper. Giggles escaped from one side of the room, and the Weather Agency people sitting across from them turned their heads toward the sound. In civilian clothing, Suh Ga-ul looked rather gaunt. The whispers continued.

"What do they do when they work overtime? Do they hold a ritual or something?"

"I don't know. It's not like they can make the weather happen."

"So then they come in to work on weekends and fret together?"

"Doesn't sharing worries lighten the stress load or something?"

A senior officer from the Launch Base Operations Division stood next to the screen and spoke with restraint. "We will begin the morning briefings. Starting today, the chief of staff will be in attendance via video. Please turn on the screen."

People's gazes all turned to the big screen covering the wall. Soon, the projector began to beam a huge image. At that moment, the people in attendance flinched. Looking out toward the people from the projector screen, Chief of Staff Gu Yemin noticed people's reactions and asked curiously, "What? Why are you all startled?"

People jumped once again. This time, it was because her voice was much too loud.

The director of the Orbit Operations Office calmly gestured at the spacenaut sitting by the projector to lower the volume.

On the screen, the chief of staff's face, filling up the entire screen on the wall, said, "Who set up the system? You have me in god mode again, don't you? I can hear my voice blare throughout the room even from over here. How should we do this? Should I come back a little later? Or can you fix the setting right away?"

Lieutenant Colonel Shim Jaesun, Director of the Orbit Operations Office, answered her question perfunctorily, "You can stay where you are, ma'am. There, please reduce the screen size."

"You've zoomed in on my face too? How big is my image on the screen?"

"We can only see your face, ma'am. We're all scared here, ma'am, so please stay still."

"You have my face filling up that entire wall? Hey, I see someone taking a picture with their cell phone."

"Oh, that's just for the Public Relations Corps' records. Don't worry about it, ma'am."

"But it's the Public Relations Corps, and I'm not wearing any makeup!"

Soon the chief of staff's face grew smaller. Bookcases appeared behind her shoulders, but they were still gigantic enough for everyone sitting in the room to find a book in their academic discipline. Now that the bookcases appeared in the background, the chief of staff's divine authority that had overwhelmed the entire room subsided, giving way to her usual intellectual face.

"You still look big like an Egyptian god, ma'am, but we'll begin now."

"Wait, Colonel Shim ... Well, never mind. Go ahead and begin. As long as I don't turn my head to the side, I won't look like the goddess Isis."

"According to the chief of staff's orders, we will begin with a briefing from the Weather Agency. Director of the Weather Agency?"

The entire room did look like something right out of an Egyptian relief. The giant goddess in glasses and the small people sitting around her. A picture where the important people are painted big while the less important are painted smaller. And the goddess occasionally opened her mouth to express her wishes.

After the briefing from the Weather Agency, the chief of staff said, "So it looks like the weather's not going to be too bad. No wind. And it would be better for it to be hot, at least until then?"

The director of the Weather Agency answered, "Yes, ma'am. Because the high-pressure system is creating a heat dome over the Korean Peninsula, the weather will be favorable."

"Great. And even the typhoons have bounced off."

The operations and technology briefings continued. Then at the end, the launch control officer offered up a comprehensive opinion on the launch.

"The conditions for the launch are favorable. Today's assessment is to go ahead with the launch."

With an impassive face, Gu Yemin placed her glasses on the table and said, "OK, great. Please do your best until the day of the launch. It seems that the Allied Space Force's launch date has been set as well, so unless the weather conditions worsen, I hope that the launch can be safely completed by Thursday, the launch day, or Friday, the backup day, at the latest. Let's do it right when it looks good instead of missing the perfect timing and ending up running around in a panic. I'm sorry that the date has been set out of the blue, but we are the Space Force. Let's not think that this is unreasonable, since we have to launch something when we are suddenly given an order. It is an order from the commander-in-chief, and the fate of the Space Force depends on it, so let's do our best. Oh, I see the Air Force liaison officer over there. The Air Force and the Space Force are closest partners, so I hope you understand what I meant just a little earlier about the fate of the Space Force depending on this launch. All right, that's all."

The chief of staff vanished from the screen. All together, people who had been sitting upright in their seats relaxed like balloon dolls leaking air. Suddenly, the briefing room was abuzz with chatter.

Everyone started to get up and leave. Park Kugyong grabbed people in the Development Corps and started asking, "So about that 'something.' The thing that'll be loaded onto the launch vehicle. What is it going to be?"

"We have no idea."

"It's going to be mounted today or tomorrow at the latest, isn't it?"

"It's coming this afternoon, or so I've heard. Once the inspection is done, we'll mount it tonight."

"Can't you tell from the data? They must have sent over the data at least."

"They'll send it over when it's time. We'll let you do an exclusive, so don't worry and just go and relax. If you're that curious, ask the Operations Division or HQ Transport Corps."

The launch day began with commotion early in the morning. Park Kugyong ran into Command Sergeant Major Jo Yeonjung at the entrance of the main building.

"My goodness," Sergeant Major Jo exclaimed. "I finally have a moment to catch my breath. It's the prime minister, prime minister."

Unable to understand what she meant, Kugyong asked, "What's going on?"

"Have they not contacted you guys in the PR Corps yet? The presidential helicopter's not coming. The prime minister's visiting instead. Go to the office and let them know."

Kugyong mumbled almost to himself, "Huh, I don't know if that's a good thing or not. We're doing all this to make it look like it's a big event, but that's kind of anticlimactic."

"That's true, but with all the chaos right now, even things that are bound to happen might not happen. It's best to do things quietly. It won't do us any good to have people be louder than the rocket itself. And it's a headache to have three helicopters in the air so early in the morning. It's better to have a car drive in quietly. Imagine having the president here. He would have to say something after the launch, and if the reporters are there, he would have to stay and answer questions. It'd be exhausting."

"Sure, well, if you say so, I suppose it is a good thing."

"Of course. Well, I'm off to do my regular job and go discipline some spacenauts that are probably dozing off right now."

Kugyong walked through the corridor and stepped into a room with the sign REPORTERS. Something seemed to be off in the room. Journalists sat complaining about having to come all the way to the base and not being allowed to cover the launch from a close distance. Sure enough, as soon as they recognized Kugyong, the reporters hurled the same grievances at him. Kugyong scratched his head. Right then, his cell phone rang. After checking his phone screen, he turned to the reporters.

"I'm here to tell you something. I just received final confirmation that the plans for a presidential visit have been switched to a prime ministerial visit."

Reporters jeered, but the booing was so much quieter than Kugyong had expected that he felt a chill run down his spine.

Stepping out of the room, Kugyong made a phone call. He had to take care of something that was even more troubling than the canceled presidential visit. He held the phone to his ear as he walked through the building corridor and into the yard outside.

"Well, the reporters are right. They're here, but now we've banned them from taking pictures during the launch. I mean, how could they have found out about that this late? If we'd known about it, we could've canceled the press coverage. Well, I suppose we couldn't have since it was the chief of staff's orders. Yes, I understand. I understand but ..."

He could see the launch area atop the hill in the distance. The rocket stood erect on the launch pad.

Kugyong spoke into the phone in a loud voice, "I'm looking at it from the outside now, and you can't really see it because it's dark. Can't we just let them take pictures? Sure, the camera might see more than the naked eye, but even then I don't think they'd be able to tell. Really? It looks the same to me. Really? You can tell? OK, yes, I got it, sir. I'll figure something out. And you'll send us the launch video taken from a decent angle? Yes, sir. Sure, you have to focus on the launch now. No, I won't call anymore, sir."

Kugyong hung up the phone and glowered at the launch pad. Weather Specialist Suh Ga-ul, who was passing by, noticed him and approached.

"Something not working out?" she asked.

"Oh, hey. Yeah, it's getting a bit troublesome. All of a sudden, we're not allowed to take pictures."

"Ah, they've prohibited photography? I heard that they'd mounted something strange. They're not allowing pictures even from a distance?"

"Apparently you can tell if you know what it is. Damn it. But you look good, SoCal. You haven't looked this cheery this past week. I'm guessing the ritual went well?"

"As you can see! The southeasterly wind is blowing! Of course, not the real southeasterly wind but the southeasterly wind in my heart."

Ga-ul shot her two hands up into the sky with a triumphant smile. There wasn't even a breeze to sway the starlight, which poured directly down onto the ground.

At her ludicrous remark, Kugyong let out a laugh and said, "Gosh, I extend my congratulations, oh, Wise One. The Weather Agency, or should I say the Magic Agency, has made a great achievement!"

"This is nothing. You should do your best too—then something will come about, one way or another."

Um Jonghyun opened the doors, which resembled those of a movie theater, and stepped into the Launch Control Room. There were no blackout curtains or seat tickets, but the inside looked something like a mid-sized cinema with stadium seating. The wall straight ahead of Jonghyun was covered by a brown curtain, and the aisle from the doors to the curtain was a gentle downward slope. On both sides of the aisle were seats akin to those in theaters.

Jonghyun quickly found an empty seat in the corner, and moments later, the prime minister and his staff entered the Launch Control Room. Everyone rose from their seats and turned to the back of the room. Chief of Staff Gu Yemin briskly walked over and greeted the prime minister and his staff. Numerous medals and badges dangled with moderation on her uniform, befitting the chief of staff's position.

Like the intelligence officer he was, Jonghyun studied people's faces with a furtive eye. Aside from the chief of staff, everyone else seemed a bit nervous. One person tossed his head from side to side as if to wake himself up. Only the chief of staff seemed relaxed and full of confidence.

"Wow, like there's nothing going on," someone whispered next to him. "She doesn't even look guilty even though she's going to launch something like *that* into space."

The voice belonged to Suh Ga-ul. Jonghyun held up his forefinger and signaled her to stop talking.

"She's a lionheart. A lionheart indeed," added Ga-ul before she fell silent.

After the greetings, people took their seats. The director of the Base Operations Division took on the role of master of ceremonies. He explained the basics about the launch and gave the order to begin.

The curtains opened, revealing a glass wall. On the other side of the glass wall was a stage where sound couldn't be heard. To be precise, sound from the other side of the glass wall could be heard by the audience, but not the other way around. Although this room where the observers were sitting was called the Launch Control Room, in fact the real Launch Control Room was up on that stage.

Large and small monitors filled an entire wall inside the Launch Control Room. Some screens showed the rocket, while others showed the path of the projectile. Another screen showed the status of the fuselage, and yet another screen transmitted the weather conditions in real-time. On the wall without any monitors hung the biggest Korean flag most people would ever see in their entire lives. The accompanying Allied Space Force flag was much smaller.

In front of the wall of monitors were desks. Each desk was equipped with an ordinary computer screen, keyboard, mouse, and other objects, including an ordinary corded phone. So aside from the three or four monitors displayed like a folding screen, the rest of the Launch Control Room looked like a typical office. On the kind of chairs that can be found in any workplace sat people who'd thrown on Space Force field uniform pants and t-shirts, wearing headsets and intently looking at the monitors.

As if they were simply continuing what they had been doing before the curtains were opened, no one even turned to glance at the audience. They were completely immersed in their work, as though the Launch Control Room inside the glass wall was the only part of the universe that existed and the seats on the other side of the glass weren't there at all.

Seeing someone on the stage chewing their fingernails and shaking their leg, Gu Yemin's face hardened for a moment but soon regained composure.

"There was a bit of confusion due to an unexpected change of the payload," she began, "but fortunately everything has been sorted out."

At her gentle voice, the prime minister sitting in the adjacent seat turned to look at her.

"That's what I heard. Thank you for all your efforts."

"As you and the defense minister know, the importance of this operation lies in the timing of the launch itself rather than the payload. We had a bit of difficulty getting a payload that was ready."

"I'm sure. I don't believe that it would've been easy to put this together at the sudden command to launch something. In any event, I hope that this launch comes to a safe completion."

While the prime minister answered, the defense minister's face darkened. He searched the screens in front of him and fixed his gaze on one. It was the screen showing the top of the rocket—the payload.

It was finally time. Looking at the people within the glass wall, it was possible to tell that the launch was about to happen. Each section performed its checks in order, and the launch control officer sent the final signal. After finishing his role, the launch control officer leaned back into his seat. Then another person sat up erect in his seat. It was the flight control officer.

"One minute to launch. The countdown will begin now."

A heavy silence fell among the audience. No one stirred. The defense minister turned to the chief of staff, who was sitting on the other side of the prime minister, as if to say something but gave up under the silence. Twenty seconds into the countdown, the defense minister suddenly leaned forward and quietly asked, "Chief Gu, is that what I think it is?"

Gu Yemin didn't answer him. She didn't even glance in his

direction. The screen in front of them showed a close-up of the lower part of the projectile.

The last fifteen-second countdown began. The number grew smaller by one. About a second after "zero," the rocket on the screen began to spout fire.

The flames soon created an enormous amount of steam. The launch pad was enveloped in clouds. But the camera located immediately below the launch pad showed a clear image of the rocket slowly lifting off.

The main screen on the front wall was switched to a view of the launch pad seen from afar. Through the rising clouds, the rocket shot up, with the sea and the island in the backdrop. Creating a trail of a long, vertical cloud that gave dimension and depth to the image, the rocket gradually sped up and soared into the sky. Some people in the seating area stood up and brought their hands up to their chest level to clap, but seeing that the people inside the glass wall were still tense, they quietly sat back down. Then, a thunderous roar swept over the launch base main building. The shock wave from the launch seemed to have reached them, seconds after the launch.

On the stage, people were still busy. Some sat with their eyes glued to the screens, while others reached for their phones.

"The first section has been safely discarded, and now we are waiting for the second section to be separated," Gu Yemin explained to the prime minister. "The orbit doesn't look bad. We still have to wait a little longer, but there shouldn't be any big trouble at this point."

The prime minister, who was a former academic, moved his eyes across several of the screens in front of him, diligently studying the images. Only when several people on the stage finally threw their hands into the air in relief did his face relax.

"Is it finished?" he asked.

Gu Yemin answered, "Yes, sir. Now you can clap."

The prime minister stood up from his seat, and others followed suit and began to clap. As it wasn't the first launch ever, or even the launch of a manned rocket, the shouts and cheers weren't particularly uproarious.

"Well, now, we have an early breakfast prepared," Gu Yemin spoke to the prime minister as though nothing special had happened. "Shall we?"

While people left the room, Jonghyun remained in his seat, looking at his phone. News articles were being posted online. They were about how, in line with the Allied Space Force's operation to destroy Pac-Man, the ROK Space Force had launched a military apparatus.

"The headlines make it sound like the ROK Space Force also shot a missile at Pac-Man, but when you read the articles, none of them say that exactly," said Ga-ul, who was reading the news on her phone like Jonghyun. "It looks like they don't know what we launched yet. The chief of staff is a formidable woman."

"Indeed. They told her to launch something, so she launched what she really wanted to launch into space."

"She's completed our long-standing project in one go. The key issue wasn't the Pac-Man sun but what we launched, right? But is that OK? A lot of people were against us launching that particular payload, wouldn't they feel tricked that we launched that?"

"Probably. But it'll be all right. The chief of staff has another gift for them. If they're concerned about approval ratings, they'll certainly be happy. The president already knew, it seems, seeing as how he canceled the visit."

"Oh, another gift? You probably won't tell me what it is even if I ask, would you? This is why they say you shouldn't befriend intelligence officers."

"Do people say that? Well, I'm sorry I can't tell you."

With that, Jonghyun fixed his gaze on his phone screen. As if in response, a message popped up.

"I should get going," he said. "I've got work to do now."

"Without even a cup of coffee?" Ga-ul asked. "It's a routine, you know. A shamanistic aspect of the Space Force. And it's not just the Weather Agency but all the other offices do it too. You have to get a cup of coffee before work if you're in the Space Force."

"I'll have it in my office."

"With the suspicious-looking people from the intelligence office? Well, as you wish. See you later then, whenever that may be."

After checking the text message, Captain Park Kugyong of the Public Relations Corps stepped into the press room. The reporters fired off another round of questions at him.

"Was that it?"

"Is it over already?"

"What was the payload?"

Rather than answering any questions about the day's launch, Kugyong calmly picked up the microphone and cleared his throat.

"Thank you for your patience, everyone. Details regarding today's rocket launch will be provided to you through a press release. However, beginning at five a.m., the head of the Space Force Public Relations Corps will personally brief you on the

Space Force Fighter Wing's operation to bomb the rear base of the Pac-Man. This was an unscheduled operation carried out in concert with the Allied Space Force, and we have just received news that the operation was recently completed. So we ask for your patience for a little longer. The coffee pots will be refilled, and sandwiches and kimbap will be provided as breakfast. I understand that you must all be very tired, but I would like to ask for your patience once again."

Around sunrise, Park Kugyong was finally able to leave the press room. Along one wall in the launch base main building, photographs of previous chiefs of staff hung in a line. At a glance, the arrangement made the portraits seem like they were images of dead people, but most were still alive.

Kugyong stood in front of the photograph at the very end, the portrait of the current chief of staff, Gu Yemin. She was one of the few female chiefs of staff and the only one with a bright smile on her face.

After standing glued to the spot for a long time, he called someone on his cellphone and said, "Things are pretty much done here now. It looks like the Ministry of Defense will take over now. I'm punching out for the day."

An announcement about the cancellation of the day's morning briefings flowed out of the PA system. Kugyong vacantly looked up at the speaker blasting the announcement, turned right around, and walked out of the building.

Chapter Two

Trash Talk

Major Park Soojin, Acting Inspector General of the Internal Review Department at the Space Force launch base, took the sandwich she had brought from home and headed up to the rooftop of the launch base main building. There was a DO NOT ENTER sign on the door to the rooftop, but it wasn't locked. As if she already knew that the door was unlocked, she opened it without hesitation. Stepping outside, Soojin noticed that someone else was on the rooftop. It was Kim Eunkyung, the planetary official who was on a long-term assignment from the Planet Management Corps at the Space Force headquarters.

Soojin was going to turn on her heels and close the door behind her, but before she could, her eyes met Eunkyung's. Reluctantly she stepped out on the rooftop.

"Just come," said Eunkyung. "There aren't a lot of places you could go to anyway."

Soojin was wearing pants and a long-sleeve blouse, but despite the heat she wasn't sweating a drop. Approaching

Eunkyung, Soojin said, "It seems that we're in a strange competition. Can't we compete over something worthwhile instead? Instead of a secret hiding spot on this secluded rooftop."

"Seriously. There's not even a bit of shade, so why climb all the way up here? I'm an oddball, but you're also something else, Major Park. I can't believe you're wearing that."

Eunkyung shook her head from side to side, unable to believe that someone would be wearing a long-sleeve, semi-formal uniform in this weather. Ignoring the remark about her clothes, Soojin responded to Eunkyung's earlier comment.

"There's not a single quiet spot around here, especially during mealtimes. Is Chief Gu Yemin going to send everyone from the Space Force headquarters over here to the launch base? The population density at the mess hall must already be the highest within ten miles of here."

"Looks like she's planning on sending more. It's easier out here. There's no need to mind other branches of the armed forces."

Soojin went and sat down on the bench next to Eunkyung and placed her sandwich bag between them. The plastic bag had misted, as if it had just been taken out of the refrigerator. Soojin waved half of her sandwich at Eunkyung, who picked up an empty bag by her side to indicate that she'd brought her own lunch.

Soojin asked, "There are probably far fewer people at the headquarters now. Don't you want to go back?"

"Trying to get rid of a competitor?" answered Eunkyung jokingly. "I've been thinking about wrapping up this long-term assignment, but the Communication Relay Station's here, which means I'd have to learn something new if I wanted to go back to the HQ. So I'm not sure yet."

"I see."

"And I don't have to walk on eggshells around people here. That's one strong advantage. That's why Chief Gu is stealthily trying to move the entire Space Force over here."

"Are the other forces really that high-handed at the headquarters?

"By the looks of it, yeah. To them, the Space Force is like some other country's military, you know. Even we say that we're like the Korean branch of an international organization, and it feels that way, at least from the whole atmosphere. The Space Force is the only armed service that frequently goes on overseas assignments, and the right to command is tied to the Allied Space Force, but despite all that the chief of staff does whatever she wants. And we don't listen to the Ministry of Defense for crap, making excuses about the line of command. Things were already iffy for us, but then Chief Gu went ahead and did that crazy thing, so things are probably awkward over there."

Soojin added, "And it seems like the Blue House is favoring us, which can't feel that great for the other military branches. Well, if she's going to keep on sending people here, they should at least build us more mess halls."

"That'd mean the worst restaurant within ten miles of here would grow bigger."

"Ah, I didn't think of that. The Space Force mess hall becoming a franchise."

With that, the conversation ended, and the two of them sat in silence for a long time, looking down toward a basketball court in the shade of the launch base main building. It was a decent one, with lines painted to mark the rectangular court and the baskets even had nets.

The court was abuzz with activity. A basketball game was going on, and people who had finished lunch stood around the court to watch.

Soojin gracelessly munched on her sandwich. Eunkyung turned to look at Soojin and let out a short chuckle.

After a while, Eunkyung said, "Those people down there, you know they're only defending in the shade?"

"Defending in the shade?" Soojin asked.

"The basketball court down there. Look closely and you'll see that they rarely leave the shade. They're only using about two-thirds of the court."

Soojin looked down at the court. What Eunkyung said was true. There were ten people playing, five on each team, and only one person was out in the sun.

"Huh, there really is just one person in the sun," said Soojin. "Let's see, it looks like Master Sergeant Han Summin. I'd have thought it's too hot to wear a ponytail in this sweltering heat, but she's held out all summer."

"She is kind of a superhuman," said Eunkyung. "I think you're the only one who can take her on. Someone who wears a winter dress uniform in this weather. What do you think? It's a rest day, so why don't you go down and show them what you got?"

"I'm short, so basketball, nah. I'll end up being a laughing-stock."

"Ah, well."

"The other team's all guys, so perhaps they're not blocking her on purpose."

"Maybe."

"And officially we're supposed to wear this uniform starting this month."

"Even Chief Gu who gave the order is probably wearing a t-shirt."

The conversation lulled once more. The hum of cicadas seemed to grow louder. Eunkyung looked up at the sky. On one side was the smirking Pac-Man sun.

"Why is the Allied Space Force still unable to take that down? Didn't they say it'd be a piece of cake?"

"I know," sighed Soojin. "Apparently something's broken and the Allied Space Force missile launch has been delayed. But where is this endless supply of cicadas coming from?"

"I'm not sure. Perhaps they woke up thinking that it was the summer already. But the United States' missile shouldn't be affected by the delayed launch, right? Don't they already have a missile or such up there in orbit?"

"Apparently that missile's broken, but who knows. It's probably universal that once you achieve a goal, your budget gets cut, so perhaps they're just dragging this out."

At Soojin's lackadaisical answer, Eunkyung gazed at her face.

Then she said, "You seem a bit disappointed about the successful launch last time?"

"Yeah, well. My life's still boring thanks to that success."

"Work starts piling up if something goes wrong, though. You want that?"

"I wasn't planning on doing this inspector general stuff forever," grumbled Soojin. "They said I needed to work at the Internal Review Department to do a hands-on investigation of actual space accidents, so I worked my butt off to come here, but there have been no accidents."

"And until now we've only been doing contract launches with foreign rockets, so we had no spacecraft to get into accidents. If an accident had occurred this time though, you could've gotten some real hands-on experience and prepared to start a new job in the private sector, right?"

Soojin took a small bite of the sandwich and said, "I didn't particularly wish for anything terrible to happen. But the higher-ups did say to try and launch anything we could, and the chief of staff readily agreed, which means that she must have realized there was enough justification for getting an increased budget even if the launch failed. Plus, it wasn't a manned rocket launch, nor was it planned for in advance, meaning this failure wouldn't have messed up the mid- to long-term plans. This was indeed a perfect opportunity in many ways."

"But if an accident did occur, everyone else would be busy out of their minds. Personally, I'm sorry you won't be able to put your talents to good use, but for others ..."

"I'm not so dumb that I'd go around complaining about it to other people," Soojin remarked.

"But you've been looking dejected, like withering grass."

"If I were grass, I would be doing well in this heat. It's just that there are too many people here. Which means I have that much more work to do. And now there are more people to hate me when I say that I've come from the Internal Review Department. Even though they won't ever have another generous IG like me."

"Maybe that's because people have just gotten used to seeing you around. Generally, you'd expect an IG to ambush you like a wild, roaring beast."

"No way."

Soojin looked down wordlessly. Eunkyung turned her head toward the mountains. The chirping of cicadas was coming from that direction. The sound, which was loud enough to interrupt conversations, seemed to have been amplified and resonated all around them. In between chirps, Eunkyung could hear the sound of the basketball bouncing.

Moments later, Soojin quietly exclaimed, "Oh! It went in!"

"What went in?" Eunkyung asked and followed Soojin's gaze to the basketball court. "You've never seen someone make a basket before?"

"I've never seen a three-point shot. Wow, I had no idea people actually made those."

"Oh, really?" asked Eunkyung. "Somebody scored a three-pointer?"

"Guess who it was. It was Master Sergeant Han Summin."

At Soojin's words, Eunkyung stretched her neck to look down at the court over the railings. Soojin joined her. They looked like they were searching for a replay screen.

"Nice, just nine points behind now!"

Someone shouted out loud. Han Summin glanced at the scoreboard. There wasn't a fancy electronic scoreboard, but one of those flip scoreboards you would see at a ping pong match sat on a desk by the court. Although, the scores ran higher than twenty-five, so it seemed the scoreboard wasn't just for ping pong.

DISPATCH TEAM 25, BASE TEAM 16.

Summin jogged backward to her side of the court. The other team's point guard approached her and held up one hand. He was sweating like a pig, face was crumpled up in a frown. He wrapped his left hand around the hem of his t-shirt, looking like he was pondering whether to take the shirt off or not.

Summin stopped backtracking. Then she sprinted three steps forward. She was quick. The other team's point guard started and stared, and at that moment the ball flew over from the other side of the court. Summin had stepped forward, expecting the ball to come that way, even before the ball was passed.

"Ah!" the point guard let out a startled shout.

Summin stretched out her hand. The ball bounced from her fingertips. The ball wasn't in her team's possession, but rather than following the ball, she ran toward the frontcourt. Everyone else flocked toward the ball. Both the offense and the defense ran at it, and the defending team took possession.

Summin was the only one standing in the frontcourt. When she reached toward the sky, the ball landed in her hand. It bounced once on the ground and slowed down as it rose to Summin's chest level. The three-point line was right in front of her toes. Summin raised her head to look at the basket. As soon as the basket came into view, she didn't even jump as she threw the ball into the air. Someone rushed over from behind her and stretched out their hand, but the ball was safely out of reach. As Summin had planned, it was on a stable trajectory.

The ball flew over the round rim and passed through the net with a satisfying *swoosh*. Something like cheers was heard from the audience, but they weren't planned cheers. Rather, they were exclamations that were somewhere between "Woah!" and "Wow!"

Returning to her defensive position, Summin glanced over at the scoreboard. DISPATCH TEAM 25, BASE TEAM 19. Now the scores were much closer.

Then she noticed her teammates' shoulders slump down all of a sudden. She turned to look at the other team and saw the point guard who'd lost the ball moments ago walking toward them, holding the ball at his side.

"Time-out!"

"Time-out in a pickup basketball game?" Technical Sergeant Jin, standing next to Summin, asked as if the idea was absurd. "We don't even have a referee."

"I just have something to discuss."

As the other team's point guard turned around, Technical Sergeant Jin quietly murmured, "Why is he so serious all the time? He is a bit strange. He's such a Martian."

After that, a player was assigned to guard Summin at all times. It was the excessively sweating point guard, the man who'd suddenly called for a time-out: Captain Lim Junggyu. He had been dispatched from the Strategy Agency at the Space Force headquarters. Everyone else played zone defense except for Captain Lim, who was guarding Summin man-to-man. Now Summin and Captain Lim were in the sunny part of the basketball court together.

The zone defense wasn't much of a defense, as most players leisurely walked around in the shade. But Captain Lim was different—only he seemed to be taking this game seriously. He did his best to mark Summin. Giving no regard to anything else, he closely followed Summin.

Summin didn't like how Captain Lim held up his two hands in an exaggerated manner whenever they were on the verge of physical contact. But what annoyed her even more was his constant talking. He didn't even make eye contact with Summin. He was always looking somewhere else, but he kept on muttering as though he were talking to himself, and the words grated on Summin's nerves.

"The ball won't come if I just keep following you around. And it'll be hard to score as many points if someone just stands in front while you're shooting. I wonder how many times you'll succeed. Sad I can't even test out my theory, what with the ball not coming anywhere near here."

Summin said nothing in response. She only went and stood out in the sun or outside the sidelines more often than before.

She glanced at the scoreboard again. DISPATCH TEAM 31, BASE TEAM 21. They were ten points behind again.

Acting Inspector General Park Soojin watched what was happening below with a concerned look.

"Looks like Lim Junggyu is harassing Han Summin," Soojin said.

Planetary Secretary Kim Eunkyung, who had been watching the game alongside her, responded, "Is he? Who is he? I don't think I've seen him before. Is he from the HQ? I feel like I should've seen him around still."

"Captain Lim Junggyu? He was at the Mars Settlement and came back a couple years ago."

"Was he involved in the uprising? Or was he with the suppression forces?"

"It's a bit iffy. Originally he was with the rebel forces, but he wasn't actively involved and ended up changing sides halfway. Only the higher-ups seem to know exactly what happened."

"Oh? A complicated man, I see," said Eunkyung. "Is that why he's so keen on running around the court alone?"

"Looks like it, right? But isn't that a bit menacing? It looks like he's specifically harassing her."

"Yeah? It's probably just trash talk, no?"

Indifferently, Soojin asked, "What's trash talk?"

"You know, athletes saying stuff to get on each other's nerves. You see it a lot in team sports. Players who aren't on camera suddenly grabbing each other by the collar in a scuffle. What's happening over there is what happens before that kind of scuffle. It happens all the time. Sergeant Han's the most delicate player in that crowd, and it would completely put her off her game if she loses her calm. So he's trying to provoke her."

"But he's far higher in rank. His military occupational specialty is strategy. I know we're just the Space Force, but Sergeant Han is also strategy, so you'd imagine that ranks would bother him. With what happened on Mars, Captain Lim doesn't know a lot of people, but if they're in the same line of work, some kind of superior-subordinate relationship must exist, right?"

"You think that'd discourage Summin?" asked Eunkyung. "Sure, she's not doing what she's trained to do, like you, since there's no spaceship or weaponized satellite for her to pilot yet, but she's the ace pilot on our base."

"An ace? She's a remote pilot. Controlling spaceships or satellites from Earth and not in outer space."

"Who cares? She's the only pilot on this base. You think it's easy taking up a valuable spot, which there's only one of, in this kind of place? It's not a given that such a position exists for someone to fill. Without her, that position will no longer exist. We don't have a anything for her to pilot yet, but they're not getting rid of the remote pilot, as you can see. I mean, you know this better than anyone."

Soojin couldn't find the words to answer Eunkyung immediately. So instead, she closed her mouth. Eunkyung quietly watched Summin down on the basketball court.

Moments later, Soojin said, "Hmm, Secretary Kim, were you just trash-talking to me? I feel like I just got trashed."

Eunkyung smiled and quickly changed the topic.

"The Space Force Academy's basketball team finishes fourth in extramural basketball tournaments with other military academies, right?"

"Right," Soojin answered. "Fourth out of four teams. It's a tradition."

"But the Aerospace High School, where our non-commissioned officers come from, their basketball team finished second or so in the national tournament. When Summin was a third-year there. There aren't a lot of women's basketball teams, but they were competing against more than three other teams. All I'm saying is, Han Summin's probably an expert in trash talk."

As the game carried on, Summin began to feel the need to stretch. She stopped mid-run to stretch her shoulder muscle, then she sprinted and stopped again to flex her ankles. When she moved into the frontcourt, she bent down to tie her shoes and slowly stood up with her back to Lim Junggyu, who was following her close behind.

Lim muttered, "Do you feel different after you warm up? Does it make you grow taller and stuff?"

Avoiding Lim's gaze, Summin murmured loudly to herself, "Can't shoot a basket but he sure can shoot his mouth off. Is he a cicada or what?"

After that, Summin began to roam the court. Unlike before, she started weaving through the eight players, creating a complex track. Lim did his best to chase her. There was about a meter of distance between the two of them for a short moment, but soon he caught up and positioned himself close enough for her to hear him talk.

But that short moment without Lim was more than enough for Summin. The ball wasn't passed to her every time she managed to lose the defense, but one in four passes did come to her. And now was one of those chances. A brief moment in time, less than a second long.

The ball left Summin's hands and drew an arc. It was on a high and stable course. People encircling the basketball court all looked up. Some of them noticed Soojin, who was watching them from up high. But in the next moment, no one remembered seeing her. As Summin's third three-pointer made the basket, the previously disorderly cheers from the crowd became coordinated.

Returning to the backcourt, Summin turned not to the scoreboard but to Captain Lim. They hadn't looked at each other while talking, but after Summin scored points, they made clear eye contact.

It was at that moment that Lim's trash talk changed.

Watching him, Soojin frowned. Unlike before, Lim began to cover his mouth with his hand.

"Do you see that?" Soojin asked Eunkyung.

"I do."

"Isn't that worrying? What is he saying, covering his mouth? I think I should go down there and see."

"You should," said Eunkyung.

DISPATCH TEAM 31, BASE TEAM 24. Those were the two teams' scores at halftime. When Soojin arrived at the ground level, the first half seemed to be over. None of the players were on the court, and instead five or six people who weren't in uniform were gathered under each basket, shooting balls. Summin was sitting with other players on the bench in the shade, catching her breath.

Soojin walked over and asked Summin, "You OK? Everything good?"

Recognizing Soojin, Summin looked at her with a befuddled

expression. It seemed like she had something to say but wasn't sure if she should or not.

"Can I talk to you for a sec?" asked Soojin.

"Sure," Summin answered.

The two of them headed to a corner of the lot and stood with their backs to the crowd.

In a quiet voice, Soojin said, "I didn't want to intervene in the game, but I was worried you might be in trouble."

When Summin didn't answer, Soojin added, "Never mind, if not."

But instead of leaving right away, Soojin watched the faraway mountains, giving Summin a little time. After a lot of hesitation, Summin begrudgingly summoned her voice.

"There is something a bit strange."

"Yeah?" asked Soojin.

"But it's not the thing you're worried about though," said Summin. "That kind of stuff happens during games, and he's not too bad. They think it makes them look tough, but they're basically softies."

"That's true."

"Not that softies aren't harmful, but that's not what's happening here. Only ..."

"Only?"

Without realizing it, Soojin had bowed her head and covered her mouth. To others, she looked like a coach giving a one point lesson to her player.

"He said something odd," Summin continued. "But I'm not sure why he said that to me, so I've been thinking."

"Is that why you spaced out for a second?"

"Yes. Oh, it wasn't like he was swearing at me or anything. But I'm not sure if it's something you'd say to a player you've been marking during a game of pickup basketball. I mean, the context of what he was saying. I would never have expected to hear it."

Summin seemed troubled. Or perhaps the expression on her face was that of someone who was asked a difficult question.

Eventually she said, "But I can't tell if I should tell someone this or not. I think I need to mull this over a bit."

Soojin quietly nodded and added, "If, if you decide that it's something you should tell someone, and if you think that I'm the right person to hear it, then you can tell me anytime. Although I do have the flaw of being the Inspector General. On second thought, actually, it might be better for you to talk to someone else. You don't have to come to me. I won't be disappointed much. I just came over because I happened to be around when I saw you, so don't mind me, you know."

"It was about a potential defector," said Summin, cutting Soojin's lengthy speech short.

"What?"

"He said someone wanted to defect. Captain Lim, he's been assigned here from the Intelligence Department at the Space Force headquarters. And I'm in the Operations Division here. We're in the same line of specialty, so that's probably why he chose me. Still, I don't know why he said this to me, but I think he had to say it now. So I should tell someone about this straight away, right? Oh, you know that Captain Lim was on Mars? And what happened over there?"

Soojin blankly stared at Summin. Then she came to her senses and asked, "The gist of it, yeah. But you trust me?"

"Of course."

At Summin's ready answer, Soojin was taken aback.

Gaining back her composure, Soojin said, "OK. That prospective defector. Did he say who it was? Who was defecting to where?"

"Not yet."

"Then you need to find out more."

Summin nodded and said, "But, it looks like Secretary Kim's heard everything."

Soojin snapped her head around. Eunkyung was standing close behind them.

Summin asked with a concerned look, "Can she be trusted?"

"Would've been better for her not to have heard it, but I think it's OK," said Soojin. "How's this for the time being? Lim Junggyu just glanced this way, so if he keeps on giving you information during the second half, then we'll assume that it's all right for both her and me to know. Sounds good?"

"But if he doesn't say anything more?"

Soojin looked at Eunkyung. Eunkyung asked indignantly, "You really think I will be the reason he stops talking? Really?"

Fortunately, Lim Junggyu kept on talking. Wherever Summin was, he stuck close to her and continued to run his mouth. Like before, his eyes were on the mountains in the distance.

Summin's footwork became more intricate, pretending to put her weight on her right foot and then immediately running to her left. She did the same in the other direction. When she did so, Lim copied her movements exactly. Naturally, Summin's movements grew even more complex.

The only problem was that the ball was nowhere near the two of them. The game had turned into a four-on-four. The ball was passed among the other eight players.

"This means I win," said Lim without covering his mouth. "The two of us just need to stay out of the way."

Summin knew his words were valid. DISPATCH TEAM 35,

BASE TEAM 24. The score difference had widened even more.

"It would kill me to know that I'm this useless if I were in your position, but, man ... Props to you," said Summin as she made a run for the basket.

Sweaty men stood under the net with their arms spread out. Summin squeezed between them. There was just enough space for her to get through, which made it easier for her to lose the defense.

Summin signaled the point guard on her team with her eyes. Then moments later, she slipped out of the crowd and stepped outside the three-point line. The ball bounced once and obediently arrived in front of her. Summin stooped and stretched out her hands to grab the ball with one foot inside the three-point line.

When she had a firm grip on the ball, she stepped her foot back to meet the other one outside the line. She looked up at the basket. At that moment, she saw someone's palm in front of her. Lim had already caught up to her.

Summin passed the ball that she finally had gotten her hands on back to the point guard and let out a sigh in spite of herself. Catching that small sound, Lim Junggyu muttered as he approached her, "It's quite fun to watch someone realize how useless she is."

But a little later, during the dispatch team's offense, Summin succeeded in intercepting Lim's ball. She didn't score, but it was more important that she had a chance to tell him her answer.

She mumbled, "What was it that I heard? Oh yeah, I heard that someone from the Mars base was particularly skilled at passing the ball to the other team."

At her words, Lim clenched his fists.

About five steps away from the sidelines, Soojin stood watching the two of them. In a voice low enough not to be heard by others, she said to Eunkyung, "He's not covering his mouth."

"Right. It just looks like the two of them are bickering."

"Maybe he was just bluffing? If he meant to confuse her, I think he succeeded."

Summin certainly appeared to have lost her concentration. She seemed lighter on her feet than ever, but her shots were not as great as they'd been in the first half.

"Or he's unhappy that she's told us?" asked Eunkyung.

"Perhaps," answered Soojin. "Or maybe they're just busy playing basketball. They seem too hostile to have just exchanged that kind of information, the two of them."

"Yeah, you're right. But from their faces, doesn't it look like Han Summin's chewing Lim Junggyu out, rather than Lim harassing Summin? Although I have no idea what they're actually saying."

As Summin retreated into the defense, she glared at the basket on the other side of the court for a long time. She had missed three three-pointers in a row, and her success rate had dropped to fifty percent. It was still a ludicrously high percentage. But considering that her success rate had been a hundred percent in the first half, it meant that her rate was precisely zero in this second half.

When Summin passed by the sideline, someone shouted, "Don't focus too much on the game. Go easy, easy."

It was Soojin. She was acting like a coach or a manager, standing on the sidelines and yelling at the players to focus on the game. Except she was saying exactly the opposite.

LAUNCH SOMETHING!

"It's harder to go easy, you know," said Summin.

Soon, someone stepped up to play the coach for the other team as well. The spectators grew more serious. Their exclamations and cheers gained consistency, and it became easy to distinguish who was rooting for which team. Casually watching a basketball game was fundamentally different from watching a game while cheering for one of the teams. Unlike when the game first began, in the second half, it felt like most of the people were siding with one team or the other and rooting for their team to win. You could see it in their eyes.

The change in the mood certainly had an effect on the players. They played even more intensely but scored fewer points. Even after a long time passed, the scores were still the same: DISPATCH TEAM 35, BASE TEAM 26. It wasn't because the defense had tightened; it was because the players felt pressured by the actively cheering crowd.

Once again, a game of tag began between Summin and Lim Junggyu. Summin seized a chance outside the three-point line in the left corner of the frontcourt. Lim Junggyu got a late start and belatedly ran over to her after disentangling himself from his teammates, but Summin had already received the much-awaited pass. It came right by her throat. As soon as she laid her hands on the ball, Summin raised both arms. Lim jumped, but his hands only pawed at empty air. Instead of jumping, Summin bounced the ball once and took a step to the right, unperturbed. This time, the ball drew an arc in the air. Returning to the backcourt, Summin glared at Lim. It was her fourth three-pointer.

"What percent is four out of seven?" Summin asked Soojin as she passed the sidelines, but Soojin couldn't give her an answer right away.

"About fifty-seven percent?" Eunkyung answered instead.

After Summin slipped away, Soojin turned and looked at Eunkyung with respect in her eyes.

"What?" asked Eunkyung.

"I'm just amazed."

"Amazed, heh. Han Summin, though, wow. She's really snooty when she's in athlete mode. I've never seen her that way."

"You said she was an ace," said Soojin.

"I know. She's really kind of incredible, you know. She went to the Aerospace High School because she wanted to be an astronaut."

"Huh? Isn't that the wrong school?"

"She's from the countryside, so her parents weren't much interested in her education apparently. They did let her do whatever she wanted, though. She had no idea that she had to test well in the college entrance exam and go to the Space Force Academy to be an astronaut, she thought that she only needed to go to the Aerospace High School."

"Oh no. But she must have realized that the school was for non-commissioned officers."

"She did, but the school did have a pilot major at the time."

"Oh."

"And the quota was just one."

"Wow!" exclaimed Soojin.

"She was exempt from paying the tuition and received scholarships and even a stipend for living costs, apparently. But afterward, even that quota was cut."

"Why?"

"Because Summin graduated."

"Wow, just like that?"

"Yeah, apparently when Summin became a second year, the pilot major disappeared from the first-year curriculum. Not because of Summin, though. They were originally going to get rid of the major but delayed a year for her. I mean, it was natural for them to get rid of it. There are no jobs, so if you keep training people in that major, their lives would go nowhere. But seeing that Summin got in, the school decided to train a pilot once last time. That's what one of Summin's classmates told me."

"That's incredible," exclaimed Soojin. "And that three-point shot was incredible too. It's different from watching it from above. How does she do that?"

"I know. It's like magic, right? Generally, people make about one three-pointer in ten or so in pickup games like this. But she makes six times that. The first one, you're like, cool, but the other five seem amazing, like they came from a different world."

"Indeed. I guess that's what an ace is. But she must have been sad after graduation. Being assigned here, only to find out that we have no spaceships. How does that make sense? Oh, but come to think of it, when the spaceship or satellite that Han Summin controls gets into an accident, I get to investigate it. So my turn comes after hers. Darn, I don't know who should be more depressed, her or me?"

"You just realized that now?"

DISPATCH TEAM 35, BASE TEAM 29. Catching her breath, Summin lowered her posture. With his back to Summin, Lim Jung-gyu was slowly dribbling with his right hand. Then suddenly he brought his left hand to his mouth.

"Did you tell the IG?"

Summin hesitated for a moment. But she maintained her pose as she said, "I did."

"What about Secretary Kim Eunkyung?"

"She heard it by accident. But this is all a lie, isn't it?"

At that moment, Lim turned around and threw the ball over Summin's shoulder. It was a pass. Someone standing under the basket caught the ball and scored two points.

Staring at Lim's face, Summin muttered as if to herself, "Heh, I knew it was all lies."

Summin took the ball and dribbled into the opposing team's court. Once she crossed the half-way line, she passed to a team-mate and began a game of tag with Lim once more. But this time around, it wasn't too long before she got her hands on the ball again. When the ball was passed to her, Summin assumed a position, looking as though she were about to dribble past him. Left, right, she tried to trick him.

Lim Junggyu wasn't easily fooled. He watched Summin's movements and tried his best to react. From left to right, and again to the left. He didn't miss the movements of the ball, but he concentrated on her feet more, as well as her shoulders, her waist, and how she was shifting her weight.

It was right at that moment that Summin's ponytail bounced up and leaned to the right—a familiar sight to someone who has been in a vacuum, like in the shuttle between Earth and Mars. Whether it was hair or a scarf, when something on one's body moved one way, it meant the body was actually moving in the other direction. Summin was lowering her posture and sprinting to the left.

Lim stepped one foot to the left. The other foot quickly followed. But in the next moment, he saw Summin move in the opposite direction.

He hadn't seen it, but Soojin, who was watching from the back, saw exactly what happened. Summin turned her head left to make her ponytail bounce to the right, and when Lim Junggyu fell for her trick and stepped left, she'd taken two steps to the right.

Summin didn't sprint far. She took two steps to her side and positioned herself in a spot free of obstacles. Then immediately she made the shot. It was her fifth three-pointer. 37 to 32. Only five points apart.

"What percentage is five out of eight?" asked Summin as she walked the sideline.

"I don't know!" Soojin shouted, her head snapping from side to side. "Good job! You're the best!"

"62.5 percent!" Eunkyung cheered Summin on with the math. Then she added, "I have to head to the Communication Relay Station. The chief of staff's orders. Told me to standby."

Summin nodded. She ran over to Lim, who wasn't in possession of the ball, and took a defensive stance. Lim didn't move as fast as Summin. It was much easier to follow him and talk. When he stopped in an empty corner, Summin also halted and again assumed a defensive position.

"The Communication Relay Station is on standby," Summin said, covering her mouth with her hand and intentionally avoiding eye contact. "You know Secretary Kim Eunkyung is the one in charge of administrative communication with the Mars base, right? She just received orders and went to standby."

Lim brought his hand over his mouth and said, "I saw the IG contacting someone. Who did she report to?"

"The chief of staff."

"Good. Now listen closely. The name is ..."

Then suddenly, Lim picked one foot up. It wasn't a quick movement, but for a second Summin nearly lost her balance. After checking the position of the ball, she assumed her position. That was when she heard the whisper. It came as Lim wiped the sweat under his nose with a corner of his shirt.

"Hwang Sun."

Summin's eyes widened at the name and quickly returning to normal. Watching from the sidelines, Soojin didn't miss the subtle change in her expression.

When the base team began its offensive and Summin grabbed the ball, Soojin suddenly called a time-out. All the other nine players looked at her with a puzzled expression. The spectators did the same. "When did the IG become a basketball coach?" They seemed to say.

"This is the chance," Soojin said brazenly as she gathered the players on Summin's team together. "You have to catch up to the other team on this offense, got it?"

It was a ploy to take Summin aside for a moment. The four other players on Summin's team looked at Soojin in confusion.

"What's going on?"

"Is she Sergeant Han's personal coach or something? Or our team's coach?"

"When were we ever a team except for now?"

"That's true."

Soojin pulled Summin away from the other players, and the two stood so close that their shoulders touched. Summin hunched her shoulders to create a shade, and Soojin made hand gestures in the air to make it look like she was giving strategic instructions.

"What are you doing?" Summin whispered, covering her mouth with her hand.

"How should I know," said Soojin. "Lim Junggyu said something important just now, didn't he?"

"He did."

"What did he say?"

Summin draped a towel over her head and looked down at the ground to fully cover her face from view. Soojin stooped alongside her to listen for her answer.

LAUNCH SOMETHING!

"Hwang Sun," Summin whispered.

Upon hearing the name, Soojin stood upright. Then she bent down again.

"Hwang Sun's defecting?"

Summin said nothing in response. It seemed that she didn't have anything else to say. Soojin righted herself and spoke loudly as if giving tactical instructions.

"You're doing good. Just do as much as you have been doing so far. We're almost there."

"But, coach," said Summin. "Even when I was on the school team, I never played this long in a game. Players have to sit out for a little while and then go back in, you know. Aren't you overworking us? I'm not just pretending to look exhausted. It's really tiring. Captain Lim's stamina is no joke."

"What are you saying? You know how important the timing is right now. Think of this as the last game of the season, and do your best."

"Jeez, which sports movie did you get that from?"

Eunkyung stood alone in the Communication Relay Station. Like the Launch Control Room, the Communication Relay Station was divided into two by a perfectly soundproof glass wall. Behind one side of the glass wall was a well-lit, everyday workplace with a bunch of office equipment, and on the other side was a dimly lit space with a high ceiling. The way the office was raised in comparison to the dark area on the other side of the glass made it resemble a small theater stage, or a studio of a broadcasting company. In either space, there was no one else other than Eunkyung.

In the center of the stage-like room in the Communication

Relay Station, Eunkyung stood under the spotlight. On the side opposite the glass wall was a huge screen, nearly filling up the entire wall. The main spectator of Eunkyung's stage and the main spectacle of another stage, Chief of Staff Gu Yemin, was on that big screen.

Gu Yemin spoke. "Secretary Kim Eunkyung, I'm sorry to make you turn on the communication device on your day off. He could've asked the Governor-General of Mars about defecting, but he contacted here for whatever reason."

"You mean the Vice-Minister of Mars, ma'am? I think it's because he wants to live. Had he requested defection to the Vice-Minister of Mars, his safety would probably not be guaranteed."

"General Lee's a rather … straight arrow, isn't he. He should relax and be a little open-minded."

"They probably think he's merciless, what with him constantly calling for a zero-tolerance policy for those involved in the uprising."

"You're right. I've been sending guidelines on handling those involved in the uprising, but I can't do much else about it since the vice-minister's power has grown too much on Mars. In any case, that prospective defector, I had a contact window made for him on Mars that didn't involve going through the Governor-General, so I don't know why he's made contact this way. Is he trying to get a rise out of me? If he thought that none of the channels we've created there were trustworthy and so decided to make contact via the only safe route he could think of, that's a lot of work for us, isn't it? Because we would have to investigate everyone involved in our usual channels. On top of that, he's distorted the communication channel this much, the Mars Governor-General will be breathing fire down my back. In any case, this is all a headache. As I'm sure you know full well."

LAUNCH SOMETHING!

"I do understand why he did what he did," said Eunkyung. "But that doesn't mean it's not a headache."

"Sure," Gu Yemin replied. Then, changing the topic she said, "You know, when we are talking to someone, we usually look them in the eye. Some people have a hard time deciding whether to look at the right or the left eye, and some just focus on either one. Right now, I can tell you are the type of person who moves back and forth between the right and the left. I mean, you might not usually, but I think you are doing that now. The angle and direction of your gaze change a lot when you shift between my right eye and my left. You see what I'm getting at? How big is my face up there that you have to move your eyes that much? You have me in god mode again, don't you? Why do people keep on doing that? Who keeps on fiddling with the setting?"

"You are awe-inspiring no matter what, ma'am."

"Geesh."

"In any event, I just received a message from Major Park Soojin. She has the name of the defector."

"Who is it?"

"It's Hwang Sun, ma'am."

"I knew it. He's not even that important but he's been in hiding for a while, and now that he has no way to escape, he wants to turn himself in. But he said he wanted to defect? Shouldn't it be surrender?"

"His nationality is a bit complicated," Eunkyung answered. "It seems that he wants to begin at a legally advantageous position."

The enormous Gu Yemin on the screen put her glasses down on the table and said, "We'll let that slide for a moment. The fact that he's contacted us through Master Sergeant Han Summin must mean that this is an emergency?"

"We have not confirmed that yet. What I have reported to you is all we know at the moment, and I will relay you the details as I get them."

"Sounds good. Everyone at the HQ is on standby now, so let's just wait. Captain Lim Junggyu, though. He hasn't changed much over there, has he? No friends, and people just avoid him?"

"There has been no official announcement regarding what exactly happened on Mars, so ... People will be careful without all the information. Also, he is certainly not a social butterfly, so it would be natural for people to keep their distance, thinking that something must have happened over there."

Upon hearing Kim Eunkyung's words, Gu Yemin fell into deep thought. Then in a strained voice, she said, "I know, but I think it's best not to disclose information on the Mars issue for the time being. There's not much we can do. Is Master Sergeant Han Summin playing well?"

"Very well, ma'am. We thought that Captain Lim was just lying to distract her at first, and Han Summin only half believed it and was focusing on the basketball game. It's hard to get her energy down now that she's concentrating."

"Good. That's why I gave her scholarships and kept her in school. She wanted to quit, you know."

"You were the principal?" Eunkyung asked in surprise.

"Happened to be."

"Why didn't you tell her to go to the Space Force Academy?"

"I felt like she wasn't going to come back to us if she left that way. That's what happens generally. You become rivals, and they never come back. And you don't need to go to the academy and be a commissioned officer to become a proper pilot. At least not in the Space Force."

"But technically you have to be a commissioned officer."

"True. I knew that going in, but I thought that I'd be able to change the system. And then time just flew by while I was occupied with other things. Master Sergeant Han must have felt very conflicted, but I'd completely forgotten about her."

"She's not much of a talker either. She always stays on the base even after work hours. She works out, but I'd never seen her so excited playing a game like she is today."

"Right? I'd forgotten how she can be. But the Space Force is going to change for real."

Eunkyung seized that moment and delved in. "You gave her a gift, didn't you?"

"A gift?" asked Gu Yemin, looking completely clueless.

"The satellite you launched last time. The unmanned equipment that requires a pilot to control."

"Did I? Well, that's confidential."

"People who do even a little bit of digging know that was for Han Summin. It's all implicit, but they also know that she's one of your people. One of the ones least likely to betray you in this base. Both Hwang Sun and Lim Junggyu probably expected to get to the higher-ups more quickly if they went through her."

"That's too much speculation. I'm close to other people on the base too. But if that's the case, then Hwang Sun and Lim Junggyu must think very little of my line of command. As if I wouldn't trust anyone else other than my personal connections."

While the chief of staff equivocated, Eunkyung received another message from Soojin. Looking at her phone, Eunkyung said, "I just received a message through a secure channel. Han Summin scored another three-pointer ..."

"Goodness!" exclaimed Gu Yemin. "Six, total?"

"The scores are 39 to 37. The main details are: Coming with family. Request for permission to board the earthbound space shuttle. In exchange for information on the source of funding for the remaining rebel forces. Extradition to Allied Space Force upon return. These are his conditions."

"Sounds like he has a lot of friends to sell out."

"It seems that he is at the spaceport on Mars, so can't we just arrest him?"

"He probably has an escape plan," replied Gu Yemin. "Since he's confident enough to designate the spot."

"I see. Another message. It says to give a specific signal if you accept the terms."

"What's the signal?" asked Gu Yemin.

"Make Han Summin throw an air ball. Ma'am, that must mean that someone other than Lim Junggyu is watching the game."

"I assumed so. There was a suggestion of swooping in and taking in everyone around the basketball court for interrogation, but I pulled the plug on that and am sitting here now instead. They must have someone relaying the information as well. The terms must have already been set, and a simple signal to proceed as planned."

"What will you do?"

"I'm not sure," Gu Yemin answered.

"We could just take him in and think about the conditions afterward."

"We could, but that wouldn't be right."

"That's why they're throwing a tantrum. They have nothing to rely upon other than your kindness. And for exactly that reason, they will never go to the Vice-Minister of Mars. Everyone knows that you can't survive if you go that way."

"That's why he hates me. Why is everyone doing this to me? It doesn't matter who's defecting, whether it's Hwang Sun or someone else, it's a big deal if the Mars Governor-General is roped in."

Eunkyung stretched her arms far out to the sides and answered with a smiling face, "It's because you're this great!"

LAUNCH SOMETHING!

Staring squarely at Lim Junggyu's face, Summin said, "Yeah, right."

"What?" asked Lim.

"The signal. You just made that up."

"Why would I?"

"To win."

"You've got some trust issues."

"I've been lied to a lot."

"Ask your coach."

Summin turned to Soojin. Or actually, she pretended to turn to Soojin and quickly spun around, putting Lim behind her. The ball wasn't passed to her. She'd tried hard to shake him off her trail, but it seemed that no one had saw her. Summin went back to running around the court as if nothing had happened. Lim did the same.

In the meantime, the ball went over to Lim's team's possession. On the way back to the backcourt, Summin passed Soojin.

"Any word?" Summin asked.

"Not yet," Soojin replied.

DISPATCH TEAM 41, BASE TEAM 39. The scores were close enough for any individual player to make the difference. But the players on both teams were having a hard time scoring points at all. Too many eyes were on them.

Lim was desperately blocking Summin. Since all the players wanted to score the winning points themselves, the chance that the ball would be passed to Summin was low. But it wasn't easy for her teammates to not pass to someone like Summin, who was quick and still full of energy.

Lim was drenched in sweat. Summin's hair was stuck to her face as well. A lock of hair that crossed her forehead in particular resembled a toupee.

"You'll be taken in," she said.

After running around chasing after Summin for a while, Lim Junggyu replied, "I'll probably be questioned. I get that often these days."

About ten seconds later, Summin said, "I don't know much but it must have been hard for you. These past few years."

"This game is harder. Let's take a breather."

"Should I call a time-out?"

"No need, no need. Everyone's having a great time. Might as well let them play."

Summin and Lim gradually slowed down. Their run eventually turned into a jog, and soon the two of them were walking side by side, almost like they were taking a stroll along the sidelines.

"Did you play sports?" Summin asked. "It's not easy for someone who isn't an athlete to keep up with me."

"Not professionally. I only started working out after I got into the academy. I played some basketball, but just in a recreational team."

"I heard it's hard to adjust to life on Earth after being on Mars."

At Summin's words, Lim asked, "Why? You interested in going to Mars? You don't have to come back. Not a lot of people who go there think of coming back anyway. Someone like you who is skilled and sought after won't be standing in the same line as people like me who can be discarded at any moment."

"A settlement, though …"

"It's not like how it was in the past. It's not the pioneer days anymore. You won't be going around shoveling and digging and stuff."

"I suppose that's true."

"Never mind if you're not interested," said Lim indifferently.

Then he changed subject and said, "I didn't know you were an athlete."

"Just in high school."

"Aerospace High School? They have a powerful women's team, don't they? Were you on the starting lineup?"

"Yeah, a bit."

"If I'd known that, I wouldn't even have come near you. I saw you idling around, so I thought you were just here to fill the head count."

"You can't just give it a hundred percent from the start. Are you all rested now?"

"No, it's only been like a minute."

Without a word, Summin sprinted out into the center of the court. Not wishing to be left behind, Lim chased after her.

DISPATCH TEAM 44, BASE TEAM 42. Soojin let out a startled scream when the person standing next to her suddenly yelled. The time was nearly up. They weren't timing the game like a real basketball game, in which playing time refers to only the time when the ball is in play, but like a soccer game, where the clock runs without stopping. Someone must have been timing the game nonetheless.

"Only three minutes left?" Soojin asked the shouter. "Somebody's keeping track, right?"

"We don't stop the clock when the players go to fetch the ball. But I'm not the referee."

"Do you stop the clock for time-outs?"

"If you tell them to, probably, since you're the IG, but please don't. You don't really have anything to say during the time-out, do you?"

Soojin sent a message to Eunkyung in the Communication Relay Station, asking for an answer regarding the defection request since there were only two minutes and thirty seconds left in the game.

A little after two minutes, Eunkyung finally sent a reply. Down by the basketball court, Soojin waved her arms in the air and walked out into the middle of the court.

"Time-out! Time-out! Referee, time-out! Stop the clock!"

People burst into complaints, both the players and the spectators alike.

Soojin called over the players on the base team, including Summin.

"You're only doing this to speak to Summin, aren't you?" one of the players asked.

"Not at all! Listen here, everyone. You want to win, right? I know that you want to win. This is not the game you thought you'd be playing when you started. We've come this far, and this is now a matter of pride."

"A matter of pride sounds a bit much," someone grumbled.

In a slightly more assertive voice, Soojin said, "That's what weaklings would say! We don't know how many more people will come to the base from the HQ, and you're just going to sound that weak? Are we just going to give up our spots to the newbies rolling in? No, we're not!"

"What are you talking about?" asked Technical Sergeant Jin with a befuddled look on his face. "No one thinks that."

"Shush, Sarge Jin, you little … Listen to me, and listen good. You all just do as I say. OK? Just pass the ball to Master Sergeant Han, got it? It's not like the rest of you are making shots anyway. Summin's scored half of those points up there, didn't she? So help her finish. OK? And Sergeant Han, let me talk to you for a sec."

At Soojin's strange order, the players on the base team looked confused. They had no idea why she was giving instructions in the first place, but they also didn't seem to think that her strategy was that bad. Summin's face went scarlet.

"Inspector General, don't embarrass me," said Summin.

"What?"

"I thought you were cool."

"Hey, hey, I'm doing all this for you, and that's what I get in return?"

Summin covered her mouth and asked, "What about the order? Have you heard?"

With a meaningful look in her eyes, Soojin nodded.

Summin pressed her again, "Have you?!"

Soojin quickly covered her mouth and said, "Yeah, yeah, I did."

"You should say it in words, you know. What kind of military sends messages by nodding?"

"I'm not in the Operations Division!"

"But you were great at calling time-outs, which no one ever calls in these games to discuss an operation."

"Someone had to. Someone has to send the ball your way to give our answer, you know."

"So you just told everyone to pass the ball to me, and then you're telling me not to score? Not just not score, but shoot and completely miss?"

Soojin looked into Summin's eyes above the hand covering her mouth. They were strong, unwavering eyes, but Summin's gaze resembled that of someone with many stories to tell, someone who was holding back her tears. Soojin had done nothing wrong, but her voice grew small for some reason.

"Just this once, please," Soojin said.

"I'll never play basketball again after today, though."

"Why not? You're great!"

"Ugh. OK, fine. Don't mind me. I'll do as you say."

In the empty Communication Relay Station, Eunkyung stood face to face with the enormous Space Force Chief of Staff Gu Yemin.

"We're all set on the Mars end, so now all we have to do is send that message."

At Eunkyung's words, Gu Yemin asked, "You've sent the word, right?"

"I have, through Major Park Soojin. That Master Sergeant Han Summin should shoot a three-pointer, but shouldn't score and shouldn't let the ball even hit the rim or the backboard."

"Good work."

For a long while, Gu Yemin remained silent. The anxiety that fogged up the mind of the Space Force's chief filled the entirety of a wall in the Communication Relay Station.

Then Gu Yemin asked, "Do you think Han Summin will do as she was told?"

Eunkyung shrugged, "I don't know, but why wouldn't she?"

"I don't think she will."

"Should I contact her again? Tell her once more not to score?"

"Should we? No, never mind. Let's let her be. It's not even a military operation, so let's not put any pressure on her. She's received the order, so she'll do as she sees fit."

"Yes, ma'am," Eunkyung answered.

At the same time, Eunkyung quickly moved her fingers to send a message to Soojin on the secure channel.

miss! do not let the ball touch anything!

LAUNCH SOMETHING!

Soojin received the message. When Summin's eyes met hers, Soojin brought her hand to her neck and made a throat slash sign while silently mouthing, "No, no, no!" Among the crowd, someone whispered, "I didn't know the IG liked basketball that much."

At those words, Soojin wiped off the silly look she had been wearing on her face.

DISPATCH TEAM 46, BASE TEAM 44. Summin, the base team's ace, stood in the center of the frontcourt. She hadn't begun dribbling yet. If she started to dribble, it'd be difficult to stop and then start again. If the chance she had wasn't perfect, she would have to pass the ball to someone else again. And that someone else would pass the ball back to Summin as the IG instructed them to, even if the timing or the build-up play wasn't great, and then they'd really end up with an embarrassing loss in the end. It meant that Summin had to take care of this herself in one go.

Summin glanced at Lim's feet, which blocked her from making a forward run. However, there was a little distance between Lim and herself. It seemed like he was giving her room to shoot the ball as she wanted.

"They said OK," said Summin, holding the ball in front of her to cover her mouth.

"You don't have to say it to me. Just give the signal."

"Saying it is the clearest way to send a message, so why do you need an additional signal? Does that make sense to you? Relay the message to your contact or not, that's up to you. We've done all we can, so this is over. Now, I'm just going to do my best for this game, so do whatever you want."

"Can you? After you received orders?"

Summin began to dribble the ball. There was a bit of space between her and the opposition, but she had to get closer to the three-point line to shoot. Lim talked as if he wasn't going to block her, but his pose was far from his words. It was like he was baiting her by giving her room. If she took the bait, she might end up regretting it a lot.

Summin tested him by trying to break through. Her movement was slight and nonthreatening. Lim's reaction wasn't slow. He wasn't actively chasing her by stepping left and right but instead chose to step back a bit and narrow her path. Turning her back to him, Summin backstepped gradually to get to the three-point line. As she stood with the basket behind her, she could see the Inspector General's strange facial expression. She wasn't sure if Soojin was worried about her or cheering for her. Regardless, Summin's feet moved quickly. Her weight shifted busily from side to side. Her movements were menacing, as though she was looking to break through rather than hope for her opponent to fall for her feints. And finally, she got her chance. When she stepped to one side and shifted her weight on that foot, Lim committed. Summin quickly turned to the opposite side. It took a little longer for Lim to catch up to her movements. It was bizarre how inertia seemed to have no effect on Summin but dragged Lim down.

Summin broke through to her left. Lim couldn't follow her except with his eyes. Summin breathed a relaxed sigh. In the next moment, Lim heard a short inhale. Summin's ankles, knees, shoulders, elbows, wrists, and knuckles each used their own strength to push and angle the orange basketball that was resting lightly on her hand. Each part of her body moved separately, but her body as a whole worked as a delicate mechanism that did not waste a single ounce of energy while launching her in a perfectly vertical position.

The following jump was only a byproduct of that mechanism.

LAUNCH SOMETHING!

Like a spring that has outlived its usefulness bouncing up into empty air, Summin's body sprang upward, having launched the ball. Her legs straightened, and her right arm stretched up in a straight line. Her right wrist curled down at ease. Her torso was slightly twisted, with her left side slightly behind the right, and her chin was touching her right shoulder. This was the scenery that the orange basketball left behind as it drew an elegant arc in the air.

"You weren't supposed to score!"

Someone yelled from behind. The sound hadn't come from the other team's supporters but from the home team's coach—Soojin. Lim looked up at the ball with a face full of despair. All the spectators held their breaths, and the senior master sergeant in charge of the scoreboard slipped his fingers behind three cards, ready to flip them over. Needless to say, under the shining Pac-Man, cicadas boisterously fired away their chirps like cosmic background radiation.

As Summin watched the ball fly away from her, a pleasant smile spread across her face.

"That's a win," she whispered.

That day, Han Summin shot seven three-pointers and led her team to victory, and nevertheless, as Han Summin had wagered, Hwang Sun boarded the earthbound space shuttle with his family anyway.

Chapter Three

Space Force Honor Guard

There was an oversized couch in the first-floor lounge of the single occupant dormitory at the Space Force launch base. It was shaped like a three-seater, but it must have been imported from abroad because each seat was wide enough to fit two average-size Koreans.

Captain Park Kugyong of the Public Relations Corps was lying on his side on the couch, resting his head on its arm, watching the television. It was a period drama. People were wearing military uniforms from the time of the Korean Empire. Black uniforms with gold buttons and red decorative bands. Kugyong turned his gaze to a photograph of the Space Force's dress uniform. The design was different, but the colors were the same. The Space Force uniform had a glittery sheen, but you could barely notice that when it was dark.

An expression of intrigue popped up on Kugyong's face for a moment before it vanished. It wasn't enough to spark his interest.

Kugyong reached for the remote and turned up the volume.

On the television, people who seemed to be members of the Righteous Army, with their faces covered by masks, suddenly jumped out behind the man in a black suit who was passing through an alley. Without a word, a Righteous Army soldier pointed his rifle at Black Suit's back, and Black Suit stopped in his tracks.

Kugyong sat up suddenly. He grabbed the remote and rewound. At that moment, Suh Ga-ul, who had been watching the television from the table in the corner of the lounge, grumbled out loud.

"There goes Captain Park Cooking again. Let's just watch the thing all in one go!"

Startled, Kugyong snapped his head around to look at her.

"How long have you been there?" he asked.

"What does it matter?"

"It's Saturday. You didn't go home?"

"I'm on night duty today."

Stone-faced, Kugyong watched the same scene again on TV and turned to Ga-ul.

He said, "You know, I think I just discovered something."

"What is it this time?" Ga-ul asked.

"That man, the man in the black suit. Someone aimed a rifle at him, and he just stopped."

"Wouldn't you stop if someone pointed a gun at you?"

"But how did he know? No one said anything. Does he have eyes on the back of his head? Or did he feel some kind of energy from the rifle?"

"The rifle made a sound."

"The click, right? The one that suggests, 'This is a firearm.' But what rifle is that? Are there rifles or guns that make a clicking sound when someone points them at things?"

"You always hear it in movies. Whether it's a revolver or what-not, when you point them, they make the clicking sound, no?"

"That's exactly what I'm saying," said Kugyong as he got up from the couch and slipped into his sandals. He walked over to Ga-ul and handed her the remote before striding toward the lounge door.

Ga-ul asked, "Where are you going all of a sudden? Looking all excited about something."

Kugyong answered, "Me? To surf the web."

"Why all of a sudden?"

"I want that rifle, so I'm going to see where I can find it."

"Huh?"

"Do you think they have one in the armory? They probably don't, right?"

"Rifles from the Korean Empire period in the Space Force ar-mory?"

"They give the latest models to the Army, older ones to the Air Force, and even older ones to us. Since we don't really have to use them."

"Do they think the Space Force is a museum or something? How come they don't give us laser guns?"

"If they did, they'd probably tell us to have fifty spacenauts share one gun. Anyhow, do you think they'd have that rifle in a museum? They probably don't have that kind of old junk even in museums. I don't even think I've seen one in the museum at the Space Force Academy. Though, they might have it in the collection storage."

"Huh? The collection storage? Can't you just buy that prop?"

Ga-ul pointed at the television. Kugyong looked in its direc-tion, and suddenly his face brightened.

"Doctor Suh, you must be a genius," he said.

"*Doctor* Suh, huh. Now I've heard everything. You must have never seen an overnight millionaire spend money before, Captain Cooking. If you like something you see, you can just buy it, so why go to all the trouble to make it yourself? Even if they say it's not for sale, if you offered enough money, they'd even gift wrap it and deliver it."

"What? You've done that before?"

"Of course. Though the money was from the company I used to work for. Oh, but there *is* a problem."

"A problem?"

"A problem about whether the Space Force at this point is an overnight millionaire or not. These days, I can't tell how much the spending limit is."

On Monday morning, Park Kugyong was eating breakfast in the mess hall when he heard intelligence officer Um Jonghyun sitting across from him say, "I heard Chief Gu asked the Ministry of Defense to purchase us an aircraft carrier."

Kugyong's chopsticks paused mid-air, and he asked, "An aircraft carrier? Who said that?"

"It was in the newspaper," Jonghyun answered. "On the back of the Space Force Fighter Wing's success, she demanded that they let her have an aircraft carrier. Not officially in a meeting or anything but through an unofficial channel apparently. Officially she said she never did such a thing and denied the rumors as nonsensical, but the word is still out there. I thought the Public Relations Corps was behind it, but guess not."

"The Public Relations Corps at the Space Force headquarters must have done it. People like me, assigned here to a subordinate unit, aren't privy to that kind of information."

"What? You've been pushed out of the core group? Isn't it a promotion to be dispatched here these days?"

"Not for the Public Relations Corps. Here, we just have to work on PR."

"Oh, but that sounds like a good thing, doesn't it?"

"I'm not much of an idyllic person," said Kugyong. "They told me to take care of this year's festival since that's what I'd been doing at the headquarters, but after that, I think I won't have anything to do for the headquarters."

"What festival?"

"The Autumn Military Music Festival."

"Oh, I didn't know it was already that time. It doesn't feel like fall at all."

"That's because the temperature doesn't matter, only the date does. Anyway, asking for an aircraft carrier, the people at the headquarters must be excited. The Navy must be fuming! Man, I should've stayed at SFHQ instead of coming here to the launch base."

"They might just ignore it because it's so absurd," replied Jonghyun.

"But there are different types of absurd remarks. She could've asked for something else, but she asked for an aircraft carrier of all things. Even the Navy wouldn't dare ask for that."

Kugyong went back to eating with his chopsticks again. The chopsticks moved quicker than before, but he kept dropping the food he picked up, and his mind seemed to be miles away.

Then he asked, "Since she asked for something as absurd as an aircraft carrier, it's possible that they'd compromise by giving us air defense artillery at least, don't you think?"

Captain Um answered indifferently, "Probably. The Air Force did take theirs from the Army anyway. It'd be a different story if there had been no Space Force, but since there is, it would be better for the Space Force to have the missiles. But this is only when we think about the technicality. Politically, isn't that a bad move? We're only turning the Navy and the Air Force into enemies. Considering the scale of things, it would be hard to go up against the Army even if the other three branches join together, and I doubt that public opinion is positive enough for the Space Force to take on the Army, Navy, and the Air Force altogether. Honestly, it seems like the chief of staff is treading a dangerously fine line."

"I'm sure she has something in mind."

"You're right. She probably does have something up her sleeve. Well, I'm sure she'll take care of the aircraft carrier. Oh, Captain Park, you should give this a thorough read before moving in. I divided up the cleaning tasks equally, but let me know if there's anything you want to change."

Jonghyun pushed a sheet of paper sitting by his food tray closer to Kugyong. Kugyong glanced at it, and when a couple of words caught his eyes, he immediately turned to Jonghyun.

"A cleaning schedule when we're only going to be living together for a couple of months? Couldn't we do away with the rules?"

"A couple of months as roommates is enough to turn people into enemies for life," answered Jonghyun. "Where did you get a couple of months though?"

"I heard they said that two months is more than enough time to build the new single occupant dormitory."

Jonghyun eyed Kugyong curiously.

"What? Two months to build a three-story building? They haven't even started digging yet."

"It's the military. You'll see it go up like the buildings in those city-building games. It'll be constructed in no time. A building that will be nice and moist in the summer and let all the cold winds blow through the rooms in the winter—in order to prevent harmful microbes and vermin from inhabiting, of course."

"Yikes. Perhaps I should look for an apartment outside the barracks."

"Well, they certainly can't erect a building in a couple months outside the barracks," answered Kugyong. "And there are a lot of people who'll be dispatched here in the meantime. I actually looked into it, but all the nice apartments in town are owned by non-commissioned officers. Things could get a bit complicated if your subordinate is the landlord."

"Do things get complicated?"

"Not necessarily, I suppose, but people say that eventually things go wrong."

With a look of resignation, Jonghyun put his spoon down.

"I see. Then I suppose I have no choice but to stay. Captain Park, are you moving in tonight then?"

"The day after tomorrow, actually," said Kugyong. "Wednesday. Today and tomorrow, I have to go to the headquarters."

"The music festival?"

"I have to wrap it up all nicely. And there's something fun to look into."

Private Lee Ja-un of the Space Force Band stood with the telephone receiver in his left hand and stared blankly at the wall across from him. On the desk was an official document from the Air Force, and there was a huge sack that took up about half of the desk full of letters, postcards, and the like. A cursory glance suggested it was the desk of a postal worker, but the contents of the entire sack was addressed to "Private Lee Ja-un (Oste)."

Entering the office of the Public Relations Corps at the Space Force headquarters, Park Kugyong noticed Lee Ja-un make a call and then slowly put the receiver back down. Eyeing him curiously, Kugyong approached his desk. Ja-un stood up and saluted, "Ascension!"

Kugyong nodded in response and said, "Hey, if you call someone and then hang up without saying anything, the person on the other end would be confused. Who were you calling? Did they say something?"

"Sir, I called the Air Force headquarters to confirm something about the military music festival," answered Ja-un.

"Huh? Then why did you hang up like that? Is it because people your age aren't comfortable with making phone calls? But you've been out in the real world, working for a while. And you're older than most other recruits."

With a look of embarrassment, Ja-un answered, "It's ... I can't understand what they are saying, sir."

"What do you mean?"

"I can't understand anything they are saying, sir."

"Why? Did they answer in a foreign language?"

His head slightly askew, Kugyong walked over to the phone on Ja-un's desk. He picked up the receiver and pressed the redial button. After a few rings, someone answered the call.

Listening to the sound coming from the other end of the line, Kugyong stared at the wall across from him. A huge wooden Space Force logo was hanging on the wall.

"This is Captain Park Kugyong of the Space Force Public Relations Corps," Kugyong enunciated every word as he spoke into the receiver. "Who am I speaking with?"

The person on the other end of the line said something, but Kugyong couldn't understand a word.

"Hmm, OK. So who am I speaking to?"

He furrowed his brows and concentrated on the sounds, but once again he failed to learn who was on the phone. It sounded something like, "Zisisouiaeinungowmehahhelpew?" It took the person on the other end of the line less than two seconds to say all those vowels.

"Owmeh? Hmm, I'll call you back."

Kugyong put the receiver down, dumbfounded. Then his eyes met those of Private Lee Ja-un who had been standing nearby.

"The Air Force is rather amazing, isn't it?" Kugyong said. "I'm sure the Air Force will do a great job of protecting our country. As for contacting them, let's just do it by email."

Kugyong took Ja-un outside. There was an old wooden bench in a corner where the sunlight pooled, and the two of them sat down. Kugyong told Ja-un to sit at ease, but Ja-un remained firmly upright.

"The Space Force is an armed force, and you've probably seen and heard a lot about how the military is, but in the Space Force, when your superior tells you to sit at ease, it really means you can relax. But then again, in about a month, you'll be sitting slumped on the bench with all that rookie tension out of your body, so I'll stop minding how you're sitting today."

Giving up on getting Ja-un to relax, Kugyong got to his main point.

"Your stage name ... Ohst? Is that how you pronounce it? It says O-s-t-e."

"It's pronounced 'Ah-sti,' sir."

"Right, Oste. Your boy band B Density seems to be still performing. You guys decided to do your military service in order, oldest first?"

"Our members vary in age, sir. And we also have foreign nationals. Currently, three of us are doing our mandatory military service, and seven are still performing."

"I see. So why did you come to the Space Force for your military service? The service period is the longest here. Was it your way of allowing other members to take the spotlight for a while?"

Kugyong looked at Private Lee Ja-un. Nervously, Ja-un answered, "No, sir. I came to serve here because I wanted to."

"Good, that's how you should think. The service period is the longest here compared to other military branches, but being here won't be too bad. Your fans will have to wait longer to have you back, though, and I'm sure that's an important factor for a celebrity."

"That's no concern, sir. I dreamed of being in the Space Force ever since I was little."

Kugyong looked upon Oste's childhood dreams with pity.

"Your dream was probably about becoming an astronaut or the like instead of joining the military band," he said. "But now that you're here, we can't get you out. We call it the military music festival, but we have to work with the honor guards for the event, you know? The Space Force doesn't even have honor guards, so we assign people from the military police to prepare for the festival, but we still don't have enough people. That's why I'm coming to you. I know that it could be a bit silly for a celebrity like you, but for other people it is an honorable position."

At Kugyong's words, Ja-un turned to him and answered in an earnest-yet-not-overly-eager voice, "Please let me do it, sir. I can do it well."

"OK, got it. I just hope you know that I'm sorry to be asking you to do something that doesn't suit you."

"No, sir. I can do anything."

Kugyong slanted his head to the side and apologized again, "I know, I know. But I still hope that you understand we're sorry about ..."

"I'm confident that I can do it well."

"Well, OK. It's good that you're into it. Sure, that's all I'll say."

Kugyong looked into this young man's face, who looked like a new recruit but also an experienced professional singer. Kugyong's eyes seemed to be saying, "What a strange kid, just like a Space Force recruit."

At eleven a.m. on Tuesday, Kugyong followed Colonel Lee Dongjin, the head of the Space Force Headquarters Public Relations Corps, into the office of the Space Force Chief of Staff. It wasn't a scheduled meeting but an impromptu one called by Chief Gu Yemin while Kugyong was talking to the colonel.

Chief Gu Yemin was tidying up a bookcase when they entered. She turned to the two of them and asked, "Should I get another bookcase?"

Colonel Lee answered, "There are no empty walls in the room, ma'am."

"I could put it over there next to the door, or I could take out that sofa and put it there, couldn't I?"

"Then we won't be able to see your face, ma'am."

Gu Yemin smiled, as if it wasn't a bad idea, and asked Kugyong, "What kind of interesting tidbit did you bring this time to annoy Colonel Lee?"

Kugyong stood tall to attention. It was a show of respect to the chief of staff who asked him a question. Then immediately he returned to his relaxed position like a limp balloon.

"It was about the honor guard demonstration at the military music festival, ma'am."

At his words, Gu Yemin let out a long sigh. Then she asked, "Should we just not do it this time? It creates so much publicity for us in a bad way."

"It's our turn to host the festival, ma'am."

"Is it? Well, that's a problem."

"But it will be different from the spring festival, ma'am. This time, we have a secret weapon."

When Kugyong answered, the chief of staff quickly put her brain to work. But no brilliant answer must have come to mind because what came out was another long sigh.

She said, "Oste? But both the Navy and the Army have idol singers. It's not a matter of having an ace up our sleeve; it's more about even meeting the basic requirements of an honor guard unit—ours is so small. Even K-pop groups have at least ten or so members these days, but our ragtag honor guard is only a little more than that. Plus, there's no stage, and all the performances are held in the military training ground out in the open, so our honor guard has nowhere enough people to cover such a large space. But I don't want to pick more spacenauts to be honor guards. We technically just need the Space Force Band for protocol. Isn't it enough to have a few guards that can squeeze into the national Honor Guard when we receive foreign heads of state? Do we really have to have enough to go and compete in the silly festival? I'd rather expand our e-sports team."

Colonel Lee chimed in, "Captain Park's idea is the solution to that particular issue. Let's hear him out."

"Really?"

Casually avoiding Chief Gu Yemin's bright and curious eyes, Kugyong held up the device in his hand with the screen facing outward. It was a military-issue tablet, about the size of a diary.

"This is a video from the United States," Kugyong explained. "It shows them supplying batteries and other goods to the space station. The Russian spacecraft in orbit gradually closes the distance between itself and the space station, and an astronaut at the space station operates a robot arm to dock the transport ship at the station."

The video showed the view from the space station—the image of a cylindrical spacecraft launched from Earth. It would've been easy to mistake the video as a still photograph if not for the Earth in the background, moving rapidly due to the revolution of the space station. The next scene showed the spacecraft seen from where the robot arm was being operated. This time, the screen showed a virtual green line across the center. It was a guideline that helped mark the precise location and position of the spacecraft, which was in a three-dimensional space, on the two-dimensional screen.

"And?" asked Gu Yemin.

"The images are not what I mean to show you, ma'am. It's the video broadcast that I wanted to tell you about. This video was live streamed for about three hours, but basically there's not much happening on screen. It's a delicate task that requires a lot of time, but they could've sped the video up and been done with it in three minutes. Instead, they streamed it in real-time for three hours. And so this video had a narrator."

The chief of staff pushed up her glasses with one hand to show curiosity.

"A narrator, you say?" she asked.

With a meaningful smile on his face, Kugyong answered, "More like a commentator or a sideline reporter, but the role is essentially that of a silent film narrator."

"That's a creative interpretation. So?"

"In terms of communications, the outer space is a silent film," Kugyong continued. "There is no sound. Not only is there no sound, but for most of this video there's nothing happening on screen. So the narrator tells the viewers where the space station is passing over with respect to Earth and answers questions that people post online. Obviously, it would be boring to simply repeat that the spacecraft is approaching the space station for an entire hour. This next video is one that our Public Relations Corps made last year for a recruitment commercial. This video has sound."

"It's a sound film," the chief of staff repeated curtly, hinting that she knew what he was going to say and urging him to go ahead and skip a few steps.

Without hesitation, Kugyong jumped ahead and said, "This is a sound film, but it was done post sync."

"You mean it was dubbed after the film was recorded? People liked this video."

"Yes, ma'am. But the production period was long for a twenty-second video. And the process was creative. I'm not sure if you remember, but you'd ordered us to show the Space Force's unique interpretation of the sounds in outer space instead of the sounds we often hear in sci-fi films."

"I did?" Gu Yemin asked in surprise. "That must have put you in a rather difficult position, though it was probably a random idea I just threw out there. So what's the next step? Are you working on it?"

"Yes, ma'am. We are developing technology that is comparable to real-time recording. We use artificial intelligence to interpret what's shown on screen and immediately provide the relevant sounds. Some of the budget from the Research and Development Center at the headquarters was allotted for this and is now under review, and development will begin next year."

"Wait," Gu Yemin interrupted Kugyong and chimed in. "So that means no narrator?"

"There will still be a commentator. Basically, nothing happens, and that'll remain the same, but now we'll be watching a video where nothing happens but at least has sound. And the role of the commentator will be different."

"OK. And it'll take several years to perfect the technique, I imagine. So what about the matter at hand? What are you going to do with the honor guards?"

At Gu Yemin's words, Kugyong reached his hand out to the tablet and played the scene he'd watched in the lounge in the single occupant dormitory. It was the scene that had made Kugyong sit up immediately on the couch—the scene where a man in a black suit was walking through a dark alley, stopping when he heard someone pointing a rifle at the back of his head.

Gu Yemin burst out into laughter. Kugyong and Colonel Lee followed suit. The laughter meant that it was good to go—it was like a big signature that spilled over the signature line and filled the entire page of the document for approval. It was that kind of laughter.

"Your name, spacenaut, is Captain Park Kugyong, if I remember correctly? Colonel Lee, let him do what he wants. What an interesting fellow. What is it that he needs? We won't have any technical problems right now, would we?"

Colonel Lee answered, "I'll be issuing an assignment order to the sound development team at the Development Center, and they can do this with the technology they have now. We would need proper sound equipment. I believe it would be best to rent it. The Public Relations Corps will take care of the rest, and we plan on getting that rifle."

"Since that was a prop for a movie, the production crew will know where to find it, I'm sure," said Gu Yemin. "I'm glad I told you to come to my office. I probably would've said no, if I had just looked at the proposal. In any case, it sounds like a plan. I'm good with everything you have there. You can go now. I have a lot to discuss with the Ministry of Defense. You know, right?"

"Is there anything you need help with, ma'am?"

"The Mars Governor-General Lee Jongro raised an issue. General Lee's influence these days is ... he's like a K-pop star to the Ministry of Defense. I think I'd better discuss it with the intelligence agency first. I did do something that could be a bit sensitive. Though, in my defense, I didn't have much of a choice."

That evening, the single occupant dormitory at the Space Force launch base was bustling with people who were moving in. Without having even changed out of his uniform, Kugyong lay on the couch. When the Planet Management Corps' Secretary Kim Eunkyung walked into the lounge with a mug in her hand and nudged his leg to move, Kugyong folded his legs and made room for her without even looking up.

"What are you doing here?" Eunkyung asked. "I thought you said you were moving rooms today."

Only then Kugyong sat up and scooched over to the couch arm with his legs tucked under him.

"I'm just lazy," he said. "Who do you have to live with, Secretary Kim?"

"Me? I don't get a roommate because I'm in planetary work. You know how it is. My work hours are Mars work hours."

"Oh, I remember your interview with *Monthly Space Force*. You said a day on Mars is a bit longer than on Earth."

"Yeah," Eunkyung answered. "Things start thirty-seven minutes later every day for me."

"Right, right. Sounds like hard work, but at least there's one good thing that comes out of it. Now we have to have a roommate and you don't."

"Well, it's not that much of a positive. I became the emergency contact person two years ago, so I can't live off base at all. I'm required to live on base, and the Space Force is supposed to provide me with an apartment or a house, but I haven't moved into one because I think it'd feel a bit stuffy. It's my loss, really. Anyway, who's your roommate?"

"Captain Um Jonghyun from the Intelligence Department."

"Oh, the new guy? Why? Is he giving you trouble?"

"No, no. It's literally that I'm lazy and I don't feel like cleaning up the room."

"But you need to pack and move out of your room for whoever else to move in."

"I moved my stuff to my new room already. I just piled up the boxes in the room and ran."

"I suppose I should be asking Captain Um whether he's OK living with you instead of worrying about how you're feeling. Stop causing trouble for Captain Um and go and unpack your stuff."

"Captain Um's not home yet. He went out a little while ago. Left for the supermarket. I'll go and unpack in a little while."

"Did you tell him that it's far?" Eunkyung asked.

Kugyong answered, "Oh, I told him about the new supermarket that's in fact about the size of a small grocery store which opened about seven kilometers from here, and that it's quick to get there with a car."

As time passed, people who had finished moving into their

dorm rooms began to gather one by one in the lounge. With everyone gaining a roommate, the single occupant dormitory felt like a college dorm at the beginning of the school year. But since everyone was an adult, they didn't seem very excited. It was more like they were in the lounge because they weren't sure what to do in the room with their roommates. As a result, the atmosphere in the lounge became that of a house party.

Wondering whether he should take action as a public relations officer, Park Kugyong was about to get up from his seat when Suh Ga-ul entered the lounge with a voice loud enough to startle everyone.

"I was going to watch a movie starring Oste," she said. "Who wants to watch it with me?"

It seemed like she wasn't aware of how loud she was talking.

Eunkyung asked Ga-ul, "Who's Oste?"

"Oh, Secretary Kim, I didn't see you there. Oste's a member of B Density. He joined our band this summer."

"I thought it was pronounced 'Ohst.'"

"Oh, dear."

While Ga-ul fiddled with the remote to get the movie to play, Eunkyung asked again, "He was in a movie? I hadn't heard of it."

"It bombed," answered Ga-ul. "It's one of those terrible choices that male celebrities make before their mandatory military service because serving a few years in the military feels like the end of the world. Though obviously it's not the end of the world."

"Sounds like you're not a huge fan, SoCal."

"Yeah, well, it'd be the decent thing to watch this film for him as people who eat from the same pot. You know what the title of the movie is? It's *Lunandalusia*. It's so embarrassing! The title is enough to make me cringe! I was like, no way, is it really a portmanteau? But when you look at the poster, there really is a moon! And the movie is set in Andalusia! I mean, wasn't it a stroke of luck that it bombed?"

Hearing Ga-ul, about a dozen people gathered in front of the television. They had been standing awkwardly not knowing where to look, so they came near the couch to see for themselves the irreparable mistake made by the new Space Force band recruit.

At that moment, Um Jonghyun returned from the grocery store with a whole case of beer and entered the lounge with a look of curiosity at the crowd gathered inside. People cheered at the sight of beer, and then it was a party.

There was no music, but the party was off to a good start. Suh Ga-ul was in charge of the remote, and the key to a good party is frequently pressing the buttons on the remote. Every time there was a scene featuring Oste, which if he had been watching would have made him blush scarlet in embarrassment, Ga-ul rewound and replayed. That resulted in a burst of laughter from the people around the couch. There were guffaws of delight. That was how this party went on. Since there was one designated person being the butt of the joke, anyone could join in.

Amidst the uproarious laughter, Kugyong half-yelled at Ga-ul, "SoCal! This is a bit much!"

"So what?" she answered. "He's a celebrity. Plus, he's not here right now."

"I'm afraid he'll find out about it. Some of the people here will meet him eventually."

"It doesn't matter. The most useless thing to do in the world is worrying about celebrities!"

"Oste loves the Space Force, you know!"

"Oh, oh, sure!" Ga-ul answered with her voice dripping with sarcasm.

Now there were about twenty or so people in the lounge. It was the largest crowd ever to have gathered in the lounge, and every one of them looked excited. Bursts of laughter kept on erupting from the first floor of the single occupant dormitory. It seemed almost absurd that the movie had bombed when it elicited such a passionate reaction from the audience.

Jonghyun tapped Kugyong on the shoulder and whispered, "I didn't know Specialist Suh was such a scary person."

Kugyong answered, "Me neither. I heard that she'd lived in all kinds of shared housing around the world, and here she literally stepped in and conquered the lounge. No one can challenge SoCal now. You should be careful too, Captain Um. Don't go strutting about thinking that you'll be left untouched because you're in the Intelligence Department."

"Darn, I should be careful."

With a pitying gaze, Kugyong watched Oste's face taking up the entire TV screen. The moment Oste spoke his line with a sober look, another burst of laughter erupted and filled the lounge.

Seeing Ga-ul roar with laughter, holding the remote control firmly in her hand, Kugyong shook his head from side to side. Then he stepped out of the lounge.

One morning about, three weeks after the impromptu lounge party, a military bus was in the Space Force launch base parking lot waiting to take people to the Autumn Military Music Festival. Looking out at the ocean that lay before her eyes, Suh Ga-ul leaned her head against the window. The weather was finally feeling like autumn. The leaves of the trees around the parking lot seemed to have reddened a little.

Ga-ul had been looking outside the window for a while when someone spoke to her without even a hello.

"That movie, the actor wasn't the problem but the direction!"

Ga-ul turned to find Han Summin sitting next to her.

"Oh, Handsome Man! Long time no see. But, what movie?"

"Lunandalusia."

"*Lunandalusia*? What was that? Just hearing the word makes me cringe for some reason. And it looked like you were a bit embarrassed to say it out loud. This tells me ... that you're talking about Oste's movie?"

Summin said nothing. Instead she glowered at the back of the seat in front of her.

Ga-ul asked, "Why are you here anyway? Does an ace pilot also get assigned to attend things like the military music festival? Wait, wait. I didn't know you also had that service uniform, Handsome Man. Stand up for a sec. Now that I look at it, this uniform looks great on someone who has the right fit for it! Why did they make the uniform that way when we barely have people like that?"

Summin remained quiet. Inspector General Park Soojin, who had just boarded the bus and was passing them by, answered for her instead.

"Master Sergeant Han wasn't assigned. She volunteered."

Ga-ul asked in surprise, "What? Someone actually volunteers for this kind of thing?"

Sitting down in the seat behind Ga-ul and Summin, Soojin whispered as though she were sharing a secret, "Sure! She's a B Density fan."

At Soojin's words, Ga-ul widened her eyes and stared at Summin. Summin turned to Ga-ul and snapped, "So behave yourself from now on. Our alliance has been practically terminated."

"I'm sorry, I had no idea," Ga-ul apologized. "But the movie's hilarious! And admit it, you're embarrassed to say the title aloud too, aren't you?"

"I'm telling you it's not the actor. His agent clearly has a terrible eye for film, and the director was even worse. If you're thrown into a situation like that, no one can fully concentrate on acting. Even the critics recognized that."

"Someone actually critiqued that movie, huh? Oh, sorry."

"Shut up, Suh *Ghoul*!"

Ga-ul turned to Soojin behind her and tattled, "This Space Force sergeant is making fun of an army civilian's name. Isn't that clearly bullying?"

"Not something Suh Ghoul should complain about, is it?" Soojin answered. "Let's just ride the bus in silence, shall we? I'm not that excited about having to be part of this at my age."

Ga-ul popped a question she seemed to have been waiting to ask.

"But seriously, you'd be good at being shooed away since you're Shoojeans, but you're the IG. Why were you assigned out of all the other people in your office?"

"Because we don't get reinforcements. The spacenauts in our office are all very busy. And don't get cute with me."

"Yes, ma'am."

Moments later, as the bus was about to take off, Soojin said to Summin, "Sergeant Han, speaking of direction, do you think the direction for this performance is going to be OK? Public Relations Corps' Park Kugyong seemed to be plotting something."

Without turning around to face Soojin, Summin answered, "I heard that too. That's why I'm going. To monitor what happens."

Unlike other years, there were a lot of civilians at the training ground of the Space Force Academy, where the Autumn Military Music Festival was to be held. From the signs and glow sticks in their hands, it seemed that many of them were B Density fans.

As soon as they stepped down from the bus, Ga-ul grabbed Summin's hand and pulled.

"Come with me. I'll show you backstage. Captain Park Cooking said we could come."

Suddenly, Summin stopped and spoke, drawing a line.

"No, what are you doing? It may be fine after the event but not before a major performance. He's probably busy preparing, so don't do anything stupid."

Looking a bit embarrassed, Ga-ul let Summin's hand go.

"OK. I was just doing it for you."

"I know, and thank you. But, next time. I'm not the only one who wants to see him. All his fans who came to see him would feel that way. I can't receive special treatment. But at least we can get good seats."

"'Kay then, I'll make sure to find us front row seats!"

The Space Force Academy's training ground was big enough to be called "vast." Like the plaza at the SFHQ, it seemed to have been designed to express the universe, with a focus on empty space. As Ga-ul had promised, Summin sat in the very front row.

Ga-ul turned to Summin casually and started when she saw Summin looking through binoculars. She waved her hand in front of Summin's binoculars to get her attention.

"When did you have the time to bring those?" she asked.

"It's a must," Summin answered.

"You want to see him that up close?"

"It helps me not see other pointless stuff too."

And so the pointless festival began. After pointless remarks were made by the pointless chief of staff, the Space Force Academy president's pointless speech continued. The music bands of all military branches stood in groups and played the national anthem. Even at a glance, it was apparent that the Space Force Band was the smallest. The one that seemed the most excited was the United States Forces Korea's band.

The event consisted of band performances and honor guard performances. The Naval Honor Guard stood in a formation that resembled a ship. Two sailors stood in the back of the formation, where a propulsion system should be located. Standing with their backs to the rest of the group, they held out their arms and spun their rifles fast in a helical shape. As they did so, the entire formation began to propel forward, gradually gaining speed. Applause erupted from the audience. The two sailors spinning their rifles had their heads turned, looking behind and walking backward.

The Air Force Honor Guard's formation was an aircraft with four propellers on the front side of the wings. These propellers moved forward instead of backward. Though it was an impressive performance, it was nothing new, as the Navy had already done something similar.

Instead of propellers, the Army caught people's attention with traditional army uniforms from the Joseon Dynasty. The choreographed movements of honor guards throwing spears into the air and catching them were also much more natural than the Air Force or the Navy's performances.

Yawning, Ga-ul was almost dozing off, but the sound of the US Forces Korea Band singing a song in Korean woke her up.

I'll cross the Pacific, cross the Atlantic, and even the Indian Ocean
To run to you when you call for me, I'll run to you at any cost.

Hearing the lyrics, Ga-ul muttered to herself, "The Americans actually could do that. Though it's a bit terrifying to imagine what they'll be holding as they run to us."

Summin still hadn't said a word. Ga-ul looked at her. She seemed nervous yet determined as she fiddled with the binoculars.

Ga-ul asked, "Why are you so anxious? Is it because your idol's about to come out?"

"I'm just worried," Summin said. "Why did they have to make him go at the end? The Space Force is so bad at these kinds of performances."

"But he's a professional. I'm sure he can handle something like this."

"But it's not his usual gig. Plus, there's no stage or lights. If he makes a mistake …"

"No one would say anything even if he does make a mistake. The Space Force's performances have been terrible every single year, but we're still here. Hey, are you listening to me? Handsome Man? Guess not."

The Space Force's performance was last. Since the host of this year's festival was the Space Force, it wasn't strange that it was performing the grand finale. Yet the members of the Space Force who were assigned to attend the event seemed rather uncomfortable. The performances weren't ranked, so there was no need to cheer for their honor guards or be disheartened. But a plainly glum aura emanated from the stands occupied by the Space Force.

Summin held her breath as she immersed herself in the world inside the binoculars.

Suddenly, she said, "If he makes a mistake, people will say that Oste messed up instead of thinking that the Space Force's performance was bad as usual."

She seemed close to tears. Ga-ul said nothing in response.

Moments later, when the Space Force Band appeared, Summin was back to her passionate self, as if nothing had happened. The binoculars were raised to her eyes, and her back straightened. Ga-ul turned around to look toward the back of the stands. She saw people in a similar pose as Summin in the civilian seating area. Even though they were sitting in different parts of the audience, their binoculars moved in perfect synchronization toward the same point.

After the Space Force Band's musical performance and march, the honor guard finally stepped up. The binoculars moved about frantically, looking for Oste, who was not among them yet. As the other military branches' honor guards had done, the Space Force Honor Guard finished its brief introductory demonstration, and the band began to play a new song. Loud shouts and screams that hadn't been heard before rang out from the audience. Roars that seemed to be somewhere between cheers and madness gradually spread throughout the stands. The binoculars that had been moving were now glued on one spot. An exclamation escaped from Summin's lips. Now that the handful of other members of the honor guard had stepped aside, Oste was alone on the Space Force Academy training grounds.

With a rifle slung across his shoulder, Oste strode to the center of the grounds and stopped. Aside from the sound of the drums, no one—not even the Space Force Band—made a sound. After placing the rifle on the ground before him, Oste stood and waited until the cheers died down. Finally, when the audience became utterly silent, Oste picked up the rifle with a swift movement.

That was when the sound was heard. *Click.* The sound that said, "This is a rifle!"

LAUNCH SOMETHING!

Ga-ul's eyes flew open wide, as did others.

When Oste moved the rifle again, a sharp and crisp sound rang throughout the grounds.

Click click clack. Click click rattle, clack click.

The sounds were familiar and easy on the ears. They surrounded the audience from all sides as if the noise were coming from somewhere deep inside Earth.

Other firearms that the honor guard used had also made sounds, but there was something unique about the sounds made by Oste's rifle. It was because sounds that wouldn't ever be made by a rifle were blended in the mix, like the *swoosh* that was heard whenever the bayonet cut through the air. The sound effects were similar to those heard in sword fights in movies, and they surely weren't coming from the short dagger on the end of the muzzle.

Everyone who heard it knew that the sounds were mechanically engineered, but it was also clear that they weren't coming from a pre-recording. When Oste tossed the rifle into the air and caught it, with its butt on his palm, the swooshing sound also stopped. It would've been nearly impossible to get the timing right if the sounds had been recorded in advance.

Because of the perfect timing, the noises that Oste's gun made seemed more real than those of an actual rifle. Sounds mixed with the murmur of an analog device which therefore carried a chill that couldn't be felt from real firearms. Strangely persuasive and impactful sounds that sent a cold shiver down the listener's spine.

The audience fell silent without being prompted. Everyone was straining to concentrate on the sounds. Oste was holding the gun that Ga-ul had seen in the period drama. It was the rifle that Park Kugyong had wanted to get, from the Korean Empire days. The uniform that Oste was wearing was also similar to what was worn back then, since the Space Force's dress uniform had been designed in the style of that period, although with a more modern interpretation. That was why it didn't look out of place.

Every time the rifle was moved, crisp clicks and clacks were heard. Everyone's eyes were on the spacenaut of the Space Force Honor Guard, standing alone in the center of the training grounds. From the not-so-fast but sharp and crisp moves to the flashy moves that continued without giving time for the audience to cheer, Oste's movements were not a millimeter off as he stood alone and performed in the vast space.

Gathering momentum from his performance, Oste then moved on to the part of the show unique to the Space Force Honor Guard. It involved spinning in a circle, like a revolving planet. Every time a full circle was completed, Oste took a big step, eventually crossing the training grounds from one side to the other. As he performed, the rifle in his hands continued to spin without pause. The swooshing sounds that expressed a rifle cutting through the air filled the entire training grounds, and unique, inexplicable mechanical sounds were adequately inserted between the swooshes. The sounds were imbued with something like madness.

The announcer broke his silence and added a commentary.

"The perpetual spinning movement represents the rotation of planets. In space, objects move in three different ways—they remain in one place, move in a straight line, or revolve around something. Through the combination of these three basic movements, the Space Force explores the universe and responds to threats to humanity."

Holding her breath, Summin watched Oste's movements through her binoculars. Spinning round and round, and then spinning round and round again. The same movements were being repeated, but the more he repeated the movements, the more energetic and stronger his steps grew. A sigh of admiration escaped from Summin's lips. Applause and cheers erupted from the audience who must have been feeling the same way.

Ga-ul, who was sitting next to Summin but outside of her field of vision, exclaimed with a thrilled voice, "That's how that's supposed to be done! It's the same performance we're familiar with, but this is really impressive. I used to think this was the silliest thing ever."

He'd been spinning so much that a slight swoon was more than expected, but Oste's steps were firm and unwavering. Without taking her eyes from the binoculars, Summin spoke to Ga-ul in a dreamy voice, as though she were murmuring to herself.

"I've never seen such a thing before either. I've seen these movements countless times since high school, but he's the first one to get it perfect."

The event ended, and everything was cleared up, but neither Suh Ga-ul nor Han Summin could be seen in the green room for the Space Force Band. Park Kugyong kept glaring at his phone and finally picked it up to call Ga-ul.

"You said you were coming to the green room," Kugyong said when Ga-ul answered.

"Summin didn't want to go."

"Why not?"

"I don't know. She's crying and everything."

"Crying?"

"Not like bawling or anything. Just tearing up. She said she only found out today that the Space Force was so amazing."

"Huh? That's a bit much. So she just went to take the bus back to the base?"

"Yeah, that's where she's headed. She says she shouldn't bother the artist."

"Artist? Well, if she says so. Then we're off as well."

Lee Ja-un, who had been listening to the phone conversation by Kugyong's side, looked at him pensively.

"She's not coming, sir?" he asked.

"No, she's not. Let's get our stuff and go."

"Do you think I'll have another chance later, sir? I really wanted to meet her this time, sir."

"You don't have to keep on adding 'sir' at the end of the sentence."

"Do you think I'll have another chance to see Master Sergeant Han Summin?" Ja-un asked.

"You actually do like the Space Force, don't you? You even know that it's best to see Summin before she becomes a celebrity."

"Call me a fanboy who wants to see his idol from up close."

With a face that said he'd just heard something completely absurd, Kugyong stared at Ja-un and said, "The popular K-pop star Oste, a fanboy? People would think it's the other way around. I just heard that Han Summin went home nearly shedding tears of joy."

Ja-un said nothing in response. Instead, he stared at the mountains far away for a few moments before picking up the bags he'd packed.

On the bus back to the Space Force headquarters, Kugyong said to Ja-un, "We did an amazing job this year. We've been doing these things for decades since the Space Force came into being, but that was the first time I'd seen it done that well. In any case, this is the last time you'll be called in to perform as an honor guard. I've been assigned to the launch base, but the chief confirmed it as well. Instead, we'll start a different program. I think it'll be closer to what you've been doing out in the real world in show business. Doing internet broadcasts and stuff. What do you think? I do think that the most important thing is whether you want to do it or not. We can't pay much for your appearances, but if you'd still like to do it, then we'll talk to your agency."

Ja-un answered, "I'd like to do the same performance next year. If the Public Relations Corps finds it necessary, I can participate in related activities. And I would be grateful if I could perform at the following year's festival as well. Also, could the Public Relations Corps purchase that rifle? It fits perfectly in my hands, and I don't think I can use a different one."

Kugyong was at a loss for words. He tried gauging the situation for a moment and, hiding his confusion, he calmly said, "Why? You don't have to do that anymore. We'll let you do something better. If there's something you'd like to do, you can tell me."

After a moment's hesitation, Ja-un skipped the explanation and answered curtly, "I just want to spin round and round."

"What?"

"Please let me just spin."

"Why?"

"That's my dream."

"Since when?"

"Since today."

"But why? Doesn't it make you sick just spinning like that?"

"A little bit, sir."

"Geesh."

Han Summin sat slouched on the couch in the lounge and recalled the performance she'd seen earlier. It seemed that the excitement of the day hadn't yet died down. Kim Eunkyung came to the lounge to get something from the refrigerator and noticed Summin.

"Still awake? Everyone went back to their rooms saying they were all tired."

Instead of answering her question, Summin said, "Secretary Kim."

"Yeah?"

"What do you think about the Space Force?"

"Huh? Why are you asking me that in the middle of the night?"

"I know it's kind of random, but I'd still like to hear your answer. What do you think about it? The Space Force."

"Well, I've been here for too long to know anymore."

"What was it like at first?"

"At first. Which administration was it? I can't even remember. I do remember thinking this though: brilliant people in a stupid system. And so every day's like an episode of a sitcom."

"Right?!" Summin exclaimed.

"That's a rather strong reaction. I didn't say much."

Eunkyung hesitated whether to sit down or not and eventually took a couple of steps toward the hallway.

Summin grinned and said, "Go get some rest. I'll be heading up to my room soon too."

"OK, have a good night. Oh, and there's one more way I would summarize it. The Space Force, I mean."

"What is it?"

"Brilliant people in a stupid system. But people who are trying to overhaul that stupid system in order to do something great.

You know, people who come here have absurd dreams. I mean, outer space? Come on."

"I will be sure to bear that in mind."

"But you're lucky, Sarge Han."

"What do you mean?"

"The thing about people trying to overhaul this stupid system—I've seen many people try to do it, but it always ends in disappointment, like in my case. The bigger the dream, the more broken the people eventually become and the more likely they are to end up just waiting out their days, looking forward to receiving their pension. But things feel a bit different these days, don't they?"

"Do they?"

"Of course! Though I don't know if that's because of Chief Gu or Pac-Man."

"Hmm, the training sessions have increased this year for sure," Summin said.

"See? That's a good thing. Anyway, I'm really off to bed now. Night."

"Good night."

After Eunkyung left the lounge, Summin returned to being one with the couch again. She dozed off for a bit but started awake and went up to her room. A little while later, the lights in the lounge turned off automatically. The refrigerator began to hum.

Chapter Four
Romantic Relationship Occurrence Report

Acting Inspector General Park Soojin sat behind the huge desk with her back to a window, talking to someone on the phone. There were two windows in the inspector general's office—one behind Soojin and the other to her right. With her gaze fixed on the pencil holder on her desk, she concentrated on what the person on the other end of the line was saying. When that person stopped talking, Soojin chimed in without a moment's delay.

"In any case, you're saying that you've broken up?"

As the person on the other end of the line began to talk again, Soojin's face turned into a slight scowl.

Then a little later, she spoke once again in a business-like voice, "So you do mean that you've broken up. You don't need to give me the long story about why. Since that's now been confirmed, your relationship will be marked as terminated. As the Inspector General, that's within my authority, and I trust you know the relevant regulations. Do not do anything rash. I have to go now."

Soojin put the receiver down and picked up a stamp from the corner of the desk. After pressing it down on a red ink pad, she stamped the top of the document that lay in a folder at the center of her desk. In red ink, the stamp read, "Relationship Terminated."

The form, made up of a table that had been filled out by hand, was titled Romantic Relationship Occurrence Report.

Soojin wrote down the date below the stamp. Then she took the document out of the folder and put it down to the side.

The next document in the folder was another Romantic Relationship Occurrence Report. Holding the receiver with one hand, Soojin checked the phone number written near the bottom of the form.

All of a sudden, the door to her office opened, and the newly transferred technical sergeant poked her head inside.

"Inspector General, are you busy?"

Soojin put down the phone and looked up at Technical Sergeant Choi Suzy.

"Not really. What is it?"

Suzy explained, "Yesterday I submitted the furlough form for our office's spacenauts for approval, and we need it approved now to get it processed in time."

"Oh, sorry about that."

Suzy stepped over the threshold and into the office. Then seeing the folder on Soojin's desk, she cordially said, "Oh, you're working on that. From the size of it, it looks like there are a lot of romancers here."

"Romancers? Is that what they call them in the combat units?"

"Is it different in the rearguard units? What do you call them here?"

"Hmm, I don't think we call them anything. Maybe 'couples'?"

"Ah, well, in the Fighter Wings, they strictly manage romancers. Every month, the chief is briefed on the status report, and the Internal Review Department puts together a list of romancers and separately reports on them during disciplinary periods, and they track down unreported romancers as well. They are probably a lot stricter because we are deployed overseas. I gather it's not that strict here?"

Soojin, who had been curiously watching Suzy, answered in a calm voice, "Why is that necessary? I mean, the thing I care least about is other people's relationship status. What's military discipline got to do with that."

"Really?"

"Since the Fighter Wings were originally part of the Air Force, perhaps the guidelines were enforced differently, but other people's relationships are no one else's business."

"Then what are you checking them for?"

"To stop people from using their relationships as excuses."

"But aren't people in relationships under special management?" Suzy asked in all seriousness.

Soojin gestured at her to take a seat in the chair in front of the desk and then sat up straight to meet Suzy's eye level. Then she calmly said, "Spacenauts are free to date. They don't even need to file a report. As long as nothing untoward happens, no one should care what they do with each other. Here, people would think you're joking if you go around monitoring who's in a relationship and who's not."

Suzy then pointed to the stack of papers on Soojin's desk and asked, "Then what are those for? Why do you even collect them?"

"For reference in case of some kind of trouble. For instance, someone could break and enter another person's apartment and tell the military police that they entered with tacit permission because they were in a relationship. That's when we can use these to check the facts. Confirming if they'd filed a Romantic Relationship Occurrence Report."

"Then what?"

"If they did file one, then it can be used to mitigate their offense. But imagine what would happen if they didn't file one."

"Then it becomes breaking and entering?"

"Exactly."

"Even if they really were in a relationship?" Suzy asked.

"Yep," Soojin answered.

"Even if everyone else knew that they were in a relationship?"

"Of course. Because that's the reason this form exists."

Leaning back in her chair, Suzy looked befuddled. Soojin gave her another example.

"Say that someone reported an assault. The assailant could say that they were in someone else's room because they were a relationship. So they'd at least be able to worm out of the serious charge of breaking and entering. But just saying you are in a relationship doesn't work in the Space Force. If you want to say that, you need to be registered. It's not as simple as submitting this form. Once the form is submitted, an official in charge has to listen to the two parties concerned and conduct an assessment. At the launch base, that official in charge is me. And every quarter we have to contact everyone who has registered their relationship to confirm whether the relationship is ongoing or has been terminated. Sure, some people try to use this form to get out of what they've done, but that won't work. Regardless of this form, all cases are to be properly investigated by the military police. It looks like an agreement with no binding force, but I think it's better to have it than not. That's precisely why this system was adopted. Also because too many offenders tried to make excuses saying that they were in relationships. But I find listening to other people's relationship troubles the most tiresome. Even after I hear about the relationships, I forget. So I have to look into them again and again every quarter. When I call to confirm, a lot of them think I'm some kind of a relationship counselor and babble on and on and on. So then I have to hear them out. Then in the next quarter, I forget all about who was dating who. I really want to pass this over to the newly transferred technical sergeant—yes, that's you, Sergeant Choi Suzy—but I can't. I could transfer the task if you had at least twenty years of experience, or else the Inspector General has to do it herself. So I'm miserable. I mean, I like that you've been assigned here, but the day you were transferred, I went home and realized that I have to keep doing this. And so that's what I'm doing now. Quarterly updates."

"Sounds like you are miserable," said Suzy.

"Extremely."

"I actually like that stuff."

"And that's why I find this entire situation utterly ridiculous. Anyway, those Fighter Wingers, why are they trying to manage people's relationships? Do they think that military discipline means preventing people from dating? Preventing stalkers from making ridiculous excuses—that's what discipline is."

"Then is there nothing else that people do here about romancers, aside from you updating the forms?"

"Nope. Everything else is up to the military police. If a criminal case occurs and the military police request confirmation, I look up the list to see if the name's on it. That's it. And I have to do all of it, and they're all a secret."

"I've heard that there are strange provisions in the regulations. Do you really accept those too? Like affairs?"

"If they register the relationship, then yes. We don't question anything else about the relationship apart from whether they are in a relationship or not. But people probably don't register those."

"Some people might."

At Suzy's words, Soojin hesitated as if she were thinking of someone specific.

Then she said, "Well, maybe."

Suzy's eyes sparkled as she looked at Soojin with respect and said, "Inspector General! You're like Pandora's box! There must be a lot of people who register their relationships and keep it a secret from everyone else, aren't there?"

"The problem is that this Pandora is someone who doesn't ever want to open a box that she's been told not to open. But in any case, Sergeant Choi, come check in with me every now and then. If you end up interpreting regulations here the way you used to in the Fighter Wing, you might end up wasting time and energy preventing one thing when it's really meant to preventing some other thing. I should suggest to the Space Force headquarters that they curb the front-line units' enthusiasm."

"OK. But I heard that Mars is much stricter with this kind of stuff."

"That's why I didn't go there. Sometimes it just feels like Mars isn't under our jurisdiction."

"I think Martians look cool. Oh, I just thought of this. Who do *you* report to if you are in a relationship?"

"Hey, too many questions. But I'll tell you since you are the special duty sergeant at the Internal Review Department. I have to report to the base commander. Or someone higher up. Practically they're just saying I shouldn't date. And Sergeant Choi, you know Specialist Suh Ga-ul in the Weather Agency? There's something I tell her often. Wanna hear it?"

"Sure! What is it?"

"Don't be cheeky."

"Oh, no, ma'am," Suzy answered. "I'll be off now!"

Early next morning, Technical Sergeant Choi Suzy stepped into the inspector general's office to drop off a report and noticed a piece of paper sitting in the center of the otherwise empty desk. It was a blank Romantic Relationship Occurrence Report.

Suzy put the report for approval on one side of the desk and left. Right next to the inspector general's office was the Internal Review Department, where Suzy worked. Seeing Senior Spacenaut Song coming into work, Suzy said, "Good thing you're here. I have a question. Our inspector general, you said she's really efficient at her job, right?"

"That's what I think," answered Song. "She predicts how things will turn out or who will come to see her with what kind of problem and puts together relevant forms and documents. And when that someone comes to see her, she gives them the forms that she had ready on the desk and tells them to fill them out. Not all the time, but it happened a few times and then rumors spread and within six months turned into legends. So everyone's kind of scared of her."

"I heard that too. So that must mean that sometime soon someone will be coming to fill out that form that's on her desk."

"Who? Coming to fill out which form?"

"There was an RROR form in the IG's office."

"Then I suppose that means there will be two people coming to see her."

Since it was too early for the air conditioner to be on, the door to the internal review department office had been left open. While Suzy and Song returned to their desks, someone who had been listening to their conversation in the hallway outside the door nodded solemnly. It was Captain Um Jonghyun from the Intelligence Department.

The Intelligence Department was located across the corridor from the Internal Review Department. While the Internal Review Department was located in the corner of the launch base main building and had two windows for the sunlight to stream in, the Intelligence Department was located on the sunless side of the building with a single window that was sealed closed except for a small ventilation hatch.

Every time he heard footsteps in the hallway, Jonghyun cracked open the door to peek outside.

"Are you expecting someone?" asked Senior Master Sergeant Jeon In-gu.

"No," Jonghyun answered.

"Are you watching people going in and out of the Internal Review Department? Who? The newly transferred Technical Sergeant Choi?"

"Not at all."

"Then, are you trying to figure out people's identity by their footsteps? You're frowning, and by the looks of it, you're guessing who's walking from the sound of their feet and checking to see if you're correct. Is that what you're doing?"

Jonghyun answered in a somewhat embarrassed manner, "Something like that."

"I used to play that a lot back in the day. When I was at the SFHQ. Although, there's no one from other organizations or higher-ups here, so there's no real need to do that. They don't still do that at the HQ, do they?"

After that, it was harder for Jonghyun to look out through the cracked opened door. Having spent the entire morning straining to hear the people walking past, by the afternoon, Jonghyun was able to recognize some of the footsteps when he furrowed his brow and listened very closely. With a contented smile on his face, at times Jeon would idle and watch Jonghyun concentrate on the sound of steps for a moment before returning to what he'd been doing.

Origami designs sent from the Mars base were spread out across Jonghyun's desk. They were some kind of blueprint, where the folds were marked with dotted lines or thin solid lines. Jonghyun was scrutinizing them when Jeon said, "I can't tell who this is."

Jonghyun looked up at him, perplexed. Then realizing that Jeon was talking about footsteps, he listened for the noise coming from the hallway.

"There are two people, right?" asked Jonghyun.

Jeon nodded and said, "The person with quiet but quick steps sounds like Master Sergeant Han Summin, but I'm not sure who the other one is. I've never heard those footsteps before. Perhaps they're from the HQ on an assignment."

Jonghyun perked up his ears and rolled his swivel chair back toward the door. Then he cracked it open to check outside. He noticed a man in full winter dress uniform disappear into the Internal Review Department office. Unfortunately, he didn't see the man's face. Then he saw Han Summin follow the man into the office.

Looking at Jonghyun's pensive face, Jeon asked, "Is it Master Sergeant Han?"

"Yes," answered Jonghyun. "I didn't see who the other person was."

"I told you I was good at this game. I wonder why she's going to the Internal Review Department. Maybe to write a letter of justification? Was it the chief master sergeant who brought her in? Though I don't think the footsteps sounded like hers."

"No, it was a man."

Jonghyun returned to his desk, looking unperturbed. The office phone rang, and Sergeant Jeon took his time picking it up.

"Well, well, Fidelity!" Jeon answered with the Army salute instead of the Space Force's. "Long time no see!"

Jonghyun stared at Jeon, who was saluting the empty space. Jeon winked at Jonghyun then turned his head to continue the phone conversation. The sound of him talking and chuckling continued.

Jonghyun went back to looking at the origami designs. After a while, he snapped his head up like a bunny that sensed a fox's footsteps. His movements were so rabbit-like that he would have pricked up his ears if he didn't have human ones. He heard the sound of someone walking in the hallway.

He rolled over to the door once again, still sitting in his chair. Through the cracked open door, he saw the backside of a man who had come out of the Internal Review Department office and was walking down the hallway. From the uniform alone it was difficult to tell who he was.

Jonghyun cocked his head to the side and wondered out loud, "Isn't that Captain Park?"

Right at that moment, Sergeant Jeon—who must have gotten off the phone at some point—poked his head out next to Jonghyun and whispered, "Which Captain Park? The military police? Oh, you mean Captain Park Kugyong from the Public Relations Corps on assignment here from the Space Force headquarters? Come to think of it, it must be him. You two are roommates, right? You must know what his footsteps sound like then!"

Jonghyun answered, "He walks around in sandals at the dorm."

"But you can tell from the way he walks, no? You can just add the sound of footsteps to his gait, and you'll know."

"Hmm, I can't really tell."

Sergeant Jeon laughed at Jonghyun's words and returned to his desk, where he assumed the position of a man not planning to do anything for the entire afternoon.

"You look elated that the director's not here today," Jonghyun said.

Sergeant Jean responded to Jonghyun's words with a beaming smile that spread across his face.

That evening, Jonghyun immediately went to his room after work without even getting dinner. As he entered the main entrance of the dorm, Park Kugyong was walking down the steps, already changed out of his uniform and into something nicer. The electric clock at the door to the dormitory building read 17:20.

Jonghyun asked, "Going somewhere?"

"To get dinner," Kugyong answered.

"In that?"

"Oh, I'm headed out."

With that short answer, Kugyong left through the entrance. Jonghyun surveyed the way Kugyong walked from behind and opened his eyes wide when he noticed that Kugyong was headed into the parking lot.

"You bought a car!" he exclaimed.

"Just a used one," Kugyong answered. "I bought it for cheap from my sister."

"Don't people say stuff when you drive *that* around base?"

Instead of a reply, Kugyong gave him a quick salute and got into his light blue sports car.

The engine roared to life, and the car slid out of the parking lot. Then a window on the third floor of the dormitory opened, and Planetary Secretary Kim Eunkyung poked out her head. Seeing Jonghyun standing at the entrance, she asked, "Was that Park Cooking's car?"

"Apparently so."

"He could've given Summin a ride."

"Is she going somewhere?" asked Jonghyun. "I'll be heading out in a little while, so if she's up there, tell her to wait a bit."

"Oh no, she left already. Said she was meeting someone. She walked down, saying she was going to take the bus, so I'm sure he'll see her on the way."

Jonghyun tipped his head to the side and shouted up to Eunkyung, "Already? Everyone's so quick to leave, and it's only five twenty. Is today some kind of special day I don't know about?"

"I was wondering the same thing. Maybe it's one of those special days that young people make up. I have no clue about new holidays on Earth that aren't marked on calendars."

Summin was walking down the hill beyond the entrance to the base when she heard a car and stopped in her tracks. She didn't turn around to look up the hill. Moments later, Kugyong's blue sports car drove down and pulled up in front of her. It seemed perfectly timed, as though they'd meant to meet up there.

Kugyong rolled down the driver's side window, and from a distance the two of them seemed to talk for a little while, but

Summin didn't get into his car. Kugyong's car disappeared toward the town, and Summin cautiously looked from side to side before heading down the hill again.

The Weather Agency's Suh Ga-ul watched the entire scene from afar through the telescope, about 1.5 meters long and mounted atop a tripod, that was installed on the rooftop of the Weather Agency building.

"Strange, those two," Ga-ul murmured. "I wonder if there's something going on between them."

Inspector General Park Soojin, who was standing next to her but outside of the telescope's field of view, asked, "Who are you talking about?

"Nobody," Ga-ul answered. "I just spy on the people in the neighborhood to test the telescope. All right, the telescope's working fine. I'll show you how to focus."

Soojin was wearing a yellow night duty band on her left arm. In her right hand was a big walkie-talkie. She asked, "Can't you just focus it now?"

"But there's nothing in the sky now."

"Don't you have one that has an automatic focus?"

"We're only the Weather Agency, not an observatory. And what you're looking for is tiny because it's an asteroid. The space probe did install reflectors on it, but it won't look as bright as the space station. It revolves around the Earth at the same speed as the moon, about sixty degrees behind it, but if I tell you that, you'll say that you don't know the moon's orbit. Oh, you have an astronomy app on your phone, right? Not the Space Force's. Right, that one. Turn it on and point your phone at the night sky, and it'll show you where the moon is passing on the screen, so you can point the telescope in that direction and use this little telescope on the side to look for the asteroid. And when you see it in the center of this small lens, you look into this bigger telescope and make adjustments. Use this to focus."

"It's too complicated," Soojin grumbled at Ga-ul's long explanation.

"Nah, you just have to do it manually," Ga-ul said. "If you can't see it through the telescope, just look up at the sky with the naked eye. You said you have good eyesight. If you see it during your early morning patrol, it might look rather romantic, who knows? And it won't be that cold tonight."

"Thanks. Although my eyesight's not great. What do I do with the telescope afterward?"

"Just leave it. It's too heavy for you to move it by yourself. And if you break it while trying, then my director's going to be in a bind."

"The Weather Agency director?" asked Soojin.

"He can't ask the Inspector General to pay for it," Ga-ul explained.

"I can pay for it."

"That's the thing. You could pay for it, but he would never ask you to. Because it's like belling the cat."

"Great. But you know when I do the night rounds, it feels like there *is* a bell on my neck. I wonder if the person on duty calls people on my route to warn them. If they feel that uncomfortable with me doing the rounds, they could take me off night duty, you know. When they feel uncomfortable because they have to ask me to do something, I'm Inspector General, but when they're scheduling night duties or sending me on assignments, I'm Acting Inspector General."

"Well, that's that, but asking you to pay for the telescope is different. Technically you're supposed to be in combat uniform on night duty, but no one says anything even if you're in service uniform. So just leave the telescope, no one would steal it. I think you're only talking now to keep me here because you're bored. I'm gonna head home now."

"Well, don't you catch on quick. But one more question. Is it safe for an asteroid to be orbiting the Earth?"

Hesitantly Ga-ul answered Soojin, "It's a satellite of the Earth now. It used to revolve around the sun, but once every fifty years, when it gets close, it gets caught up in the Earth's gravity and orbits a few times before it gets released again. Of course, it's not as close as you'd think. And the possibility of it hitting us? Well, I don't know. It's really far to even consider it as being in the Earth's vicinity."

"Do things like this happen a lot?"

"An asteroid getting caught up in the Earth's gravity and orbiting for a while happens all the time, but you don't see one this size that often. That's why those grandstanders at Allied Space Force took advantage of this opportunity and had reflectors installed on it. When you think about it, it's pretty much the same thing as Pac-Man. But of course, when others do it, it's all terrible and must be shot down; when you do it, it's great! This is actually Captain Um's area of expertise. But in any case, make sure to get a look at the asteroid before it disappears. When it comes back, you'll be too old, and your eyes will be too dim to see it. I'm off then."

Still on night duty at the Launch Base Operations Division, Soojin closed the book she'd been reading and took off her glasses as she turned to the clock to check the time. It was three thirty in the morning. She turned to the monitor on the desk and tapped one side of the screen, pulling up a table titled "Base

Vehicle Entry and Exit." Soojin put her glasses back on and examined the table. Then she murmured to herself, "Not back yet, hmm."

She stealthily got up from her seat and grabbed her cap and a walkie-talkie. The non-commissioned officer and spacenaut also on night duty were dozing side by side at the desk across from her. Deciding not to wake them, Soojin quietly left the office.

As Soojin tiptoed down the steps, trying not to make any noise, the spacenaut on night duty who had looked to have been asleep straightened his back. With eyes wide open and sparkling bright, as though he had been awake this whole time, he picked up the phone and made a call.

"This is the night watch," he spoke into the phone. "The night duty officer is on outside patrol."

He hung up and dialed another number.

"This is the night watch. The night duty officer is on outside patrol."

Stepping out of the entrance, Soojin put her earphones in. A soft voice of a man flowed out of them. It was a radio show emceed by Lee Ja-un.

"Oste's *Let's Raise the Density!* This is Spacenaut First Class Lee Ja-un, and I'll be your host tonight. You've all been waiting a long time, right? For an entire week, I've been dying for today to come. It feels like time passes way too slowly. Is it because I'm a spacenaut doing the mandatory military service? Speaking of spacenauts, what kind of things come to mind when you hear the words 'Space Force'? I was told an interesting story today, about how to tell whether you are in the Space Force or not.

LAUNCH SOMETHING!

First, you go to the nearest pantry cabinet. Considering that there are pantries in both the military and ordinary company offices, you might still be confused about where you are. Second, open the cabinet and see if there's a choco pie. And third! Rip open the wrapper and take a bite of the choco pie. If you think, 'Oh my gosh, this is the most delicious thing I've ever had!' then you're in the base. But if you think, 'Damn, why did I open this? I need to eat this now,' then you're not in the military. Well, well, isn't that great? Today's first song is as sweet as a bite of choco pie, and it's sung by the young Oste before he understood why people ate things like choco pies. Lone Orbiter!"

The outside patrol was a piece of cake. Not a single guard was dozing at the guard posts. Signing the patrol log, Soojin said to a military police officer on night guard duty, "Everyone's guarding the posts so well, sharp-eyed and all. People might mistake us for the Air Force, you know."

Soojin headed up to the rooftop of the Weather Agency building, where the telescope had been positioned. As Ga-ul had told her, she opened the app on her phone and pointed it at the sky. Stars appeared on her phone screen. Unfortunately, it was cloudy and hard to make out the stars in the actual sky. Pushing her hands into her pockets, Soojin stood quietly by the telescope.

"And she says she works for the Weather Agency," Soojin muttered. "I don't know if she didn't tell me that it was going to be cloudy on purpose or because she didn't know."

She looked out into the night. Below the horizon, she saw a light approaching the base. It was the road to the main entrance. Soojin turned the telescope in that direction and looked into the eyepiece. Without even having to fiddle with the focus, she could plainly see an approaching vehicle.

"That must be where SoCal was spying," mumbling to herself, Soojin removed her earphones. A blue sports car came into the telescope's field of view. It stopped midway up the hill before reaching the top. Then someone got out of the car. It was Han Summin.

Soojin took her phone out of her pocket and checked the time. It was 4:10 a.m. She looked into the telescope again. After dropping Summin off, the car glided through the entrance gates. Then it stopped in the parking lot by the single occupant dormitory. Under the lamplight, Park Kugyong got out of the car and glanced toward the main entrance.

Kugyong took something out of his pocket. From the light it shone on his face, it must have been his phone. Soojin turned the telescope toward the hill outside the main entrance. Summin was now beyond the top of the hill and walking down toward the gates. She opened her bag and fumbled through it. The inside of her bag grew bright. She must have been looking for her phone, it seemed. Without taking it out, Summin slung her bag across her shoulder. Then she trudged toward the main entrance.

"Those two must be who SoCal was talking about when she said two people were acting strange earlier," Soojin murmured to herself. Then feeling self-conscious about talking to herself out loud, she put her earbuds back in. She left the telescope and walked down the steps of the Weather Agency building.

"Regardless, it's good that they're both home now."

The next morning, Jonghyun took the hiking trail up to the base main building. Making sure that no one else was in sight, he took out his phone and checked the message he received through the secure channel.

LAUNCH SOMETHING!

MASTER SERGEANT HAN SUMMIN, AT 03:58, EXITED A CAR WITH LICENSE PLATE NUMBER ENDING 6628 ON THE ROAD TO THE BASE MAIN ENTRANCE. CHECK THE MAP FOR THE EXACT DROP-OFF LOCATION.

Jonghyun stopped walking and clicked open the map. Then he tilted his head to the side.

"She got out this far from the base?"

When he'd finished his hike up the hill, he saw Kugyong driving his car toward the base main building. Jonghyun checked the license plate: 3246. He waited a moment. As Kugyong got out of his car, Jonghyun approached him and asked, "What time did you come home last night? I thought you were only going out for dinner."

"A little after four," answered Kugyong. "Were you up waiting for me?"

"Why would I do that?"

"I went to my aunt's house, then my cousin's daughter fell sick, so we had to go to the ER."

"Oh no, is she OK?"

"She's better. But I feel like I'm dying. These days I pull one all-nighter, and I'm dead tired for two days."

The Public Relations Corps office was located on the first floor. Jonghyun parted ways with Kugyong at the building entrance and went up to the second floor. He turned right at the top of the steps, toward the Operations Division, instead of left, where his desk in the Intelligence Department was. The door to the Operations Division office was open, and when Jonghyun approached, Soojin, who was sitting at her desk still wearing her yellow night duty band, nodded as if she had been expecting him.

In a low voice, she greeted him, "Captain Um, come in."

Hiding his surprise that she seemed to have known he was coming, Jonghyun answered, "You were on night duty. You must be tired."

"You're here to ask me something, right? Will you wait a bit? I'll be getting off work when the operations staff come into work. Let's meet outside quietly. In the backyard."

Looking a bit put out, Jonghyun turned and was about to head towards the end of the hallway where the Intelligence Department was when his eyes met Han Summin's, who was standing right behind him. It seemed that she was coming into work. Summin saluted him, and his response was a quick nod before stepping to one side to let her pass. Without a word, Summin entered.

After trading places with the person on the next shift, Soojin waited for Jonghyun by the basketball court at the back of the main building. Jonghyun emerged from a back door with an awkward expression on his face. When he came near enough, Soojin spoke in a near whisper.

"Park Kugyong's car came into the base at 4:10 a.m. Han Summin arrived five minutes later. There is a bit of a gap, but they returned together. Kugyong let her out on the hill in front of the main entrance."

"Is this a presumption?" Jonghyun asked.

"I saw it."

"How?"

"I just did."

Jonghyun eyed the Inspector General's face. Her eyes were intelligent and astute.

He asked, "About the Romantic Relationship Occurrence Report …"

"Is that why you were peeking out into the hallway all day?"

"Is our pilot Han Summin and Captain Park ...?"

Soojin answered, "No. They just happened to come to the Internal Review Department office at the same time. Captain Park was there to pick up a base parking permit."

"Ah."

"Summin was there to report that she's been contacted by a private enterprise about working for them. That's a sensitive issue, isn't it?"

Jonghyun nodded and said, "So she reported it herself."

"You knew about it?"

"Well, yes."

"Chief Gu must have gotten a scare, but Summin won't betray her. The reports filed to us will be sent over to the Intelligence Department by the end of the day, and the chief of staff should've already received them. Chief Gu Yemin launched a real doozy into space, but things seem much too quiet since. That thing she launched, it was for Summin, wasn't it? I'm a bit jealous. Summin has people taking good care of her."

Feeling a bit uncomfortable with the direction of the conversation, Jonghyun changed the topic and said, "So they're not in a relationship, those two?"

"How would I know? The only thing I will confirm is that they didn't file the report, but I shouldn't even be telling you that. I'm only telling you because I figure things would get more annoying for Summin if the Intelligence Department begins to take an interest in this. But Park Kugyong and Han Summin—isn't it a bit suspect that the two of them pretend to come home at different times that late at night? People do think that kind of stuff is suspect, right? I don't really have a feel for what the norms are regarding things like that. I mean, the two of them do look good together, even when they're just standing next to each other."

Jonghyun answered, "I don't think that's it, though."

"Yeah? I see. You sound certain, which probably means that Chief Gu and the Intelligence Department have decided to manage Summin's private life as well. Well, you don't need to say any more about it. I'm not interested. Do what you Intelligence Department people need to do. I'm off now. I'm going to sleep all morning and go out and have some fun in the afternoon."

Soojin left with light footsteps, and Jonghyun disappeared back in through the door he came out of.

In a hallway on the first floor of the launch base main building, there was a bench under the window that overlooked the backyard. Kugyong had been lying on that bench on his side, and when Soojin and Jonghyun parted ways, he sat up straight like a roly-poly toy. Then, as if deciding to pretend that he hadn't heard their conversation, he shook his head and lay back down.

Kugyong had spent the entire morning hiding in inconspicuous places taking naps, and by lunchtime he was all smiles as he headed down to the mess hall with colleagues from the Public Relations Corps. After eating, on his way to return the tray, Kugyong saw Summin. Quickly putting the tray on the return counter, he tried to strike up a breezy conversation with Summin.

"Do you listen to Oste's radio show?"

"Of course," answered Summin.

"Is it popular among his fans? I wonder how his fans are reacting to it in internet forums."

"They're interested. Then there are some people who criticize it. Is that what you wanted to ask me? You're not even in charge of that stuff anymore."

"I'm not, but I'm still curious."

"It's nothing to do with your work anymore, but you're still curious, and so you're asking me about it ... but why are you moving your arms so much? What we're talking about and your gestures are completely out of sync. What's going on?"

"I'm just practicing," answered Kugyong. "The Public Relations Corps always has to deal with people."

"But I mean, the words you're saying aren't about anything that would make you point a finger at yourself and then at me. And earlier, as you were saying that bit about the Public Relations Corps having to deal with people, you pointed at your watch."

"No, I didn't. But anyway, if there's anything the fans want, relay that info to me, would you? It'd be hard to do much about it, but we could at least do enough to suggest that we're listening to their opinions. That's what the HQ Public Relations Corps guys told me anyway."

"Yeah, sure. Though I don't think you need to be dancing while saying that. I don't think you're drunk ... is something going on at home? Did you wake up in the morning to find a scratch on your expensive car or something?"

"No, nothing like that. Have a good day, then."

"Could you please not wave your hands at me like that? Just tell me to salute or something."

Eating the side dishes on his tray, Jonghyun nonchalantly glanced at Kugyong and Summin talking. Kugyong was doing most of the talking and gesturing, but the two of them seemed quite close. Technical Sergeant Choi Suzy, who was sitting across from Jonghyun, signaled with her eyes to Suh Ga-ul sitting next to her and voiced the same thoughts that were in Jonghyun's head.

"Looks like he's thrilled to see her. Even though we all see each other every day."

Ga-ul answered, "Indeed. I thought Handsome Man was busy these days with training, but it seems like there's some kind of spectral energy encroaching on her. We should do an exorcism. Oh no, now I'm talking like a shaman. Don't tell any of the Weather Agency people about what I just said. I'll get in trouble. I'm serious."

Secretary Kim Eunkyung from the Planetary Management Office, who was sitting a seat away from Jonghyun, said, "You sure she's busy with training? Doesn't she become a free agent in the coming spring?"

Ga-ul asked, "Does she? Does her mandatory service end next year? But she won't go anywhere, will she?"

"You never know," Eunkyung said. "If a corporation is only willing to add a one to the first digit of her salary, she won't be going anywhere, but who knows what'll happen if they tack on a zero?"

"Companies do that? I wish they'd take me."

Eunkyung answered indifferently, "A private company might. They can give a signing bonus of the amount it would cost to train a spacecraft pilot over ten years and get someone who can be put into the field immediately. That'd be a win for them."

"In simple calculations, that could be, but she wouldn't have a license. No pilot can do business without a permit from the Allied Space Force."

"Unless she goes to Mars," said Eunkyung. "It's still pretty much a lawless zone there, so it's good for people with skills, apparently."

"Oh, really? I wonder if they'd buy my planetary meteorology degree there."

"Careful—the Intelligence Department is watching you."

At Eunkyung's words, Ga-ul said, "Captain Ohm Jonghyun's a good guy, so it's OK."

Eunkyung let out a chuckle and said, "So you've now accepted Captain Um as part of the family too, huh? And he's Captain 'Ohm' now?"

"The vowels were just a bit confusing. Um Jonghyun. Ohm Jonghyun. Figured I'll just stick with the 'o.'"

Jonghyun wasn't upset from the jesting but felt a bit uncomfortable being the topic of conversation. He picked up his tray and rose from his seat.

"Have a good lunch, ladies," he said. "I'm going to head out now. You can continue with your conversation."

Ga-ul said to Eunkyung, "See? He's so gentle."

Later that day, at five p.m., Kugyong was the first to enter the mess hall and finish his dinner. He left the hall and headed to his car, which was parked in the lot in front of the main building. Rummaging through the driver's side front door pocket, he found something and fished it out. It was a hospital parking stub marked with the exit time of "2:30 a.m." After checking the timestamp, Kugyong place it back into the front door pocket, put the seatbelt on, and turned on the engine.

Summin checked the twelve screens in front of her. She was wearing thin headphones with a mic and held a controller in each hand. The controllers had three joints each and were fixed on the arms of the pilot's seat. There were devices attached to the ends of the controllers which detected pressure whenever the pilot clutched them or let go, and they were designed in the shape of robot arms.

That wasn't all. Summin's feet were connected to devices as well, although the devices on her feet each had a different shape, which suggested that their uses differed. One of them looked exactly like the controllers in her hands, aside from the fact that there was no grip on it.

A voice came through her headphones.

"Close combat simulation. Setting the controllers to combat mode. Right hand, arm one; left hand, arm two; right foot, arm three; left foot, starting device. The current mission is 'Defense to Death.' The enemy spacecraft is armed with weapons permitted by international treaties. It has two arms angled at 180 degrees. First a preemptive attack and then defense. Contact with the enemy spacecraft in thirty seconds. Pilot, standby. Begin countdown."

Summin glared at one of the twelve screens. She could see a clear outline of a cylindrical frame with three massive robotic arms placed at 120-degree angles. Summin alternated between clutching the controllers in her right hand and left, and the long shields equipped on two of the arms twitched in turn. There was about a one-second delay between Summin's movements and the movements of the mechanical arms.

The enemy weaponized satellite was shaped like what could be described as a generic robot, with a head attached to shoulders and two arms. You could see an outline of its waist. Instead of legs, however, it had nozzles. On the biggest of all twelve screens, Summin could see the enemy spacecraft gradually approaching. It was a red robot holding an ax in each of its hands. On another screen, the orbits of the two spacecrafts were marked. They were growing closer.

Soon the enemy was near enough to fill up the entire screen. It raised its arms over its head with an ax in each hand. Summin

LAUNCH SOMETHING!

moved her arms outwards, pushing the long, narrow shields that the satellite she controlled held in its hands outwards. Doing that obscured her view.

Walking out of the remote pilot station holding her headphones in one hand and roughly taking her hair down, Summin grumbled out loud.

"A defensive operation doesn't make any sense. It takes time for the control signal to reach our satellite, so I can't wait to see the attack and then react. No matter how effective my defensive pose is, the offense is at an absolute advantage. Even if I react immediately, what I see on the screen is already something that happened a second ago. So considering that it takes another second for what I do to reach the spacecraft, the offense will always be two seconds ahead of me. So this is just ridiculous."

Sounds came from the headphones. Instead of wearing them properly on her head, Summin put them to one ear.

"We'll reduce the lag time on Earth to less than 0.5 seconds. The attackers would not be in orbit—they'd also be remotely controlling the robot from Earth, so technically they shouldn't be twice as fast."

Summin raised her voice and answered, "Please, do. But I still think it'd be the same even if the lag time was reduced to 0.5 seconds. It's not like in the past when the robot arms were slow. Now we're fighting with arms that are amazingly quick to react. Imagine that this was happening on Earth instead of in outer space. If I'm fighting someone, and that person reacted half a second later than me, would he be able to hit me even once? So please don't put me in a position where we have to defend. Let me go into action only when we're on the offensive."

"I know we're at an absolute disadvantage, but you never know what kind of complications will arise," said the voice in the headphones. "We have to make necessary preparations."

When she returned to the dorm, it was already late evening. Summin walked straight into the lounge and slumped down into the couch. She lay there, boring a hole into the ceiling. There were a few other people in the lounge, but they didn't dare talk to her.

Soon, someone broke that silence.

"Handsome Maaaan! What are you doing on Christmas?"

It was Suh Ga-ul's voice. Without even turning her head toward Ga-ul's direction, Summin answered hollowly, "Training."

Everything was tolerable before the words left her tongue, but those two syllables immediately evoked regret and annoyance. Including her time spent on the high school basketball team, she'd been tied to that word for much too long.

Perhaps concerned at the emotion, or lack thereof, in Summin's voice, Ga-ul asked, "On Christmas? The entire base is going to be closed."

"Really? Then, I'll sleep."

"You'd be in big trouble! When you wake up, you won't have anything to eat. The mess hall's going to be closed, and so is the base exchange, I'm pretty sure. And you don't even have a car."

"I'll just buy some food in advance."

"But it's Christmas! You can't just eat anything!"

"Stop beating around the bush and say what you want."

At Summin's words, Ga-ul giggled and asked, "Want to party?"

"Here?" asked Summin. "A party on the base? I don't know if that's going to be fun. Well, I suppose some choco pies would be great."

"No, no," Ga-ul said. "At Shoojeans' apartment in town. You haven't been, have you? She has a yard and everything. It's really nice."

"Gee, I know we're only the Space Force, but what kind of spacenaut would go to the Inspector General's house to party? Oh, that's right. You're not a spacenaut."

Summin's jibe only seemed to ignite Ga-ul's fervor to persuade her.

"But Oste's going to be airing a special episode on Christmas Eve. We're going to get together and listen to *Let's Raise the Density!* Or more likely we'll have it on in the background."

"Will the party involve someone shamelessly poking fun at Oste? Then that party might end with a fight."

"It's the Inspector General's house, so even a pilot wouldn't dare hit me there, don't you think?"

Summin didn't answer. She did seem a bit persuaded. With a contented grin, Ga-ul spoke, thinking that her next words would ultimately win Summin over.

"We're going to invite Captain Park Cooking and a few others."

Summin remained quiet. After waiting a few more seconds, Ga-ul was ready to give up and turn around when, as if it just suddenly occurred to her, Summin asked, "Why are you so bent on throwing a Christmas Eve party in the middle of nowhere? Be honest. You're on duty on Christmas day, aren't you? And no one said they'd switch with you. Am I right?"

"Jeez, you found me out," answered Ga-ul.

When his name left Suh Ga-ul's lips, Kugyong had been just about to enter the lounge, looking as though he'd just woken up from sleeping all evening. However, he stopped in his tracks and stood outside the door, leaning in to eavesdrop on what Ga-ul and Summin were saying. Feeling somewhat awkward about appearing in front of them just when they were talking about him, he tiptoed back the way he came.

Walking up the steps, Kugyong fumbled through his pockets for his phone. As soon as he entered his room, he put earbuds into his ears and lay down on his bed as though it were sucking him in. Oste's radio show, which he'd paused earlier in the day, continued.

"... There are a lot of questions about why the Space Force is acting as though it is part of some other country's military. Let me explain it in a way that would be easy for everyone to understand. The Space Force is not a branch of the armed forces that defends Korean territory. The Allied Space Force was created through an international treaty called the Kessler Syndrome Prevention Treaty, which was designed to prevent a series of explosions in the orbits where satellites and space stations are located. In movies, it looks like things are just floating in empty space, but satellites are always moving at a tremendous speed: Mach 25. The fastest jet that can be manned by people fly at a speed of Mach 3, so Mach 25's extremely fast, right? That means a single screw from an old satellite is like a bullet when it hits a working satellite. Imagine what would happen if an entire satellite were to explode! It would be like thousands of bullets bursting out into space, right? Some of them might even be as big as cannonballs.

"Imagine what would happen if other satellites ran into those shards and fragments. They'd also explode. Creating thousands of fragments again. All the satellites up in space would be destroyed in no time. So if a series of explosions occurred today, when there are so many satellites up there, it would be impossible to launch more satellites or space stations into space. To prevent that from happening, we have to ensure no satellites explode. We have to make sure nobody launches missiles from Earth to shoot down satellites and prevent satellites from crashing into each other. That's what the Kessler Syndrome Prevention Treaty is all about, and that was why the Allied Space Force was created. Korea joined the treaty, and that was how the Republic of Korea Space Force was born. Man, that's a lot of information. It's rather complicated, isn't it? So how do we wage war in orbit? That was another question. I asked others, and they said that it's straightforward—close combat is the safest. Get close to your enemy spacecraft, break their engine or control device, and then push them down toward the Earth. Primitive, right? But apparently you need state-of-the-art equipment for such primitive combat. Even building a spacecraft on Earth is tremendously expensive, let alone launching it into space. And having a pilot that can control the spacecraft becomes especially important, right?"

Kugyong vacantly stared at the ceiling.

"He's good," he muttered to himself. "I couldn't explain that properly even after all these years."

He tossed and turned for a bit and soon drifted into sleep.

The next morning, Kugyong woke up with a start as though an alarm clock had gone off. He rushed to wash his face, put his clothes on, and quietly left the room so as not to wake his roommate.

"So hungry. It's only six a.m."

The exchange store at the entrance of the dorm wasn't open yet. He headed to the mess hall, only to discover nobody was there yet either.

However, when he drove up to the base main building, in the

parking lot was the Inspector General's car. Kugyong got out of his and headed inside. When he knocked on the door to the Internal Review Department office, Soojin answered.

Opening the door, Kugyong asked, "Inspector General, you here already?"

"Captain Park, what's up? You weren't on night duty."

"I didn't have dinner last night, so I woke up early because I was too hungry. Do you have anything to eat?"

Soojin pointed to Technical Sergeant Choi Suzy's empty desk and said, "You could probably find something in there, but she's not here …"

Finding a bag of chips in Suzy's desk, Kugyong fumbled to open the bag and spoke with the pretension of someone calm and composed and not in a hurry to shovel food into his mouth.

"Why are you here this early?" he asked.

Soojin answered, "I got off night duty and slept for about sixteen hours from yesterday morning, then my back hurt too much."

Instead of words, the sound of Kugyong munching on chips filled the gaps in conversation.

After a while, Soojin said, "I thought, since I came to work this early in the morning for the first time in a while, I was going to sit here elegantly and read a book or something, but a subordinate who rarely comes up to the second floor deigned to come all the way to my office and is making all the noise in the world eating a bag of chips."

"Oh, was I doing that? Sorry, my brain was numb. Now I've come to my senses."

"Yeah, Captain Park. Now that you've come to your senses, don't hover around Han Summin, you know. Even if you run into her by chance, just try to avoid her. For at least three months. Or else, you'll be investigated."

"Yes, ma'am."

"You catch on quick."

"They work, these carbohydrates," Kugyong said, suddenly talkative. "I can suddenly understand everything."

"If you've filled your stomach, go downstairs and take a nap until people come to work."

"Got it."

Kugyong put his hand on the door handle, about to leave, but turned back around to Soojin and asked, "Sergeant Han's not going anywhere, right? She seems a bit troubled these days."

"Well, someone did say that they'd pay her well on Mars. And they'd treat her well too, better than here at least."

"What would you do, Inspector General?"

"If it were me? I don't want to go to Mars, but if someplace on Earth contacted me, I might go there. She'll figure it out on her own, in any case. You go worry about your own self, Captain Park."

That evening in town, through a small window in a building stairwell across the street, intelligence officer Um Jonghyun was surveying a coffee shop. It was a small place, and all the chairs were facing the street, so it was a perfect place for him to read people's lips.

Jonghyun took out his cell phone. The conversation between Han Summin and the owner of the car, license plate number 6628, was being relayed to him via messages through the secure channel with a slight time lag.

PILOT ASKS ABOUT THE ORBIT COMBAT DEVICE STRATEGY. ASKS ABOUT CONTROLLING ROBOT ARMS.

EXTERNAL CONTACT GIVES ADVICE.

After a series of such messages, finally the thing that everyone at the Space Force had been worried about appeared on Jonghyun's phone.

EXTERNAL CONTACT OFFERS PILOT A JOB. PRESENTS CONDITIONS. PRESENTS MINIMUM GUARANTEED BENEFITS AND ASKS FOR PILOT'S OPINION.

NO ANSWER FROM PILOT.

PILOT SAYS SHE'LL THINK ABOUT IT. REPEAT. PILOT SAID SHE'LL "THINK ABOUT IT."

Space Force Chief of Staff Gu Yemin sat on the massage chair in her living room, listening to music, as her cell phone continued to vibrate. Annoyed, she reached out and grabbed it. There was a secure message from the sender LAUNCH BASE COMMANDER. The subject line read, EMERGENCY: REPORT ON PILOT AND EXTERNAL CONTACT.

After scrolling through some of these "emergency" messages that were being relayed live to her phone, Gu Yemin placed her cell phone back on the table and closed her eyes with a relaxed face. She seemed confident that nothing urgent was going to happen that she would have to handle.

Trying hard not to stare out the window, Han Summin answered the man in his fifties sitting next to her.

"I'll think about it."

"Please do," he said. "It's a great opportunity. Once again, what I told you earlier is just the minimum guaranteed conditions. You should know that it's definitely going to be more than that."

"OK," Summin answered curtly.

LAUNCH SOMETHING!

The man said, "And today's going to be our last meeting."

"Excuse me?"

"There's too much of a risk for us to keep on chasing you. Even when headhunting, there is a line we shouldn't cross since we don't want to turn the Space Force into our enemy. But we're nearly stepping on that line right now, so we won't be moving forward anymore."

"I see."

"I had fun talking to you, though, Master Sergeant Han. I can tell from your questions how much you love what you do and how skilled you are in that area. I can tell without having to actually see you in action."

"Then couldn't we continue our talk for a little longer?"

"That's actually why I'm putting a stop to it now. The conversation itself has been great for me too, but I got to thinking that perhaps the reason you decided to meet with me is that I'm an experienced pilot-turned-company executive. Isn't that right? You don't need to answer that question. But why is it that I get the feeling that that's really all this was? To be honest, when you said moments ago that you'll think about our offer, I got the feeling that you weren't really going to consider it at all, rather you were saying that so that I'd show up again and answer more of your questions. Or am I wrong?"

Summin answered, "No, no. I really will think about it. But I do have one thing that I really want to ask you."

The man grinned. His face was relaxed out of resignation. Like the expression people make the moment they let go of an obsession over something. Seeing the look on his face, Summin's own face hardened. She knew that this really was the last meeting.

The man said, "I think I got your answer. You don't have the slightest inclination to leave the Space Force, do you?"

Summin said nothing in response. She only let out a long sigh.

Looking relaxed, the man said, "I reported to the company that I've been doing a good job of convincing you, but it looks like I've been a fool."

"I'm sorry, sir."

"Heh, well, now it's certain I've been played. Hahaha. No need to apologize. I really did have fun talking with you. I'm jealous of the Space Force for having such a tenacious and capable pilot. Well, then, I think this is the end of our talk."

Summin studied the man's face with regret. The man shuffled the papers he'd taken out back into the briefcase. Then he put both his elbows on the table and naturally clasped his hands in front. With a face full of smiles, he said, "From now on, why don't I answer your questions for a bit? Today is our last day anyway. In return for allowing me to have a wonderful dream even for just a little while, I'll answer all your questions. Would an hour be enough? Starting now, it's your time, so ask me any questions you have."

Summin nodded to express her sincere apology and gratitude. Then she fished something out of her bag and put it on the table.

"Then I'll trespass on your kindness, sir."

Seeing the unexpectedly thick, frayed notebook Summin placed on the table, the man burst into laughter.

"I had no idea you were hiding such a huge list of questions! Hahaha, goodness. Had I not realized this today, you would've gotten me to meet you at least five more times! Wow, look at that, you've even drawn diagrams."

"I really wanted to hear about this stuff. And I've learned a lot from you, truly. I think it was me who crossed the line. I shouldn't have taken it this far, but every time you've given me tips and know-how, I applied it in training, and my results improved remarkably. I've been selfish, thinking that I would never have a chance to meet someone like you ever again."

"Haha, it's fine. It really is. I appreciate your brutal honesty more than anything. In fact, I'm quite flattered. I'll remember you, Master Sergeant Han. I've seen many talented pilots, but that notebook, that's just incredible."

The following message appeared on Jonghyun's phone:

EXTERNAL CONTACT: "WILL KEEP ON WATCHING" "INCREDIBLE" "HAVE SEEN MANY PILOTS" "WHAT KIND OF PERSON ARE YOU?"

Similar messages were relayed to Gu Yemin's phone as well. Of course, the information given to her was better organized than that given to Jonghyun or other intelligence officers. But Gu Yemin had already gone to bed feeling satisfied, without giving a thought to the messages on her phone.

On Mars, a little while after Han Summin and the driver of 6628 parted ways, a military officer in his forties wearing the Space Force combat uniform plunged his hand into his pocket and pulled out his phone. With one hand, he checked the message he received moments ago.

FIFTH ATTEMPT TO BRING OVER THE PILOT FAILED. MISSION TO ABORT BASED ON ONSITE ASSESSMENT. SPACE FORCE INTELLIGENCE IS TIGHTENING SURVEILLANCE. WILL DISBAND ALL MISSION NETWORKS AND LIE LOW FOR SIX MONTHS.

The Space Force officer had two stars on each shoulder of his uniform, and as one of his hands pushed his phone back into his pocket, the other hand held a gun that gave the impression of being frequently used.

He muttered, "Those guys who return to Earth really never stray from the stereotype. Pushovers. *Tsk*."

Then, looking down in front of him, he said, "Thought that was going to be something breaking your way? No such luck. In fact that was not at all relevant to what's happening here right now, so you may as well just give up. And so, what was it that you were going to do? You want to defect?"

The muzzle of his gun was pointed at a man with a shaggy beard kneeling on the ground. The man's hands were tied behind his back, and blood trickled down his forehead.

The kneeling man nodded.

The man in uniform ruthlessly booted him.

"Answer me. You want to defect?" the two-star Major General of the Space Force asked again in a cold voice.

As he struggled to sit himself up, the man answered in a hoarse voice, "I have useful information. It will be of help."

The Major General stared into the face of the kneeling man. For a long time, neither of them spoke.

Eventually, the Major General opened his mouth and asked, "What are you going to sell out? The location of the hideout?"

"Yes, sir."

Major General Lee Jongro, the Vice-Minister of Mars, AKA Mars Governor-General, answered with a stoic face, "A hideout, huh? No thanks, I don't need that. You have nothing to give me, right? And I don't think this is the time for you to negotiate anything. You should've said that before I came into this room with the SWAT team."

Kang Taejin, a remnant of the rebel forces who had been in hiding, swallowed hard instead of giving a response. Even that small act seemed painful.

Lee Jongro said, "You didn't even consider negotiating until this moment, did you? You probably thought that since I'll be heading to Earth soon, you'll be able to find some way to survive by coaxing whatever pushover the new governor-general is, right? You have no plans to start another rebellion, and there was no 'great cause' from the beginning. You should've sought asylum instead. Like that crafty Hwang Sun, you should've sold your information when you could and ran away to somewhere I couldn't get you. But nothing comes out of regret, does it? Now it's all over."

The captive squeezed his eyes shut. A tear seeped out as a million emotions crossed his mind.

When he opened his eyes again, the barrel of the gun was now further away from his face than it had been. But before he could let out a sigh of relief—right at the moment he'd inhaled a breath—the Mars Governor-General's arm stretched out toward him again, bringing the muzzle of the gun right to him. Without a moment of further hesitation, the Governor-General pulled the forefinger that had been resting on the trigger.

The Governor-General spat out some harsh words as he opened fire, but Kang Taejin didn't hear them.

The launch base of the Republic of Korea Space Force was at peace. The next morning after Han Summin met the headhunter for the last time, and the morning after that, the uncompleted Romantic Relationship Occurrence Report remained on top of the Acting Inspector General's desk.

Technical Sergeant Choi Suzy noticed it when she entered with documents that needed to be approved and asked Soojin, "Should I file this away?"

Soojin shook her head.

After Suzy left the office, Soojin murmured quietly, "Let's just leave it. Since a terrifying person is coming from all the way across the universe."

Surprised by her own voice, her eyes darted left and right, her mouth agape.

The morning sun, positioned too low in the sky, seemed to be stealing glances at her. It was the sun that seemed to be laughing as though it was having fun all the time. The artificial structure that was providing a reason for the survival of Space Forces all around the world, quietly peeking into the Space Force launch base.

Chapter Five

Strict but Flexible

There were windows on three walls of the base commander's office. Each window was big, designed without giving an ounce of thought to privacy or security. No curtains had ever been provided. The office wasn't larger than the chief of staff's, but there were no bookcases, and it was so well-lit that it looked at least 1.5 times bigger.

Lieutenant General Song Keunki, Space Force Launch Base Commander, sat in an enormous chair behind an enormous desk. Sunlight poured in through the windows on to his back and sides. There was a heavy conference table in front of his desk, and although the conference table was round and had no seat at the head of the table, it didn't mean much since the commander sat at his own desk.

Lieutenant General Song said, "Since this is a sensitive issue, I hope we can deal with this in a strict but flexible manner."

Sitting at the table, Acting Inspector General Park Soojin half-turned to the base commander and twitched her shoulders.

Then immediately, her right hand holding a pen shot up into the sky. She wanted a say.

"Yes, Major Park?"

When the commander acknowledged her, Soojin turned around fully and asked, "What do you mean by 'strict but flexible'?"

The three other people sitting around the table—the provost marshal, the chief of operations, and Captain Um Jonghyun from the Intelligence Department—all held their breath simultaneously.

The commander cleared his throat and solemnly answered, "The Internal Review Department, the military police, and the Intelligence Department will be jointly handling this, so naturally it will be strict. Flexible means that you should all adjust the pace of the investigation."

Soojin wanted to confirm the commander's intent once more. "So we should make an obvious fuss about the investigation to make it seem intimidating to people on the outside, but we should do it slowly. Cooperate without rushing."

The commander glowered at Acting Inspector General Park Soojin. Her words had sounded confrontational, but there was no emotion behind then—she wasn't being sarcastic, and there was no hint of her challenging his authority. She only seemed to want accurate instructions. The commander made the decision to answer her generously.

"I'm saying you shouldn't jump to conclusions. Crosscheck thoroughly. It's clear that this is a major incident. Firearm data was transmitted to the interplanetary shuttle. The intelligence must have confirmed it?"

Captain Um answered without hesitation, "Yes, sir. We confirmed that firearm data was transmitted to the emergency parts production equipment on the earthbound interplanetary shuttle that left from Mars. We also confirmed that our base was the point of transmission. These are indisputable facts."

Soojin interrupted him, "Could you explain that in more detail? What were the steps involved? First, what is 'emergency parts production equipment'?"

"It consists of a 3D printer with connected robotic arms. If a shuttle that takes months travelling between planets breaks down, the only way to repair it is to do it on the spaceship itself. But no one knows which part might break down, and it's impossible to carry all the weighty replacement parts. So the spaceship leaves with a small amount of 3D printing material and blueprint data. If they need something, they can make it right there on the ship. They print out the parts with the 3D printer and put it together with the robotic arms."

Even after Jonghyun finished explaining, Soojin said nothing in response. Instead, she kept on scribbling in her notebook.

Silence continued. Everyone in the room was waiting for Soojin to finish. On the desk in front of her were five pens in a variety of colors and two highlighters, also in different colors. Using a blue pen and a set square, she drew a neat rectangle around the word "3D printer."

Finally, Soojin asked, "So it's like form and matter, and they can add the form part from a long distance?"

"Yes, ma'am," Jonghyun answered. "We can transmit data from Earth or Mars. They have most of the data for parts originally used in the spaceship, but there may be times when they need to make something else. Like when you need the latest parts."

"And someone used that data transmission program to send

over firearm data? The data was only received, though, right? They didn't actually make the firearm?"

"That is correct. We checked the operation records and the materials inventory. It was never printed."

When Jonghyun finished talking, Soojin once again began to write something down in her notebook. Silence filled the air once more. Everyone's eyes were glued to Soojin's hands. Impatiently, the provost marshal flexed his shoulders for a moment, then with a sigh, he brought a glass of water to his lips.

After taking notes, Soojin put the pen down and turned to the commander.

"It's a big incident, but marginally so," she said.

Lieutenant General Song Keunki nodded slowly. Sunlight poured onto his colossal physique.

"You're right," he said. "It looks like the Space Force headquarters will be investigating this incident. But since nothing actually happened, they've given us the courtesy of conducting a preliminary investigation on our own."

"For how long?" asked Soojin.

"Two days."

"And after two days?"

"HQ will take over, and it'll be out of our hands. HQ won't be able to do a cursory job if they want to stop the Allied Space Force from intervening. Major Park, after the meeting I presume you'll share those minutes you're making with us, right?"

After writing "two days" in her notebook, drawing an arrow next to it, and writing "SFHQ intervention" above the arrow, Soojin answered half-heartedly, "I'm sure Captain Um will write up the minutes and share them. Even though he doesn't look like he's writing anything down, he'll send a report right after the meeting. The Intelligence Department is tremendously capable. Although it is a problem that they sometimes create meeting minutes they shouldn't and get caught. In any case, my notes are personal and nothing you could use for reference."

Soojin finished writing and turned to the provost marshal this time. While everyone in the room was watching Soojin take notes, it seemed that she'd gained control of the meeting.

She asked, "And it's certain that the suspect is Professor Cha Gwanyoung?"

"From the surveillance camera footage, it's actually unclear whether it is Professor Cha Gwanyoung or not," answered the provost marshal. "We don't see his face. It looks like him, but the evidence is too tenuous to designate him as a suspect."

Finishing up his answer, the provost marshal glanced at the commander's face.

Soojin retorted, "Whatever we designate him, he was the only one hovering around the Communication Relay Station at that time. And it doesn't make sense that the guard at the main entrance didn't leave records of an outsider entering the base, unless he knew the person, no? Suppose the person who looked exactly like Professor Cha Gwanyoung was not actually Professor Cha Gwanyoung. In that case, the guard at the entrance needs to be held accountable, but that's preposterous. So I'll first go with the rational reasoning—that the guard didn't leave a record because he knew the person. I'd appreciate it if I could get access to the footage immediately after this meeting. I'll contact the Military Police Corps. And Professor Cha Gwangyoung's residence is in the nearby town, right? Have you met with him?"

The provost marshal answered, "I didn't see him personally, but I did contact him."

"Oh no. So you've told him that he's under suspicion. What did he say?"

"He denied it."

"What about his alibi?"

Looking a bit peeved, the provost marshal answered, "He said he would've been video conferencing at the time. With someone in Europe."

"Exactly who was in this meeting with him?"

"He said it was a sensitive call, so he couldn't say. He did say that the call can be confirmed for certain if this turns out to be something ... big."

Soojin half-turned her head toward the commander and asked, "He means that he'll answer when the SFHQ comes to confirm after two days. So what should we do? Should we just consider this two-day preliminary investigation an investigation to check if things like this are bluffs or not? Or should we just trust his statement and proceed?"

Um Jonghyun swallowed hard. The commander shook his head from side to side. It was a firm expression of denial, but the movement was subtle, not at all vigorous.

Soojin nodded and said, "Got it, sir. I will leave the task of confirming the video conferencing up to HQ. What do we have then? Is there someone to confirm his alibi?"

When Soojin directed questions to him again, the provost marshal sat up straight and answered, "No, there is footage from a surveillance camera in town that was pointing in the direction of his house, but it's too far to see anything clearly."

"Far?" asked Soojin. "How far?"

"About five hundred meters?"

With that answer, the provost marshal pushed the tablet from under his notebook to the center of the table. The screen was almost completely black. It would have appeared that the tablet was turned off had it not been for the faint streetlamps and a silhouette of the low mountains behind the town. In the bottom left corner was a timestamp with the last digit rapidly changing, indicating that it wasn't a still photograph. Aside from the timestamp, nothing was moving on the screen.

"Five hundred meters from his house at night?" asked Soojin. "It seems evident that it won't be of any help, so why did you bring this up?"

"We checked the video, from two hours before the incident to two hours after, but couldn't find anything that caught our eyes. If he'd driven a car, the headlights would've been on, and if he'd walked, at least the door light would've come on. Unless he intentionally turned it off when he went out."

Soojin began to jot something down in her notebook once again. The four other people in the room once again watched her hand move, as though they were being silently punished.

Soojin said, "So all this to explain that the footage isn't helpful."

"No, no," the provost marshal protested, as if he'd been waiting for that comment. "There's something you can see."

"What is it?"

"Look here," the provost marshal pointed to one spot on the screen. "You can see that a beam of light is coming from his living room. All the other lights in the house are off, but there's a faint light from something like a computer monitor, which coincides with what Professor Cha said about staying home."

There was a dim light. Below, the timestamp was still moving. The closer she looked at it, the more Soojin felt that she could detect the color of the light changing bit by bit, but the changes were not significant enough to be notable.

Soojin glared at her notebook. Then she stretched out her hand toward the black pen on the desk but stopped, making her mind up not to use it.

"Well, I don't think I need to write that down," she said. "Well, then let's get to it, shall we? You can send us this video too, right? I'll take it along with the surveillance camera footage you mentioned earlier."

Soojin took her pens and highlighters and put them into her pencil case one by one. No one said the meeting was over, but it felt like once she was done putting away her pens, everyone should get up and leave.

Before she was done, the commander spoke in a hurry.

"Major Park, let me just say this in advance. I'm against referring to Professor Cha as a suspect. Over the years, he contributed a lot to the Space Force, and it's our duty to protect his reputation."

Soojin didn't answer him right away. Instead, she slowly zipped up the pencil case, tucked her notebook and set square under her left arm, and stood up. Then she turned to the commander and asked in a voice utterly devoid of emotion, "Then how should we refer to him?"

The base commander said nothing in response. Soojin saluted the commander and strode out of the room that did not have a single bookcase.

On their way down the hallway towards the staircase to the second floor, Um Jonghyun asked Soojin, "Inspector General. I'm sorry to be asking this despite being in the Intelligence Department, but is there some kind of context I'm missing? Both the commander and the provost marshal were so ... Just who is this Professor Cha Gwanyoung?"

"It's nothing. He was just a couple years ahead of the commander at the Space Force Academy."

At her words, Jonghyun exclaimed, "Ah, he was in the Space Force."

Soojin stopped on the stairs and looked up at Jonghyun, who was standing a couple of steps behind her. She said, "Now he's a grade two civilian employee. We call him a professor, but he's not really a professor. He retired as a colonel, took about a year off, and then came back as a researcher. People still call him colonel and all."

"That's why this case needs to be handled carefully."

"Well, not really, but let's just say that there are some people who will go easy on him. Whether you will or not will be decided for you by the Intelligence Department chief. So, take your instructions from him and follow them."

Soojin grinned and continued heading down the steps. After walking four steps down, she stopped and asked Jonghyun, "Oh, Captain Um, your major was not origami but satellite analysis, wasn't it?"

"Yes, ma'am."

"I think I've read about it in *Monthly Space Force*. It was about looking at satellites in Earth's orbit and reverse engineering the design, right?"

"Right. Although I look at far more satellites that are in Mars' orbit these days."

"I suspected you'd been recruited to look into Mars, but that's a conversation for another time. I actually wanted to ask you about something else. Reverse engineering whatever is in the Earth's or Mars' orbit. The act of looking at something that's in orbit, though … how do you do it exactly? I was on night duty a little while ago, and I tried but failed to see the asteroid in the Earth's orbit. Bad weather and all. But the person who loaned me the telescope told me that it'll just look like a tiny dot in the sky anyway."

"Right," Jonghyun answered. "We use better telescopes, but that's just about what things look like."

"So you look at that tiny dot to figure out the shape or structure of the satellite, right?"

"It seems like you understand pretty well."

"And when you study it intensively, you find out how it folds or unfolds, and even the diagram of what it looks like when it has been completely unfolded."

Jonghyun chuckled as he said, "That's exactly what I do. Although I do a lot of other intelligence related tasks as well."

The smile vanished from Soojin's face as she asked, "This is my question. To find out all of that information, all you need is a dot, right?"

Jonghyun nodded and answered after a pause, "That's what astronomy is. There's close to zero possibility of getting more clues, so we have to figure out from one dot whether that's a single planet or a double planet. If it is a double planet, then how long its revolution cycle is, how many moons it has, and of the moons that circle it how many layers of Saturn-like rings the largest moon has. That kind of stuff."

"Right. It's not like you can see its shape even when you enlarge the photo, but it's about getting all kinds of information from the light. I think I even read that there is a study of those planets' weather conditions."

"That's what Suh Ga-ul majored in."

"Oh, I must have heard it from her, then. I think a lot of my knowledge on astronomy came from her, which, now that I've realized it, feels rather dubious."

"I don't think you have to worry about that. She's definitely not in the Space Force because she has nowhere else to go."

With a meaningful look, Soojin agreed, "Right. The Space

Force is packed with talented people like her. Anyway, if we look at a dot closely enough, we'll be able to figure that out too, right?"

"By 'that,' what do you mean exactly?"

"His alibi. Cha Gwanyoung."

Jonghyun stared at the ceiling, looking a bit befuddled, then his eyes opened wide as he looked at Soojin.

Soojin said, "OK. I was just trying to see if it made sense, but your face says it all. How long will it take to get the results?"

With a blank look on his face, Jonghyun answered without confidence, "It would probably take all night, I think?"

"Good. We need the results by tomorrow. It would probably be better for you to do all the prep work when there's no one else around, wouldn't it? You would have to work with AI, right?"

"Huh? Right. Yes, you're right. But Inspector General, how did you even come up with this idea? You're talking about what I'm thinking about, right?"

"I don't know how I came up with it. Maybe it's all to do with my habit of reviewing my notes. Anyway, I'll get permission to use the necessary AI, so go have your dinner and wait for me to contact you."

Soojin drove up to the Communication Relay Station on the hill next to the launch base main building, and found that fortunately, Secretary Kim Eunkyung was on duty.

As soon as she set her eyes on Soojin, Eunkyung grumbled, "I have no idea what's going on. It's already hours past the Mars office's work hours."

"Did they tell you to standby as well?" asked Soojin. "It didn't sound like it was that big of a deal, not yet anyway."

"It's only a big deal for me. Having someone like me be on standby is the easiest way in the world to deal with stuff."

"Sorry to hear that. So what's going on in the shuttle?"

"Everything's still hush hush. They've kept it a secret from the passengers, and the crew is quietly searching to see if anyone's brought in bullets."

"Bullets?" asked Soojin.

Eunkyung simpered and said, "You can't make gunpowder with a 3D printer. Or shampoo or toothpaste."

"I thought it was an all-powerful machine."

"Major Park, you have no idea what a 3D printer does, do you?"

Soojin widened her eyes and shook her head. "Not knowing hasn't really caused any trouble for me."

"It won't cause trouble for you as long as people don't know that the Inspector General has no idea what a 3D printer does. Everyone's been talking about how intimidating the Inspector General is, but when it comes down to it, you know only what you need to know and nothing else. You're good at hiding what you don't know."

"It's not like I mean to come across as intimidating. I didn't come up with that image of me, other people did."

"Sure, sure. In any case, I'm saying that since bullets can't be printed, if someone had planned to print a firearm from the 3D printer using the secretly transmitted data, then they would've smuggled in bullets separately. So if bullets are found, this gets blown up into something huge. The identity of the culprit will be revealed as well, but it could be difficult to figure out who's behind it all. Even if they don't find the bullets, the whole situation is still going to be a bit sticky until the vessel arrives on Earth."

"Sounds like you'll have to be on standby for a while, Secretary Kim. And the spaceship crew too."

"I hope they can find the bullets soon—otherwise I'm worried I'll be on standby for a long time. Oh, but the incident is good news for you, though, isn't it? Finally you'll be able to investigate something."

At Eunkyung's words, Soojin shrugged.

"I'm not sure. There hasn't really been any 'incident' yet."

"But it looks like you're hoping for one."

"Let's just see. But I can't just sit and watch until then. Speaking of which, can I use the AI here tonight?"

"Our computer? Tonight? Why don't you do it now? It's nighttime on Mars, so we're all off duty."

Soojin lowered her voice and said, "It's kind of confidential. I can just write up a request, right?"

"You can, but I can't just let a non-expert like you operate that expensive piece of equipment. You'd need an operator. Our team's already working overtime, so I can't ask an operator to come into work that late. And I can't really do it myself tonight either."

"Ah, then I'll just bring someone in from the Intelligence Department."

"That'll work. Captain Parachute's good at that kind of stuff. People say he was parachuted in to get to where he is, though I actually heard that they had to kowtow and beg him to come. Even in the Intelligence Department, it seems like he's a big deal."

At her words, Soojin smiled enigmatically and asked, "Captain Um Jonghyun, huh? I'll ask him if he has time."

"Why are you smiling like that? Is it that exciting?"

"It's nothing. You should go think about getting off work."

"I will. As soon as I write up your request form. Let's see, most of this stuff I can fill out ... Oh, what are you going to do with the computer?"

"Watch some TV."

"All night?"

"All night."

Shaking her head, Eunkyung said to Soojin with a concerned voice, "Let's just write 'intelligence task.' A secret 'don't ask don't tell' operation. Tell Captain Um not to leave anything on the computer about what you two do tonight. What I mean is … never mind. I'll tell him myself."

Cha Gwanyoung looked out his window. An elderly man in a suit stood at the gate with two younger men who seemed to be his secretaries. A black sedan was parked on one side of the street. It was well-polished—an indicator that the man wanted to impress others and boast of his high social status.

"I don't think they're here for delivery," he murmured to himself. "Who are these people?"

His daughter, standing next to him, shrugged. Cha Gwanyoung headed outside. When he appeared at the gate, the elderly man in a suit greeted him warmly.

"Ah, isn't this Professor Cha Gwanyoung? I stopped by without an appointment, but thank goodness you are home."

Gwanyoung racked his brains but came up blank—he didn't know this man. He rarely had guests these days. But he still welcomed the visitor. He smiled candidly, as though he'd known this man for a long time.

"You should've called at least," Gwanyoung said. "I am mostly at home these days, but I do go out occasionally. I'm glad that you didn't make this trip in vain. But pardon me, may I ask who you are?"

He wasn't sure why, but this was clearly a battle that he

couldn't lose. He had to be bold and kind now and find out the reason for this tension between them afterward—Gwanyoung was true to his ingrained habits. *Someone who came to see me with bad intentions wouldn't have greeted me that way*, he thought.

The guest answered, "I'm sorry to be introducing myself so late. I should've visited you earlier to say hello. My name is Lee Gwangsam. I'm no one important, just an old man serving as a provincial assembly member in the countryside."

Gwanyoung opened the gate. Lee Gwangsam took a business card from one of his secretaries and handed it to Gwanyoung. As he did so, he bowed in a way that didn't seem subservient at all. It was the gesture that was second nature to an experienced politician.

Gwanyoung said, "I'm sorry I rushed out and didn't bring my business card with me. But what brings you here? If you're not too busy, would you like to come inside? It's only a humble house, but it would be better than talking out here on the street."

Lee stepped inside the gate as if he had been waiting for the invitation. Then he walked straight toward the house.

"You have a cozy little yard. People retire and start a farm these days, but that's all very hard work. I think it's best to tend to a small garden instead. There's no need to go through the difficulties of farming, harvesting, and trying to sell produce that's not up to par."

A little while later, the two of them were sat facing each other on the living room sofa. Lee's two secretaries remained outside by the car, talking among themselves.

With a generous smile, Lee Gwangsam looked outside the window for a moment before speaking up.

"I used to love reading mystery novels when I was young. My preferences were a bit bloody in those days, so I read a lot of hard-boiled British mysteries. I even thought about how great it would be to have a retired colonel in our town. Have you read any British mystery novels yourself?"

"No, I haven't read much," answered Gwanyoung.

"I see. British mystery novels always feature a colonel. Not a colonel still serving in the military, but a colonel who's more like a village leader. Sometimes he's the murder victim; other times, he's a suspect. Every town has a colonel. If they were on active duty, they would've been untouchable, but the colonels in these mystery novels are just civilians. Like a church pastor or a schoolteacher. I wonder if local aristocrats became colonels in the United Kingdom in those days. I'm sorry for rambling on like this, but I just remembered that when I saw you, Professor Cha."

"I was a colonel, but I had no idea that was what colonels were like. Local aristocrats in the past are like city or provincial assembly members these days, though, don't you think? I would love for you to stay and chat, but I'm sure you've got a busy day with government work, so may I ask what your visit is about?"

At Cha Gwanyoung's polite question, Lee Gwangsam fidgeted with the teacup and slyly changed the topic.

"Ah, sure. I've digressed. Then I shall move on to the reason I came to visit. I came to ask you something."

"What is it?"

"When a distinguished person like you comes to a humble little town like ours, the townspeople get curious, you see. As you know, everyone here is looking for an opportunity to leave for a bigger city."

Gwanyoung tilted his head, with no clue as to what Lee was getting at.

"That doesn't seem strange to me. Only the young people look for a chance to get away. When you get to my age and you no longer need opportunities, it's a dream to retire to a quiet little town."

"Hahaha, is it? But even then, this town doesn't have much to look at, nor is it a great place to live. Half the town has become a bedroom community for the Space Force. You would know, Professor Cha. I've heard that you've filed several complaints about the noise from the Space Force base."

"Is that why you've come to see me personally?"

"No, no, sir," Lee answered. "My secretary told me when I said I'd like to pay you a visit. I do a little research on people I'm going to meet. Oh, it's nothing like a full background check, just getting the basic information that's out there. My secretaries are the ones who'd get into big trouble if a provincial assemblyman like myself goes around saying the wrong things. But, hmm ... I've read that you were mainly at the headquarters in the Space Force. And you have connections there. You weren't at this base for very long ..."

"Anyone in the Space Force visits the launch base frequently, regardless of where they are stationed."

"That's what I mean. But there's something that people who've served in the Marines like myself can't quite grasp. Why would a distinguished person such as yourself retire to this town when you don't really have any connections here?"

Gwanyoung wasn't sure how to answer that question. He had no idea about the provincial assemblyman's intent behind this question.

Lee then said, "I will then ask you directly. I've already gone on and on for too long."

"Sure, what is it?" Gwanyoung asked.

"Are you interested in next year's election?"

"Excuse me?"

"I'm asking whether you have plans to run for the provincial assembly seat. The ruling party has a strong respect for you. And you provide counsel for the Ministry of Defense these days, too, don't you? You've been on the news a few times since the two suns situation came about. With someone honorable like you in town, sir, I cannot but be concerned as an incumbent. That's why I've come to see you. To ask you whether you are planning to run for a seat in the provincial assembly, and, if you are, which party you'll be running for."

For a moment, Gwanyoung felt his head go completely blank. The provincial assemblyman smirked as he brought the teacup to his lips.

Suddenly Gwanyoung burst out with a laugh. It came out without his realizing, releasing all the tension that had been built up until now.

"Goodness, me! That's why you're here!"

"Yes, that's why I'm here. I'd like to hear your answer before I leave."

Gwanyoung walked over to Lee Gwangsam and grasped his hands.

"Mr. Assemblyman, I'll do my best to help you if there's anything I can do. About the election, I mean. And with your administration as well. I have no desire to run at all."

Lee Gwangsam looked askance into Gwanyoung's eyes.

"Do you mean it?"

"Of course, hahaha! I had no idea that there was such an election. Had I known that it would have worried you so, I would have come to see you first."

An awkward silence filled the room for a moment. Seconds later, Lee Gwangsam let out a generous laugh, and Cha Gwanyoung followed suit. He was now laughing out of courtesy, but he felt half sincere about it. He glanced at Lee Gwangsam and noticed that the man's eyes were devoid of mirth, even amidst uproarious laughter.

But that didn't matter. As long as Lee wasn't here about the incident.

That night, Um Jonghyun was in his room in the single occupant dormitory waiting for a call. Park Kugyong, who had gotten off work a little late, walked into the room in his dress uniform. Since it was also his room, Kugyong had entered without knocking, and Jonghyun had jumped at the sound of the door opening, but Kugyong didn't seem to notice.

Seeing that Jonghyun was dressed to go out, Kugyong asked, "Are you going somewhere?"

"There's something I have to do. I have to deal with the stuff you gave me earlier."

"Is it something urgent? I thought it was censoring films and TV shows and stuff."

"Is the Intelligence Department in charge of censoring stuff in the Space Force? That's not it, though. It's because of Professor Cha Gwanyoung."

"Oh? I'd heard rumors about that, but what does that have to do with TV shows? Ah, I shouldn't be asking an intelligence officer things like this, I know. Anyhow, I knew he was going to be trouble at some point. Has he done something major?"

Jonghyun swiveled his chair around toward Kugyong.

"You know him well?"

"Not well, but he's one of the people who call us to file complaints. When the Base Research and Development Center performs engine tests and stuff, he calls the PR department."

"Why the PR department?"

"Because our phone numbers are everywhere, and it's hard to find the numbers for other departments. He's an artist, or so he says. He either takes pictures or does paintings. When we do engine tests, it generates steam. Once, he called and said he was doing a landscape painting or something outside, but then clouds mushroomed out of nowhere, making him lose all inspiration and whatnot. So he calls every now and then to ask if we can let him know the engine test schedule."

"He called more than once?"

"He calls once every three months or so, but not for the same issue. He complains about all kinds of stuff. Sometimes it's about noise, other times it's the` steam causing sudden rain showers. He's also from the Space Force, so I have no idea why he complains about stuff so much."

Jonghyun asked, sounding like an intelligence officer, "Perhaps he's not happy with the Space Force these days? Like how the chief of staff is a woman."

"That could be part of it. Chief Gu Yemin has many friends but also a lot of enemies. If she didn't want enemies, she'd go along with things as custom dictates, but she doesn't. Since it looks like the Space Force is doing well these days, the media has a demand for people who either advocate for or criticize the Space Force. They always need at least two people on each side, so it's not a bad career choice. It looks like Colonel Cha's decided on being a critic."

"Is he a neutral party, though? He's working for the military."

"The HQ PR Corps is monitoring the situation, but they're just leaving him be. A bit of a fight makes for a good show."

"I see," replied Jonghyun, "but as for criticism, being a critic might just be a role you create for yourself at first, but if you keep at it, don't you come to believe in what you're saying?"

Kugyong rolled his eyes left and right as he traced back his memories. Then he said, "Now that I think about it, that sounds about right. These days, he's pushing for intercepting the Pac-Man sun. Saying that the reason the Allied Space Force hasn't shot it down yet is that it's a trick to continue this Space Force fad around the globe. Then he ended that argument by asking about what we're going to do with the dying polar bears in the meantime. He's not completely wrong. We're just watching him for now since he's not directly attacking the ROK Space Force, but it looks like he's become rather serious these days. Some feel he's too much of a fan of the Mars Governor-General and that he's doing all this to go into politics."

"Does he not believe that it's because of the treaty, that we can't just get rid of Pac-Man?" asked Jonghyun as he changed into a different shirt. "That's the reason the Allied Space Force was created—forbidding launching a missile to destroy anything that is in Earth's orbit, whatever it is."

"But aren't we going to shoot it down eventually? It's a bit far away to say that it's close to Earth. So it's all a bit iffy. Aside from figuring out the best time to shoot it down, is there any reason we're keeping it up there? No matter how much debate there is, there's not going to be another conclusion, and we can't just let it stay up there forever. They'll shoot it down at some point. When it's advantageous."

"I suppose so."

"Oh, speaking of Cha being a fan of the Mars Governor-General just reminded me of something. Professor Cha's daughter is a real professor, and she is an Oste fan. Last month, he called the PR department and requested Oste's autograph. He was suddenly polite and all."

"Huh. Did you get her his autograph?"

"He said he was friends with the base commander, so what could we do? When he calls, he never fails to mention it. He starts the phone call with 'I'm a friend of the commander.' He gets a free pass like that, but it will eventually get him into trouble. Thinks he's still a colonel. How do you think they are going to handle this upstairs?"

"I'm not sure. They're thinking about it."

"Yeah, well. I didn't know I was helping out with something to do with Professor Cha Gwanyoung, but since I did help, let us know what happens. The PR Corps needs information if we have to clean up after him. And please, please don't leak info about suspects to the wrong people. Credibility is our asset, and it's hard if you keep giving us information that will be corrected later."

Jonghyun nodded and swiveled back to face his desk. Minutes later, his phone rang once, and he took his bag and left the room.

The next morning, Soojin left the launch base main building with sunken eyes. Suh Ga-ul, on her way in, noticed her and approached.

"Inspector General, have you been studying overnight for a test?"

"How great would it have been if you were a weather specialist who knew to ignore me when I'm looking too haggard."

"Indeed. Why did I turn out like this, I wonder. You probably weren't on night duty again. Did you have a lot of work? Did someone do something?"

"Just watching movies all night."

"Sorry?"

"No, wait. Just watching a computer watch movies, TV shows, and videos on the internet all night. Wait, that's not quite it either. Just watching the back of the head of an intelligence officer watching a computer watch movies all night. I ... don't know what I'm saying anymore."

"I have no idea what it's for, but it sounds like a real bore. Are you off to take a rest?"

"More like going to take a shower. We've done all the preparation, now it's time for the real work to begin, but I don't know when that's going to start, so I have to come back and stand by. I hope it all begins soon. It'd be a disaster if I start dozing off."

"I'm sure you'll be fine. Use all the energy you have left, and good luck! I'm off to arouse a southeasterly wind."

Soojin headed to her house in town to take a shower and lay down on her bed for a moment, where she ended up nodding off. Two suns bore through the cracks between the curtains that covered the window, but Soojin was fast asleep.

A little later, she started awake. Reaching out her arm, she fumbled for her phone to check the time just as it rang. It was Technical Sergeant Choi Suzy from the Internal Review Department.

Soojin picked up the phone and said, "I fell asleep. Is the commander looking for me?"

Suzy answered, "No, the commander hasn't said anything, but the Intelligence Department called. They said that Professor Cha Gwanyoung was loading luggage into his car."

"Oh geez. Trying to run away? That's a terrible move. Is the commander at the base?"

"Yes, ma'am. He's in his office."

"I should head up then. I'll be there in ten minutes. Contact Captain Um Jonghyun and the Operations Division. Tell them I'm convening a meeting."

"Should I contact the military police as well?"

"No, if you call the Operations Division, they'll figure out what to do."

Soojin drove up to the main building. When she stepped onto the second floor, the entire span of the hallway, from the Internal Review Department to the Operations Division, was abuzz with excitement. She noticed that Captain Um Jonghyun was cornered against a wall by the director of the Ground Operations Office and the provost marshal.

When Soojin appeared, Jonghyun sent her a pleading look for help.

Noticing the look of distress in his eyes, Soojin asked the other two, "What's going on? This isn't where you should be."

Major Chun Unsil, Director of the Ground Operations Office, spoke angrily, "The Intelligence Department overstepped its bounds."

"What do you mean?" asked Soojin.

"Moments ago, the military police stopped Professor Cha Gwanyoung's car. But the order came from the Intelligence Department, not the provost marshal."

Soojin asked Major Chun, "Stopped his car? Where?"

"By the bridge that leads off the island. They barricaded the bridge and started an inspection. They got him at the checkpoint, and then they reported to the base military police. When I asked the bridge checkpoint who ordered them to keep Professor Cha in custody, they said it was Captain Um Jonghyun. It was an order from the 'Military Police-Internal Review-Intelligence Joint Response Team.' Has such a team been created without my knowledge?"

The provost marshal remained silent, but he too didn't seem all that pleased. Again, Soojin looked at Jonghyun as she answered Major Chun.

"There is no such team yet, but it looks like Captain Um did take necessary measures. Professor Cha should not be on a bridge headed off this island at this time. We would've been left pawing the air. Can we just agree on this now, then doesn't that make that order one given by the Joint Response Team?"

The provost marshal asked, "On what grounds are we supposed to be holding him? The military police were the ones who actually blocked the bridge and took him into custody, but was that a measure founded on a legal basis? It wasn't what the commander instructed us to do—"

Before his speech turned into a lengthy one, Soojin cut him short.

"Is the legal affairs director in his office?"

"He's coming," answered Major Chun Unsil.

Soojin nodded and asked the provost marshal, "How long can we hold Professor Cha at the checkpoint? About half an hour?"

Instead of an answer, the provost marshal shrugged his shoulders. Soojin understood the gesture as "We have some leeway."

"Then let's go to the base commander's office," said Soojin. "Let's sit down and figure this out."

Soojin took the lead and headed to the commander's office with the provost marshal, Major Chun Unsil, and Captain Um Jonghyun in tow.

The commander was sitting in his chair. He didn't even ask the four other people in his office to sit down. His face was full of annoyance—it was clear that he'd received a call from Cha Gwanyoung.

He barked, "Didn't I tell you to take extra care and treat him with respect? Or was that too much to ask?"

The provost marshal's face hardened. The director of the Ground Operations Office seemed rather triumphant.

The commander continued, "Is the intelligence director coming? I'd like to hear from him about what happened, but I was told it'll take at least an hour for him to get here. So are you going to explain this to me, Captain Um? Or you, Inspector General?"

"I will, sir," Soojin spoke up without hesitation. "We did take care to treat him with respect, but given the situation in which he attempted to leave the island, this has become a serious problem. We are not at the stage of considering him a suspect, but this would grow into a much bigger issue than it is now if we let a person under investigation disappear. Someone needed to take the necessary measures, and the Intelligence Department first assessed the situation and took action—"

"On what grounds?" the commander interrupted. "Taking him into custody when we don't consider him a suspect? You've already come to the conclusion that he was running away. Don't you watch the news? He's busy with all kinds of work. He's not someone who's confined to the island. If he's late for his schedule today, are you going to take full responsibility?"

"It is difficult to see his departure from the island as a simple business trip," Soojin answered. "Because there's a discrepancy in his statement."

"What discrepancy?" the commander snarled at Soojin.

Putting a pile of documents on the round table, Soojin said, "His alibi has been blown."

At her words, the base commander, the director of the Ground Operations Office, and the provost marshal, who had been taking it in turns looking at Soojin and Jonghyun, all snapped their heads in Soojin's direction.

"I think we have about twenty-five minutes left until Professor Cha is released. So let me explain as quickly as possible. Last night, I analyzed the video that recorded Colonel Cha Gwanyoung's house on the night of the incident. The footage from the surveillance camera taken about five hundred meters away from his house. I consulted with Captain Um Jonghyun, as his expertise is in satellite analysis. As you know, he is tasked with analyzing satellites in orbit that have been deployed by foreign countries, and he says that these days he mainly analyzes satellites in Mars' orbit rather than the Earth's. That should be enough background information. I would like to get straight to the point, but I do need to explain this part, so please excuse me. Analyzing a satellite begins with looking at a video of the satellite to figure out its shape. You might think that it's not too difficult since there is a video of the satellite but, by a video of the satellite, I mean a video of the dark night sky with just a tiny dot. Am I correct, Captain Um?"

Jonghyun nodded.

Soojin caught her breath for a moment and continued, "If anything I am saying is wrong, please interrupt and correct me. I will continue. His task is to look at a small dot and figure out precisely what it is. How, you may ask. First, he measures changes in the magnitude of light. This is a basic astronomical research method. You can find even minute changes in apparent magnitude, and a computer can draw this on a graph. If you observe a satellite for a long time, you eventually get a repeating pattern, and that becomes a cycle."

Soojin shuffled through the documents and found a piece of paper with a graph of changes in apparent magnitude, which she pushed toward the commander.

"From this point to this point is a single cycle, and from this point to this point is the next cycle. To find out the shape of the satellite, the key is to identify a cycle, from here to here. From this, it's possible to reverse engineer the shape of the satellite."

Major Chun chimed in, "Isn't the order backward? The graph of the changes in apparent magnitude is the result, and the shape of the satellite is the cause, but you're looking at the result to figure out the shape. That's possible? Just from this graph?"

Soojin answered, "Good question. That's exactly the point. And what you're thinking is correct. Just from this graph, it's absolutely impossible to figure out the original shape of the satellite, no matter what you do. Just from this graph, that is."

"Then what?" asked Major Chun.

"If we try to solve this like an essay question using only this graph, it's impossible. But we can solve it if we treat it as a multiple-choice question."

"But there are no choices."

"You make a list of possible choices. You position a virtual light source so that you have a light shining on the satellite from the same direction and at the same angle as the sun. Then you put an orb in the position of the satellite in question. You set the rotation period the same, all virtually, and draw a graph. Let's say that's A. Then, you use a cone instead of an orb and draw a graph of changes in apparent magnitude. That's B. Then you use a hexagon, and then a cylinder, and so on."

"Wait," the provost marshal interrupted Soojin, "but those are all just choices that you make up yourself. What's the point of comparing those with the original graph?"

Soojin lowered her head to look for the documents to show them next and answered in a calm voice, "There is a point, sir. Because it's not a question with four choices."

"Then what is it?"

"Consider it a multiple-choice question with about five hundred choices. Like this."

Soojin slid pieces of paper toward the commander. Every

page contained dozens of graphs of changes in apparent magnitude. Soojin continued.

"There are hypotheses. Since there is a list of known satellites, we don't need to start from scratch. We can virtually place all known satellites in the same position as the target satellite, have them exposed to a light source, and simulate changes in apparent magnitude. One of them would eventually produce the same pattern. Of course, there is a chance that you still might not find the same pattern. However, Captain Um's task is to identify completely new types of equipment. In that case, he won't have a model satellite to use as a reference. Then what does he do? What do you do, Captain Um?"

Jonghyun answered, "I would have to create about ten thousand choices and run simulations."

"Just ten thousand?"

"Even a hundred thousand choices are possible. There are other methods too, such as dividing up the target satellite into parts and analyzing them. For instance, traditional spaceships have a cylindrical body with a conically shaped module for the return trip. At the other end of the cone would usually be a nozzle. So we can use the graph of changes in apparent magnitude for the cylinder as a base, and separate the pattern of changes in apparent magnitude resulting from the conical structure. The patterns for basic shapes are well-known, so it's easy to analyze them. Even for complex structures, if you consider them as combinations of basic shapes, it's not impossible to analyze them."

Soojin held up her hand to stop Jonghyun.

"Since we don't have a lot of time, let's wrap things up here. If we get any farther into it, it becomes much too specific. Back to what I was saying earlier, the key here is the principle of the reverse engineering method. You're not just looking at the results and backtracking from there. You have to first record all the patterns through simulation, and then compare those patterns with the pattern of the target you wish to identify. The trick is in handling a tremendous amount of data in a short amount of time—with the help of computers, of course. If you have a kid or a niece or nephew who's studying for the college entrance exam, you would probably know how kids who aren't good at math just pick C for all multiple-choice questions and then use their remaining time to solve the questions worth four points. You simply substitute as many answer choices in as you can. It's exactly the same thing. You put in numbers from one through a hundred to see which one gives you the right answer. Kind of like figuring out lock combinations too. You can try all different combinations of numbers, one by one. If you have enough time."

The commander leaned back into his chair. Both the provost marshal and the director of the Ground Operations Office also relaxed, as if telling her to continue.

Soojin got to the point.

"If you understood all that, you'll find the rest easy to understand. When you look at the video provided by the provost marshal taken five hundred meters away from Professor Cha's house, you can only see a dot. But in the Space Force, a small dot is enough. And thankfully, it wasn't a still but a video. It's possible to graph changes in apparent magnitude, and when you put it through a spectroscope, that dot is separated into three or four dots. We didn't do the latter and only did the simple method. Last night, I borrowed the AI from the Communication Relay Station and made it watch TV all night."

The commander let out a short exclamation at her words. It was a sign that he understood what she was getting at. Nodding, Soojin confidently moved on with her explanation.

"First, we made it watch movies. We got all the movies we could get our hands on and played them to draw graphs of changes in apparent magnitude. In the mind of the AI computer, we created a small room equipped with a TV that's similar to the one in Colonel Cha Gwanyoung's living room, turned that TV on, and seated the AI on the virtual sofa. Then we pressed the play button. It takes less than a second to watch an entire film, and we couldn't edit or process the movie files as we wanted, so we just played them in their entirety. We made tens of thousands of those rooms in the AI computer's head to watch tens of thousands of movies at the same time. All this happened inside the AI. As you probably assume, the issue was not in watching the movie but in getting hands on those movies. Captain Um used the Intelligence Department's know-how to get them, and I decided not to ask for details. Ah, I also believe he received help from the PR Corps. After the AI finished watching movies, it watched TV shows, specifically all the shows that were aired within the given time on the night of the incident. Then we made it watch stuff that wasn't on the list input by Captain Um. Animations, documentaries, performances, music videos, and commercials. Then we made it watch popular videos online. Eventually we came to the conclusion that there was a limit to what we could find the AI to watch, so we had it look for such videos on its own. That was much more efficient. Secretary Kim Eunkyung, who is in charge of the AI program, told us not to save anything that the AI watches. From what I saw out of the corner of my eye, I think I understand why she said that. In any case, what did Captain Um Jonghyun, the AI, and I do last night? In sum, this is what we did. We watched all the videos that a resident of this island could get their hands on and watch at the time of the incident. All of them."

"Did you find it?" The commander asked.

Soojin nodded. "We converted them into graphs of changes of apparent magnitude, and we found the one with the same pattern as the graph that we drew from the faint light that was coming from Professor Cha Gwanyoung's living room that night."

"Ha! That's just astonishing. How did you even … OK, so what was it? You're saying that it wasn't a video conference call for a fact?"

"Correct, sir. It was a movie, which was what we began with. But it wasn't in the database that Captain Um first provided the computer, so we only found it after going through the entire process and allowing the AI to search for videos to watch on its own. As a result, it took a long time to find it. How should I say this … it was something that the AI thought of only after it had learned to become somewhat of a cultural critic."

"What was it?" the commander asked.

Soojin answered, "The AI had to become a certain type of a fan …"

"No, the title of the movie."

"Ah, it's a Korean film titled *Lunandalusia.*"

The moment the title came out of Soojin's mouth, Major Chun Unsil let out a snort in spite of herself. All the eyes in the room turned to her. Major Chun regained her composure quicker than it took the AI to watch a movie.

The commander asked, "Director Chun, you know the movie?"

Soojin nodded at Major Chun, and she answered, "It's a movie starring Oste. Private Lee Ja-un, who is serving in the Space Force Band at the headquarters, starred in the film before entering the Space Force, but it bombed in the box office."

"What? From B Density? He was in a movie? But why would

Colonel Cha Gwanyoung be watching that at that time of ... Oh ..."

The commander let out a long sigh before he could finish thinking out loud. Soojin pushed a sheet of paper that contained information on the movie toward the commander and finished up.

"His daughter, Professor Cha Minyoung, once asked Captain Park Kugyong in the PR Corps to get Private Lee Ja-un's autograph. She sent several gifts along with the request, although the actual request was made by Colonel Cha Gwanyoung through the PR Corps. Professor Cha Minyoung does not live with Colonel Cha Gwanyoung, but ..."

"She comes once a week to take care of chores around his house," the commander finished Soojin's sentence for her. "OK, I understand what you're saying. I see it now. So after you found all of this out, you went to get some rest while Captain Um monitored Colonel Cha's house."

Jonghyun answered, "Yes, sir. Since his alibi of attending a video conference at his home was blown."

The commander stared at Jonghyun. His face was an odd mix of emotions—trust on the one hand and resentment on the other. Or perhaps it looked that way because of the different angles in which the natural light streamed into the room from three directions.

"Provost Marshal," the commander spoke with a voice stained with resignation. "You should go in person."

"Yes, sir," the provost marshal answered.

"Go get Colonel Cha. Bring him to my office immediately."

"What should we do with the vehicle?"

"Seize it and search it. Don't let him drive himself. That's how you get into an accident."

At lunchtime, Soojin took a bag of steamed corn up to the roof of the launch base main building. When she opened the door, Secretary Kim Eunkyung was sitting on the bench, where she always sat.

"I thought I heard that you've been frequenting the mess hall."

"Oh, hey, Soojin," said Eunkyung.

"You don't like the mess hall?"

"I just went a few times to meet the new people. Now that I've spent all my socialization energy for the year, I can't go back until next year."

"Oh no, there can't be two queens of this rooftop."

"It's a world with two suns in the sky, haven't you heard?"

Soojin sat down next to Eunkyung. The two of them looked up at the sky. And as if they'd planned in advance, they each held up a hand to shade their eyes from the suns, then looked down at the shadows cast at their feet.

"I guess it won't be too long until we're left with just one shadow," said Soojin. "The other's just a strawman anyway. I feel like I should cherish it for now."

"I don't think I'll miss it."

"This could be the Space Force's heyday."

Neither of them spoke for a while. Soojin took an ear of corn out of the bag, picked off kernels one by one, and popped them into her mouth.

After a long silence, Eunkyung said, "So, Cha Gwanyoung's been arrested?"

"We brought him in with all the respect in the world. The commander's very devoted to treating his colleagues with kindness."

"He's really not like a spacenaut. Some might mistake him for an airman."

"And the Air Force would be confused by that statement."

"I heard that someone saw Cha Gwanyoung cursing the Space Force as he went into the commander's office," said Eunkyung.

"Oh no," Soojin said. "What kind of a curse?"

"I think it was directed at the chief of staff. Like, how long does she think she can pull strings like this, why is Pac-Man still left up in the air, aren't we just leaving it up there using the international treaty as an excuse because we know that shooting it down isn't going to lower the temperature on Earth, it would be better for the vice-minister of Mars to take charge of the Space Force, yadda yadda yadda."

"He's certainly a conservative commentator."

"Indeed. He's a semi-pro conservative commentator now, considering how he criticized the SF even while he was being taken in."

"Whether we shoot the Pac-Man sun down or not isn't really up to the chief of staff, though."

"Nor the vice-minister of Mars."

There was another long bout of silence.

Abruptly Eunkyung turned to Soojin and asked, "What's going to happen with Cha Gwanyoung now? Why did he transmit the firearm data?"

"I have no idea," Soojin answered. "I'm just a soldier on a checkerboard. The Space Force headquarters will continue the investigation. I assume that they'll get to searching the shuttle soon too."

"They probably will. If his accomplice on the shuttle finds out about Cha Gwanyoung's arrest, they might destroy the evidence. That is, if there is an accomplice."

"Well, well, the Space Force now has an opposition. It's like we've only just surfaced from the depths of anonymity."

"Because it makes money. For the first time in history. And it's true that Chief Gu Yemin is walking a dangerously thin rope. At least until now, that rope remained taut, but it won't stay that way for long."

"Really? I think it will."

"Things will probably change when *he* comes, don't you think?"

"Ah, *him*. He's on his way, right?"

"Probably."

"Do you think he'll shake the rope?"

"That rope will probably fall limp at his feet, even if it looks like he didn't do anything."

"Yeah, I suppose we'd be lucky if he doesn't do anything."

Eunkyung then said, "But you know, a checkerboard just has pieces, not soldiers. Technically, you'd say a pawn on a chessboard. I don't think I've heard anyone say a 'soldier on a checkerboard.'"

Soojin answered, "I'm like a soldier, and a chessboard is also checkered. They're practically the same thing, so what does it matter?"

"Well, you know, such a basic error makes you look so ... normal. You're the high and mighty Acting Inspector General of the Space Force launch base!"

"I told you it's all an invention that other people have conjured up. It's nothing, like that Pac-Man sun. It's just all a made-up image."

"Speaking of your image, there's a rumor going around that you're now a basketball coach. People are saying that you were once a player too or something—you injured your knee and gave up on playing on the national team right before the selection?"

"Whaaat?"

Unable to hold it in, the two of them burst into laughter. Once the laughter died down, the rooftop became dead quiet again. Like a battery-operated toy running out of juice.

As lunchtime came to a close, Soojin said, "What the heck does it matter anyway. Let them believe what they want."

"Sure, sure," answered Eunkyung. "I'll keep it a secret."

Soojin brought a kernel of corn to her mouth. A plane flew by somewhere far above. A basketball was bouncing in the court far below.

Chapter Six

Throwing Away a Stuffed Bear

Park Young-ah looked into Kim Eunkyung's eyes, slowly tilting her head to the left and then to the right. Eunkyung's gaze, however, didn't follow Young-ah's eyes.

"Are you listening to me?" Young-ah asked.

Eunkyung straightened her face and replied, "Of course."

"Then I'll continue. Our program will be developed in time for when Earth-Mars communication opens to the public. Mars welcomes these types of projects, so there haven't been many issues there, but I'm not sure how it'll work on Earth since there are a lot more regulations. In any case, our goal is to air it on both Earth and Mars simultaneously."

Eunkyung added, "Since the market size would be tripled."

"Right," Young-ah continued. "From our standpoint, it doesn't make sense to give up on the Earth market. Plainly, that would halve our profit, and we'd lost like seventy percent of our viewers. The test broadcast will begin for the thirty percent on Mars first, but when we were getting investments, we had to proceed with the project on the premise that the Earth market would be completely open. So we'll probably have about a year or so between the Mars test broadcast and broadcasting on Earth."

Kugyong, who was listening to the conversation, chimed in, "A year's barely enough time."

Young-ah answered, "Oh, I meant a year by Mars time. I've only just returned from Mars, so I keep making these mistakes. It'll be more like a year and ten months in Earth time. So not unrealistic."

"Ah," Kugyong exclaimed as he looked up at the clocks on the wall. There were three clocks displayed in the Communication Relay Station. Two round analog clocks on the left and the right showed Korean Standard Time and Mars Settlement Time, and between them was a digital clock that showed Mars Settlement Time converted into Earth time—each day on Mars was twenty-four hours and thirty-seven minutes long in Earth time.

The auditorium-like area of Communication Relay Station beyond the glass wall was empty. Only an orange light was on, like an open stage.

Eunkyung said, "You haven't started the test broadcast on Mars yet, have you?"

Young-ah answered, "No, we have to wait for the private communication networks to be opened. We're thinking of starting at the next Opposition."

Eunkyung nodded, but Kugyong asked, "What's that?"

Eunkyung answered, "It's when the sun, Earth, and Mars are positioned in a straight line. You know how the Earth and Mars revolve around the sun—when these two planets are moving on the same side, it's called Opposition."

Young-ah explained, "On a clock, it's like twelve o'clock. When the hour hand and the minute hand are in the same place.

Both planets are the closest to each other. And it's called Conjunction when the hour hand and the minute hand are on opposite sides, like twelve thirty. It's when the Earth, the sun, and Mars are lined up in that order, and the Earth and Mars are the furthest apart from each other."

"Oh, so the distance between the planets keeps on changing?"

As this realization dawned on Kugyong, Eunkyung shook her head at him.

"Have a little interest in planetary work, you know," Eunkyung said to Kugyong. "I guess reporters don't ask the PR Corps about that. When Mars and Earth are the closest, it takes about three minutes for the speed of light to reach Mars from Earth. Twenty-one minutes when they are on the opposite sides of the sun. You know how there's a bit of a noticeable delay when you're making an international call? It takes a little time for what you say to reach the other person, and the same length of time between when the other person says something and that reaching you. During interplanetary communication, that delay ranges from somewhere between six and forty-two minutes."

"Really?" asked Kugyong out of astonishment. "That must be really frustrating. Don't administrative orders also go through this channel? Are all orders transmitted that way?"

"There's nothing we can do about it," answered Eunkyung. "There's no way to send radio waves faster than the speed of light. It takes a similar amount of time to control satellites remotely. You should study more, really. From what Ms. Park's saying here, it sounds like more and more people are going to be asking about it next year."

"So it takes at least six minutes to ask a question and receive an answer? How do you carry on a conversation? It must take an entire day to have just a single meeting."

"That's why planetary civilian workers deal with the calls. We compile ten, twenty questions and ask them all together, and the answers come all at once as well. It would take an entire day to go back and forth with just one question and answer at a time. Even when we lump the questions together, it's all the same in that there's still a delay in receiving the answers. Looks like you really had no idea about any of this."

"I just thought we exchanged documents for things like that," said Kugyong.

"There is a lot of back and forth with documents as well. For more important things, there's a system to contact Mars directly, but everyone says that their stuff is the most important in the world. Just like how things are here on Earth—people like to schedule a meeting when they could just send over files."

"Yes, well, meetings are considered a marker of job performance, so it makes sense," Kugyong said. Then he turned to Young-ah and asked, "But what do you mean that the broadcasts have to start at Opposition?"

"It's when the delay's the shortest," answered Young-ah. "Just six minutes. From then on, the delay will grow to forty-two minutes. So we take that period of time, from the shortest to the longest delay, as a season and air a show. The first episode would be a pilot, and it'll be just six minutes long. The episodes will grow longer over time, until the last episode, which will be forty-two minutes. We'll make the episodes short initially, like advertisements with intriguing content to draw people in, and then end the show with the longest episode. If we go the other way around, from Conjunction to Opposition, then the first episode will be forty-two minutes long and the finale only six minutes, which wouldn't be great. So that's why we have to begin at Opposition."

Eunkyung chimed in, "It's not just the length of delays that change over time. The relationship between the two planets changes as well. The interplanetary shuttle runs during Opposition too, so the politics and economies of the two planets grow closer. Sort of like a festival period."

Young-ah followed up and said, "During the conjunction, meaning when the two planets are on the opposite sides of the sun, shuttles don't run, and communication itself becomes infrequent. Since there's a significant delay, you know. So we become two isolated planets, and around that time, another kind of festival begins on Mars."

"They celebrate that period?" asked Kugyong.

"There's a thing called the Conjunction Festival, which lasts for about a week. It's gotten longer in some places, and they go on vacation for two weeks or so. It originated from the disruption in communication between Earth and Mars because of the sun being between them. Started in the pioneer days. The signal sent to the Mars-bound shuttle breaks up when it passes the sun. The reception's not great, and sometimes erroneous signals get sent, causing the shuttle—that expensive spaceship—to malfunction. So around this time, they just turn off the communication equipment. They put the shuttle on autopilot, and the people on Earth in charge of communicating with Mars used to go on vacation. That tradition has lasted."

Eunkyung let out a sigh and further explained to Kugyong, "Before the rebellion, that is. The rebellion occurred right when Mars was outside of the Earth's influence. Since the planetary officials on Earth were on vacation, our city on Mars had to rule all on its own. They had full authority for the time being and, using that, they declared independence, set up their own autonomous assembly, and joined the alliance of Mars cities."

Young-ah then said, "And the rebellion was suppressed. Bru-tally."

"Brutal's kind of a strong word," said Eunkyung.

"It's true that they used excessive force to put them down. It was clearly an offensive operation."

"Because we were outnumbered by far. Offense was our de-fense."

Kugyong looked from Young-ah to Eunkyung and back. There was a sudden chill in the air. He quickly tried to steer the conversation in a different direction.

"So Ms. Park, your request to the Space Force is to test air that show from here in the Communication Relay Station?"

Realizing what Kugyong was doing, Young-ah answered in a cheery voice as if nothing had happened. "Yes. Since the pub-lic communication network isn't open yet, we don't have any-where else to test it. And the higher-ups seem to like it because they think it's an employment benefit for planetary officials."

"Why is that a benefit?"

Although Kugyong's question was directed at Young-ah, Eunkyung answered instead, as if to say that she was also back-ing off since this was a business meeting.

"Delays during international calls on Earth are frustrating," Eunkyung said. "When there's a delay of about half a second, you instinctively think that it would be polite to say something, so you start talking, but then you end up stopping the other per-son from talking. Imagine what that would be like if the delay were six minutes. It wouldn't be a big deal if it were thirty min-utes, but six minutes, or ten minutes, those kinds of short delays are just enough time to make you uncomfortable staring at the screen. And it's too short a time to go do something else. Plus, sometimes we actually handle confidential reports, so it's not really ideal for the person in charge of communicating to leave their seat. Meaning we have to just sit here and stare at the other person on the screen. This is the number one stressor for planetary workers. To the point where whether you can take this agonizing suspense decides whether you'll be able to do this work or not. So the higher-ups are saying that they'll provide us with content we can watch during that time."

Kugyong asked, "You mean, watching the same six-minute video over and over again?"

"If this becomes part of broadcasting," Eunkyung explained, "other people will probably make dozens of six-minute, ten-minute, fifteen-minute-long videos."

"There are tons of short videos out there even now," said Kugyong.

"That's true," Eunkyung responded. "But there are numerous content producers as well, and they will have to keep on making stuff to survive. Plus the business model for free content is different from our proposal. I'm sure the competition in that industry is fierce and feeling out new markets is something they do all the time."

As soon as Eunkyung finished talking, Young-ah said, "There will be a number of channels, so the viewers will stay interested. This is a rather important factor since it impacts commercial pricing. In any case, this is all theoretical, and there is a lot we don't know unless we actually try it. For instance, we won't know whether it would be best to provide six-minute-long content during the six-minute delay. Some people might pause the show and then come back to it. Considering that, a five-minute or a five-and-a-half-minute video might be better. So we can't *not* do a field test, but there's only a handful of places where we can run the test. In Korea, there's the relay station at the central government and the one here. That's why we're asking for your help. It looks like upper management is likely to review the project positively, so I think something will eventually be worked out. But … Secretary Kim, are you listening to me?"

Young-ah tilted her head to the left and right again as she asked.

Without moving her gaze, Eunkyung answered curtly, "Of course."

Kugyong cocked his head as he looked at the two of them.

Eunkyung bluntly asked, "Ms. Park, but isn't the pool much too small for the test broadcast? If it's just the government and here, that is."

"Oh, that's not all," Young-ah answered. "Korea was a bit unique in that we contacted the government, but the Korean Space Force isn't the only one we have in terms of Space Forces."

"You mean you have the Allied Space Force?" asked Eunkyung as she turned to look at Park Kugyong. Kugyong nodded.

Eunkyung asked Young-ah again, "What did you promise them?"

"A positive and progressive image about advancement into space. What the Space Force Public Relations Corps does."

"Wait, what?" Eunkyung exclaimed. "Are you saying that I'll be watching a TV show that promotes the Space Force for an entire year?"

"Not at all. You can relax. We haven't even made it yet. We'll only be able to start working on that once we get the money from the Space Force. We'll start with something more neutral. So you can just give us your honest feedback. Since we'll be doing this with all the Space Forces around the world, you won't need to worry about whether what you say will have too big of an impact."

"I thought light of it, but it's a very ambitious project, isn't it? If it involves all the Space Forces on both planets."

"Sorry to be subjecting you to this kind of experiment, although this ambition didn't start at our company. It's time for the Space Force to begin a new chapter, but these days people say that the most terrifying thing in the world is the Space Force."

"Not as terrifying as the Space Force on Mars, for sure," said Eunkyung.

Later that day, on her way back to her room, Eunkyung noticed an excavator parked by the side of the single occupant dormitory. People in safety helmets were standing around. There was a small wooden stick tied to the end of the bucket, and when she looked more closely, it seemed that the person in the driver seat was writing in the dirt with the stick.

One of the people watching looked at his watch and shouted to the operator, "Come on down now! We really have to get back to work!"

Moments later, the driver's side door opened, and the operator wearing a safety helmet jumped down. It was Han Summin.

After returning the helmet to the workers, Summin walked out of the construction site. Then noticing Eunkyung from afar, she bowed to say hello.

Eunkyung held up her right hand in response and asked, "What's going on?"

"Oh, they're building the new dorm," said Summin. "It'll take about a month or so. A month! Can you believe it?"

"No, I mean, what were you doing here?"

"Personal training. The simulator's under maintenance today."

"You were training here?"

"Something like that. My regular training is like operating three of those at the same time though. Are you getting off work now?"

"Yeah."

"You're working too hard. You should go take a rest."

"You should too, Sergeant Han. Since your equipment's under maintenance."

Summin bowed her head with a bashful smile on her face and walked up toward the base main building. Then she stopped and turned to ask Eunkyung, "Secretary Kim, are you going to the Christmas party? I heard there's going to be a party at the IG's house. Suh Ga-ul told me."

"Oh, that. I don't think so. You go and have fun."

"You should come. If you're getting off work now, you should be free that evening considering the shifts."

"Thanks. I'll see."

Summin looked into Eunkyung's eyes. Then curiously, she turned around to look behind herself. There was nothing behind her.

"Secretary Kim, is there something behind me?"

"Huh? No, there's nothing."

"I thought you were looking at something. Never mind. Have a good night!"

That night, right as she was about to fall asleep, someone knocked on Eunkyung's door. She opened the door to see Ga-ul standing there. It wasn't often that people visited Eunkyung uninvited, so she was suddenly wide awake.

"What is it?" Eunkyung asked. "I don't know what I'm doing on Christmas yet."

Ga-ul said, "Did I wake you? I'm sorry. I'm not here about the party. I just wanted to say the temperature's going to drop by twenty degrees Celsius in the morning."

"Oh, twenty degrees?"

"It's abnormal. Though it'll be the average temperature in other years, so technically it's normal. Just wanted to tell you to dress warm for the weather. You'll have to dress like it's the coldest day of the year in the middle of winter. You have winter clothes, right? Not like you took them to get dry cleaned and never got them back or anything?"

The next morning, the temperature did drop to ten degrees below zero. Eunkyung stepped out of the dormitory wearing the thickest jacket she had and turned to look up toward Ga-ul's room. Then she pulled her hat down over her eyes.

The temperature at her workplace—the Communication Relay Station—was adequate as per usual, which meant there was expensive equipment there. Eunkyung took off her coat and hung it on the back of her chair before checking up on what she needed to do that day. There were documents for approval submitted from the Public Relations Corps from after she left work yesterday.

Eunkyung flipped through the pages one by one, then she suddenly looked up and stared at the chair across from her. Then she breathed out a sigh.

After taking care of work for the morning in Mars time, she left the Communication Relay Station to find the sun high up in the air. Eunkyung dialed a number on her office phone.

"Yeah, it's me," she said when someone on the other end of the line picked up. "It's starting up again. I'm seeing it again. Yeah, that."

When Eunkyung arrived, Soojin was already sitting on the bench on the rooftop, shuddering in the cold.

"Do we really have to meet on the rooftop every time?" asked Soojin. "On this freezing cold day?"

Instead of answering her, Eunkyung got straight to her point.

"It's here again. It was gone for a while, but it started back up again. What do I do?"

"The teddy bear?" asked Soojin, as she reached out and waved her hand in front of Eunkyung's eyes.

Eunkyung said, "It's not there now. What you talk about doesn't stress me out, so it's fine. It happens when I talk to people I don't want to talk to."

Soojin nodded as if she just remembered and said, "I thought you didn't like talking to me. When did it start?"

"Yesterday."

"Yesterday? Were you talking to someone that you didn't like?"

"Yeah, there was someone from a media agency that the PR Corps brought over."

"Oh, her. I scanned through her file. You didn't like her?"

"She's half Martian."

"Oh no. And was there anyone else?"

"I saw Han Summin for a few minutes, and it was there too."

"You don't like Summin either?"

"I do," Eunkyung answered. "But we were talking about something that stressed me out. So I went to bed early, but Suh Ga-ul came and woke me, so it appeared before her face too."

"Well, I understand that happening," Soojin remarked.

"And I saw it again this morning."

"This morning? Aren't you usually alone in the Communication Relay Station around that time?"

"Yeah, but it was on the screen."

Soojin buried her hands deep into her pockets and thought hard about what Eunkyung was saying. Then she suddenly looked up and asked, "Are you saying that it was beyond the screen? Like on the Mars side?"

"Yeah, there was a difficult situation. Because it's such a headache, it's all confidential. But this is really troubling. If I get even just a little stressed, it shows up right away."

"You said it was a huge teddy bear, right?"

"Yeah."

Soojin took her hands out of her pockets and stretched them out wide. Then she quickly plunged her hands back into her pockets and said, "About that big? The teddy bear."

"Bigger," Eunkyung answered.

"Wow."

"Like I told you before, I can hear people fine. It's just that I can't see their faces. When it gets worse, Teddy erases the sound too, but that only happens when it gets really bad."

"Oh man, I think planetary work conditions are just too poor. The job is too lonely. Everyone else lives twenty-four-hour days, but you live twenty-four hour and thirty-seven minute days, so you can't even socialize with other people, and you're isolated like you're living on a completely different planet. So unless it's people you see often, you have to think, would it be OK for me to call this person at this time?"

Eunkyung stared at Soojin, who was voicing her complaints for her. Though her face was frozen because of the cold, there was no teddy bear in sight.

"So what should I do?" she asked Soojin.

"I'm not sure," Soojin answered. "But could we go inside first? Even if the teddy bear does appear, it won't make the weather warmer."

As soon as it was time to get off work that evening, Soojin drove over to the single occupant dormitory. Then she walked up to Eunkyung's room. When she knocked on the door, Eunkyung cracked the door open and poked out her head. At that moment, Soojin realized that no one had ever seen inside Eunkyung's apartment—or rather what some called a room and others called an apartment.

"Can I come in?" she asked. "It's not really a conversation for the shared lounge."

The door opened. Not all the way, but just wide enough for Soojin to squeeze through.

The suite was spacious and clean. For someone who has lived there for years, Eunkyung didn't have a lot of furniture, and everything was well organized. It was undoubtedly better furnished and decorated than all the other rooms in the same building—the bright wine-colored wallpaper, mustard blinds, and sprightly plants were inconceivable for people who thought of the dorm as tentative housing.

Eunkyung closed the door quietly and asked, "Wanna sit down?"

Soojin looked down at the chair but remained standing as she said, "I finally get to see your suite. It looks great. It's not too small for you, is it?"

"It's OK. They did build it when there was nothing else around here. Well, there's still nothing much around here now, but there was literally nothing around back then. When I first came here, this felt like a four-person suite."

"So, where is it?" Soojin asked.

"The teddy bear? In that room. Open the door, and you'll see it."

"You didn't pack it away and just left it out in the room?"

"No, I didn't leave it out so much as ..."

Soojin strode toward the room. Back in the days when each

person had a suite to themselves, this second room had been used as a study, but now with two people assigned to each accommodation, most used it as another bedroom.

"Well, Let's see what it looks like," Soojin said expectantly and reached for the door handle. Then she pushed it open without hesitation.

The door opened ajar, but could go no further because of something behind it. Soojin poked her head inside, before pulling it back out and turning toward Eunkyung.

"What *is* this?"

"The teddy bear. Well, it's ... like that."

Soojin squeezed herself through the doorway. In the room was a dark brown teddy bear, slumped down on the floor with the back of its head touching the ceiling. It was a giant teddy bear. It wasn't standing upright—it was sitting on the floor, yet it was so big that it couldn't even hold its head up high, which was bent forward.

Soojin came out of the room and asked Eunkyung, "Why is this here? I feel like bringing that in must have violated at least one regulation. What is it anyway? Is something that size still called a teddy bear?"

"It was a gift," Eunkyung answered. "From him."

"Goodness. So you lived here for all those years with that in there? If *he*'d given that to you, it must have been here for over fifteen years, no? Secretary Kim, I know nothing about psychology, but I think I might have a cure for your condition. You should throw that thing out. I feel like that must make something better."

Moments later, Soojin and Eunkyung were sitting on the floor, looking up at the teddy bear that took up the entire room. The teddy bear had pitch-black eyes and long limbs. Each of its eyes, made to look like it only had a black pupil, was as big as the mug Soojin held in her hands. It was carelessly bent and squeezed into the room, but it also seemed to be expressing something with its body, from the way its limbs were positioned. The emotion it aroused was close to melancholy.

While quietly staring at the teddy bear, Soojin suddenly stopped and turned to look at the door to the room. Then she asked Eunkyung, "How did you get it in here in the first place? Did it fit through the door?"

"It has no bones. If you can get the head in somehow, the whole thing can eventually squeeze through. People helped me to get it into the living room originally. Some people from the Development Corps brought it over on a truck."

"It must have come on a truck when it was delivered at the main entrance too."

"Yeah, well."

"You must have gotten a call about a present and gone to the main entrance to pick it up. What did you think when you first saw it?"

"It was shocking," Eunkyung answered.

Soojin said, "It must have taken up at least half of the living room."

"So I moved it into this room, which I had to empty first. I nearly died doing all that myself. I struggled to push its head in first and then the rest of it, only to realize that it wasn't sitting like it is now but folded the other way around."

"Like it was bending over backward?"

"Yeah. So I left it that way for several days but couldn't stand looking at it that way any longer, so I flipped it around. It was so heavy."

"Geez. So did you ask him?"

"Ask who what?"

"The person who gave that to you. What was he thinking sending that thing? He must not have thought about the value of the real estate that it would take up."

Eunkyung's eyes became wistful.

She said, "It must have been a mistake. I think he was thinking about sending a smaller teddy bear that is still oversized. Like, as tall as the bookcase when sitting down or something."

"It was custom-made, right? Maybe they miscalculated the size."

"Probably. I guess he ordered a bigger one than the regular ones so that it would look substantial even when sitting down. Although he made a calculation error, probably because he lives on Mars."

"What do you mean?" Soojin asked.

"Ceilings are higher on Mars," Eunkyung answered. "Since gravity is much weaker on Mars, if you jump wrong, your head can hit the ceiling. So after two years of living on Mars, he probably forgot how high ceilings are on Earth."

Looking at Eunkyung, Soojin calmly asked, "By two years, you mean Earth time?"

"Yeah. A little over two years. Two years and two months or so."

"Meaning not one year on Mars or two years on Earth but 780 days of Mars and Earth's conjunction period?"

"Right."

"So two years after he left for Mars, the Earth and Mars grew close enough for him to return to Earth for the first time in twenty-six months, but instead of coming himself, he sent this."

Eunkyung answered with a flat voice, "Will you not narrate this sad story in that official tone?"

"Well, I don't want to tell it crying. When he left, he must have promised that he'll be away for one conjunction period and return immediately."

"Everyone who leaves for Mars says that. Though none of them return."

"You probably didn't know whether to cry or laugh when you got that."

"We were pretty much done by then. I don't know if he sent it to ask me to wait another twenty-six months or if it was a parting gift. He probably didn't know himself either. But regardless, I decided not to wait."

"You say that, but you did let it take up a bit too much of your real estate. Isn't it pretty much the same as letting another person live here?"

"It's less awkward than living with a person. It doesn't use the bathroom, and it doesn't snore."

Soojin stared at the teddy bear without a word. Eunkyung put her mug down on the floor and leaned back against the wall.

After a long while, Soojin spoke first, "Let's throw it out."

"OK," Eunkyung answered.

"Do you want to donate it somewhere?"

"Let's just throw it out."

"Should we cut it up and get it out in pieces?"

"Aw, no, that's a bit … If it gets cut up, I don't want to see it. If not, the next time it appears as a hallucination it might be all mangled up. At least now it's cute."

"Ah, I see your point."

"And I want to give it a nice send-off. When I think about it, Teddy didn't do anything bad to me. It only appears in my hallucinations to help me not see the person I don't want to see and not hear the things I don't want to hear. It's on my side."

LAUNCH SOMETHING!

Early the following day, in Korea time, the Allied Space Force Press Office made an important announcement. Through the United Nations' mediation, the use of weapons to destroy the Pac-Man sun was negotiated. In other words, they were going to launch a missile to shoot down the second sun.

In the evening, the lounge of the single occupant dormitory of the Space Force launch base was bustling with activity for the first time in a while. They were gathered to watch the news.

"So they finally decided to launch a missile," Eunkyung said, standing awkwardly behind the couch. "I suppose this is the right time."

Sitting on the couch and looking cynical, Ga-ul added, "There's nothing more to do. There was a cold snap, and the temperature began to drop, at least for the northern hemisphere, so regardless of whether it's true or not, it will be less and less convincing to argue that this summer's heatwave was a result of that thing."

"It's different for the southern hemisphere?"

"A lot of the budget comes from the northern half. Anyway, the Pac-Man sun has to be destroyed right about now, so the Space Force can pretend that destroying it has dropped the temperature. Like you said this is probably the perfect time."

Han Summin, who was sitting beside Ga-ul and watching the news with a concerned look on her face, turned around and asked, "Would that result in getting our budget cut? That'd be a big problem."

Noticing the worried look on Summin's face, Eunkyung smiled and said, "There's going to be a second season to this show, though."

"A second season?" Summin asked.

Impatiently, Ga-ul chimed in, "She's talking about the second moon. The asteroid that had the reflectors installed on it. Looks like the Allied Space Force is really looking into it. Those asteroids usually get caught up by Earth's gravity and remain in orbit for a while before they get pushed out. They say that one at Lagrange point four or five in the Earth-moon system has become stable, but it's difficult to stay that way because of solar perturbations. This one is on the line, but it's lasted for a while, so they're keeping an eye on it, thinking that it could amount to something. They're acting as though they're not interested, but I can feel them constantly looking sideways at it."

"What could it amount to?" Summin asked.

Ga-ul hesitated for a moment but soon looped her arm around Summin's neck and spoke in a grave voice.

"Pulling it in close like this. Course correction. You know, the project that the US Space Force has been really pushing to earmark a budget for. Sending a spaceship to an asteroid to install a propulsion system. The theory is that correcting the asteroid's orbit slightly with a low-propulsion rocket can cancel out the perturbations caused by the sun. That's what they want to do. And if it succeeds, the asteroid will become a satellite that they can use at some point. It'll be their real estate. Anyways, Handsome Man, it's been a long time since I've had you in my arms. I heard you were training a lot these days, and I can feel it in your muscles."

"Hey, let me be," said Summin. "But is that really a doable project? I heard that it was impossible this time around but maybe possible next time it comes back into Earth's orbit. Like in fifty years or so?"

"That's what I don't believe. Seeing how the Allied Space Force has been boasting about that project to install the reflectors, I wonder if they placed something else on there too. Though I haven't seen anything to back my theory up. I just don't think they're going to wait another fifty years."

"What do you mean, something other than reflectors?"

"A propulsion system," answered Ga-ul. "I think they've already put it there."

Summin exclaimed, "What? You're such a conspiracy theorist."

"They put the reflectors there. Who's to say they can't put in a thruster?"

"Where did they get the money for it?"

"Well, I don't know!"

As Ga-ul and Summin argued, Eunkyung stepped toward the hallway and said to Summin, "Sergeant Han, go to bed already. Only the Public Relations Corps and the Intelligence Department were busy today, but starting tomorrow, the entire Space Force will be running around for about a week. Considering the Orbit Operations director's personality, that office is going to make a pretty big fuss about all this, I'm sure. And there's no need for an ace pilot like yourself to fret. The Allied Space Force is certainly not the kind of organization to let a once-in-several-decades opportunity slip through their hands. I'm sure they're preparing for the next thing. They'd have to take a risk, but no military likes risks. Ah, I should really go to bed."

As she was about to step onto the staircase, Eunkyung heard Ga-ul tell Summin, "She's probably going to go and watch the news alone in her room. We *are* taking up all the good seats."

Eunkyung smiled at that.

Early next morning, on her way to work thirty-seven minutes later than the day before, Eunkyung saw the huge teddy bear waddle ahead of her. It was about fifteen steps ahead.

Turning to look at the construction site by the road, she noticed the excavator and walked toward the lot where Summin had previously been practicing with it. It was well-lit by a nearby streetlamp. No one must have worked here since, because the picture that Summin drew with a small stick on the excavator's bucket was still there.

It was the Space Force emblem. The lines weren't crystal clear, but anyone could tell what it was. For a long time, Eunkyung stood staring down at it. Then she spoke to the long-limbed teddy bear that was now stood ahead of her.

"Wow, just where did someone like Han Summin come from? I don't think I could draw this if someone gave me a pencil and paper. Isn't this crazy? Didn't she say that she controlled three of these at the same time?"

That day, the view of Mars on the screen at the Communication Relay Station was entirely full of the teddy bear. It looked like the teddy bear was smiling, but it was really just slumped down with an impassive look. Ban Segyung, the Mars communications officer whom Eunkyung saw every day, asked questions and gave her answers as usual on the other side of the screen, but Eunkyung couldn't see her face at all because of the bear. Eunkyung was obliged to ask questions and give answers while staring at the teddy's face.

"Secretary Kim, you look more tired than usual today. Are you OK?"

Even Segyung's concerns sounded like words coming from the teddy's mouth. Without an answer, Eunkyung gave an awkward smile. That was the only thing she could do.

Around the time the hands on the Earth clock pointed to the beginning of the workday, the office phone rang. It was Soojin.

"How is it today?" she asked.

"It's filled up the entire screen," Eunkyung answered. "I've been working this whole time staring at it."

"You really hate the other person that much?"

"Apparently. I thought I really liked Ms. Ban. But man, I haven't even gotten a glimpse of her all day."

"I'm sure it's not her but what's behind her you hate."

"I guess. If I do hate it that much, I think it's not bad that I don't see it."

"Are you going to keep the teddy then?"

"No."

"Then let's postpone. I'm ridiculously swamped today. I have no idea why the Internal Review Department is so busy."

"If everyone's that busy, I don't think I can ask people for help. Let's deal with it after we shoot down Pac-Man. It's not like something terrible is going to happen if we delay getting rid of it."

"Sure, OK. Anyway, I don't think it's something we should discuss on the phone, so I'll see you after work!"

Later, at a time that was a little early to call night but already pretty late to call evening, Soojin was still in her uniform in the lounge, which unlike the previous evening was almost completely empty.

To the nearly dozing Eunkyung, she said, "So that's the problem, right? You are a civilian employee responsible for communicating with Mars, but the entire screen is covered with the teddy bear."

Eunkyung answered, "I wonder if I've come to hate anything related to Mars."

"Perhaps it's just stress from work. I mean, who enjoys working?"

Eunkyung slowly shook her head. She seemed deep in thought.

"No, because I know exactly when that teddy bear started appearing again."

"When was it?" Soojin asked in a calm voice, carefully studying Eunkyung's face.

"Remember the day Cha Gwanyoung was arrested? We met on the rooftop. And I told you then. That *he* was coming back. I didn't think it meant much when I said it, but later, it kept on popping into my head. Like, 'Ah, he's really coming back. Finally.'"

"Yeah?"

"I think it was around then that I started seeing the teddy again. Because he was the one who gave it to me. It's been stressful to think that someone I considered dead to me is actually going to be here again. It's brought on indigestion and insomnia too. And I think it's this stress that sort of transfers to other people when I have to deal with them. Originally it was the stress from thinking about him, but now I hate hearing anything about Mars, and I get irritated. But then I'm in charge of communicating with Mars, so I wonder if I can do this. Because it means I'm letting negative perspectives get mixed into what's supposed to be a neutral interplanetary communication network for my own personal reasons."

"There's another communication channel in the government. This isn't the only one, and when you consider the entire planet of Earth, it's one of myriad channels. You told me that was what that producer said. So don't overthink it."

Soojin thought that Eunkyung was close to tears. Eunkyung said nothing in response. She only sat blankly staring outside the window.

In a low voice, Soojin comforted Eunkyung.

"Instead of the teddy bear, should we get rid of *him* when we have the chance?"

Eunkyung turned to Soojin, looking radiant.

On the morning of Christmas Eve, the missiles that the US Space Force launched in the name of the Allied Space Force headed for the Pac-Man sun, which had been shining in Earth's sky for over six months. The missiles hadn't been newly launched from Earth; ones that were already in orbit simply belched fire and changed course, so there were no spectacles to be seen on the television.

Just like everyone else in the world, all the spacenauts at the ROK Space Force Launch Base stopped what they were doing and gathered in front of televisions or computer monitors in groups to wait for the second sun to disappear. In the early evening, US Eastern Standard Time, when the first sun had set, it was time for the second sun to shine alone in the sky. It became clear that the people in the Americas would directly experience sudden darkness when the second sun was shot down, but people in other regions wouldn't—they had to watch it being aired on television.

There was no spectacular scene yet, so the news was full of expert panels and commentary. Just an hour of watching the news was enough for viewers to realize that the same things were being repeated, but the members of the Space Force kept their gazes fixed on the screens.

Just as Ga-ul had predicted, and as many other people had discussed, the project for capturing the "second moon" asteroid was mentioned occasionally during the broadcasts. The Allied Space Force Press Office's video of the spaceship that was to be deployed as part of the new project was much more impressive than the live-stream of experts giving commentaries.

In addition, words and phrases like "the international treaty," meaning the one that had become the basis for the establishment of space forces; "Kessler Syndrome"; and "collective defensive system expanded to the orbit" continued to appear on the screen in captions. The news was full of information that even the members of the Space Force would hear maybe once a year, such as how the treaty and the missile launch were contradictory, why it took such a long time to come to the conclusion of launching missiles, and in what direction the Space Force should pursue its policy in the future.

Eunkyung had the news on the big screen inside the Communication Relay Station and watched it alone. Then it came—the moment sudden darkness fell.

A scene in which several missiles, which were invisible to the naked eye because they were so much smaller than the Pac-Man sun, exploded and at once completely erased the gigantic structure in outer space; a scene where brightly lit foreign cities suddenly succumbed to darkness, as if a lightbulb had blown or someone had turned off the light switch.

Eunkyung watched the same scene repeat about three times and picked up the remote to turn off the news. Like the darkness that suddenly fell over the foreign cities, a sudden silence fell in the Communication Relay Station. Eunkyung let out a quiet sigh and slowly walked toward her office.

"It was such a fragile structure."

That night, there was a Christmas party at Soojin's house in town. It was a Korean-style party, so no one was standing—everyone sat on the floor, eating, and drinking.

When Eunkyung arrived, people cheered loudly. Looking a bit embarrassed, she went and sat down in a corner.

Ga-ul dominated the scene as usual. She was also the only person in red, suitable for the holiday season.

"Captain Park Cooking, I'd never imagined you to be this kind of person, but you seriously went and got sashimi on Christmas Eve? Yikes. Well, everyone, look what I brought! Tada! This cake! Those of you who think that this is nothing special are the ones that try to beat the traffic every weekend, rushing home to the city, but our IG who also lives in exile in this countryside would know! How hard it is to bring over something like this! Am I right?"

Soojin didn't even look in Ga-ul's direction and said, "All right, which wine should we start with today? Captain Um is the designated driver, so no alcohol for you, which means we need five glasses? I only have three wine glasses. I suppose Ga-ul and I can use cups."

"Aw, why me?" Ga-ul whined. "Why do you hate me even on Christmas?"

"Because you organized the party," replied Soojin.

"I should've brought a glass."

Summin sat looking apathetic, but it didn't take long for her to join in the conversation. When Kugyong started unraveling stories about Oste, her eyes sparkled with interest. Um Jonghyun now looked like a full-fledged intelligence officer, meaning he cast suspicious glances now and then even while socializing with others. He was, as Eunkyung had once described to Soojin, a person who knew exactly where to look even in awkward situations—someone who was always polite and sophisticated no matter what role he was given to play.

Eunkyung was the only one who couldn't mingle with the others. As the party became rowdier, Soojin turned to glance at Eunkyung from time to time. She certainly wasn't a hologram—she was eating the same food and drinking the same wine—but she seemed out of place, like someone who was living in the time of another planet. It felt as if someone looking through the viewfinder of a camera would either only see Eunkyung or the other five people.

"Captain Ohm! The Intelligence Department would know. What are our prospects like for next year, is the Space Force gonna be poor again?"

When Ga-ul brought up this question, everyone's eyes landed on Jonghyun. Jonghyun glanced at the Inspector General for a moment, but he must have thought answering such a confidential question was inappropriate because he quickly turned his gaze to the wine bottle.

He said, "I don't really have any intelligence on that matter, but when you listen to what the Allied Space Force Press Office is saying—meaning if you look at their attitude rather than their words—it doesn't look like they're in a rush. It feels like they're confident. Right, Captain Park?"

"Yeah, well," answered Kugyong, "There are things that they are making quite public, so it feels like they're going to do something. The ASF Press Office has always been very cautious, so they don't just say anything without clearing it first. They're much more diplomatic than we are since they're under the direct influence of the treaty."

"Yay!" Ga-ul cheered at his words. Possibly because she was feeling tipsy, her gestures seemed even more animated than normal. "Then let's relax and keep on drinking!"

Once again ignoring Ga-ul's words, Soojin offhandedly asked Kugyong, "Why's the Public Relations Corps so busy these days? I knew you'd get busy sooner or later, but what's the issue now?"

"That's a good question. It's actually nothing important. We're busy with new promotional materials. Oh, there's going to be new souvenirs in the gift shop by the main entrance. The Pac-Man sun lamp used to be in great demand, but now we have to take that out. So we're getting new promotional products, and it's all changing in a rather orderly manner which feels like everything was planned in advance."

"What's the new item?" Soojin asked.

"Or-me-tee Or-me-tee," Kugyong replied. "It's a new asteroid character. All sparkly. The design isn't something that will sell in Asian countries, so I don't know if it'll generate much profit. But it'll help the Space Force survive next year—having the asteroid to deal with, I mean. Not the Or-me-tee Or-me-tee goods."

"Or-me-tee? As in meteor? Is that such a good idea—when asteroids start coming toward Earth and become meteors, doesn't that get a bit worrying?"

"Well, yeah," Kugyong sarcastically answered, "There's that trivial matter."

At that moment, Ga-ul suddenly jumped into their conversation. Peeved by Soojin not responding to her excitement, she seemed determined to join in.

"See, I said they didn't just install reflectors on it. They might really be working on installing a thruster."

"That's news to me," answered Jonghyun in a serious voice.

"Me too," Kugyong agreed with his roommate. "In any case, it'll orbit around Earth with the reflectors until next summer at least. We have to work hard and milk it as much we can until then."

Ga-ul swallowed her words at his response. It seemed that she didn't have enough evidence to counter Kugyong's expert opinion. Instead, she quickly changed the topic, ensuring she still had control over the conversation.

"Didn't they say that he was coming back next year? The Mars

Governor-General. He was a two-star, wasn't he? I wonder where he's going to go. He's definitely the cream of the crop."

Soojin carefully studied Eunkyung's face. She was relieved to see that Eunkyung wasn't distraught. At least, not on the surface.

Unable to avoid Ga-ul's gaze, Eunkyung reluctantly opened her mouth and said, "Indeed. There are rumors about how other generals exaggerate their experiences to receive stars, but there is no such controversy for the Mars Governor-General."

"He's going to remain influential even when he's back on Earth, right?"

"I guess ... Did you know that the most difficult thing for a Mars officials to do is to create a method for getting approval signatures? Because there are about fifteen people or so whose signatures are needed for projects over a certain budget."

"Fifteen?"

"That's actually the tip of the iceberg," Eunkyung explained. "There's the Space Force's approval process, and then the Korean Ministry of Defense, the Allied Space Force Finance Team, the Mars Occupation Force Command, the Mars City Hall, the Prime Minister's Office, and the UN Headquarters. It's a hodgepodge of everyone, and the chain of command is so convoluted that it's impossible to implement an automated approval path. When important forms come over from Mars, I spend from thirty minutes to an entire hour struggling over which organizations and agencies I need approval from, even though I'm not the one who filed the forms."

"But why?"

"Because people get so sensitive over where they are in the chain of command. Tons of people complain all the time about why they're before this person or that. Some quibble over ranks, while others quibble over administrative grades. Secretariats of treaty organizations are above member country governments, and the UN is above treaty organizations in certain cases but not in others, and Mars is a whole other problem. Everyone makes a fuss trying to be a step above others."

"Yikes, that sounds like a rather extreme job. Kind of like performing ceremonial rites at the Pantheon."

"Makes me want to smash and tear everything down. Plus, the whole chain of command isn't fixed. As time passes, certain institutions ascend the hierarchy while others come to exist in name only. The treaty secretariat used to be the real authority, but then the Allied Space Force won that power game—things keep on changing, so we have to keep watching to see how the power dynamic changes. It'd be much better if I could simply do this by people's years of experience in the field. The whole seniority rule, there's something to it. It shouldn't just be criticized."

"Wow, you must be an expert in ranking people in the Space Force," Ga-ul exclaimed.

"Of course," Eunkyung answered.

"So, what's the latest trend in the chain of command?"

"Oh, right. That was what I was getting at. In the past few years, there's someone who's been pushed up about five ranks in the approval process."

"Who's that?"

"That man. If you call him Mars Governor-General, you might get into trouble—the Vice-Minister of Mars. He's been treated like a hero since he suppressed the rebellion."

"Wow, so he's coming home in all glory! He's going to be pretty popular back here, I bet. He's relatively young and is already a two-star."

"By the looks of it, yeah. He's the only field commander in the

ROK Space Force who earned his reputation as a real spaceman, not a member of the Fighter Wings."

As she finished the sentence, the excitement in Eunkyung's voice faded, and her voice grew quieter.

In the early hours of the morning, the five people who lived in the single occupant dormitory returned home in Um Jonghyun's car. Everyone headed to their rooms immediately, except for Eunkyung, who remained outside for a while.

"I'm going to sober up before I head upstairs," she said.

"You didn't drink much," Jonghyun remarked.

"I'm old."

As a cold breeze brushed past her face, Eunkyung's feeling of an oncoming hangover decreased, and she felt herself become wide awake. Her heart didn't settle down as easily, however. It was because of longing, as well as regret.

Eunkyung crossed the parking lot and took a long stroll to a spot without any streetlamps. Then she looked up at the night sky. The asteroid caught between the Earth's and the moon's gravities was lighting up the night sky. It was dim, but its light contained hope, just like a star decorating the top of a Christmas tree.

The teddy bear left Eunkyung's house the evening after Christmas. Kugyong and Soojin struggled to pull the gigantic bear's head out of the room, and Teddy ended up with a long scratch on one of its eyes. Soojin positioned her body to shield Eunkyung from seeing the bear's scarred eye.

Jonghyun joined them after getting off work late, and the four of them pushed the bear out of Eunkyung's apartment door. Summin was passing by when she noticed the back of the bear's head poking out into the hallway and took a picture.

"Wow!" Summin exclaimed. "What is this?"

"A gift from an ex-boyfriend." Soojin answered in a loud voice like it was the most natural thing in the world. "Isn't it gigantic?"

Eunkyung covered her face with one hand, expressing her embarrassment with a rather exaggerated motion.

Then with a look of determination, she said, "I'm going to live a new life starting today."

Summin asked, "Are you going to start dating again?"

"No! I'm going to live a life with a second room!"

"Oh, I'm a bit jealous of you for that."

A small truck was waiting in front of the single occupant dormitory building. The teddy bear barely made it down the stairs and squeezed out of the building's main entrance. Laid spread eagle in the open space, it was much bigger than Soojin had imagined.

"Oh no, his eye," murmured Eunkyung as she looked down at the teddy bear from the steps.

Soojin jumped at her words and said, "Just forget you saw it. Other than that, he hasn't got a scratch anywhere. His limbs are all intact, and he looks adorable, all spread out like this."

They loaded the bear onto the cargo bed and tied it down tightly. The teddy bear sat looking back from the truck.

"Could we move it so that it can sit looking to the front instead of the back?" Soojin asked.

The truck driver and everyone who helped move Teddy out of the building and onto the truck shook their heads.

"His head isn't fixed, so it won't face the direction you want it to anyway," answered Kugyong. "I think that's probably the best we can do."

Soojin nodded.

The truck driver revved up the engine, and it was now time

to part. As if saying goodbye to an actual person, Eunkyung stroked the bear's arm.

"Take care, and don't come back."

Soojin watched her sympathetically. Others watched in confusion as Eunkyung said goodbye to the bear, not knowing the reason for such a sad parting.

"How long do we have to stand here?" Kugyong asked, and Eunkyung withdrew her hand begrudgingly.

"I'm done now," she said. "Let's let it go."

"Oh, OK."

Kugyong, Jonghyun, Soojin, and Summin stood in a line, looking toward the main entrance. With her hands deep in her pockets, Eunkyung was a couple of steps ahead of them and looked up at the teddy bear sitting on the truck bed.

"I'm off then!" The truck driver shouted, and the truck began to move forward. It sped through the parking lot and toward the base's main entrance. The giant teddy bear sat tied to the truck bed, looking out back. His head bounced up and down every time the truck lurched. It almost looked like it was nodding.

Ga-ul was walking to the dormitory when she noticed the bear on the truck, and she stared at it curiously.

When the truck stopped for a moment before passing through the main gate, Eunkyung raised her hand above her head and waved.

"Goodbye."

The four people standing behind her followed suit, waving their hands and saying, "Goodbye."

The truck passed through the main gate and went over the hill. When Eunkyung finally put her arm down, Soojin said from behind her, "OK, now it's time for you treat us to some Chinese noodles!"

LAUNCH SOMETHING!

"Can I come?" Summin asked.

Ga-ul came waving her hand, thinking that the five of them had been waving at her, and shouted, "I'm here! Were you all waiting for me?"

Soojin answered in a voice bright with mischief, "Of course! Let's go for some Chinese noodles!"

Ga-ul moaned, "You know I don't like Chinese noodles!"

"Do I?"

"As a planetary official, how are the long-term prospects for the relationship between the two planets?" Park Young-ah asked Kim Eunkyung.

It was the first meeting for the test broadcast of videos that would be aired during the communication delays between Mars and Earth. There was a small camera placed on one corner of the table.

"What do you mean by long-term?"

"Well, over fifty years?"

"Ah, so in terms of the history of civilization," Eunkyung said and fell into thought.

Young-ah looked relaxed. She didn't press Eunkyung for an answer, and she didn't seem at all uncomfortable with silence. She would've made a great planetary official. Eunkyung peered into Young-ah's face. There was no teddy bear this time, so she was able to study her face in detail.

Eunkyung opened her mouth and said, "Ultimately, I believe the relationship will become antagonistic."

"I see," answered Young-ah with a look of surprise. "And why is that?"

"Because they're too far from each other. They won't be able to overcome the physical distance."

"Your position is exactly the opposite of this project that I'm working on."

"No, not really. I do think that it is great to make efforts to overcome the distance. Of course, your primary purpose is in making money, but ultimately your work will help reduce the differences between the two planets. However, since you're asking about the long-term results, I believe that ultimately the differences between Earth and Mars will be impossible to overcome."

"Are the differences that great?"

"From having communicated with people on Mars on a daily basis, I can confidently answer yes. There is a huge comfort sharing the same kind of routine with others—a feeling that we are all living in the same world. But a minimum of a six-minute delay between asking a question and giving an answer is a difference that will be very difficult to overcome. It doesn't feel like we're living in the same world. Creating content to bridge this gap is a meaningful task. But honestly, it makes me wonder, would it really be a pleasant experience to see someone on the other side of the universe looking at something else, as soon as they finish talking, to pass the time during this six-minute delay?"

"That does sound quite hopeless."

"I don't think it's hopeless. I think we're going to thrive, each on a different planet. It's not too bad to have two independent worlds in this universe. But ..."

"But?"

Young-ah stared at Eunkyung's lips with the calm yet tenacious gaze of a documentary filmmaker. Only after a pause that seemed about as long as the delay in communication between Earth and the moon, Eunkyung's lips began to move again.

"But I don't think people from these two different worlds could fall in love with each other. I mean, there will certainly be exceptions. But those exceptions will be a very small number compared to the number of people on each planet who hate the people on the other planet. As if ..."

"As if?"

"As if there's a giant teddy bear as tall as the ceiling sitting between the two of us now."

Exactly two weeks later, there was news of an arrival at the space station orbiting Earth. It was the special interplanetary shuttle *Pilum*, which carried General Lee Jongro, the former Mars Governor-General, officially known as the former Vice-Minister of Mars of the ROK Space Force. Rumors circulated the Space Force headquarters, the launch base, and among the overseas Space Force Fighter Wings about how he was highly likely to be promoted to a three-star lieutenant general as soon as he landed and how there would be a large-scale change in personnel accordingly.

The Space Force radio show *Let's Raise the Density!* hosted by Oste also heavily covered this issue.

"Everyone, he's finally coming! You've all heard it in the news, right? General Lee Jongro, the former Vice-Minister of Mars, has finished his service on Mars and is heading back to Earth. I'm already so excited. At *Let's Raise the Density!* our goal is to successfully pull off an interview with Lieutenant General Lee Jongro in the next year. You'll all be cheering for us to do so, right?"

Unfortunately, just two weeks after the Mars Governor-General returned to Earth and resumed his duties, *Let's Raise the Density!* was canceled. Private Lee Ja-un, a.k.a. Oste, was ordered to focus solely on his Space Force Band duties. Letters requesting the show's resumption flew in from all around the world, but Lieutenant General Lee Jongro did not reconsider his decision for a second. His answer was always the same: "Is this Space Force Entertainment? Tell him to focus on playing band music."

Among the petition letters sent from all around the world was a letter Han Summin sent under a fake name—Han Jumin—which she posted during leave at her parent's home. It was an insignificant act she took as a fan of Oste. Yet, anyone in the Space Force looking back on this act several weeks later, as the ROK Space Force came to resemble the strict and rigid Mars Space Force, would understand such illicit action could in fact be a big deal.

Chapter Seven

Peace-Preserving Design

"Chief of Staff Gu Yemin."

Space Force Chief of Staff Gu Yemin heard a voice calling her but didn't look up and answer right away. The same voice then called her again.

"Chief Gu."

The air was thick with tension. There wasn't room to breathe. Gu Yemin took her glasses off and put them on the table. She then turned her head toward the voice and answered, "Yes, Mr. Assemblyman."

"There is no one here but us. However, I'm not asking personally but as a representative of the people, so I hope you can answer me to the best of your ability. Do you understand? Answer me, please."

National Assemblyman Kim Mugyong, a member of the National Defense Committee, pressed her. Unlike what he'd said about them being alone, he sounded as though he were aware of someone listening in on them.

Gu Yemin answered, "I haven't exactly heard the answer to my question about what this meeting is about, but OK, yes I understand."

"Then I will ask. Who is the Republic of Korea Space Force the enemy of?"

After taking a moment to organize her thoughts, Gu Yemin answered before Kim Mugyong could open his mouth again.

"Theoretically, we are no one's enemy."

"You have military power, but you are no one's enemy? Is there no one who considers you a threat? Then what do the enemies of the Republic of Korea think of the ROK Space Force?"

"Mr. Assemblyman, in principle, the ROK Space Force is not an independent organization. We belong to the Allied Space Force, and according to the treaty, the Allied Space Force has control over us. Therefore, we do not directly target the forces that are hostile to the Republic of Korea. If you consider the authority that —"

Kim Mugyong interrupted her.

"Why then do we have a military branch that does not pose a threat to anyone? Isn't the Republic of Korea Space Force operated with our taxes? Aren't spacenauts of the Space Force drafted from our country? Or are they mercenaries? Please respond."

"The Military Manpower Administration drafts our spacenauts."

"So, if the people of the Republic of Korea serve in the Space Force, and if our hard-earned taxes are used to pay for its budget, shouldn't the Space Force exist for the benefit of our country?"

"Mr. Assemblyman, the position of the Space Force has been clear since its establishment. It states that the Space Force only contributes to the benefit of our country indirectly, and its priority is in maintaining the security of Earth's orbit as a member of the global community. The fact that this also benefits the Republic of Korea is the idea behind the treaty that has been agreed upon both domestically and internationally, and therefore—"

Kim Mugyong interrupted her again.

"Do the two fighter wings under the Republic of Korea Space Force guard Earth's orbit? Or do the planes fly in the atmosphere and get deployed overseas?"

"The two fighter wings you mentioned are part of the Allied Space Force and are under the direct control of the Allied Space Force Operations Command. They are not military power that our Space Force can employ in our operations and—"

"Why does the Space Force have fighter wings? Wouldn't it be more efficient for the Air Force to operate them directly? Are you that confident in the necessity of the fighter wings?"

"Mr. Assemblyman, the Air Force also has tanks. In the same way, the Army also has aerial forces. The Navy operates several satellites. This is the same for any military in the world. The only unique authority the Space Force has is in independent orbit operations. To achieve the Space Force's goal, we have some aerial and land warfare service components."

Gu Yemin looked around the conference room. In particular, she scrutinized the faces of the commanders of other military branches, seated in the back row. Not a single one of them stepped up to support her.

Kim Mugyong continued, "Chief Gu, I'm not asking these questions to hear the same trite answers again and again. Present here are members of the assembly, the commanders and staff of each branch of the military, the Minister of Defense, and other relevant officials, and we are all aware of that information. Think about the people of Korea, the people. Don't just think about your own position. Remember that everyone here must always represent the public and give straight answers. Do you understand? Answer me, please. Do you understand?"

"What is it that you mean to ask?"

"Last autumn, you launched a rocket using the Space Force's budget, is it true?"

"Yes, we successfully launched a rocket," Gu Yemin answered.

"And that's covered by the Space Force's power to conduct independent orbit operations that you previously mentioned?"

"Yes, sir."

"It's a weaponized satellite, is it not?"

"It is, sir."

At that moment, Kim Mugyong paused for a moment. It was a signal that he was going to land the punch that he'd been building up to. He stared at the impeccable face of the chief of staff of the Space Force.

After the pause, he asked, "And who is the satellite the enemy of?"

As if the question wasn't at all a difficult one to answer, Gu Yemin promptly replied, "It is no one's enemy."

"Chief Gu, you said that the Republic of Korea Space Force does not prioritize the benefit of our country, have you not?"

"I have."

"Then can you ignore what the Korean government considers to be common sense?"

"I'm not sure exactly what you are asking, but in general, that is not the case."

"Am I correct in understanding that even if you prioritize the ideology of the Allied Space Force, in a general sense, the ROK Space Force still cannot take actions that go against the good sense and judgment of the Korean people?"

"That may differ depending on the issue at hand," Gu Yemin answered. "For instance, when you get into the concept of territory or jurisdiction, the considerations of the government of each country and the considerations regarding Earth as a whole could emerge in different forms."

"No, I'm saying, in general, the ROK Space Force shouldn't simply sit and watch what the Allied Space Force is doing if the Korean people believe that the actions of the Allied Space Force go against our ethical beliefs. When we signed the treaty, we delegated authority to the Allied Space Force because there was a general agreement that the Allied Space Force is ethically no worse than any individual nation. Is that right?"

"That is correct, sir."

"Chief Gu."

"Yes, Mr. Assemblyman."

"Regarding the first weaponized satellite that the Korean Space Force has."

"Yes?"

"Why does it look like *that*?"

Gu Yemin didn't answer him. She knew what she had to say, but she felt that it would be better to not say it. Kim Mugyong moved on to his next question.

"Fine, then. Let me reword my question. The Ministry of Defense of the Republic of Korea had objected to the design of that weaponized satellite, isn't that correct?"

Gu Yemin answered briefly without a pause, "That is correct, sir."

"What was the reason for their objection? In fact, I believe that most of the military officials present here today have objected to that design. Am I correct?"

"Yes, sir. However, the opinions of other military branches were not subject to consideration."

"Just answer the question instead of trying to insert your own position. Why did everyone here object to that design? Regardless of whether their opinions mattered in the decision to finalize the design for the satellite, what was the reason for their objection?"

Gu Yemin hesitated for a moment. But she didn't seem hard-pressed. Impatiently, Kim Mugyong pressed her again.

"Do you not remember why?"

"I remember," Gu Yemin answered.

"Why did they object to it? What was the most important reason?"

"It was that the design was unsightly."

"Was it simply that the design was unsightly? Or was there more to it? Speak up."

"The main objection was that it looks like an enemy robot from comics or cartoons. The biggest objection was that it didn't look like a good robot that would fight on our side. The issue was that instead of a design that included a head and two arms like the weaponized satellites owned by other countries, we chose a design with a cylindrical body and three arms attached at 120-degree angles. After I reviewed the objections, I dismissed them within my authority as the chief of staff of the Space Force."

"Why did you dismiss them?"

"Because they did not need to be taken into consideration."

"Why not? Chief Gu, what are you expecting to invade with that weaponized satellite?"

"Invasion is impossible. It is outside the scope of the operation of the satellite in question."

"Then why didn't you choose a design for preserving peace instead of a design for invading Earth?!"

LAUNCH SOMETHING!

Gu Yemin stared into Kim Mugyong's face. All eyes in the room were on her. Yet, she did not seem the least distraught. Her face only reflected traces of weariness.

She answered, "Space isn't suited for symmetry, and—"

Kim Mugyong cut her answer short once again. For a split second, anger flashed in Gu Yemin's eyes.

"Chief Gu. Just get to your point instead of beating around the bush. Or do you not have a point? Do you not have your point all prepared in your head?"

Gu Yemin calmly answered his question in a voice that some might have mistaken as being wounded, "Because a peace-preserving design does not exist." Then she said, "And I would like to hear an answer to my question, particularly due to security issues. What exactly is this meeting? Are there going to be minutes of this meeting recorded somewhere?"

Kim Mugyong sat back in his chair. His gesture suggested that he had got something useful out of Gu Yemin. As he leaned back into his chair, he glanced over at the Space Force three-star general sitting in one corner of the conference room. Lieutenant General Lee Jongro, the former Vice-Minister of Mars, sat with his head tilted in curiosity, showing no regard for Kim Mugyong's gaze.

After the long meeting finally came to a close, Lee Jongro said to Kim Mugyong, "Oh, well, I was a bit curious. Do people use the word 'curious' these days in Korea? It hasn't become archaic or anything, has it? Anyway, I thought it was strange. Because there are peace-preserving designs. In this case, a three-armed robot is more suited for defending the peace. I was curious why she didn't answer that way. I mean, I'm sure she didn't because you exasperated her by asking all those questions. Speaking of which, why did you do that?"

For a long time after Lee Jongro left, Kim Mugyong stared at the door which Lee Jongro had walked through with a look of embarrassed frustration on his face.

"What a crazy bastard! He's the one who arranged for all this to happen, but now he's trying to act all innocent?"

Having just finished training, Han Summin left the remote pilot station still wearing her headset. Her hair was slick with sweat.

"Master Sergeant Han, the inspector general's looking for you."

Summin turned to the messenger. It was Senior Master Sergeant Shin Minhyung of the Orbit Operations Office.

"Right now, sir?"

"She said to come right after your training session. Go wash up first."

After Summin changed into a g-suit that resembled the Air Force's flight suit, she climbed the stairs to the second floor of the launch base main building. When she knocked on the door to the internal review department office, Technical Sergeant Choi Suzy stood up to greet her.

"The IG's looking for me?" Summin asked.

Suzy nodded and gestured with two hands toward the inspector general's office. Thinking Suzy's action was a bit strange, Summin walked to the office door, opened it, and cheerfully said, "IG, were you looking for me?"

A stranger was sitting at the desk. The furniture in the office was also arranged differently than a few days ago. Having at first only poked her head in, Summin cautiously entered. From outside the office, she heard Suzy whisper, "It's the new inspector general. Go ahead."

As the confused Summin walked into the room, the door

closed behind her. A middle-aged woman with the insignia of a lieutenant colonel on her uniform sat behind the desk, looking over some papers. As if quietly enjoying Summin's confusion and embarrassment, she assumed an indifferent attitude.

The newly appointed inspector general, Lieutenant Colonel Kim Su-in, remained silent for a while until finally she put down the papers on the table and looked up at Summin.

"No salute?"

Summin quickly saluted her superior with a sharp and restrained gesture. When the inspector general nodded, she let her hand fall to her side and relaxed her shoulders.

"I heard you were looking for me, ma'am," said Summin.

Lieutenant Colonel Kim stared at Summin for a moment before she opened her mouth.

"Master Sergeant Han Summin of the Orbit Operations Office in the Operations Division. You are a non-commissioned officer in charge of remote piloting. Seems like on Earth they train pilots who are not academy graduates. That's good, I suppose."

"Thank you."

"Oh, don't thank me yet."

Summin's face hardened.

The new IG continued, "It seems you were close to Inspector General Park Soojin. They must have taken extra care of you since you are the only pilot on the base. Meaning they must have had high expectations. And the chief of staff seems to be making extra effort to look after you as well."

Offering no comment, Summin stared into the Inspector General's eyes. There was a unique ribbon on the left side of her dress uniform. A red planet against a black background. It signified Mars from the pioneer days, which was in fact no longer red. Next to it, the shield-shaped ribbon of white against a blue background seemed to signify suppression of the rebels. Summin didn't know the meaning of each ribbon, but she remembered seeing something similar in promotional materials about the suppression of the Mars Rebellion.

In a high-pitched voice, Lieutenant Colonel Kim said, "But Sergeant Han, is it appropriate for a pilot who's been receiving so much support from the Space Force to harbor ill feelings about the way the Space Force is run? That's rather shocking to me."

"I'm not sure that I understand …"

"Want me to read it? Let's see. 'I am a civilian who has recently learned about the Space Force through Oste. Listening to Oste's radio show, I came to learn a lot about what the Space Force does and why we need it, which I've always found difficult to understand. I came to have positive thoughts about the future that the Space Force has in mind. I also learned that the budget for the Space Force, which comes out of our taxes, is used for good purposes.'

"Let's skip this middle part, and well, oh, this is a good one. 'Honestly, the public's perception of the Space Force improved thanks to Oste, and it seems like an unfair decision to both the host and his fans to suddenly cancel the show without any explanation. I hope that the Space Force will take appropriate measures in the coming days.' Yadda yadda yadda. What was the name of the sender? Oh, right, civilian Han Jumin."

Summin swallowed hard.

The Inspector General continued, "I know that you sent this thinking it was a trivial matter. But I'm frankly surprised that you would do such a duplicitous action. Since coming to Earth, a lot of things have been surprising to me. Isn't the Space Force rather eccentric? No need to answer that. But as a matter of discipline, write an official letter of explanation regarding your action before you go. I've heard that you're an ace pilot, but I don't know you, and there are issues regarding the dignity of the Space Force, so I hope that you don't try something like this again in the future. Sounds like the Orbit Operations Office will be getting busy soon, so you won't have the time to, anyway. You can go now."

Summin saluted the Inspector General and turned around to open the door. As she was about to leave the room, she heard the Inspector General's voice behind her.

"Oh, and you have full combat gear, right? Do thirty laps around the training ground wearing it before you leave work. Report to Major Park Soojin."

"Geez, is this the proper military or something? That's way too hardcore!"

Suh Ga-ul complained as she sat on the bench watching Summin run laps around the training ground.

"SoCal, if somebody hears you talk that way, you might become the first weather specialist at the Space Force to run laps around the training ground in full combat gear," Internal Review Officer Major Park Soojin said impassively, looking in the same direction as Ga-ul.

"I don't even have combat gear."

"You think she had some? She borrowed it from the military police."

"No one else other than the military police has it?"

"Not the full set, I don't think. And she's technically an officer so it's not like she could use the enlistees."

"But seriously, doesn't that constitute unnecessarily harsh treatment? She must have ordered Summin to do that, thinking of what they do on Mars. But the whole thing weighs three times heavier on Earth."

"Who can you complain to, even if it is wrong? The inspector general is the one who ordered her to do it. And it's not unreasonable to have a soldier train in full combat gear."

"It's unreasonable considering that we're the Space Force. Especially a punishment that's so overtly insulting."

"It's not punishment but physical training. As usual, the Space Force is the odd one out."

"What if she injures her knees? And more importantly, what do we gain from publicly humiliating a pilot like that? She's ultimately irreplaceable."

Soojin slowly crossed her arms and answered, "Actually, the easiest jobs to replace these days are remote pilots."

"Why?" Ga-ul asked.

"Summin herself would know best. From what I heard from the SFHQ Operations Division, apparently, it's extremely difficult to win against artificial intelligence because of the delay in remote response times. Even if the AI is a bit dumber than humans, an AI that responds immediately in the field has a huge advantage. And these days AI is not even less intelligent than people. But do you know what the scarier thing is? Very soon, it'll be smarter than us."

"But the whole system is based on human pilots. It'd be difficult to reorganize the entire thing in a year or two."

"They will have to change a lot of things."

"Exactly."

"No, I don't mean that it would be difficult because they have to change a lot of things, but that they will start changing a lot of things from now on. Summin and her toy are Chief Gu's projects, and if they decide to do away with them, it is because they're getting rid of Chief Gu Yemin. Since the new administration has flown all the way over here from Mars, they'll try to do that much at least. Oh man, why am I discussing all this serious stuff with a mere weather specialist from the Weather Agency?"

"Ouch, that hurts. A mere weather specialist?"

"I'm saying this in all seriousness, though," Soojin said. "Pretend you haven't heard this. If you spread rumors, then I'll start doing my job as an internal review officer again and conduct an investigation into the Weather Agency, so take care."

"I wouldn't be surprised if that investigation has already begun."

"Hey, speaking of which, what the heck is wrong with you guys at the Weather Agency? We haven't actually started any investigating, but we've already got a pile of dirty laundry on you guys nonetheless. Didn't I tell you to stop believing in all the superstitions?"

"We can't help it," answered Ga-ul. "You know that any agency that launches rockets has weird superstitions. And all those superstitions wind up at the Weather Agency. On top of that, it's kind of a national tradition. In the Joseon Dynasty, there was the Office for Observation of Natural Phenomena, and they worked on everything from astronomy to selecting auspicious dates and looking for propitious burial sites. You know why we are superstitious? Because the higher-ups keep on asking the Weather Agency for a southeasterly wind. If nobody wanted a southeasterly wind, we could simply tidy up and organize our data and serve it on a platter. And I wish we could do that. But we keep being asked for a southeasterly wind. Probably for the next century. So just accept the reality."

"Well, the inspector general has a hard time accepting that."

"Why are people from Mars all like that? They've got to let their hair down and be more rational, believe that faith brings blessings and stuff. They're so stiff."

"I have no idea what you're talking about, but in any case, wrap things up as soon as you can. I have to follow orders if they tell me to do something. And I'll die if I have to run laps in full combat gear. She's only managing to do that because she's Han Summin."

"Yes, ma'am," Ga-ul answered.

As she ran, Summin straightened the helmet that had tipped over her forehead. She wanted to retie the chin straps, but it wasn't easy because she was holding a rifle. The backpack was heavy, but the gas mask dangling by her legs was more annoying.

She glanced over at Ga-ul and Soojin, who were sitting on the bench. When she had finished a lap, Ga-ul was gone, and only Soojin remained. She noticed people here and there watching her from the buildings around the training ground, and although she didn't think it was humiliating, they did get on her nerves.

The following day, when she reported for duty at the remote pilot station, Senior Master Sergeant Shin Minhyung greeted her.

"Heard you had to do some evening jogging yesterday."

"I feel completely refreshed," Summin answered.

Minhyung smiled awkwardly. He wasn't much of a conversationalist.

"Today, you're on standby," he said.

"Excuse me?"

LAUNCH SOMETHING!

"Not an order from the Internal Review Department. It's a directive from the SFHQ."

"What does the directive involve?"

"Replacement of the controls. It'll be done by tomorrow, so until tomorrow … what should you do? Ah, you can study wartime tactics and strategies."

"What's wrong with the controls? Are they broken?"

Minhyung answered without hesitation, "They're replacing the entire flight control system."

"Really? Are they scrapping the system I've been using?"

"No, no, it's much too expensive. We'll have it installed somewhere else as backup."

"In the next room?"

"Probably. It's too heavy to move far. HQ instructed us to test the new system first, so you have to get used to the new machine. Get ready."

"The instruction came from the HQ? From the chief of staff?"

"It's probably from the director of the Orbit Strategy Development Agency."

"The Orbit Strategy … what's that?"

"You know, the new agency that was created recently. A temporary position for General Lee Jongro."

As soon as she heard his name, Summin inhaled a big breath of air.

Then she asked nonchalantly, "Why is it a temporary position?"

"Probably because they've already decided on his next appointment. He's going to be there less than a year, so it'd be a bit mean to push someone out just so that he can have a position for a brief period. That's a pretty reasonable position for the time being."

"What's his next appointment?"

"Chief of staff. Then probably another big wig position after that. All right, enough chit-chat for the morning. Go sit at your desk and study tactics."

The new flight control system came two days later. Summin still had to use both arms and legs to control the spacecraft with the new system, but unlike the original system, she didn't have to use both arms and a leg at the same time to control the three arms.

"This is a shift-method system," commented Sergeant Shin upon examining the system. Other people from the Orbit Operations Office were gathered around the equipment.

Lieutenant Colonel Shim Jaesun, Director of the Orbit Operations Office, remarked, "It only lets you control two arms at once. But you can choose which arms to control."

Sergeant Shin asked, "Have we been consulted about this in advance?"

"Consulted? This is the first time I'm seeing this."

"It's pretty much a control system for a two-armed weaponized satellite but with an additional pedal. Are they planning on not using the third arm then?"

"Hmm, I don't think that's it. It'll depend on how you use the system. There is an additional arm, so if you decide to use it, you can shift the system by 120 degrees and change which arm is controlled. So you can't really say that you're abandoning the third arm entirely. What do you think, Sergeant Han?"

Summin quietly looked down at the control panel attached with unfamiliar buttons and devices. Then a little later, she answered in a determined voice, "I think it's like what you said, sir. If it has two arms and a head, then you have a front and a back, which means you're only ever fighting with half of what you have. But our satellite isn't like that. Since there's no backside, really. Or top or bottom. It seems suitable for space."

Shin chimed in, "But is it better than the original system? Even if they change it, it's …"

"Well, I think I'll have to try it out," said Summin. "It could be better than we think. Should I go for a ride once it's all set up?"

However, the results weren't great. Four hours later, Summin slowly walked out of the control room with the headset dangling around her neck. The first words out of her mouth were: "I feel sick."

Lieutenant Colonel Shim strongly agreed, "Just watching is hard enough. The moment you shift the robot by 120 degrees, all the screens in the Orbit Operations Office shift by 120 degrees, so the operators were going nuts. I don't think this is going to work. Do you think we can overcome this issue by changing the display? So that the screen would stay fixed even when you're shifting."

Sergeant Shin approached them with a look of concern on his face. His face was also pale.

He said, "I don't think that's the problem."

"It's not the biggest problem, but it is a problem," said Lieutenant Colonel Shim. What do you think, Sergeant Han?"

As she organized her thoughts, Summin used a towel to wipe her hair, slick with sweat.

Then she said, "Like you said, I don't think that's the biggest problem. I think the shift system itself is kind of fun. Still, it's obvious that it wasn't developed specifically for our satellite. It's a system for a two-armed robot, with an additional gear attached for controlling the third arm. It doesn't feel complete. It almost feels like the third arm is superfluous, which is a minus rather than a plus. I wonder if this is a system they're introducing temporarily as we change over to a two-arm system, although it could be that we just haven't been able to get the best out of it yet. But ..."

"But what?"

"The virtual enemy satellite in the simulator. It's gotten much stronger than before. Where's that data from?"

Lieutenant Colonel Shim answered, "It's apparently from a satellite deployed in Mars orbit. It's not ours."

Unable to hide her surprise, Summin asked in a somewhat nervous voice, "That's already been deployed in the field? Then I think that's a bigger problem. If the enemy is at that level already, I can't win even with the old control system. It seems more like a hardware issue than an issue with the control system. There's a huge difference in the satellites' performances."

"You think so? I'll have to confirm with intelligence first, then. Whether this is an authentic simulation or not."

As soon as Shim finished his sentence, Summin asked, "Do you know what that thing that came before the last one was? The two-armed robot with hand axes. I really couldn't take it on. It didn't seem particularly powerful, but it responded much too quickly for me."

At her words, Colonel Shim and Sergeant Shin exchanged a look. They seemed to be waiting for the other to speak up.

Summin pressed them, "What is it? Is it confidential?"

Colonel Shim nodded at Sergeant Shin and begrudgingly opened his mouth.

"You mean it was particularly challenging to fight it?"

"You saw. I got crushed. What is it? Is it a new satellite? It didn't look special on the outside."

Colonel Shim stared straight into Summin's eyes and said, "It was AI."

"Really? Well, I guess I expected that."

"It's not a satellite controlled by AI on Earth but one that's been mounted with AI. You've seen that satellite before, but AI's been mounted on the hardware."

"Oh, so it was set to have no communication delay at all. That makes sense."

"Well, it was your first time. No one wins on their first try. Let's work on it."

But the next day and the day after that, Summin's record didn't get any better. She lost all the simulated battles for an entire week straight. Her shoulders drooped as if reflecting her sagging spirits.

From the parking lot, Kugyong watched Summin pace in front of the launch base main building with a blank look on her face. Then he got into his car and left.

After he arrived and parked his car in front of the communication relay station, he walked up to the office to find Eunkyung getting ready to head home.

"Captain Park, you always come right when I'm about to get off work," she complained.

"Oh, I miscalculated the time. I'll come back tomorrow."

"Forget it. What do you need?"

"What I always need. The interplanetary communication delay content. I need a lot of signatures, so I brought the documents over in person."

"A lot of signatures?"

"Contract after contract after written confirmation after agreement."

"You bring over all these forms as if I'm pestering you to bring them to me."

"Exactly."

"Exactly what?"

"I filled out all of them and brought them over, so all you need to do is to sign them. You'd want to grab someone by the collar if you had to actually read these documents."

Kugyong laid out the documents on the table. Eunkyung set her bag down and rolled her chair over.

Five minutes later, Kugyong, who had been staring up at the ceiling as Eunkyung signed the papers, suddenly asked, "Secretary Kim, about the rebellion. Do you know the details?"

"The Mars Rebellion? Doesn't the Public Relations Corps know all about that?"

"I know what generally happened, but I don't really know the specific details of how things happened. It's like …"

"People are hushing and covering things up?"

"Yes."

Examining the papers on the desk, Eunkyung explained, "It happened during Conjunction. Taking advantage of the fact that all authority was delegated to the Mars municipality, the city council declared independence. And it joined an alliance of new settlements called the Mars City Alliance or something, but it was immediately suppressed. Those are the details. You think there's more to it?"

"Sure," Kugyong answered. "Why are they being all secretive about something like that? General Lee Jongro has become a war hero, but considering the fame he gained, none of the specifics about the rebellion have been disclosed."

"Oh, that. That's because it was legitimate."

"What was?"

Eunkyung looked up for a moment to meet Kugyong's eyes. Then she shifted her gaze back to the papers and calmly said,

"They call it a rebellion, but as I told you earlier it happened when all authority had been delegated to the city, and it was voted on at the city council. So everything was done legally in terms of the procedure. It was a democratic process rather than a rebellion."

"What? Really?"

"But it's also a bit ambiguous. Because it wasn't *not* a rebellion either. The problem was that the whole system was too lax. The city council used those loopholes in a very legal manner. It was legal, but anyone can see that it was illegal. I guess this is what you want to know in terms of the details—what were the higher-ups in the Space Force and the government thinking at the time?"

"Right," answered Kugyong. "And what the Martians were thinking."

"Everything was all up in the air. Because it was legal. But the government couldn't just sit by. Because it was a betrayal."

"So, what did they do?"

"They didn't do anything. Since there's no communication between Earth and Mars during Conjunction, no one on Earth knew what had happened on Mars. When the communication was back up and running, it was already over. The rebellion occurred, and it was suppressed by the commander of the occupying forces. The city council was dissolved, and there was a request for approval of a military government system. There was public outrage on Mars for a bit, but it didn't last long."

"Why not?"

"There were ninety-eight spacenauts in the occupying forces on Mars, but the population of the direct-controlled municipality was twenty thousand. About two thousand citizens would've been active participants in the rebellion, I'd assume.

And about twenty spacenauts of the occupying forces joined the independence forces. But despite that, Lee Jongro successfully suppressed the rebel forces."

"I didn't know they were so outnumbered. How did they suppress the rebels?"

At Kugyong's continued questions, Eunkyung set the papers down and looked up at him.

"By force. Brutally. If a trained army decides to use weapons, about a hundred soldiers can apparently subdue about five thousand people. Everyone on Mars knew how to handle weapons during the pioneer era, but they probably doubted that the Space Force would actually open fire. It would've been quick—over the course of about an hour or so? And about five hundred ended up dead."

"What happened after that?" Kugyong asked curiously.

Eunkyung answered rather apathetically, "Feels like you're enjoying the story too much. What's with all these questions? Is it because those crazy returning Martians are spoiling the vibes here?"

"Yeah, well."

"It was all hush hush on Earth. Not because they were trying to hide something but because it felt a bit off. The Mars occupying forces did take care of everything, but they shouldn't have done it that way. But we also couldn't have Martians declare independence. So here on Earth, people became intentionally disinterested. Because it was bothersome to think about it."

"That's how General Lee Jongro became the Mars Governor-General."

"He shot to prominence while everyone on Earth turned a blind eye. Earned stars within a short amount of time. That man, he's full of ambition, so he probably enjoyed it. They shouldn't have let him gain so much power. Or they should've stopped him from coming back to Earth."

"You knew him?" Kugyong asked.

"A little. But you know what? He only got to where he is now because everyone on Earth pretended not to notice him, but now that he's back, he's all angry about how Earth has been neglecting Mars. Hasn't he already picked a fight with the Public Relations Corps? About why we're trying to recreate the space age with the asteroid when we already have the Mars Settlement? The PR Corps is only doing it because the Allied Space Force told you to, but the Martians have suddenly returned and are acting with this deep-seated resentment. Snapping at people for God knows what. Rather insufferable, isn't it?"

"You don't know the half of it. It's been brutal."

"Satisfied? Now that you know the inside story?"

"Yeah, more or less. That was how things were all connected."

"OK, now that you know everything, come over here so I can grab you by the collar. Captain Park, tell me honestly. You put these papers in here hoping that I'd just sign them without giving them a thorough read, didn't you?"

"Oh, oh. You wanted to read each one? Oops."

"Captain Park Kugyong? Where are you going? Come here and explain this. You intended to come as I was about to get off work, right? If you play this kind of trick on me, you really might live to regret it, you know."

Kugyong left the communication relay station and was driving back to the launch base main building when he saw Summin up ahead the road in full combat gear.

"The inspector general again?"

Hearing a voice behind her, Summin looked around, and after realizing that it was only Kugyong, she turned back and kept on walking. Kugyong drove his car slowly behind her and asked, "Why don't you have a rifle?"

Summin answered half-heartedly, "Because they don't just hand out weapons."

"Huh?"

"It wasn't the Inspector General. I'm just going to go for a run for a bit because I have a lot on my mind."

"What? I don't know what kind of things you have on your mind if you're wearing all that by choice."

As Kugyong was talking to Summin, following her slowly from behind in his car, Technical Sergeant Choi Suzy from the Internal Review Department scurried over and stopped in front of Summin.

"Sergeant Han," Suzy addressed Summin.

"What is it?"

"The Inspector General saw you on her way home and called me to tell you to not wear the full combat gear."

"What are you talking about?"

"She said it looks like you're protesting. Rebelling against her. And honestly, it does look that way. I think it would be best if you didn't."

Summin stopped in her tracks and looked up at the sky for a moment. Then she looked from Kugyong to Suzy and then back.

"OK. I suppose I shouldn't."

Summin then got in Kugyong's car and headed to the single occupant dormitory. There, she half sat, half lay on the couch in the lounge, blankly staring at the ceiling.

"I'll leave your backpack and helmet here," Kugyong said, looking down worriedly at Summin, who remained silent.

LAUNCH SOMETHING!

Half an hour later, when Kugyong passed by the lounge on his way back out, Summin was still on the couch, having not moved a muscle.

Worriedly, he asked, "You OK? Is it the Inspector General?"

Summin answered lethargically, in a barely audible voice, "I don't care about the Inspector General. IG's are all like that."

"Then what's going on?"

"I can't tell the Public Relations Corps because it's confidential."

"Well, then ..."

"I'm getting crushed these days."

"Huh?"

"I feel like the unfortunate Japanese admiral who went up against Admiral Yi Sun-sin all those centuries ago. Maybe I should've just gone to a private company."

"What? That bad?"

"I was just thinking about this now, but Admiral Yi Sun-sin must have been a terrifying man. When I'm up against him, my future seems hopeless. It's not an issue of being crestfallen after battle—I just literally don't know what I'll do in the future. It's pretty bad if my career ends here."

"What are you talking about? Are you talking about General Lee Jongro?"

"What are *you* talking about? I'm talking about Admiral Yi Sun-sin."

Gu Yemin set the report down on her desk. It was a confidential document titled "Space Force Academy Graduation Ceremony Plans." She picked up a pen to sign it, but she put it back down upon noticing another signee above her own, with the rather long title of "Director of the Orbit Strategy Development Agency."

Gu Yemin pressed a button on her phone to summon her aide. Then she spoke into the receiver, "Have the director of the Office of Administration come to my office."

The aide answered from the other end of the line, "Yes, ma'am. He's at the academy right now. Should I call him right away?"

"No, have him come to me as soon as he gets back."

"Yes, ma'am. You also have a guest now. It's Lieutenant General Lee Jongro, Director of the Orbit Strategy Development Agency."

"Right now? At my office?"

"Yes, ma'am."

Gu Yemin mulled something over quickly before answering, "Let him in."

Lee Jongro, the former Vice-Minister of Mars, strode into the room. Gu Yemin sat while Lee Jongro stood with his legs slightly apart and saluted her with a sharp gesture.

"Looks like you've already adjusted to Earth's gravity," said Yemin.

"I requested that the artificial gravity on the shuttle be equal to that of Earth."

"I see. You arrived on the express shuttle, *Pilum*? That must have been hard on the other passengers. Raising the gravity at once instead of gradually over the course of two months."

"It's good if people adjust quickly. This is my first time in your office."

"It's a bit too cramped, isn't it? That's why I see people in the conference room instead of here."

Lee Jongro looked around at the bookcases lining the walls and answered, "It's good. Like a library."

"Is it?"

"Oh, I mean that as a compliment. There aren't so many books on Mars. They're not rare, but we don't print a lot of hard copies."

Lee Jongro stood by the bookcases, examining the spines.

"Sure," said Gu Yemin. "Now to business."

Lee Jongro turned his head to Gu Yemin.

"There was the return ceremony, and I've seen you a few other times, but I wanted to pay a visit in person to ask you how you've been doing."

"That can't be it. It's fine to start with small talk, but you can get straight into business."

"Really? Then should I start?"

"Go ahead."

Lee Jongro lowered his voice and said, "We gave you intelligence, but there was no response."

"Intelligence?"

"I believe we gave you intelligence about the sunlight reflector terrorism about three months ago. Regarding the so-called Pac-Man sun."

"Ah, yes. You did."

"I believe three months was long enough to respond."

"It was plenty."

"And the intelligence wasn't sloppy. It's impossible to confirm now that the Pac-Man sun been blown apart, but at the time, the intelligence was detailed and specific."

"Was it? As you said, we don't have the Pac-Man anymore. If there are documents left, the Allied Space Force will take care of them."

Nonchalantly Lee Jongro took a couple of steps to the next bookcase.

Then he pulled out a book and shuffled through the pages

as he said, "I'm sure you took care of everything. Did you take care of the other matter yourself as well?"

"Which matter?" asked Gu Yemin as she looked at her diary to check her schedule. If they had not been talking, it would've appeared as if they were in a library, spending time separately.

"Hwang Sun."

"Hwang Sun, you mean the man who escaped from Mars? Didn't the Allied Space Force take him? He's probably under investigation."

"So you don't know what's going on, at least officially."

Gu Yemin closed her diary and put her glasses down on her desk. Then she stared at Lee Jongro as she said, "We should've started with small talk. I don't know how it is on Mars, but on Earth, we often talk about the weather as small talk. Recently there has been a lot to talk about the weather."

Lee Jongro answered, "Weather is not a trivial matter on Mars."

"Well, then, shall I change the topic? What about rumors?"

"Sure. Sounds interesting."

"There are rumors that people you've brought over from Mars are giving someone a hard time. A non-commissioned officer."

"I doubt it's just one or two non-commissioned officers who are having a hard time. Officers and enlistees are probably having a hard time as well."

"I hope you don't give Han Summin a hard time. It doesn't look good."

"Training is supposed to be hard."

"You were trying to poach her through a private company, and since that failed, it just looks like you're just trying to break her."

LAUNCH SOMETHING!

"No."

"Really? Then let's finish our small talk right about here and get to the business."

Lee Jongro closed the book and put it back on the shelf. Then looking at Gu Yemin, he said, "What is it?"

Gu Yemin got up from her desk and took three long strides toward Lee Jongro. She looked up at him. His face was menacing. There was stubble on his cheeks, and his hair, which was too long for a spacenaut, wasn't neatly brushed back. But the look suited him. He seemed a little out of place, like a wild animal clothed in a uniform, but still natural.

Like a scholar, Gu Yemin said, "I get to ask you finally. About the suppression of the Mars Rebellion at Conjunction."

Lee Jongro answered, "Ah, an old story. I believe I submitted a detailed report on the matter."

"I've read it. Several times. I know the details to the point I could write an entire novel based on it. But there were holes."

"Were there? What was missing?"

"The list of deaths among the rebels. It was much longer than the list of the wounded. Normally it would've been the other way around. I was surprised because the report was quite detailed. It described at length who died and how. That put us in a bit of a difficult position. The families of the deceased wanted to know the details, but our answer from the beginning had been that it's impossible to discover any more information. But in fact, we did know, thanks to your report. We knew, but we couldn't possibly tell others. So despite what we'd originally planned, we had to conceal what we knew."

"Are you berating me for having burdened you with unwanted knowledge?"

"Never. You wrote it well. The more detailed reports are, the better. I assumed that whoever was in charge must have been quite competent to organize all this in such a whirlwind of events. Very capable, in fact. But you know, even that detailed report wasn't perfect."

"That's how it always is."

"Is it? Unlike other parts of the report, details regarding forty-three deaths were left rather vague. Oh, if it had been another report, the entire thing would've been that vague. But the report the Mars occupying forces submitted was excessively detailed. That's why those cases caught my eye. It was almost like they had been written up by someone else, like an entirely different report."

Lee Jongro said, "I thought you were going to get straight to the point, but it feels like you're still dodging the issue. Please, go ahead with what you really want to say."

Gu Yemin folded her arms and stared up at the former Mars Governor-General. Then she calmly continued her story.

"I looked into those forty-three cases and found something interesting. I mean, the places of their deaths weren't just random. When I looked at the times and locations altogether, they all seemed to be in the path of one person's movements. The manner of deaths wasn't anything like shooting in combat either but more like an execution."

"What's your point?"

"Was it you?"

Gu Yemin had finally got to the point. Lee Jongro met her gaze. Then he grinned and looked elsewhere.

"That's what you wanted to ask?"

"It's the only thing I wanted to ask. Everything else I say to you—whether it's a top secret or an operational command—is small talk. Meaningless stuff. Stuff I have to say because it's work."

The two of them stood with their gazes locked for a long time. Nothing interrupted their silence.

Lee Jongro was the first to make a move. Abruptly, he walked over to the door with light steps, as if Earth's gravity, which was three times heavier than the Martian gravity he'd been used to, wasn't at all strong. As he grabbed the door handle, a snort seemed to escape from the back of his head.

Without turning around to look at Gu Yemin, he said, "I really like this room. I think it'll look bigger without all the books."

Gu Yemin retorted, "A house without any furniture or traces of life does look bigger. Want me to find you a model home?"

The next afternoon, about fifteen people were seated in the audience seats in the back of the Command and Control Center at the Space Force headquarters. About ten of them were in military uniform, while the rest were in suits. Among those in suits was Lee Jongro and Assemblyman Kim Mugyong. Chief of Staff Gu Yemin was in front. The same people who had been at the mysterious meeting in the conference room a few days ago were gathered again.

"This meeting was called by Chief Gu?" asked Kim Mugyong.

"Apparently so," Lee Jongro answered without even looking in his direction. "I don't know what she plans to do."

"Does she have some secret weapon?"

"I wouldn't know, but that would only be digging her own grave."

"I heard that she was going to demonstrate the weaponized satellite's abilities. If she shows something impressive, opinion toward her could become more favorable. Particularly with some kind of advanced equipment."

"We'll see," Lee Jongro uttered.

Meanwhile, the tension over at the remote pilot station at the launch base was palpable. The simulation training session was about to be live-streamed to the Space Force headquarters. Summin looked preoccupied, as she had for the past week.

She asked, "Are they going to hear the sounds too?"

Senior Master Sergeant Shin Minhyung answered, "No, we're going to cut the sound."

"Thank goodness."

"But still, watch what you say since it's going to be recorded. Who knows who'll see it later?"

"Will do. You can start it up when you're ready. I'm good to go."

In the Command and Control Center of the Space Force headquarters, two giant screens and four smaller ones filled an entire wall. The commanders and staff of the Space Force, as well as the invited guests, sat watching the screens.

"Let's start," said Gu Yemin. The order to begin the training session was delivered to the remote pilot station at the launch base.

"Are we finally going to see the weaponized satellite in action?" asked Kim Mugyong.

Lee Jongro looked at him as if he'd said something ridiculous.

"Obviously, it's a simulator," he said. "If we move the arms on the actual satellite, the entire world would find out its shape and functions."

"You mean it's never been put into action? There's never been an actual field training session?"

"No. No one knows what our card is, so it's still a dangerous hand. Once we flip the card over, no one will fear it. But I imagine we'll shortly see why the satellite is no big deal."

The screens lit up with the simulation. It wasn't an intriguing start, as the entire process of two satellites in orbit approaching each other was complex and monotonous.

"Skip the approach and get straight into combat."

At Gu Yemin's instruction, the two satellites grew closer at a much faster pace, as if they'd teleported.

Then a voice came over the speakers.

"Approaching. Deceleration initiated. Decelerating. Approaching engagement distance in five minutes. Will initiate combat."

It came from the launch base. At that moment, the protective panels that had been covering the Space Force's weaponized satellite surface fell off, revealing the arms folded inside. There were a total of three arms. Each arm had three joints: one where the arm was connected to the body, one in the middle of the arm, and one at what seemed to be a wrist. The powerful shoulder joint could move accurately in any direction. The hands were shaped like tongs—not as sophisticated as a human hand but capable of grabbing and ripping things apart.

Two of the three hands held shields. The shields were remaining parts of the protective panels that had fell off moments ago and weren't shaped like regular shields—they were long and narrow, barely wide enough to cover the mechanical arms on the outside. Experts just looking at the satellite mounted on a rocket waiting to be launched would have recognized that it was quite unique. These shields were the reason why the satellite launch had been suddenly closed to the public.

There was a spear-like weapon on the third arm. The arm wasn't gripping the spear; rather, the spear was attached to the wrist.

Soon the enemy satellite also began to transform into combat mode. It looked like it was made up of the top half of a robot connected to a spaceship. It had a head with a face and two arms attached to what resembled human shoulders. It only had four fingers, but its hands were similar to human hands. It looked like a "good robot" that people would imagine to be "on our side."

The enemy satellite had axes in both hands. Once it was fully transformed, the enemy satellite quickly changed directions. The audience held their breaths watching the opposition control nozzles protruding from all parts of the enemy satellite belch out flames, allowing it to turn quickly. The two satellites were much faster than they had expected.

"She's going to show them actually fighting each other? That would go over well," Kim Mugyong murmured.

The enemy satellite engaged the ROK Space Force satellite. Using the boosters on various parts of its body, Summin adjusted its position and spun around to approach the enemy. Two long, narrow shields cleverly blocked the enemy's attacks. The audience was mesmerized by the two weaponized satellites—it almost didn't matter that one was the enemy. The enemy satellite may have looked more like a good robot, but the sinister-looking Space Force robot's movements were so sophisticated and accurate as to be intriguing.

It wasn't easy to follow the action with the naked eye. Every time the pilot "shifted," the images on the two big screens in the Command and Control Center suddenly spun 120 degrees. Then it would spin 120 degrees again. Watching the image spin was torture for the laypeople who didn't know anything about weaponized satellites; it wasn't a walk in the park for the experts either. As the image quickly spun left and right, everyone in the Command and Control Center soon looked as if they were all going to be sick. Only Gu Yemin and Lee Jongro sat impassively staring at the screens.

LAUNCH SOMETHING!

The combat didn't last five minutes, but it was enough time to wipe out the Command and Control Center with motion sickness. Seeing as how Lee Jongro's lips were pursed in a straight line, even he seemed a bit nauseated.

"Let's go once more."

At Gu Yemin's casually spoken words, the audience in the Command and Control Center began to stir.

"Chief Gu, let's take a break," someone said from the back. His voice was filled with desperation.

Gu Yemin curtly answered with a question, "In what kind of training session do you take a break after fifteen minutes?"

Far fewer people actually watched the second combat. Most sat looking at the floor, avoiding looking at the screens, as if just thinking about the shifting scenes made them sick.

Lee Jongro had no choice but to take on the role of commentator. It was hard for him to watch as well, but he couldn't let a training session that could work to his advantage just slip on by.

"Our satellite malfunctioned. In a mere three minutes of combat, it has lost two arms and the main engine."

"Then what will happen?" asked Kim Mugyong, his head turned to the back of the Command and Control Center.

Lee Jongro answered, "Once the engine failed in our weaponized satellite, the enemy pushed it toward Earth. It will remain in orbit for a few days before it burns up completely in Earth's atmosphere."

The result was the same for the next combat, and the one after that.

"Crushing defeat for our satellite. It is inoperative. Five consecutive defeats. As you have seen, our satellite's response is noticeably slow. You all saw how it received injuries from the enemy's attack and then moved its shield. It seems to be a problem arising from the fact that its response speed isn't up to par. The enemy is being controlled directly in orbit, while our craft is remotely controlled by a pilot on Earth. It seems the time delay is the reason for our loss."

At Lee Jongro's explanation, people nodded in understanding. Someone from the crowd asked, "How long is the delay?"

"About 0.4 seconds."

"0.4 seconds. That would be a critical difference in combat at that tempo."

"Right," Lee Jongro answered. "I am not sure if it's a difference that can be overcome. Unless we completely change the method of combat."

At that moment, Gu Yemin took her glasses off and placed them on the table. She turned around and said, "We'll take a break and resume in thirty minutes."

In the waiting room that acted like a reception room on the second floor of the Command and Control Center, major military policymakers sat slumped in exhaustion like defeated soldiers. Watching them, Lee Jongro grinned contentedly. His smirk came off as more bitter than contented because he was feeling nauseated, but he was certainly pleased.

Kim Mugyong noticed him and asked, "What is Chief Gu thinking? Why is she doing all this? Is she doing this out of spite?"

"Do you think she's that kind of person? I'm sure she has something in mind, but ultimately it won't go as she thinks, seeing as how it looks now."

"Indeed. It already looks like the game's over. Do we really have to go back in and watch that again? I think we're all ready to walk out."

"Really?" asked Lee Jongro. "Then please, don't let anyone leave just yet."

"Why not?"

"Don't you think it'd be best to put an end to all this today?"

"Ah, you're right."

The Command and Control Center was full of people once again. With a hardened expression, Gu Yemin scanned the faces of the people sitting in the audience.

She said, "Thank you for waiting. We had to replace the flight control system. What you saw before the break were operations conducted according to a new suggestion by the Orbit Strategy Development Agency. What you will see now is the operation conducted using our original system. The communication delay to the weaponized satellite is 0.38 seconds, which is exactly the same as before."

Kim Mugyong sat aslant in his seat and raised his voice, "What difference does that make? Don't try to keep us here for no particular reason. Let's just get to the point."

"That's our plan," Gu Yemin replied. "We'll just do this once."

At the launch base, Summin sat in front of the old flight control system, set up in the room next to the main remote pilot station. This system involved using two hands and one leg to control all three arms on the weaponized satellite simultaneously. Her other leg was used to adjust position or move a short distance using the boosters.

"I don't know if I can do this right," Summin spoke into her headset. "It's been about ten days since I last used this system."

The tension was thick in the Command and Control Center at the Space Force headquarters. Not because people were concentrating on an actual military operation being carried out in the field—which was what the room was designed for—but because of the apprehension and unease that enveloped the room.

Gu Yemin said, "The control method you saw before the break used only two arms at a time, while the third arm was at rest. The pilot can choose which two arms to control, and that way, we can distract and confuse the enemy. Of course, as you've personally experienced, us on Earth also become rather disoriented and confused."

Lee Jongro added, "Just as the chief of staff said, this was the method that we suggested from the Orbit Strategy Development Agency. But frankly, we also understand that this is a mere corrective measure. My tentative conclusion is that there is a limit to the strategy of deploying a weaponized satellite in orbit. Instead of directly controlling a weaponized satellite, it may be more prudent to concentrate our resources in strengthening the intelligence operations on other satellites, as—"

"Well, it looks like they're ready," said Gu Yemin, cutting Lee Jongro's speech short. "Let's take a look."

A familiar scene unfolded in front of the spectators' eyes. The approach of two satellites was skipped once again. Soon, the Space Force weaponized satellite unfolded its three arms. It was the same robot-looking design, but this time it had one shield and two spears.

At a glance, the critical difference between the two flight control systems was that the screen did not shift. The pilot's screen was fixed in one direction. Occasionally the image spun quickly to one side, but it was slow enough for people to follow—it didn't jump 120 degrees like before.

Concentration ran high in the audience. It was possible to see the robots in combat in more detail than before. Gu Yemin began to explain what was happening on the screen, possibly thinking of the concept of the silent film narrator she'd once discussed with a young officer in the Public Relations Corps.

"Much easier to sit and watch, isn't it? Our remote-control pilot is Master Sergeant Han Summin. She's a top-class pilot. Many organizations both in Korea and abroad coveted her, but we've been able to keep her in the Space Force so far. As I've explained earlier, the conditions for the simulation are exactly the same, including the limitations from the time difference delay. The only difference is that we are now using the older version of the flight control system. She has trained with this version for a much longer period. It's only been about ten days since the new system was installed. So I believe that it would be inappropriate to judge the limitations of a human pilot without seeing this. Here, we're now approaching the enemy. I'll stop talking, so you can just watch from now on. Since there are several combat strategies, I don't know how things will unfold. I believe Sergeant Han has only recently confronted this level of artificial intelligence. I hope she has found a way to counter it. It's starting now."

As they'd seen in the five previous simulated combats, the enemy spacecraft was astute, agile, and hefty. The robot-shaped enemy spacecraft slowly moved counterclockwise, and the friendly weaponized satellite controlled by Summin was turning clockwise, operating its three arms and looking for a chance to attack.

Summin knew the general pattern of the enemy spacecraft's attacks, but it wasn't easy to block the swinging axes with the long and narrow shield. As always, it was because the reaction speed was slow. She responded as fast as she could, but her spacecraft was getting helplessly beat up.

Sticking close to the enemy, Summin would watch for an opportunity, then put a little bit of distance between the two spacecraft. Several times, she approached and then backed away. On one side of her screen was her fuel gauge.

During the skirmish, Summin regained the feel for the old control system—about three minutes into the combat, her satellite's somewhat awkward movements became much more natural. Summin spoke into the headset as if to assure herself.

"Here I go."

Contrary to what Sergeant Shin had told Summin earlier, her voice was transmitted to the Command and Control Center of the Space Force headquarters.

The three-armed Space Force "robot" suddenly increased its fuel consumption and sped toward the enemy. With the shield in front, it targeted the enemy's body with the tips of the spears on its two hands. It turned counterclockwise, and the distance between them narrowed.

The handsome enemy satellite bravely blocked the spinning attack of the friendly monster. Although the friendly monster showed some flashy moves, the enemy spacecraft's response was too accurate—it turned on a booster, putting a bit of distance between the two. It couldn't throw off the friendly monster or avoid its attack, but it was able to delay the attack. It wasn't a long time, but it was enough. The enemy swung the two axes in its two hands without hesitation and blocked the two spears targeting its body.

But that wasn't the end. Immediately after blocking the attack, the enemy drew close and swung an ax into one of the arms holding a spear. The Space Force craft didn't lose the arm altogether, but it now looked pitiful with an ax stuck in it. The enemy craft let go of the ax in its other hand and latched onto the friendly robot's wrist. It now had the Space Force satellite's second spear-holding arm in a tight grip, rendering it useless as well. Boosters on both satellites began to belch out flames. The combat was an intense physical match, like two wrestlers trying to get the upper hand in the ring. Tangled in an unsightly mess, the two satellites spun on screen. Kim Mugyong sneered.

At that moment, Summin's voice was relayed to the Command and Control Center over the speakers.

"I got it!"

"Got what?" asked Sergeant Shin. "Are you going on a suicide mission toward the atmosphere?"

"No, that could work, but I'm going to do some subtraction—three minus two."

Upon hearing her words, General Lee Jongro, Director of the Orbit Strategy Development Agency, snapped his eyes open wide. The confidence in his face drained, and his expression hardened.

Everyone was looking at the screen. The Earth flashed behind as the two robots span dizzyingly, yet people didn't feel as light-headed and sick as before. The background was moving fast, but the enemy in front of the Space Force satellite remained fixed.

"Oh!" Kim Mugyong let out an exclamation.

A mechanical arm was quickly approaching the head of the sleek enemy satellite. The arm belonged to the Space Force satellite. It was the robot's third arm—the one that wasn't damaged at all.

Everyone in the room gasped. It wasn't out of admiration or

sorrow. It was more the instinctive reaction of being caught off guard.

The two satellites had their arms locked, but the Space Force craft had one more arm. It came from a place outside human intuition about combat. The arm held a shield, but it wasn't destined to only hold a shield. It could grab things and also let things go.

Summin worked the controller in her left hand. When she opened her fist and swung her arm out, the robot arm in the simulator flung its shield into space. Summin didn't hesitate to input the next command. An arm stretched out toward the enemy spacecraft's head. In the next moment, the three-armed monster ripped off the head of the enemy.

Sound doesn't travel in space, and it was the same in the simulation. Still, people imagined that they heard a noise at that moment. The sound of something being crushed and torn apart—*crunch*.

A small explosion occurred on the enemy spacecraft. Its boosters were still activated, but the two arms went slack after it lost its head.

A hand holding up a decapitated head, a realization that the supposedly friendly satellite looks like a monster while the enemy satellite looks like a hero, the feeling of being on the villain's side, and finally the rushing pleasure of victory.

"This is the end of the demonstration," said Chief Gu Yemin, turning to look at the people in the audience. As usual, her voice was calm and composed, but her face was much more relaxed than before.

Right at that moment, the pilot's voice was transmitted to the Command and Control Center.

"Phew. I got it."

LAUNCH SOMETHING!

The voice was full of heartfelt relief. It brought a smile to Gu Yemin's face.

"You can turn off the audio now," Gu Yemin said.

Then looking into the faces of the policymakers in the audience, she made her point.

"The spacecraft that our pilot defeated just now is one that will be deployed in Mars's orbit, where regulations on deploying satellites are relatively weaker. The data on the enemy satellite was provided by Director Lee Jongro of the Orbit Strategy Development Agency, the former Vice-Minister of Mars. But as I said, that spacecraft hasn't yet been deployed and it will certainly not be deployed in Earth's orbit anytime soon due to regulations—the Space Force is tied to international treaties, and as a result, oftentimes, we can't do as we wish, contrary to what the citizenry may think.

"Therefore let me sum up the significance of the simulation training that you have just witnessed. The Republic of Korea Space Force has already deployed a spacecraft into orbit capable of overpowering one of the most advanced weaponized satellites that will be deployed in the next two years. In addition, we have the tactical control system and the pilot to operate the spacecraft. Is the design of the spacecraft a 'peace-preserving' one? I'm not sure. I hope that the Ministry of Defense continues to work on that. This is it for today, and as before, I am happy to answer all your questions in a confidential briefing. Tell me when and where, and I will attend. Have a safe trip home."

The first person to leave the Command and Control Center was Lee Jongro; Gu Yemin was the last.

After returning to her office, Gu Yemin slowly paced in front of the bookcases, deep in thought. As she walked a few laps from the door to the desk, her steps grew quicker.

When the phone rang, she swiftly walked over to the desk with the eagerness of a newly appointed officer and snatched up the receiver with one hand. Dozens of service ribbons decorated her uniform, attesting to her experience and accomplishments as the head of the Space Force.

"So there is some movement? Great. Continue reporting to me."

When she put the receiver down, the room had the silence and stillness of space. Books of various disciplines filled the bookcases, which in some ways was a better testament to Gu Yemin than the decoration on her uniform.

Chapter Eight

The Logic of the Jungle and the Logic of Civilization

The mess hall at the Space Force launch base tended to be crowded only during lunchtime. Despite the large number of people dispatched to the launch base from the Space Force headquarters, the mess hall wasn't a popular joint for dinner.

Suh Ga-ul was sitting in one corner of the empty mess hall eating her meal. In the seat diagonally across from her sat Park Soojin.

"SoCal, so why are you sitting there instead of directly across from me?" Soojin asked. "Are you avoiding me?"

Ga-ul answered, "No, not really. But I do feel a bit self-conscious being buddy-buddy with an internal review officer."

"Since when?"

"Since a little while ago. Look around. No one's sitting anywhere near us. Only I dared to come sit this close to you."

"I'm not the inspector general anymore."

"Right, you're scarier now," Ga-ul said. "Oh, I was just thinking this, but doesn't it feel like someone's gone missing recently?

I don't think I noticed this earlier because the entire base has been in disarray."

"Who? I haven't noticed."

At that moment, Park Kugyong, who had been sitting behind Ga-ul back to back, cut into their conversation, "Captain Um's on vacation."

"Holy cow!" Ga-ul jumped and turned around. "Captain Park Cooking! How long have you been sitting there?"

"Just a little while."

"Could've given a bit of indication that you were there. Captain Ohm, though. He's got skills. Going on vacation amid this chaos."

"Apparently, he had vacation days rolled over from the previous year," said Kugyong. "The Internal Review Department gave him a talking to. He said he has to use them by the end of the month."

Soojin, who had been listening to their conversation indifferently, looked quizzical at the mention of the Internal Review Department.

"The Internal Review Department did? I said that?"

"Or it was the new inspector general," answered Kugyong. "Anyway, he left saying that he was obligated to go."

In a sudden, sparky tone, Ga-ul asked Kugyong, "Where did he go? It must be nice to go on vacation during the off-peak season. Is he going overseas?"

"I doubt it. The entire process for going abroad is too cumbersome."

"Then where in Korea?"

"Not sure. Sounded like he was going with his girlfriend."

"Captain Ohm has a girlfriend?"

"I didn't really ask, so I don't know. I only saw a picture on his cellphone screen."

"Ooh, a photo?"

Soojin was about to say something, but she shrugged her shoulders instead and put her spoon down on her tray.

"It's probably a picture of a celebrity. In any case, I'm heading home. Enjoy your meal and have a good night."

Um Jonghyun gazed into the face of the woman sitting next to him. On the round, window-side table were two full cups of black tea. The chairs were positioned so that people sharing the table faced the window rather than each other. Jonghyun had to turn to the side to see the woman's face.

The woman ran her hand through her hair without avoiding his gaze and continued what she was saying.

"It's a stereotype to think that Martians are creative. They are creative, but it is different from the artistic creativity that people on Earth often associate creativity with."

"Different how?" asked Jonghyun in a gentle voice. Rather than a question begging for an answer, it sounded like filler to show his interest in what she was saying.

The woman answered, "Creativity for survival? Something like that. Some time ago, I tried to get my mom's notes organized and published into a book on Mars, which didn't work out. I brought it with me this time because I thought it might be possible on Earth. The notes are something like a dictionary for Martian words. Redefined meanings of objects. What do you think?"

"Just from what you said, I'm not sure if it'll be of interest."

"You don't think so? It was rather useful on Mars. She belonged to the pioneer generation, my mom. She'd been on Mars since right after the atmosphere modification program was completed, when there were barely enough resources to survive, so she was part of the generation that had this craving for objects."

"Kind of like a deficiency?"

The woman looked up at the sky outside to organize her thoughts for a moment. Then holding her hand up, palm facing down, and rocking it slightly left and right to express that perhaps "deficiency" was going a bit too far, she said, "It's a bit different from a deficiency. Because she didn't think that she'd never have those again. It was more of a pure longing. Like, literally, 'How nice would it be to have this?'"

"Couldn't they have made these items? Or wasn't there enough materials?"

"They sort of did make them. There weren't any materials—at least not the materials that the objects they needed were originally made out of. So they made substitutes using the materials that were left over from making other objects. Say, if they wanted a chair, but they didn't have the materials or the space to make a chair, then they'd make something that would function as a chair and put it in a place that wasn't really designed for a chair. That was how they got by."

"That's how they used their creativity."

"Right. But the key here is not creativity but rather practicality or insight into the essence of the objects."

"For instance?"

"What do you think is the essence of a chair? It's an object with one to four legs perpendicular to the floor and a flat board that is parallel to the floor, and sometimes it has a back piece. But during the pioneer era on Mars, there were times when it was impossible to have a chair with legs that were perpendicular to the ground. In which case, they probably made chairs with legs that protruded from the wall and were parallel to the ground. That means, legs were no longer an essential part of a chair, and only the part about a chair being a fixed, flat board that lies parallel to the ground which can support one's weight by one's buttocks and parts of one's thighs remained true. As long as you can secure a flat board that is parallel to the ground, it becomes a chair. So my mom refined 'chair' and described the structure and function that she had taken for granted as an Earth person. Like what was good about having four legs on a chair; what kind of materials were used to make it; and what the advantages of having a chair were. She did that for everything that she wanted to have back. A house, a car, scissors, a park, a social system, and more."

"It must have been like a philosophy book."

"It was kind of like a philosophy or sociology book, but it all fell under the umbrella of practicality. Because it was all about making things that functioned the same when it was impossible to find suitable materials. If you knew why a certain object came to have a certain shape, you would know exactly what can be substituted or not substituted. That was how they tried to found a nation as well."

"Oh."

"Surprising, isn't it? But it was inevitable. Because they didn't have the right materials, just like for all the other things they wanted. There weren't enough people, and there were no traditions or symbols or something pivotal that could arouse patriotism in people. There was none of that."

"So, you're saying they came to have a 'creative' view of the state," Jonghyun asked in a serious voice. Despite the thorn in his words, his tone was soft and gentle.

The woman answered, "They only wanted a good nation. I am

not from their generation, but that's what I believe. The vision of the Mars settlers during the pioneer era wasn't that strange. For people who were forced to survive in a harsh environment, they weren't very defensive—they were moderate. Even around the time I started school, Mars wasn't a terrible place to live. People were hopeful and optimistic. They had rosy prospects for the future. Because there was hope that they'd be able to live in the greatest world in human history."

"But not anymore?"

"No. Not anymore. That only lasted until the rebellion."

The woman—Woo Jeyoung, a native Martian who came to Earth on an interplanetary shuttle around the same time as Lee Jongro—turned and stared at the men in suits who stood blocking the door. Then she turned back to the black-suited Republic of Korea Space Force intelligence officer sitting next to her.

"You people call it a rebellion, right?"

Without a moment's hesitation, Jonghyun flatly answered, "It was a rebellion."

"But still," Woo Jeyoung said, "it was a revolution that followed completely legal procedures. It happened during Conjunction, and all authority had been completely delegated to the directly controlled municipality on Mars. Mars residents followed the legal procedures to decide on declaring independence."

"Ms. Woo, that wasn't following the legal procedures but exploiting loopholes in the system. People often delude themselves, but the law isn't that lax. Stringing together several provisions cannot override the fundamental objective of the law. The regulation on delegating authority during Conjunction does not provide the right conditions for doing something colossal like declaring secession. It requires more than just putting all the puzzle pieces of procedures together and getting approval;

people are supposed to be able to intervene and make a logical and reasonable judgment. Ultimately the issue would have been judged by the high court, but there wasn't an ounce of possibility for the rebels to have gotten their way. I don't believe this is your first time hearing this."

Jeyoung looked rather emotional. But her voice was utterly devoid of emotion, when she asked, "Will there ever be a high court trial? Based on which legislation or regulation did the occupying forces' commander peremptorily massacre Mars residents? Does the fundamental objective of the law you mention tolerate those kind of atrocities? Is there anyone in the Space Force or the government who can officially say that? They must have filed reports to Earth, haven't they? Do you know how desperately we waited on Mars for a reasonable response from Earth? People we used to see every day were executed. It was a city with a population of twenty thousand. Not everyone knew each other, but we've all seen each other once at least. It's a small town. We didn't have much on Mars, but the most valuable thing we had was human life. Before that day.

"That day, I learned for the first time that among us were people who thought nothing of human life. I didn't know that the Space Force would execute settlers. How could I possibly have thought that? Mars was a place full of optimism. But that man strutted in like he was someone important and went berserk. We knew who he was because we'd seen him around since we were young. He used to come to school during safety training days. Some kids dreamed of joining the Space Force because of him. But in an instant, he turned into a slaughterer. Most people couldn't even do anything because they were so shocked. The happy and exciting play where we'd each had a role had come to a sudden end.

"But then when communication resumed, you know what the government on Earth did? They made Lee Jongro the Governor-General of Mars. They set up a military government and had that murderer run it. Some people said that Earth couldn't do anything when it was Conjunction. Because it was too far away. I believed that too. But Opposition came and went, and Conjunction came again. And even when the next Opposition rolled around, nothing changed. The Space Force simply turned a blind eye to the situation on Mars. They let things on Mars go on as they had been."

Jonghyun curled his lips into a slight smile, but there was a look of embarrassment on his face.

"Why don't we talk about this later?" he said. "I hope you know that we feel sorry for it."

"Who's we? Who feels sorry?"

"Well, I mean, some people do."

Jeyoung stared at Jonghyun's face without a word. She only inhaled and exhaled several times, taking deep breaths and letting out deep sighs. Jonghyun remained quiet as well, but his breath was shallower and quicker than hers.

After a long silence, Jeyoung finally opened her mouth.

"You're more cold-hearted than I thought."

"I don't think I have a response for that."

"No, I know that you have your given role and position. I actually knew who you were."

A look of genuine surprise appeared on Jonghyun's face for a moment before it disappeared without a trace. "Me?" he asked.

"Yes. It's been a long time. About seven or eight years. Oh, in Mars years. When I was young, I read an article in a science publication on Mars about an Earth kid who had a real way with his hands. He'd won an origami contest, and I believe he was about the same age as I was. There was a picture of his prize-winning work too. It was an origami bird about as big as my fist, and he'd folded it with a single piece of paper the size of a six-person table. The bird was spreading one wing and grooming the inside feathers. How amazing that someone could fold something like that out of a single piece of paper, I thought. Someone like that actually exists in the world. Something like that actually happens in this universe when I can't even properly fold an origami crane. I didn't forget his face for a long time after that. Earlier. When I heard your name, I didn't connect it with the article straight away, but I remembered as we were talking. I didn't think it appropriate to bring it up during our earlier conversation, though. You're him, right?"

Jonghyun said nothing in response. He only gazed at her.

Jeyoung continued and said, "I used to imagine what that boy had become now that he was older. I had no idea he would be working for Gu Yemin."

When Jonghyun finally opened his mouth, the words that came out were not friendly, like something the boy from the old picture would have said, but businesslike and blunt, like something a Space Force intelligence officer would say.

"Why did you come here of all places after you got off the interplanetary shuttle? It seems that your close relatives are either in Seoul or Gyeonggi Province, and you don't have a particular connection to this place."

"You ask that, but you already know, don't you?"

"Know what?"

"You've been doing that. Answering my questions with questions. Well, I did expect that someone would be spying on me since I got off the shuttle. I worried about what might happen when the people spying on me revealed themselves. Would they kill me? Lock me up? That's why I couldn't go to places like my mom's old home. That would also put my relatives in danger. I came here not for a particular reason but because I didn't have a plan. Because I didn't know that my mission was going to be suspended."

"Wait, by 'mission,' you mean the mission involving these?" asked Jonghyun, as he pulled something out of his briefcase. It was a photograph of four bullets.

"So you found them."

"I've already compared them with the firearm data transmitted to the emergency parts production device on the interplanetary shuttle. They were the right fit."

"You're right. I mean, the person who was supposed to use those. That was me."

"This is a good start," said Jonghyun. "Who were the targets?"

"I'm sure you know."

"Then what was the objective? To create chaos?"

"I suppose you could say that. The targets could've been eliminated anywhere at any time, but the reason we'd decided to do it on the shuttle was for maximum impact."

"You were prepared to die," Jonghyun said calmly.

As if she were talking not about herself but a stranger, she said, "I had no choice. The shuttle was big, but nonetheless, there was nowhere to escape."

"But why was the mission suspended? As you said, it doesn't look like there was a plan in place to suspend the mission. Specifically speaking, there wasn't a procedure for ordering the suspension of the mission. The moment you boarded the shuttle, communication was completely cut off between you and the organization on Mars. Am I wrong?"

"You're right. There was no other way. We're a small organization."

Jonghyun asked again, "So why didn't you go through with the mission? Did you have a change of heart?"

Jeyoung turned to look out at the blue sea that lay beyond the window and said, "Why? Were you disappointed that nothing happened after waiting for me to print out a revolver?"

"In a way, yes."

The beach looked peaceful. It was cold outside, but about a dozen people lay on the sand in their swimsuits. Two people were actually wading into the sea to go for a swim.

After another long silence, Jeyoung said, "You look like you have all the time in the world, but you're getting more impatient, aren't you?"

"Not really," Jonghyun replied.

"I don't believe you. I'm sure this is an urgent matter. I really haven't done anything since arriving. I didn't meet with anyone, and I didn't try to contact Mars. No one has come to see me. The reason you allowed me to land on Earth even after you found the bullets on the interplanetary shuttle was to arrest my contact, isn't it? You must have spent a good sum on tailing and monitoring me. Foreign organizations must be involved as well since you would've had to spy on me from the space station. So you suddenly coming to see me and telling me that you're with the Space Force makes me think that you are pressed for time."

"It doesn't matter what you think."

"Well, then, I'll take that as confirmation. It'd be more convenient for you if I bring this next point up now, wouldn't it? You were right. I had no idea that people already knew about the firearm data, but before I carried out the mission, someone gave me a signal to stop."

Even though he had just said that he wasn't particularly

impatient to get information out of Jeyoung, Jonghyun's eyes gleamed for a moment.

"Who gave you the signal and how?"

Jeyoung let out a small laugh. "I can't just tell you that. They have no connection to me whatsoever, so you won't be able to track them down. We were on the same shuttle for three months from Mars to Earth, but I'd never even dreamed that we were connected. Oh, you already know who sent the firearm data, right? I think I heard that you've arrested Cha Gwanyoung and his people. Aside from this mission, there isn't really any other connection between us. We were like polar opposites. We are still. We live on different planets so we don't really have to face each other. They probably were using us anyway. Any kind of chaos would have given them a reason to attack the Space Force politically. And our ultimate objective was to create chaos, so we happened to be in cahoots."

"Just as I expected," said Jonghyun.

"Mr. Um Jonghyun, it would be easier for us both to stop dancing around the issue. You're curious about the passenger who gave me the signal, right? The person who knew that I would fall into a trap and so aborted the mission before it took place. Because the organization that person belongs to had some kind of a bigger picture in mind. I've actually been curious about that the entire time I've been on Earth. About who they are. I have no way to find that out, but the Space Force does. Right?"

Jonghyun simply nodded without betraying his feelings. Then he asked cautiously, "What is it that you want? I'm sure it's not just to find out who they are."

Jeyoung answered, "Immunity. On paper."

"We don't have that kind of system here."

"Even if you don't have that kind of system, I could make

our negotiation public when things get worse. You can report to your superiors and let me know when it's ready. I'll tell you then who to send the documents to. When I confirm that the documents have been delivered into good hands, I'll tell you the shuttle room number of the person who gave me the signal. And you can trust me on my promise. I have no reason to cover for someone who supports the likes of Lee Jongro."

Jonghyun slowly got up from his seat. After giving a look to the men at the door, signaling them to continue to keep an eye on Jeyoung, he told her, "Stay in this area and don't stray too far. You are staying in this neighborhood, right? You'll need someone to look out for you for the time being. Even on Earth, the Mars Governor-General can take action."

Jeyoung looked up at Jonghyun and nodded.

For the first time in a long while, the lounge on the first floor of the single occupant dormitory at the launch base was bustling with life. The topic of conversation was General Lee Jongro. Suh Ga-ul sat in the center of the couch, flanked by Han Summin and Kim Eunkyung. Kugyong pulled up a chair and sat down near them.

"Where did you hear that?" Eunkyung asked Ga-ul.

"The senior master sergeants from the Development Corps were talking about it during their cigarette break after lunch. They had to disband quickly when the command sergeant major walked by."

"Geez, you can't keep anything a secret," muttered Eunkyung, shaking her head.

Summin, who secretly relished listening to other people's love stories, chimed in with a sparkle in her eyes, "Is it true? You and General Lee Jongro? Wow."

"What's so 'wow'?"

"I just can't really picture you two together. Wait, wait, so then the man who sent you that giant teddy bear? That was him?"

Eunkyung answered as if she were talking about someone else, "It was such a long time ago. When I think about it now, it makes no sense."

Ga-ul asked, "Did you have to file a Romantic Relationship Occurrence Report too? What did you do back then when you went on dates around here?"

"Why? You think we would've gone sledding on the frozen rice paddies in the winter? It wasn't that long ago. Pretty much the same as now."

"But wasn't that back when people still had CD players?" teased Ga-ul.

Summin piled on, saying, "No, cassette tapes, cassette tapes!"

"Hey, hey!" Eunkyung protested. "Sergeant Han, I told you not to befriend this one."

Kugyong sat chuckling as he watched Eunkyung wrap her arms around Ga-ul and Summin's necks in mock choke holds.

Ga-ul asked with her face buried in the crook of Eunkyung's arm, "Are you in touch with him these days? Secretary Kim, you've got to do something. The Space Force will end up as a real armed force at this rate. This wasn't the Space Force I wanted to join."

Flexing her arm around Ga-ul's neck, Eunkyung answered, "He's not the person I once dated. I don't know him anymore."

"Has Mars ruined him?"

"Ruined him? Hasn't he become a great man?"

"Whatever it is, it's clear that he's not a spacenaut anymore. He's too much of a military man to be in the Space Force!"

Eunkyung loosened her arms, letting Summin and Ga-ul go,

and said respectably, "Give him a break. Mars is a treacherous place. The whole social logic must have been different from Earth. We've gotten too used to the logic of civilization. Living on a whole new planet during the pioneer era, he must have had to follow the logic of the jungle at times, don't you think?"

Ga-ul blurted out, "But you must have broken up with him because you also couldn't accept how he'd changed!"

"Geez, you really are something, shooting off your mouth like that."

"See? This is the reason I'm here at the Space Force. Because I can say things like that. What the heck is the logic of the jungle, which he thinks is fine to force on us!"

"The logic of the jungle? It's when a bigger object and a smaller object are traveling routes which are bound to crash into each other, so the smaller object quickly steps aside to avoid a collision."

At Eunkyung's succinct summary of the logic of the jungle, Summin asked, "Then what about the logic of civilization?"

Turning her head to Summin's direction, Eunkyung said, "That's when a bigger object and a smaller object are traveling routes which are bound to crash into each other, so the bigger object quickly steps aside to avoid a collision."

"Wow!" Summin exclaimed.

"You really like saying 'wow,' huh? The important thing to remember is that both types of logic work fine in different parts of the world. We try to opt for the logic of civilization, but for a planet on the other side of the sun, the logic of the jungle might have been more justifiable, more natural."

Ga-ul chimed in, "But this is Earth! How can he suddenly force the logic of Mars on a Space Force that has been living happily ever after on Earth?"

In a calm and composed voice that sounded somewhat sentimental, Eunkyung answered, "He'll stop. He'll run ashore soon enough. He's going to have a bit of a problem building his career on Earth."

Kugyong, who had been listening to their conversation so far, spoke for the first time, "What kind of problem?"

"He does everything himself," said Eunkyung. "He's not good at controlling situations from behind the scenes. It'll be hard to succeed in a civilized world if he carries on that way. He's more like a tribal chief. Did you know that people have described charisma as being the powerful magnetism tribal chiefs have? He's someone who goes and resolves issues on his own, so he's great at inspiring devotion and arousing strong emotion in the members of his tribe. But that's it. There can't be two chiefs in a tribe, and we already have one."

Ga-ul bluntly said, "I knew you didn't break up on good terms!"

Gu Yemin answered her phone in the back seat of the official vehicle of the Space Force chief of staff.

"Do as Woo Jeyoung asks and make preparations so you can track down her contact as soon as you find out which passenger it was. Oh, and reinforce the security around her."

Um Jonghyun's voice came from the other end of the line. "Ma'am, wouldn't it be better to have her take cover somewhere safe? There will be a security issue if we bring in more guards. They would know that we've begun to move."

Gu Yemin answered with silence.

Jonghyun said, "I see. That's what you want."

"Do you believe her?" Gu Yemin asked. "I'm not so sure that

I do. In any event, Woo Jeyoung isn't that big of a threat for Lee Jongro, so nothing serious will happen. Increase the security around her sufficiently. A little excessively, actually. That will make them curious enough to act first."

"Yes, ma'am. You mean we should stir things up?"

"Exactly. Since they've unsheathed their swords, they're going to cut something, whatever that may be. Before something terrible happens, we have to figure out whether they're just going to be slashing the air or cutting someone's head off. I'm heading to the launch base now to make it look like something's going on. In any event, make a fuss as you move."

"Yes, ma'am. But will it be safe? Ultimately we might be putting Woo Jeyoung in danger."

"She is already in danger. Since the moment she stepped foot on Earth, she has been in a precarious situation. We have to take responsibility and protect her. But I don't think she's the one that Lee Jongro would consider the biggest problem at the moment, so respond with poise."

Lee Jongro was staring at the piece of paper in his hand. Wrinkles formed between his brows.

"Gu Yemin was the one who drew up this bill?" he asked.

Inspector General Kim Su-in of the Space Force launch base, sitting next to him, answered, "She drew it up and actively pushed for it."

The two of them were sitting inside a running van. The spacenauts occupying the driver's seat and passenger seat were in combat uniforms, each with an automatic rifle slung across their shoulders. Lee Jongro was still in his dress uniform, while Kim Su-in was wearing a service uniform as usual.

It was already dark outside. Two other vans followed Lee Jongro's. The windows on all three vans were tinted so dark that it was impossible to see in from the outside.

Kim Su-in explained, "The day after the report on the suppression of the rebellion was filed, General Gu Yemin apparently went around divulging information about a recovery plan. The following week, she tabled a more specific plan."

"Her plan was to deploy allied forces into our city on Mars. Is this even possible? There's no way our allies would interfere in our domestic affairs. Or at least that's what we'd reasoned at the time."

"It seems there was a fifty-fifty chance in reality. Due to particularities of the alliance treaty during the pioneer era, it could have been done if the Korean government had asked. Particularly the United States."

"I would've been completely blind to this had I not returned here," said Lee Jongro. "Then the reason that the government didn't make the move was because of compensation?"

"It seems that way."

"Makes sense. They would've had to pay to bring in another country's military, no matter how close-knit the alliance treaty had been during the pioneer era. But Colonel Kim, isn't this suspicious?"

"Sir?"

"Why is this document in my hands at this precise moment in time?"

"Oh."

"Not 'oh.' Why did this document come to your attention this evening? You must have been tracking it down for a while."

"You are right, sir. It's possible that the chief of staff intentionally slipped us this information. To see how we respond."

LAUNCH SOMETHING!

"Right? Let's wait and see."

The three vans had been speeding along the road, finally stopping in front of a vacation home by the shore. Over twenty spacenauts filed out of the three vans.

Um Jonghyun went to the door to meet the reinforcements. When he opened the door, Lee Jongro strode inside. He pushed aside Jonghyun, who had stood awkwardly blocking the entranceway, and walked into the living room without even taking his shoes off.

"General, what brings you here?" Jonghyun asked, his embarrassment showing plainly on his face. For a short moment, Lee Jongro glared at Jonghyun.

Then glancing at Woo Jeyoung, he said to Jonghyun, "What do you mean? I'm the reinforcement you requested. I've been hearing rumors about how the Mars Governor-General has been idling since he returned to Earth, so I came personally. Is this the terrorist suspect from the interplanetary shuttle? We can bring her in, I assume?"

Jonghyun couldn't answer him. With troubled eyes, Woo Jeyoung looked from Jonghyun to the former Mars Governor-General.

"We'll take her then," said Lee Jongro and nodded at Lieutenant Colonel Kim Su-in. Armed spacenauts approached Woo Jeyoung and yanked her up to her feet. They roughly pulled her arms behind her and handcuffed her. When Lee Jongro stepped out of the front door, the guards followed him. Without even time to put her shoes on, Woo Jeyoung was dragged out by the spacenauts. Jonghyun hastily tried following them outside, but Lee Jongro stopped him at the door.

"We'll take her," he said.

He bent down to pick up a pair of women's shoes by the door.

"I'll take these. And I'll report to the chief of staff. I'm sure you will too, but the more reports the better. Have a good night."

Even before the reverberations of his voice subsided, the door slammed shut. Seconds later came the revving of engines. Regaining his senses at the sound, Jonghyun hurriedly opened the door and looked outside, only to see the vans carrying Lee Jongro and Woo Jeyoung turning onto the main road.

Footprints covered the entire living room floor. Only the manuscript of the book written by Jeyoung's mother was left, suddenly seeming wildly out of place on the sofa where Jeyoung had been sitting.

"So they got us," said Park Soojin.

Everyone else working at the interplanetary communication relay station at the Space Force launch base had gone home, and all the lights were off but for a single fluorescent lamp. Three of the people gathered were in civilian clothing—Kim Eunkyung, Um Jonghyun, and Park Soojin.

The chief of staff's official vehicle was parked in front of the communication relay station. Her aide-de-camp was standing in the hallway outside the office.

Instead of responding to Soojin's statement, Gu Yemin read over the text message on her phone and relayed the new information she had received to the three other people in the room.

"He's going to eradicate the forces supporting the Martian rebels and he wants to reinvestigate the incident involving the transmission of firearm data by Colonel Cha Gwanyoung."

Soojin asked, "Is that about General Lee Jongro?"

"Yes," Gu Yemin answered.

"So he will personally uncover the information that Woo

Jeyoung was about to trade us," Soojin said. "Meaning, even if we unearth Woo Jeyoung's contact he'll have a head start and be able to cover his tracks. At the same time, Lee Jongro's declaring that Cha Gwanyoung and his cronies are not connected to him."

Jonghyun added with a bitter look on his face, "That means now Woo Jeyoung's information won't help us find out about his plan. She'll have nothing to bargain for her life with ..."

Gu Yemin took off her glasses and set them on the table, then fiddled with her empty mug. She didn't simply fiddle with the mug but made it spin round and round on the table, as space-nauts tended to rotate everything they touched.

When the mug stopped spinning, Gu Yemin asked, "Then what could it be? We've certainly seen Lee Jongro and his people making a move after Han Summin crushed the simulated enemy satellite in the demonstration. He didn't come to Earth for nothing. He's planning something. Don't you think so, Secretary Kim?"

Eunkyung nodded, "He must have a plan. He was ruling over Mars like a king. Someone like that wouldn't decide to return to Earth for no particular reason."

"That's what I'm saying," said Gu Yemin. "He couldn't have cast aside the position of Mars Governor-General only to be the chief of staff of the ROK Space Force, not even of the Allied Space Force. I don't think I would've given up a dream job like that."

Then she turned to Jonghyun and asked, "Did he take Woo Jeyoung to the SFHQ Military Police Corps?"

"Yes," Jonghyun answered.

"What about the immunity document? Did you draft it?"

"Thankfully, it hadn't been delivered yet."

"Thank goodness. Had Lee Jongro come a little later, things

might have gotten even worse. Particularly with that piece of evidence on paper."

"Indeed. Since the tables have turned on him, the Vice-Minister of Mars and his people have taken the position of victim."

Deep in thought, Soojin murmured to herself, "So now we can't even use the Woo Jeyoung card to call General Lee Jongro's bluff, although we knew it wasn't going to be of much use. What do we have left?"

Silence filled the room. No one spoke or felt the need to say something to break the stillness.

A little while later, Gu Yemin rose from her seat. "Well, I've been 'out for a drive' for too long now. I should go and see how Woo Jeyoung is. You should all go and rest since you'll all have to be at work tomorrow. If something happens, I'll contact you through Captain Um."

Everyone went out to the building entrance to see the chief of staff off. The field officer on night duty, who must have received the message that the chief of staff was about to leave, was bringing Gu Yemin's car out in front of the communication relay station. The strong headlights from the car swiftly swept across the people standing in front of the station.

Kim Eunkyung took a step forward and called to the chief of staff. "Ma'am."

"Yes?"

"I wasn't sure whether to ask you this or not, but the target of this case, the person that Woo Jeyoung was going to kill. Who exactly was it?"

"Why?"

"There's something that's been weighing on my mind," Eunkyung explained. "My instinct tells me that if General Lee Jongro personally set out to make a move, it is because he needed to take a specific action. But it seems strange that he neutralized a card that we couldn't even have used against him from the beginning. He's not the type to get directly involved in something like that."

Gu Yemin smiled with a hint of curiosity and said, "Huh, really? Captain Um!"

At her command, Jonghyun quietly whispered to Eunkyung, "We believe they targeted an associate of the Vice-Minister of Mars on the interplanetary shuttle that Woo Jeyoung was on. He has been with General Lee since the suppression."

"You mean Colonel Park Junmyong?" asked Eunkyung. "The one at the Academy right now?"

Jonghyun nodded, "Yes."

"See, that's odd."

Eunkyung's response sparked a great interest in Gu Yemin.

"What's odd?" she asked.

"It seems strange that the Mars rebels targeted someone like Colonel Park. It's true that he was a close associate of the Vice-Minister of Mars and that he helped maintain the entire occupying force system, but ... well, his reputation is a bit weird. Like, he's a good worker, but he's not really the Governor-General's right hand or anything. Did General Lee bring Colonel Park Junmyong to Earth to plot something? I don't know. Someone like him is rather easily replaceable. I don't know how the Space Force headquarters sees this situation, but this is what my instincts as a planetary official are telling me."

Gu Yemin and Um Jonghyun looked at each other.

"So what does that mean?" Gu Yemin spoke out loud to herself. "Does he have another card up his sleeve? He took Woo Jeyoung away not because he wanted to get rid of the traitor but because he didn't want her to divulge the actual target?"

Jonghyun nodded in agreement and said, "I think you should see Woo Jeyoung as soon as possible."

The car carrying Gu Yemin sped over to the military police interrogation room at the Space Force headquarters. There, the Space Force chief of staff found Jeyoung sat crouched in a corner of the room, leaning against the wall with her head drooped. Gu Yemin stood quietly for a moment and watched her from behind, unable to call out her name.

Then finally, she said, "Ms. Woo Jeyoung."

Woo Jeyoung must have been awake because she instantly turned toward the voice that called out to her. Gu Yemin thought that she looked scared.

She consoled her in a calm, subdued voice. "It shouldn't have come to this. I'm sorry."

Jeyoung said nothing in response. Gu Yemin couldn't see her face clearly because it was dark, but she thought that Jeyoung was holding back her sobs. Yet the voice that reached her from the shadows moments later didn't seem to be choking with tears.

"What do you mean it shouldn't have come to this?"

Gu Yemin answered calmly, "Everything from what happened this evening to what happened all those years ago."

A long silence continued as the two women were locked in a wordless power struggle. It was the kind of heavy silence that erases the markings on the clock face, making a short period of time feel much longer or a long period of time feel much shorter.

Gu Yemin thought that Woo Jeyoung had immediately recognized her voice. Like memories from long ago. Memories that suddenly come to mind, even though you didn't know that you still had any memories to recall. Memories that made your face and neck grow hot, making you want to vomit what you had forced down all those years ago. But there hadn't been a hint of sadness in Woo Jeyoung's voice. Or anger or darkness or rage.

Gu Yemin was the first to break the silence again. "Can you answer me this one question?"

"What more do you want?" Woo Jeyoung asked. "I heard that the information I was going to trade is no longer useful or needed."

"Just one question. Since charges have been brought against you, we can't do anything at the moment, but I will make sure that you're not subjected to unreasonable treatment. So answer me this one thing."

"Is it conditional?"

"No. Not at all."

Jeyoung looked up at Gu Yemin. As the light finally shone on Jeyoung's face, Gu Yemin thought she could read the memories of the time that had gone astray.

With a look of resignation, Jeyoung nodded and said, "What is it?"

"The target."

"Excuse me?" asked Jeyoung in a feeble voice.

Gu Yemin asked in more detail, "On the interplanetary shuttle, who were you going to shoot?"

A faint look of something came alive on Jeyoung's utterly disconsolate face. It was curiosity.

"What?"

"That's what I want to know."

"You mean, you don't know who the targets are?"

Gu Yemin answered in a calm voice, "We do. But there is a bit of uncertainty. So I wanted to confirm. Who were the targets?"

"Chloe Waters and Oren Cosby, of course."

Concealing her surprise, Gu Yemin spoke evenly, "I see."

"Who else could it have been? Why? Did the Governor-General say otherwise?"

"You've been a great help. I hope that I can repay you for this."

"Chloe Waters and Oren Cosby. They're both civilians. They first arrived on Mars as American citizens, but they acquired residency in our direct-controlled municipality and gained Korean citizenship. They served as civilian strategy advisors for the Vice-Minister of Mars about two years ago in Earth time."

From the launch base communication relay station, Kim Eunkyung reported on the information she had obtained from the Mars city government. Gu Yemin watched her on the main screen in the Command and Control Center at the Space Force headquarters. On one side of the large screen next to Eunkyung stood Park Soojin, waiting with something in her hands.

"Major Park," Gu Yemin addressed her and asked, "where are they now?"

Soojin answered, "After they arrived on Earth via the shuttle, they took the next available flight to Korea. We haven't found any trace of them leaving the country. It seems safe to assume that they are still here."

"He probably brought them over for a purpose, so it makes sense that he'd keep them close."

"Captain Um's investigating the issue right now, trying to see if they are inside the Space Force. I don't think he's found anything yet … oh, here he is now. Captain Um, did you find anything?"

Jonghyun appeared on the screen and turned to face Gu Yemin.

"I believe I've found them. They have been using fake identities, and I need to confirm, but I found that the same fingerprints that had been registered on the interplanetary shuttle were used in one other place."

Gu Yemin asked, "Where was that?"

"The Center for Intensive Research on Information Strategy, ma'am."

"Lee Jongro's playground? The Orbit Strategy Development Agency has been submitting report after report on how we need to scrap the plan to bring in additional weaponized satellites and shift to an information warfare centered strategy."

Soojin responded, "He really meant it, huh?"

Gu Yemin turned to her staff, and asked, "It's clearly illegal to sneak civilians into major military facilities under fake identities, isn't it?"

Someone cautiously answered, "If it's true, then yes, it's illegal."

"Well then, send someone over to arrest them, confiscate everything, and restrain them if necessary. Do it as soon as possible."

From the other side of the screen, Eunkyung watched Gu Yemin give the orders to her staff. Then Eunkyung covered the mic on her headset and asked Soojin, "What do they do at the Center for Intensive Research on Information Strategy? Is it a research center?"

Eyeing Jonghyun, Soojin hesitated giving her an answer. Jonghyun nodded at her, signaling that it was OK to divulge the information. Relieved, Soojin whispered to Eunkyung, also with her hand over the mic on her headset.

"They're involved in information warfare. It *is* a type of research, I suppose. They're busy studying hacking."

"Hacking?" Eunkyung asked, furrowing her brows.

"The weaponized satellites in orbit. Other countries control them remotely like we do. So they're working on intercepting the signals and neutralizing the satellites."

"They call that information strategy? That's not intuitive at all."

"Indeed. But it's doing rather well. The ROK Space Force lacks spaceships, but we're good at making a mess of remote-control systems. Kind of like, if my spaceship is going down, I'm taking your spaceship down with me; but hey, we don't actually have a spaceship, while you do. That kind of a fight."

"And Lee Jongro's Orbit Strategy Development Agency is part of that?"

"Yep."

"So they're not actually developing anything."

"It's for destroying stuff, not developing stuff. People call it the Orbit Sabotage Development Center. Wait, but Captain Um, from the look of things, shouldn't we all get going as well?"

Long before sunrise, the road to the Space Force Center for Intensive Research on Information Strategy was packed with vehicles from the Space Force headquarters. There weren't enough cars to create a traffic jam, but it looked like one as the main gate was shut, turning the road leading up to the gate into a parking lot.

About a dozen vehicles were lined up in front of the huge, barricaded iron gate. Inside the vehicles were members of the Space Force Military Police Corps and Intelligence Department, unable to do anything, waiting for someone to give them an order.

"Don't leave the vehicle. Just stay put."

"But it's an order from the chief of staff."

"So we came here. The gate is closed, what else can we do? Three-Star doesn't want us in."

"But the chief of staff is his superior."

"You can't compare them based solely on that. The three-star has the Ministry of Defense backing him. I guess the chief of staff probably has some other high-ranking government official behind her. And who knows if there's someone from the Blue House behind Three-Star as well? But we don't know who they are. No one knows. So how do we work out who's higher? We can't, can we? So just stay put. The higher-ups will sort things out among themselves and then tell us what to do next."

While this conversation took place in one of the vehicles, Soojin's car came to a stop at the back of the line. She'd driven here from a place that was much further away than the people who were already at the gate. Jonghyun sat in the passenger seat, talking to someone on the phone.

After the short phone call, he hung up and said, "General Lee has personally stopped them from entering."

"He's standing over there?"

"He went inside a little while ago."

"Really? I wonder what the chief of staff is going to do."

Gu Yemin looked down below her feet. She could see the buildings of the Center for Intensive Research on Information Strategy neatly tucked into the wooded surrounding. The main structure was a three-story building—it wasn't tall, but it's big square shape could be seen better from above than on the ground.

Looking at the cars lined up before the gates to the center, Gu Yemin murmured, "Didn't they originally make that side road long and twisted to make it less visible from the main road? When did they pave a straight one? With that long line of vehicles, now everyone in the world will know that there's Space Force buildings here."

The rotors roared, but everyone aboard the helicopter heard what she said through headsets. In a more serious voice, Gu Yemin continued, "The fact that he's going to these lengths of insubordination means that he's trying to buy time. Which means he's doing something important right at this moment. You hear what I'm saying? Get in promptly and restrain him!"

The helicopter immediately flew over to the three-story building and hovered over the square-shaped rooftop. Instead of descending, ropes were lowered from the helicopter. Armed agents slid down onto the building. Then after all the agents had been dispatched, the helicopter rose into the air, twisted slightly, and landed on the facing empty lot. As soon as it hit the ground, Gu Yemin leaped out.

"The rescue agents are in the building." Jonghyun relayed the information he'd received via a text message to Soojin. "They're the first ones to be deployed since they're a special forces unit."

When Gu Yemin finally entered the room occupied by Lee Jongro and his associates from Mars, he was locked in a struggle with a rescue agent who was there to arrest him. They were both gripping the agent's rifle. Lee Jongro was the only one resisting; everyone else stood quietly in a corner. On the floor, another rescue agent whose face was covered in blood was regaining consciousness with the help of a colleague. Other agents stood surrounding Lee Jongro, who was still holding out. They were all armed, but no one was pointing their firearm at him.

"You can stop now," said Gu Yemin, who was in dress uniform, to Lee Jongro, who was in civilian clothing. Gu Yemin dragged a chair over from the side of the room to sit down and took her time crossing her legs. Lee Jongro finally let go of the rifle in his hands.

Even now, no one rushed to arrest Lee Jongro. They didn't know what had happened overnight, but to most spacenauts, Lee Jongro was still a hero and a great man.

"What have you been plotting here?" asked Gu Yemin. "Take a seat, first."

She gestured at the rescue agents to take a step back. The room was full of computers and monitors. Red and green lights flashed here and there.

Straightening his disheveled shirt, Lee Jongro answered in a still excited voice, "I didn't know you were going to be here so quickly. And in person at that."

"You're not the only one who knows when to make a move. Those two must be Chloe Waters and Oren Cosby. What kind of technicians are they? Did they hack into our weaponized satellite?"

Lee Jongro slumped down on the chair behind him. His movements were unbridled as always.

"That's just a toy," he answered.

"So something bigger," said Gu Yemin. "How big is big enough to pique your interest?"

"I suppose you'll find out during your investigation."

"I'm sure I will. But it would be easier if you told us."

Lee Jongro let out cheerful laughter and spoke as if what was happening was a joke. "Whatever the plan, you're still going to arrest me."

Gu Yemin brushed back her hair, tousled by the helicopter ride, "Don't worry. You just need to decide whether to go gracefully or disgracefully."

"Well then, I think it would be best for me to go voluntarily. I'm not as strong as I used to be. So, shall we? Should I get in the car? Or is there a helicopter waiting for me on the rooftop?"

Gu Yemin looked into Lee Jongro's face as he leaned forward, ready to stand up. He seemed much more relaxed than before. It was the face of someone who had calmed down and realized that there was no reason to rush.

"Seems like you've done it. Whatever you were planning to do."

"I have. Just barely."

"Why are you going to such lengths to do this? Even coming all the way to Earth."

"I was intrigued by people who were obstinately insisting on starting the entire project of space exploration from square one."

"What do you mean?"

Without responding to Gu Yemin's question, Lee Jongro suddenly got up from his seat and strode out into the hallway. His face was beaming with a good-natured grin. The agents who'd come with Gu Yemin hesitantly followed him from behind.

"Is it this way? That way?" As if this situation was nothing of importance, Lee Jongro asked for directions from the agents who were there to arrest him.

Hearing his voice from behind her, Gu Yemin raised her voice impatiently, "What are you doing? Restrain him. And take him to the car, not the helicopter."

Once Lee Jongro was gone, the people who had been waiting at the entryway to the Center for Intensive Research on Information Strategy finally filed into the room.

When Um Jonghyun entered the room with Park Soojin, Gu Yemin turned toward them and grumbled, "We made a monster in Mars and brought him back home. I suppose I'd expected it somewhat. Go and find out exactly what he's done. It could be a matter of urgency."

It took less than five minutes to find out what Lee Jongro had done. Jonghyun approached Gu Yemin, who was sitting relaxed in the center of the room, and briefed her on the information he'd received from the experts.

"It seems like he's changing the orbit of the asteroid."

"What?"

"It seems that the Allied Space Force planned on permanently capturing the asteroid, and there are a number of devices installed on it that have not been disclosed to us. Lee Jongro succeeded in hacking those devices from this facility just moments ago."

As if she'd just thought of something, Park Soojin added, "If my memory serves me correctly, Cosby and Waters served as advisors in the US Space Force. It's possible that they stole information related to the original project of capturing the asteroid. Or they might have participated in the development stage and planted something there."

"So they hacked into a device installed on the asteroid and then activated it from here at our facility?" asked Gu Yemin.

Jonghyun answered, "Yes, ma'am. It's been activated. We have to look into it more, but it seems that we cannot abort or reverse it."

A frustrated silence filled the room.

"That's a problem. And you're saying that device seems to be a thruster?"

At Gu Yemin's question, Jonghyun—the intelligence officer who according to rumors had been parachuted into his position in the Space Force—answered with a hardened face, "It seems that the command input into the device is related to the asteroid's orbit—very likely a propulsive device. In sum, General Lee Jongro returned to Earth to change the asteroid's orbit."

About twenty people in the room all closed their mouths simultaneously. A heavy silence fell over them. Numerous thoughts popped into people's heads at the same time, but they all boiled down to the same thing: the most disastrous situation imaginable when it comes to an asteroid orbiting Earth.

Gu Yemin called to her aide-de-camp, "Get me on the phone with the Allied Space Force Operations Command. Through the hotline. Now."

Chapter Nine

The Front Line of Humanity

Park Kugyong's blue sports car was in the parking lot of the public relations building, which was located immediately inside the main gate of the launch base. The biggest military exchange store on the base was in the lobby of this building, and it also served as a souvenir shop for visitors. Kugyong sat at one of the tables outside the store, blankly staring towards the main gate.

As she about to enter the store, Park Soojin noticed Kugyong. She approached him and asked, "What are you doing here at this time instead of working?"

Kugyong turned to Soojin and said, "Oh, IG."

"Slacking off? You might get called to the Internal Review Department."

"Aren't *you* back to being the Acting Inspector General? I heard that Lieutenant Colonel Kim Su-in was removed from office."

"I am. But I plan on continuing the position in her spirit. So, you, spacenaut, what's your rank and division?"

Kugyong smiled, "No, no. I'm working. Since all the higher-ups stormed into the base, the civilian tours have been canceled. I contacted each and every visitor, except for one I couldn't reach."

"So you're waiting for that person?"

"Yeah, it'd be a bummer to come all the way here, only to be turned away at the main gate. They might post something on the internet about something suspicious happening on the base. I figured the least I could do was explain what happened and give them a souvenir."

"How long are you going to sit here and wait?"

"I think until about half an hour after their tour was supposed to start."

Soojin turned to the store, saying, "All right. Have fun."

There weren't a lot of goods on the shelves—there were beverages, snacks, instant noodles, and daily necessities like shampoo, but no alcohol. Soojin grabbed a bottle of green tea and headed to the counter. On the way, she noticed Han Summin, looking for something on the candy bar display.

"Sergeant Han."

"Oh, Inspector General."

"What are you doing here?"

"I'm looking for mint chocolate. It used to be around here. I wonder if it's sold out."

"Oh, no, that wasn't what I ... Let's talk over there. Get what you need and come see me there."

Soojin paid for her tea and went to sit down at Kugyong's table.

Kugyong asked, "Did you happen to get me one?"

"What am I, your servant?"

Two minutes later, Summin approached the table and slumped down in the chair next to Kugyong.

"They're no longer carrying mint chocolate," said Summin.

Kugyong asked in surprise, "They had mint chocolate here? Who eats that?"

"I do," Summin answered impassively. "Man, this was the only place that had mint chocolate within a fifty-kilometer radius."

Kugyong then asked Summin what Soojin had been wanting to ask.

"Sarge Han, but shouldn't you be piloting the weaponized satellite right now?"

Summin twisted open the cap of a bottle of sparkling water, letting out a long fizz, and said, "It's not a truck. I don't have to steer it at all times. I turned on the booster a little while ago and placed it in the transfer orbit, so I don't need to touch it for a while. It'll fly there on its own. Don't they teach you all this at the academy? Pilots can't be the only ones who learn this stuff."

"I knew that," Kugyong said. "That's not why I was asking. Aren't the VIPs here watching? I thought you'd be glued to the steering wheel like a truck driver."

"That's why I ran away. They were all sitting there watching. As if that'd make things go better. If they needed some kind of sorcery, they should just go to the Weather Agency. They're the experts in that kind of thing."

Soojin chimed in, "But our satellite, if it goes *there*, it can never come back, can it?"

Summin eyed Kugyong, wondering if she could say something like this in front of a public relations officer.

She faced Soojin but eyed Kugyong as she answered in a voice utterly devoid of confidence, "If we raise our satellite to the orbit where the asteroid is located, it'll probably use up all the fuel. So I don't think they've decided whether to put it in the target orbit or not."

Conscious of the look Summin gave Kugyong, Soojin explained, "The Public Relations Corps knows what's going on in general. That's why I asked you to come over here."

Kugyong grumbled, "Everyone always treats me like a civilian. I already knew that the Allied Space Force has suddenly gone cold on us because of the mess that General Lee Jongro made. Which makes me wonder—as I doubt there is much cooperation between us and the ASF at the moment, it must have been the chief of staff's decision to deploy the weaponized satellite, right?"

Summin nodded. "One of the Allied Space Force's satellites started up before ours. It has a sturdy engine and a huge fuel tank, so it'll get there fine. Our satellite isn't bad, but it can't make the return trip. The ASF hasn't told us whether it sent just one satellite or whether there's a second. If they sent two, we don't need to deploy ours as a backup. It's literally the only weaponized satellite that we have in this country. Man, it's a shame. But we're the ones who made the mess, so I don't think there's much else we can do other than deploy our satellite if we have to."

Silence swept over them, as if someone had made a joke that fell flat. All three sat wordlessly, looking out the window at the main gate. There was no one coming in or out of the public relations building. It was a quiet day.

Soojin cautiously broke the silence, "But, hmm, Summin."

"Yes?"

"About the asteroid."

"What about it?"

"Is it really possible for it to crash into Earth?"

Rather than giving a straight answer, Summin hesitated. Kugyong avoided eye contact, appearing uncomfortable to be part of this conversation. But when Summin started talking, he couldn't help but land his eyes on her.

"That's another thing that the ASF is refusing to tell us. They're keeping quiet about what exactly they installed on the asteroid, how much fuel it has, what its capacity is, whether it's armed, and so on. I can't say for sure, but seeing as Lee Jongro went ahead and started up his plan, I assume they decided that it's possible for the asteroid to crash into Earth."

"So we have to stop it," said Soojin.

Kugyong explained, "Regardless of whether it's possible for the asteroid to hit Earth or not, at least Lee Jongro has succeeded in showing that this asteroid, which the Allied Space Force has been putting so much weight behind, could become a threat one day. Unlike the relatively safe and stable Mars. That's why the higher-ups are saying the Public Relations Corps have to find some kind of angle to explain that the asteroid is safe. We don't even know if the whole plan to stop the asteroid will remain confidential or whether the ASF will suddenly go public with it since they haven't told us anything. If they do go public with it though, we have some information we could release to divert attention from us. After all, it was the ASF that mounted whatever equipment on the asteroid. Speaking of which, Sergeant Han, why not get a few headshots ready this time? Ones with you looking all spiffy."

Summin snapped, "No thanks. I just wish this would all go away. Why did they have to install audience seats in the remote pilot station? Ugh. If they wanted to show me support while I worked, they should have just sent me mint chocolate bars."

Soojin and Kugyong said nothing response. The peaceful atmosphere of the afternoon hung heavy over the entire launch base.

Moments later, Summin glanced at the clock on the wall and got up from her seat.

"Well, enjoy the rest of the morning. I have to go and pretend to be steering the satellite."

"Want me to give you a ride?" Kugyong asked.

"In your flashy blue sports car? You know it's pretty embarrassing to see it parked in front of here, don't you?"

"There are lots of visitors here, so people will just think it belongs to a civilian. It's more inconspicuous here than in the dormitory parking lot. Or, there was a military police vehicle parked outside just now—I could hot wire that."

Summin let out a chortle and shortly put an end to the conversation.

"It's fine. I'll walk."

Having arrived at the launch base, Space Force Chief of Staff Gu Yemin succeeded in herding the guests who had been camping out in the remote pilot station into the Launch Control Room. This room was located in the launch base main building, and with its glass wall and stage-like layout, it was where visitors had previously watched the launch of the weaponized satellite.

Since the room had been made for an audience, Gu Yemin had to show the guests something to keep them in their seats. Therefore she filled the stage with people who were usually involved in launching rockets—people who had nothing to do with the current operation in progress. It was a ruse to make it seem as though the extras on stage were making critical decisions that would have a profound impact on the mission that was being carried out by Han Summin and the Orbit Operations Office. But all they were doing was monitoring the orbit of the asteroid.

"It's fine," said Gu Yemin. "Most of them came thinking that the mission would last a mere two or three hours, so they'll want to go home when they realize that nothing is going to happen for ten or twenty hours. They've all got busy schedules."

At her words, Lieutenant General Song Keunki, the launch base commander, nodded. "Yes, ma'am. Then we will lead all the relevant people to this room."

"Does 'relevant people' include the president?"

"No, ma'am, I thought …"

"No, no. You should bring the president here too."

"Pardon?"

"It'll all be to no avail if the president heads somewhere else. Because everyone else will follow. Direct him here when he arrives. You should probably arrange everything in advance with the presidential secretariat. Let's do what we can to not distract anyone who is actually working."

There was a huge Korean national flag hanging on the wall, and next to it was a screen that was slightly smaller than the flag. On the screen was a two-dimensional chart of the three-dimensional orbits of the asteroid and the ROK Space Force's weaponized satellite. The most eye-catching thing was the asteroid's orbit, which was colored red. The asteroid, which had been at Lagrange point 5, had gradually moved to Lagrange point 1—directly between the Earth and the moon.

Being the point where the gravitational force from both Earth and the moon were exactly equal, Lagrange point 1 was on the route that the moon-Earth shuttle took in order to save fuel. An object at Lagrange point 1 was like a tightrope walker up in the air—the slightest push in either direction would make the object fall, either toward Earth or the moon.

Summin sat in one corner of the remote pilot station, watching the image of the asteroid at Lagrange point 1. The screen that she was watching the image on was much smaller than the one in the Launch Control Room, and all members of the Orbit Operations Office sat huddled around her. The chief of staff had gotten there moments ago as well.

"Is there any new information?" asked Lieutenant Colonel Shim Jaesun, Director of the Orbit Operations Office. Gu Yemin slowly shook her head from side to side.

"It doesn't look like the ASF is going to divulge anything. They seem to be assuming that we know everything and are only asking to feign innocence. We've explained that it was a mutiny, but they're nowhere near ready to believe us. It is true that the asteroid was hacked from our facility, but it wasn't done by someone on our side."

"Then what about General Lee Jongro?"

"It would be best for everyone if he tells us everything, or if his cronies do. But he's keeping his mouth shut. Both him and the Allied Space Force—I can't tell if they're not saying anything because they're bluffing, or whether they actually have a card up their sleeve that they're keeping concealed until the end."

Right at that moment, the director of the Orbit Operations Office received a report from an operator in the remote pilot station and relayed the new piece of information to Gu Yemin.

"Chief Gu, we have an update from the ASF. They gave up on intercepting the asteroid with a missile as the results of such an action are impossible to predict. And one of the ASF's weaponized satellites in the transfer orbit has entered the parking orbit. As soon as it's ready, we'll have it displayed on the screen."

Gu Yemin couldn't hide her surprise as she said, "It's already in orbit within reach of the asteroid? That was quick."

The director of the Orbit Operations Office added in a tense voice, "They're admitting that missile interception is ineffective. They'd said that they were seriously considering launching a missile, despite it breaching the treaty."

"That means there could be two possibilities," said Gu Yemin. "Either they think that the asteroid isn't a big enough threat to breach the treaty by using a missile, or as you said, they decided that a missile was useless. If it's the latter, then that's troublesome. Since that means they don't have the firepower to destroy the asteroid or the capacity to take out the propulsion device on the asteroid with precision. It seems the only solution left is to send something directly over to destroy it. Well, let's wait and see."

Time passed. Everyone, except for Gu Yemin, sat staring at the two or three monitors in front of them, but no one in the room was making any real contribution to resolving the situation. A little while later, the director of the Orbit Operations Office reported another piece of news to Gu Yemin.

"I just received an analytical report from our strategic information line, but it's a bit ambiguous."

"What did they say?"

"They said it seems the Allied Space Force have at least two more satellites deployed in the lower orbit that could be moved to the asteroid's orbit. But neither has the capacity to make a short-range attack."

Turning to him, Gu Yemin spoke as if to herself, "That's why they didn't deploy those? They're useless because they can't attack at short range?"

"It seems that way, ma'am."

"That means they've planted a short-range weapon on the asteroid. Although now it's become a hostile force. Then we should also get into the asteroid's orbit."

Gu Yemin turned to look at Han Summin sitting in the corner.

Staring at the barely changing image of the ASF satellite on the screen, Lieutenant Colonel Shim, Director of the Orbit Operations Office, said, "We'll make preparations."

Captain Um Jonghyun went down to the room where General Lee Jongro was incarcerated. He wasn't in a facility belonging to the military police or the Internal Review Department but in a basement conference room in the museum building at the Space Force headquarters. The room didn't receive any sunlight, but it was spacious and comfortable for someone arrested for treason.

After flashing his ID and a special order issued by the chief of staff to the military police officer standing guard, Jonghyun pushed open the conference room door and walked in. Lee Jongro was standing, looking at a wall calendar, when he heard the door open and turned his head.

"Oh, it's you," he said. "Don't get me wrong. I'm not counting the days. It's just that this is the only interesting thing to read in here."

Jonghyun approached the table in the conference room in silence. As he took several documents out of his briefcase, he said, "*Monthly Space Force* should be there somewhere. There it is on the floor."

"I told you, the calendar's the only interesting thing in here. I don't know what people were thinking, publishing that magazine. Thankfully you seem to have brought me something to read. Good timing. I think I might even find the Space Force regulation book entertaining at this point."

"I don't have much to show you."

"You don't?"

"Though there is something that I'd like to hear from you."

"I didn't know you were so uninteresting."

"Would you like to sit down for a moment?"

"I just got up, so I don't want to sit back down again. Let's just continue as we are."

"Sure. I'll sit, and you can remain standing. First, I have some news. The Allied Space Force decided to send an investigation team to look into this incident, but our chief of staff refused to let them for the time being."

"I see. So I won't have an opportunity to receive a fair investigation. Is that what she wanted you to come here to do? To threaten me?"

"It's more complicated than that. The Allied Space Force is outraged. The ASF believes that you are the beating heart of the ROK Space Force, and therefore they cannot comprehend the fact that you acted outside of the ROK Space Force's chain of command. Once the ASF starts the investigation, they will soon find out the truth, but I don't believe that we're at a point where we can say whether the ASF's or our investigation will be favorable or unfavorable to you."

"In any event, you're saying that the ROK Space Force is stalling and the investigation is not moving forward," said Lee Jongro. "I suppose that means preparations are being undertaken to ensure things will go in a way that would be most unfavorable to me? That's not very interesting."

"Well, then. The next piece of news I have is about Chloe Waters and Oren Cosby, who you brought over from Mars. I'm sure you would've assumed this already, but the situation they are in cannot even compare to yours. Since they have no connections here whatsoever, and the fact that they were at our facilities is a problem in itself."

"Sure."

"They're currently being kept in separate quarters, but I've been hearing reports that they're being rather vocal about their uncomfortable situation. Their complaints started at about the same time today."

Lee Jongro asked Jonghyun in a voice devoid of intrigue, "So what? I'll be seeing them soon? That's absurd."

Jonghyun said, "They seemed quite interested in the fact you're being kept in fairly comfortable quarters. We didn't plan on bringing you here. We only did because we received an order from the Ministry of Defense. But things then began to unfold in a weird direction."

"What's so weird?" asked Lee Jongro, lowering his voice. "Just get to the point."

Jonghyun glanced at Lee Jongro and continued, unfazed, "You weren't planning on protecting Waters and Cosby all the way to the end, were you? Since they were just mercenaries. I found something interesting during the investigation. There was an escape route planned for the two of them."

Jonghyun pushed a piece of paper on the table toward Lee Jongro, who glanced at it but soon turned his eyes away.

"It's not something I knew about."

"Whether you knew about it or not isn't important. Waters and Cosby probably thought that they would be guaranteed a safe escape. Since this wasn't their fight. But things didn't go as planned. My point is this: Waters and Cosby will remain silent for the time being, but they won't stay loyal to you to the end. Since being caught wasn't in their plan."

"That sounds plausible. So?"

"So it's perhaps time for you to tell us."

"Tell you what?"

"Well," Jonghyun said, "first, what did the Allied Space Force mount on the asteroid? Tell me exactly what you know. It's not your secret, so I figure it wouldn't be difficult for you to divulge that information."

"Ah. That's a good question. But there's no way I could know anything about that."

"No, we believe that you do know. If you could at least tell us about the thrust power of the rocket installed on it, that would be very helpful."

"So you don't know what's been installed on the asteroid, but you are sure that there's a rocket. It must be moving, huh? Interesting. But you're overestimating me in thinking that I would know something about it. Overrating someone like that risks turning them into some type of superhuman. Because you're not looking at what in fact one person did but instead are thinking, 'That person might even be able to do this or that,' whatever 'this or that' is. It's not unusual to make assumptions, but you have to think of what's possible—one person can do several significant things when he puts his mind to it, but he can't do all of them at once. No matter how great a person is, he has to make a choice. The moment you believe that one person could do everything, you end up making a monster out of thin air. Do you think I'm a monster?"

After hesitating whether to answer the question or not, Jonghyun used his most business-like tone and asked in return, "What else should I think you are?"

"Well."

"Should we just trust that you didn't mean to hack the asteroid, that the asteroid won't actually crash into Earth, that you wouldn't have thought to actually destroy Earth? Should we just wait and see what happens?"

"Do you always assume the worst-case scenario?"

"I'm a member of the Space Force. I've been mainly trained to respond to worst case scenarios."

"Trained to respond to worst cases? The Korean Space Force is prepared for worst case scenarios? And you of all people?"

Lee Jongro suddenly burst into laughter. His laugh continued for a little too long for him to be laughing at what he just said.

Jonghyun simply watched him without saying a word. Then he grabbed his briefcase and started filing the documents back inside. After packing everything, he got up from the chair without hesitation.

"It seems like you have nothing to say. That's fine. I won't be wasting your time or mine. I will ask someone else these questions. There's Waters and Cosby, and a few others. It is less stressful for us to investigate them; there's less pressure. It is rather daunting to be interviewing you. But your answers to a few simple questions would make things easier for us, and that's why I asked you, although I wasn't seriously expecting you to answer them. Have a good evening."

Jonghyun opened the door and was about to walk out of the room when Lee Jongro asked, "You, your name's Um Jonghyun?"

Jonghyun stopped.

Having succeeded in keeping Jonghyun in the room, Lee Jongro added, "I know that the Mars Cities Alliance tried to recruit you, but how did you end up in this hole of a place with the ROK Space Force? If you'd gone to Mars, you would've had better prospects. You could've been something better than even the Vice-Minister of Mars. They might have made you the strategic analyst of an alliance of fourteen mid- to large-sized cities. You would've been able to do a lot of fascinating things."

"I didn't want to go," Jonghyun answered. "That kind of place isn't my cup of tea."

"You didn't want to go. OK, I can see that. It's far away, dangerous, and you can't come back whenever you want to. If you couldn't adapt to the environment, you'd have ended up frittering away before you could return to Earth. You must have heard story after story about people who ended up wasting their youth and became nothing more than ordinary. But so what? That scared you?"

"Well, I hadn't thought that it was scary, but now that I've heard you say all that, I suppose I might have been scared."

"You smart ass. Captain Um, you know who I am? I have wandered through space. I have protected space, instead of those snowflakes who are Space Force in name only and have never even left Earth. I didn't spend years walking on eggshells around people, worried that my choices might boost or derail my career. You think a snowflake like you jabbering a few sarcastic words as a threat would scare me?"

At his words, Jonghyun stopped and closed the door he had been about to exit. He then turned to Lee Jongro and said what had been on his mind for a long time.

"General Lee Jongro, you weren't protecting anything, only trying hard not to lose the fistful of power that had been in your clutch. Going as far as to ruin yourself in the process of trying not to lose what small power you had to someone else. That was why I didn't go to Mars. Because I don't have much to gain from a place like that. Open your hand and look—what do you have there now? There's nothing but your palm lines. I'm sure those lines predicted that you'd become a hero. I was honestly impressed by you, but after you returned to Earth, what did you grasp with your hands? You grabbed Earth by the throat."

Jonghyun's words weren't enough to persuade him to give up any information, but Lee Jongro remained quiet. He'd impulsively stopped Jonghyun from leaving, but such a dramatic move would have been more suitable if the chief of staff had personally come to see him. He thought that he shouldn't have spoken in a fit of rage to a young officer with minimal military experience, who'd only gotten his position by being parachuted in.

Having said what was on his mind was enough for Jonghyun. Now he could leave the room.

With a slight smile on his lips, Jonghyun walked out the door. Lee Jongro turned to the calendar once again. The door closed.

Walking down the long corridor, Jonghyun called the chief of staff to report on the meeting.

"I don't think he will talk. He showed no reaction even when I told him that the people he'd brought with him from Mars will suffer. He won't speak, at least not in the next few days."

Emotion lingered in his voice.

As Gu Yemin listened to Jonghyun, something like a glint of sympathy appeared in her eyes. It remained there for a while, but it vanished entirely as soon as her lips parted.

"I see. So he no longer has any allegiance whatsoever to the Republic of Korea Space Force."

"No, ma'am."

"He did all this, not to send a message but as an act of revenge. He didn't return to Earth to prove himself but to show how powerful he is. That's a shame. He was a strong and tenacious man."

"But what exactly is he revenging? He was never a victim."

"I assume it was because he was never treated as a real hero. Resentful that people on Earth never truly showed him respect for dedicating half his life to Mars. I didn't think he went to Mars for respect. He used to be an adventurer, full of curiosity.

But then one day, he must have realized that he made the wrong choice. And he probably wanted someone to persuade him that he wasn't wrong."

"It would be best to forget him," said Jonghyun.

"Yes, you're right," replied Gu Yemin. "You can pull out now, Captain Um. There's no time to waste on him. We have to go destroy whatever it is that has been installed on the asteroid."

That night, heavy snow fell across the Space Force launch base. The Weather Agency had accurately forecasted the snowfall, but no one complimented them on a job well done—the entire Space Force's attention was focused instead on outer space.

A look of concern rested on Gu Yemin's face as she watched a snowplow clearing the paths. The base commander, Lieutenant General Song Keunki, stood by her side, looking apprehensive. Their breath slowly fogged up the window. When the fogged-up window got to the point where it became too blurry to tell the cleared paths and the blanket of snow apart, Gu Yemin turned away.

"Our weaponized satellite," she said, "Will it work properly? We've only run simulations, so I'm uncertain whether it will operate as we expect it to."

Lieutenant General Song tilted his head to the side and answered, "I don't think we need to worry about that. We should go ahead assuming it will perform well no matter what."

"We should, shouldn't we. You've confirmed the exterior of the satellite incurred no damage during the launch?"

"We've confirmed it through the Allied Space Force satellite. We asked them to maintain a certain distance from our satellite, so we don't have high-resolution photos but can confirm there's no damage or dents. But that's not the issue. The question is whether combat will unfold in the way it did in simulation."

"The time delay between the control command input and output will be much longer, won't it?"

"Yes, ma'am. It's much farther than the orbit that our satellites are usually deployed in. We assume there will be a delay of two seconds at the very least."

"Are we prepared for the changed conditions?"

"We're still performing simulated training. But bluntly speaking, it won't be of use. If we really will be engaging in combat with an AI-mounted spacecraft."

"Sure," Gu Yemin said. "If there's a two-second delay, I could even win against Han Summin, with a bit of luck on my side."

Lieutenant General Song answered, "No, you would definitely win."

While the two of them remained deep in thought, the door opened. Lieutenant Colonel Shim Jaesun, Director of the Orbit Operations Office, rushed in and reported in an urgent voice.

"We just received a message from the Allied Space Force."

"What is it?"

"They've requested that we prepare for combat."

"Prepare for combat? What about the satellite they deployed ahead of us?"

"It apparently became dysfunctional when it arrived and had to abort."

Gu Yemin's face hardened.

"So there is a combat-ready weaponized satellite on the asteroid?" she asked. "Is that what they said?"

Lieutenant Colonel Shim answered, "Yes, ma'am. They've agreed to share all the data. We'll have it soon in the Operations Division."

Walking to the door, Gu Yemin asked, "They're giving us all of their data? The high and mighty Allied Space Force is going to give us that? That means this is really serious."

"As of now, it looks that way."

"Who should I talk to at the ASF? I'd like to talk to them personally."

A few minutes later, Gu Yemin entered the remote pilot station looking resolute. The director of the Orbit Operations Office leaped to his feet and studied her face, and the rest of the people in the room turned to look at the two of them.

The director of the Orbit Operations Office asked, "How did it go, ma'am?"

"Where's Sergeant Han?"

At the chief of staff's question, Senior Master Sergeant Shin Minhyung answered, "She's training via simulation in the next room."

The chief of staff nodded and commanded, "Let's prepare for action. Get this remote station set up and call her in—she can continue the simulated training here. Base Commander Song should focus on handling the visitors in the Launch Control Room. Contact the base command sergeant major to check combat readiness of our satellite. Starting now, the entire Space Force should be in emergency preparedness mode."

Base Commander Song asked the chief of staff, "What did the Allied Space Force say?"

Gu Yemin answered him, as though she were addressing the entire room and even the entire Space Force.

"The Allied Space Force is sending us all the data they currently have on the asteroid. We'll have it soon. There are two pieces of important information that have come to light. One, the thruster mounted on the asteroid is powerful enough to threaten crashing into Earth. Two, the Allied Space Force deployed AI-mounted combat equipment to protect the asteroid, so I assume the combat equipment is a weaponized satellite. The ASF believed that the system on the weaponized satellite was completely separate from the thruster and therefore could not have been hacked by Lee Jongro, but moments ago, this satellite suddenly became active on its own and incapacitated the weaponized satellite the ASF sent to intercept the asteroid. Since the satellite that has gone rogue is an old model, its performance isn't outstanding. But the key issue for us is the time delay between command input and output. Because the time delay is so long, the ASF's weaponized satellite was destroyed soon after engaging with the rogue satellite."

"Are they sending us the data on the rogue satellite as well?" asked Sergeant Shin.

"Yes. The ASF's Strategy Analysis Team will analyze the combat data and share that with us."

No one else asked questions. The atmosphere in the remote pilot station grew heavy. So heavy that Han Summin, who opened the door to the remote pilot station and walked in, noticed and stopped short.

Upon seeing the ace pilot enter the room, Space Force Chief of Staff Gu Yemin said the last lines of her speech:

"Everyone, let's pull ourselves together and do our best. We are now the front lines of humanity."

The chief of staff issued an order of emergency preparedness, but even in the Space Force there were only a handful of people who could make substantial contributions to resisting the impending threat.

Soojin drove her car through the base's main gate and headed to the Weather Agency. The snowplow had cleared the roads, but a dusting of snow already covered the path in front of the Weather Agency as she entered the parking lot, noticing a few familiar cars.

In the office of the Weather Agency, traditional *pansori* music flowed out of the speakers:

"The wind is the heavens' mysterious deed
so how could a mere human bring about the wind"
Zhou Yu asks Kong Ming
"A man can only plan but the heavens achieve
You can only do what you can
and the rest is up to the heavens"
"I shall go up to Mount Nanping and pray for the wind"
Making a promise to Zhou Yu, Kong Ming goes to pray for the
southeasterly wind
With a troop of five hundred soldiers
With a troop of five hundred infantry and one hundred and twen-
ty elite soldiers
Zhou Yi awaits further command as spirits fly high
and soldiers stand guarding their position
Zhou Yi rides alongside Lu Su to the mountains
His soldiers build a three-tier platform with red soil from the
southeast—
the size of the rectangular and circular platform is 240 zhang in
length
and each tier is three chi high, totaling nine chi
On the first tier he put the banners of the Twenty Eight Mansions

On the blue banner are the seven animals that symbolize the seven stars of the east
and the banner is placed to the east
on the black banner are the seven animals that symbolize the seven stars of the north
and the banner is placed to the north
on the white banner are the seven animals that symbolize the seven stars of the west
and the banner is placed to the west
on the red banner are the seven animals that symbolize the seven stars of the south
and the banner is placed to the south
Zhou Yi examines the sixty-four hexagrams of the sixty-four sides and lines up soldiers in eight ordinal and cardinal directions
He positions one soldier to the rear left holding the treasured sword
and another to the front left holding the incense burner
to have all see all the banners of the Twenty Eight Mansions

"Is this it?" Soojin asked as she entered the office of the Weather Agency.

Kim Eunkyung, who had been talking to Park Kugyong, heard her voice and turned.

"Come in," said Eunkyung.

Soojin said, "There's nothing here. I thought there was going to be a big ceremonial ritual or something."

"That's what I thought too," said Eunkyung. "It's the Weather Agency, so I came thinking they might be doing some rites or something, but nope."

Suh Ga-ul came into the office from another room. The moment she noticed Soojin, she shouted, "Oh no! She can't be here!"

Her voice was so loud that Eunkyung was embarrassed for Soojin, but Ga-ul didn't seem to have realized she yelled.

Soojin asked, "Why not? I'm not here to inspect anyone."

"It's bad luck," Ga-ul responded. "Having someone who doesn't believe in this stuff come here, you know."

"Who believes in this stuff?" Soojin asked, looking from Eunkyung to Kugyong.

Shrugging her shoulders, Eunkyung said, "Well, I kind of want to believe in it today. SoCal, I hope you can do something."

"Well, the entire Weather Agency's working right now. Don't you see how busy we are? I'm not here because of the emergency preparedness order."

"Why are you so busy?" Soojin asked.

Ga-ul answered, looking dumbfounded at being asked such an obvious question, "We correctly forecasted the heavy snowfall. Right down to the precise time it would begin, but no one's interested. Even before the chief of staff issued the emergency preparedness order, the entire Weather Agency was on emergency duty because of the snow."

"You get more attention when you're wrong. No one cares if you're right."

"You tell us not to believe in jinxes and enjoy making fun of the Weather Agency. But look! Even you come here when there's nothing else you can do. You've got to be sensible and believe in spells and stuff, right? 'A man can only plan, but the heavens achieve.' Even Kong Ming says so."

"Oh, is this the 'Song of the Red Cliff'? That's why you're playing this *pansori* music. The southeasterly wind just started blowing."

Soojin went and sat down on an empty chair. She listened carefully to the tune playing in the background.

"I would never have expected the Weather Agency to be so focused on the weather at a time like this. Especially now the asteroid has become a guided missile."

"I doubt it'll lead to total destruction. I wouldn't go so far as to say it's a guided missile."

"Well, you seem at ease."

"Not really," Ga-ul said, "But if we all go down together, then it doesn't matter much, does it? I did think of something to do once the snow stops. In preparation for the destruction of the world."

Soojin looked up at Ga-ul and asked, "What is it?"

"I'm going to organize all Earth's meteorological data. I'm considering how I could compile information to make it possible for non-Earthian meteorologists to understand. I don't know if I'll have enough time, though."

"What would you do that for?"

"I don't know. But if one day some alien meteorologist happens to find it, they might be able to figure out what the weather used to be like on Earth before its destruction, don't you think?"

"Heh, they say a physicist imagines intelligent alien beings to be physicists. I guess the Weather Agency's version of an alien is an alien weather specialist."

"Well, you must think of an alien acting inspector general, IG."

"No way. That's the most ridiculous alien imaginable."

Eunkyung chimed in, "Come to think of it, I think the alien that I imagine is an alien planetary government official. Park Cooking, have you ever imagined something like an alien PR officer?"

"Not really," answered Kugyong.

"But I don't think we'll need it," Ga-ul once again raised her voice. It wasn't to steer the conversation in her direction, but nevertheless the three people in the room looked over at her.

"Information about Earth's weather for alien weather special-ists, I mean," said Ga-ul.

Eunkyung asked, "Why not?"

"Because Handsome Man will take care of everything."

"I know. But we've never prepared for something like this. There's no precedent, and the conditions have changed. Even for someone like Han Summin."

"You'll see. Handsome Man doesn't get nervous."

"You say that with complete confidence."

"Of course, I know. She's an ace. You know what an ace is? People think it's someone who has the best record, or the per-son who scored the most goals in a season. But I realized some-thing while watching Handsome Man. How should I say this ... An ace is someone who scores a goal when your team is in des-perate need of one. Spectators tense up when they see the ball in the air heading towards the goal, and they cheer like crazy when it goes in, but an ace is the kind of person who scores the goal and just thinks of it as nothing special. To people like that, skill is just a tool and practice is just a precursor. Doing exactly what is necessary when it needs to happen is something spe-cial that can't be explained by skills or training. Instead of feel-ing pressured, they just naturally take care of the problem as if they'd been designed to handle that kind of situation from birth. Oh man, I must be going crazy or something. Am I in love with Handsome Man? I didn't think I'd gone that far."

Blankly staring into Ga-ul's face, Soojin fell into deep thought. Then quietly she murmured, "Doesn't everyone love her?"

"No," Ga-ul flatly answered and disappeared into the adjoin-ing room.

"How could they have failed?" asked Summin, looking at the small screen that was protruding toward her face. "It's not like the ASF's satellite is second-rate."

She was sitting in the pilot seat with everything configured to the right setting.

Looking at the same image on a different screen, Lieutenant Colonel Shim Jaesun, Director of the Orbit Operations Office, answered through the headset, "Perhaps because the ASF satellite has a head?"

"Hmm. It was incapacitated after being hit on the head, but if it didn't have a head, the rogue satellite could've damaged something else."

Lieutenant Colonel Shim organized his thoughts for a moment and offered his opinion in a rather business-like voice, "It must ultimately come down to reaction speed. I can't think of anything else. I don't know when they planted that satellite on the asteroid, but doesn't it look ancient? If we can hit it, then we'd be able to overpower it quite quickly."

"Regardless of whether it's an ancient device or not, due to the delay in response times, wouldn't it be difficult for us to hit it more than once unless we also have AI on our satellite, which we don't."

"So, what do we do?"

"We have to attack first."

"And if it blocks the attack?"

"How about if we design a sequence of attacks? We have three arms, so as we've seen before, a two-armed robot won't be able to restrain us completely. General Lee Jongro saw the simulated combat between our three-armed satellite and a two-armed opponent, so if he input some new sequence of attacks to be activated when the rogue satellite became active, as the ASF suspects is the case, the rogue satellite would know not to try holding down and restraining our satellite's arms. It'd probably instead aim to deflect our attacks."

"So we'd have to design a series of attacks?" asked Gu Yemin. "So that the guarding spacecraft can only respond in a way where it has to restrain two of the three arms on our satellite?"

"If we input a sequence of attacks, it would become difficult to block three arms with just two. And it's not the latest AI that's been mounted on the asteroid. If we could continue to attack without giving it a chance to strike back …"

"It could end up revealing a weak spot."

The snow stopped early in the morning. Around the same time the ROK Space Force's weaponized satellite reached the asteroid's orbit. Upon hearing the news as she woke up, Summin reviewed the attack sequence she'd practiced on the simulator.

Now, the ROK Space Force satellite did not have enough fuel to return to its original orbit. It only had fuel left for combat, and even that was barely enough.

"This is the second combat for the enemy spacecraft," said Gu Yemin. Then she asked, "What did the ASF say? Have they analyzed how much fuel the rogue satellite has left?"

The director of the Orbit Operations Office answered, "It seems it has more fuel than we do."

"Oh no. So time isn't going to increase our chance of winning."

"The longer the combat goes on for, the more disadvantageous it will be for us."

"We'll have to end this swiftly then."

Summin's face was displayed on a screen in the corner. She seemed relaxed as usual.

Gu Yemin was careful about making even the slightest movements, afraid that some might think she was nervous. She maintained a comfortable sitting position and only shifted her body slowly and with relaxed movements. The same went for her breathing—she made sure not to let out a long exhalation.

Um Jonghyun pushed open the door to the remote pilot station and entered just in time for the action. He quietly went and sat down in the corner. A little while later, the ROK Space Force's three-armed weaponized satellite unfolded its shield and arms, which had been hidden by the exterior frame. This was its very first time entering into attack mode in the months since it was launched. And it would also be its last.

Everything in space is fated to do one of the three things: remain still, keep going straight in one direction, or revolve around something. And when this whole thing was over, the ROK Space Force's satellite wouldn't simply drift away into empty space—its fate would be to continuously orbit Earth.

"The satellite is now active and ready. Pilot, test movements." The voice belonged to Senior Master Sergeant Shin Minhyung.

At his words, Summin moved each arm attached to the control device and briefly spoke into the microphone, "Everything's in working order."

The director of the Orbit Operations Office gave the next order.

"Skip the position control booster test."

Summin answered, "Skipping the position control booster test."

"Discard all shields. Equip three proximity weapons."

"Equipping three spears, one in each arm. Discarding the rest. Three, two, one, discarded."

"Stand by."

LAUNCH SOMETHING!

"Standing by."

The asteroid appeared on the pilot's screen. It was too small for its shape to be clearly defined, but the numbers appearing below it confirmed the asteroid's movement and relative distance from Earth.

The same image was transmitted to the main screen in the Launch Control Room, where the important people were gathered together. Everyone fixed their eyes on the screen and held their breath.

Another object appeared on the screen. It was the rogue satellite—much smaller yet showing up as being much hotter than the asteroid.

The director of the Orbit Operations Office summarized the situation.

"The enemy spacecraft is in sight. It is exposing an arm that it had unfolded in the previous combat."

The numbers below the rogue satellite indicating its movement and location suddenly changed from white to yellow.

"It has seen our satellite," the director of the Orbit Operations Office continued. "The rogue satellite has changed position. We've detected that its boosters are active."

His voice rang throughout the remote pilot station. The chief of staff held up her forefinger to point upwards first and then towards Han Summin, as though pressing an imaginary button. It was an order to begin the mission. Seeing this slow and restrained gesture, the director of the Orbit Operations Office reacted without hesitation.

"Activate boosters. Target, the enemy spacecraft. Charge in preemptive attack position."

"Activating boosters. Initiating attack."

The screen vibrated a little. The ROK Space Force weaponized satellite suddenly gained speed, but not even the slightest change could be detected in the vast space projected on the screen.

"Reaction delay is 2.217 seconds. Stop fuel injection."

"Stopping fuel injection," Summin repeated. "The time lag's shorter than I'd expected."

There seemed to be a hint of a smile in her voice—which might have been an illusion, but it was at least clear she wasn't anxious.

Moments later, the rogue satellite grew big enough on the screen for the spectators to recognize its shape. It meant that it was closer. The screen showed the rogue satellite looking at the friendly satellite, wielding its weapons.

The director of the Orbit Operations Office gave the next order.

"Launch the proximity weapons at low speed at an interval of 0.3 seconds."

"Launching proximity weapons. One, two, three."

"Good. Initiate rotation. Clockwise."

"Rotating in surprise attack mode."

The image on the screen slowly began to move counterclockwise. The three spears flying at the rogue satellite seemed like they were also slowly rotating. And finally, combat began.

Summin carefully studied the rogue satellite's two arms. With the axes it held in its hands, the rogue satellite blocked all three spears one after the other. One, two, three. Its arms were now in positions that Summin had expected, leaving its head fully exposed.

The three arms on the ROK Space Force satellite attacked the enemy's body all at once. The arms were positioned at roughly 120-degree angles; each had been manually arranged by Summin. The three arms on the rotating satellite frantically struck the rogue satellite. It might have looked as if the attacks were random, but each was a calculated move. As minute adjustments had to constantly be made, Summin couldn't just swing the arms without looking exactly where they landed.

That was why this was undoubtedly a lopsided fight from the beginning. If the rogue satellite had been given the time to observe and respond to the attacks, it would have been almost as if it was predicting them two seconds ahead of time. For the ROK Space Force satellite to keep up with the blows made by the AI-mounted rogue satellite, Summin had to make moves by imagining what would happen two seconds later. A whole two seconds.

According to the sequence input by Summin, the ROK Space Force satellite's arms moved either altogether at the same time or separately at short intervals, and before anyone knew it, she had blocked the proximity weapons in the rogue satellite's hands. Summin had hurled all three weapons away as soon as the combat began, but the arms in themselves were still powerful weapons. Particularly so since ROK Space Force had no reason to hold back, knowing that the satellite would be of no use after this combat.

Two minutes into combat, the rogue satellite began to let up a bit. Since there was no screen showing the fight from a third-person perspective, it was difficult for people who weren't experts to understand what was actually going on, but the ROK Space Force's weaponized satellite was using its three arms as three sets of huge teeth, biting off parts of the enemy spacecraft from three directions. It almost seemed as though they'd never operated as arms.

"We have a chance to win," whispered Jonghyun, sitting in the corner of the remote pilot station.

The command sergeant major sitting next to him answered in a low voice, "Not yet. We have to keep going this way to the end without making a single mistake. I'm not exaggerating—it really has to be that way."

The screen showed images after a delay, which meant that what people were seeing had already happened far away in space. On Earth, people only saw the results. The same images were being relayed to the Launch Control Room and a screen at the Allied Space Force. Even the screen that the remote pilot herself was watching relayed the same images, although the delay was slightly shorter.

The ROK Space Force satellite attacked with terrifying ferocity, but it couldn't afford to let up for even a fraction of a second. Summin matched every assault by her opponent, thinking, *So far, so good. That one was fine, and that next one. Things are going well so far. But only so far.*

Things were certainly going the best way imaginable, but the slightest change in the balance was sure to make the situation extremely difficult to fix.

"Huh!" Summin's voice rang through the headset. Without realizing, Gu Yemin leaned forward slightly. Everyone else in the room did the same.

"I missed," said Summin. "The AI changed pattern!"

Her voice was urgent, saying only the words necessary to relay the relevant information. Realizing that it couldn't win using the current pattern of movements, the AI program on the rogue satellite changed its attack and defense patterns. This meant that Summin's flow had been interrupted, and the two-second delay between the command input and output could now turn the tables. It was what everyone in the remote pilot station had been worried about.

But Summin spoke in a calm, dry voice, "Responding manually."

It was now free hand-to-hand combat, no longer adhering to a planned sequence of movements. An unchartered territory that hadn't been prepared in advance. A situation in which Summin had to instantly respond to an opponent's moves that were impossible to see in real-time. The only thing on Summin's side was her intuition. Based on the last three minutes of data, she had to preempt the enemy spacecraft's moves that would only be visible on her screen two seconds later.

The screen displaying the ROK Space Force satellite's status showed the damage it had received. An alert popped up, but Summin couldn't afford a glance.

She instead checked the amount of remaining fuel and turned on the boosters. The display moved chaotically. The rogue satellite disappeared from view, and instead, vast space unfolded in front. When Summin swiftly activated the control device, the rogue satellite appeared on the screen once again. It was a bit smaller, as it was slightly further away.

"Resetting the combat situation. Changing pattern. The enemy will attempt to grab the friendly spacecraft. Launching a preemptive attack."

As Summin said those words, she flew her spacecraft toward the rogue satellite at maximum speed. She stretched out two of the three arms to attack her opponent's body. Summin needed time to confirm the success of the attack, but even before the result of the move was transmitted to the screen, she had input her next moves.

It was clear that the AI was reacting with a different sequence of movements than before. Contrary to Summin's expectation, however, the rogue satellite didn't try to grab onto both her satellite's two attacking arms. Instead, it made a compromise, grabbing one arm and fending off the other one. Then it moved its free arm to block the third arm, which Summin had set to deal a finishing blow.

"Oh!"

Someone's voice was heard through the headset. It was the moment Summin's plan went south. The AI program on the enemy spacecraft had accurately blocked Summin's attack with its free arm. Summin's face hardened.

"Oh no," someone else exclaimed in terror, unable to hold back.

It was what everyone wanted to scream into the air but had been suppressing for as long as possible. The exclamation hadn't been loud, but it had been piercing.

The resulting scene was transmitted onto the screens—two of the arms controlled by Summin were now restrained, and as the rogue satellite flexed its arms, it broke them both off. As before, the image was transmitted to the screens in the remote pilot station, the Launch Control Room, and the office of the Allied Space Forces.

Everyone grew quiet. Even those who had been nervously fidgeting kept still. Not a single sigh, gesture, or exclamation could be detected. Had a broadcasting company been streaming this, a voiceover would have said, "And now a word from our sponsors!" at this point.

Sitting in the corner of the remote pilot station, Jonghyun

squeezed his eyes shut. Gu Yemin couldn't even blink. No one dared inhale a breath—the air was thick with tension.

At that moment, a voice flowed out of the speakers.

"Got it."

It was Summin. Gu Yemin snapped her head towards the screen showing Summin's face—Summin's peaceful face.

"What's going on?" Gu Yemin asked. "What happened?"

Summin moved her foot to slightly change the position of her satellite. The camera transmitting the images to the main screen now pointed up, showing the scene that had been obscured from view.

One of the ROK Space Force's two arms—one of the arms that had just been ripped off—was lodged deep in the place where the enemy's head should have been.

The rogue satellite was no longer moving. That image was Summin's answer to Gu Yemin's question. Summin was the only one who had seen her opponent's demise.

Pulling out the arm from the rogue satellite that had once been friendly, Summin said, "The front line of humanity is still standing strong."

A good demonstration of just how far ahead Han Summin was from her peers is the delay it took for observers to understand what had happened: about seven seconds after defeating the rouge satellite, cheers finally erupted from the crowd. From that seven second time delay, Um Jonghyun, Space Force's Captain Parachute, calculated that Summin was at least 3.5 light-seconds ahead of other humans.

Jonghyun joined the cheering crowd with a roar. This was also the first and the last time most of the people in that room saw the Space Force's chief of staff let out a celebratory yell.

"Excuse me. It's not over yet."

At Summin's voice, everyone in the room stopped cheering and returned to their seats. The room grew quiet in a fraction of a second, and in the embarrassed silence, some people burst out in nervous laughter.

Only Summin spoke in a serious voice, "Someone please contact the Allied Space Force and tell me how to access the thruster system on the asteroid so I can move it to safety."

Looking gaunt, Gu Yemin opened the door to the conference room in the basement of the museum building. Lee Jongro, who was sitting and staring at the wall, turned to look at her. Gu Yemin went and sat down in the chair closest to him and gazed at the empty table without a word.

After a long silence, Gu Yemin was the first to speak.

"I wondered who was going to crack first, and it was Oren Cosby."

Lee Jongro hesitated whether to say anything in response, then answered, "I'd assumed as much."

"So you knew he'd crack first."

"He worked under me."

Another long silence followed. Gu Yemin's eyes were back on the table.

"Is it over?" Lee Jongro asked, unable to hide his curiosity. Gu Yemin slowly turned her gaze over to him.

"We figured out almost the entire escape route you had in place for Cosby and Waters once they were finished with hacking the system planted on the asteroid and the AI-mounted satellite. It was an impossible way to escape. I assume you weren't going to let them get away so easily?"

LAUNCH SOMETHING!

"I know nothing about that."

"Still making excuses even at this point?"

A weak smile appeared on Gu Yemin's face.

"You couldn't stop it could you. Is it over?" Lee Jongro asked again.

"Are you satisfied?" Gu Yemin asked in return.

"I'm not sure."

"The entirety of humanity is about to be wiped off the face of the universe."

Lee Jongro's face seemed somewhat peaceful.

"That's not true," he said. "We still have Mars."

"Heh. Sure. Of course. We still have Mars."

"It'll take shorter than you think for Mars to reach Earth's level of civilization. And people will return to Earth in the future."

"But did you have to go to these lengths?"

Wordlessly, Lee Jongro stared at Gu Yemin. After slightly parting and closing his lips a few times, he finally answered, "I had no choice."

"No, that can't be true. You had no other choice than to crash an asteroid into Earth to draw our attention to Mars? None at all?"

"You don't have to understand."

"Sure. And I don't want to understand. Well, let's get back to work."

"Work?"

"We have to sort things out. You mentioned Martians eventually returning to Earth, well they'll be curious about this."

"About what?"

"Was it you who first suggested this, or was it Cosby and Waters?"

"Oh, which came first. They didn't bring the information about the asteroid to me, per se, but they sure did talk about it a lot. They bragged about it. Saying that the Allied Space Force was doing something suspect, and that they'd been involved. They said they had no idea what they were working on at the time, but eventually found out it had to do with the security system for the equipment that was to be planted on the asteroid."

"And they'd planted something? Kind of like a Trojan horse?"

"They're dubious personalities. They made huge profits through similar schemes."

"So you planned all this upon hearing that?"

"Not immediately. I'd been too busy then. I simply hired them as civilian advisors. Though I didn't give them anything to do and only paid them. But that was fine, since it wasn't my money."

"It seems that they'd wielded enough power to get on Martian extremist group's list of assassination targets, but from your position, I suppose they weren't very important. What happened after you hired them as advisors?"

Lee Jongro answered, "They must have thought that it could make them some big money, because they brought me detailed information. Detailed enough for me to draw up a specific plan."

"And so you drew up this grandiose plan."

"No matter how skilled those two were in what they did, executing the plan wasn't up to them."

Gu Yemin leaned back into her chair. Anyone could see that she'd spent the entire night in nervous suspense. Watching her, Lee Jongro's facial expression grew even more relaxed.

"You did well," he said. "Much better than I'd expected."

Gu Yemin looked at him as he said those words.

Taking her silence as a response, he continued, "It was just that I planned it all for so long, and I acted so quickly."

"Is that so? So if I had more time, you think I would've been able to thwart your plan?"

"I'm certain that you would have. But you were too obsessed with the idea that your monster of a weaponized satellite would ever be effective out there in space. Probably because of the pilot, I assume. Master Sergeant Han Summin. Ultimately, she's the reason everything turned out this way."

Gu Yemin slumped into the chair comfortably. She now appeared much too relaxed. Lee Jongro's eyes wavered. Soon he looked wary. The haughty confidence that had been exuding from him vanished entirely.

"Han Summin's the reason everything turned out this way," said Gu Yemin.

Lee Jongro didn't answer her. Instead, his eyes widened slightly.

Gu Yemin leaned forward and said, "That was probably the biggest crisis I've faced. Do you know what I'm talking about?"

"So it's not over."

"Oh, it is over. But not in the way you wanted it to end. Let me ask you one more time. Do you know what the biggest crisis I've faced in my entire career was?"

Lee Jongro faintly shook his head. It was almost as though he'd moved involuntarily. Gu Yemin smiled as she looked up at the ceiling.

"It was when you tried to recruit Han Summin through a private company. At the time I wasn't worried at all since there was little chance that she'd be won over. But when I look back on it, I feel weak at the knees. Even if the odds were close to zero, had I lost Han Summin then, how would things have turned out today?"

"I see. So you've succeeded. But how? The time delay would've been no less than two seconds."

"Two-point-two seconds, to be precise. It was simply impossible. I have no idea how she made it work. I saw it, but I can't understand it. It's a matter of instinct, so she would be the only one who knows. But do you know what makes me feel even more faint? That I'd almost lost Han Summin once before that. When she was a first-year at the Aerospace High School. That was a close call. I honestly thought she was going to drop out. I miraculously managed to help her graduate."

Lee Jongro pursed his lips. Gu Yemin was about to continue in all excitement, but she stopped, seeing how he wasn't at all responsive. Wearily, she got up from her chair and said goodbye to Lee Jongro.

"I'll see you again. Although, we may be meeting in a much smaller room next time. There won't be any magazines, so no need to worry about that."

Lee Jongro squeezed out a smile. It was a bizarre smile forced out of stubbornness, not wanting to admit that he'd lost.

"This is not the end. That incident will come back to bite you."

"That incident?"

"The fact that I'd given you advance intelligence on the Pac-Man solar reflector terrorism."

Gu Yemin turned a deaf ear to his words. Instead, she chose the welcome relief and peace that had come to greet her at the door.

Remote pilot Han Summin lay on the couch in the first-floor lounge of the single occupant dormitory and blankly stared at the ceiling. Suh Ga-ul noticed her as she walked into the lounge and went over, sticking her face right in Summin's.

"Handsome Man! What are you doing here? Why are you lying here looking as if the world has ended?"

"I'm done for."

"What are you talking about? Haven't you heard? No one's done for!"

LAUNCH SOMETHING!

"I trained like a devil to pilot that satellite, but it was a single-use spacecraft! I tried really hard to get it back again, but … Man, what am I going to do now?"

At Summin's words, Ga-ul turned to the group nearby sitting at a table watching television.

"Captain Park Cooking! Didn't you say that the Public Relations Corps is going to publicize what Summin did? It looks like she has no idea about that. Isn't she going to be a world star now?"

Kugyong readily answered her, "Of course! HQ said they were going to send someone over, but I refused. Told them this was my turf."

Soojin, who had been sitting across from Kugyong, sided with Summin. "But what Summin said is true. Whether she's a star or not, the Republic of Korea Space Force no longer has a satellite. Oh, that reminds me. My spacecraft accident investigation …"

"What's that?" Ga-ul asked.

Eunkyung blandly answered, "Soojin's in the same boat. Her life's goal was to build a career investigating spacecraft accidents and then leave the Space Force for a lucrative private company, but the only spacecraft we had was heroically destroyed in combat the first day it was put into action."

"Oh, that makes sense," Ga-ul said. "That's what I meant that day. That it was unlucky for Shoojeans to be there at the Weather Agency. Someone who was wishing for an accident to happen was in our midst! I knew I felt an evil force lurking among us."

At that moment, Jonghyun entered the lounge and caught Ga-ul's last few words.

"Are you talking about me?" he asked.

"Oh, here he is," Eunkyung said. "The chief of staff's unseen right hand."

Jonghyun shook his head at Eunkyung's words.

"That rumor's been plaguing me. What's all this about being parachuted in unseen? Geez. Why is Sergeant Han lying there like that?"

Ga-ul answered, "I don't know. She says it's because she no longer has a spacecraft to pilot."

"Oh, I see," Jonghyun said. "I'm sure she'll get one in a little while. She'll be hailed as a hero and soon be too busy to do anything because she'll be summoned here and there. Is it OK to leave her like that?"

"A hero?" Summin snorted, staring into the ceiling. "I'm screwed. Completely screwed. I trained so hard to pilot that satellite. In a few years, AI programs will catch up and surpass me."

She sounded utterly dejected.

Jonghyun offered a word of consolation, "I saw mint chocolate bars at the exchange. Three different kinds."

Summin's grumblings stopped immediately. Kugyong also had his own news.

"Oh, Oste's resuming his radio show. *Let's Raise the Density!* is making a comeback. He said he'll be here in a few days."

Summin sat up from the couch at lightning speed.

"Really?" she asked.

"Why would I lie? I'm pretty sure that you'll be on the show."

"What? For real? Oh my gosh, this is crazy! I must have done something great in my past life or something!"

At Summin's words, everyone in the lounge snapped their heads around toward her.

"What? In a *past* life?"

Soojin looked at her ludicrously, but Summin sat confused, asking, "What?"

The Pac-Man sun was gone, but the following year's spring was still short, and the summer still long. The Earth gained a new satellite much earlier than expected, but the Allied Space Force didn't want to make a fuss out of it. A new administrative system was to be introduced in Korea's direct-controlled municipality on Mars. A civilian vice-minister of Mars was expected to head over from Earth, but as the interplanetary shuttle was unable to take off in time, the trip had to be delayed for about two years.

People would later speak of Earth as a planet that should've been destroyed back then. The international treaty remained firm in place, and the Republic of Korea's Ministry of Defense remained uneasy about the Space Force. At every chance, the chief of staff requested the purchase of a spaceship and an aircraft carrier and continued to relocate people to the launch base. Two weeks into the new year, the construction of the new dormitory was completed, but because there were so many people who had been dispatched to the launch base, most spacenauts still had to share a suite with a roommate. The food at the mess hall, of course, was no better than before.

All things in space move according to three laws of motion: remain still, continuously travel in one direction, or revolve around another body. Using a combination of these three motions, the ROK Space Force strove to protect humanity from all things that threaten the peace and safety of the world. Of course, of these three motions, they particularly favored revolving round and round.

The revolving front line of humanity would remain strong as for a long, long time.

Author's Note

The inspiration for the first page of this novel was the ridiculous heatwave in the summer of 2018. I say this to clarify that this novel was not influenced by the US president's idea of the Space Force that was announced afterward.

I received an interview request from a magazine titled *Air Force* because I was a writer who had formerly served in the Republic of Korea Air Force. During the interview, I thought, "Huh, what kind of military is this?" I wasn't overjoyed about having to do the interview, but it turned out to be very entertaining. As you may know, the Air Force has a relatively laid-back atmosphere compared to other military branches. Sometimes, to the point where you'd think, "Are we really supposed to be doing this?" I expanded on that idea of a "strange military branch" with the addition of a sci-fi element to create the atmosphere of the Space Force in this novel. The Republic of Korea Space Force does not exist in reality, so I hope there is no misunderstanding about people who are in a similar line of work.

The storyline about the Korean settlement on Mars, which is an essential part of the novel, was written based on the basic elements introduced in my novella titled "Conjunction Holidays," published in the sci-fi anthology *Because We Still Have Time* (Hankyoreh Publishing, 2017). In short, those elements were related to the idea of a "single civilization that has settled down on two different planets," including the Martian calendar, the daily changing time difference, and the changes in the Earth people's perspective of the Martians and vice versa. They pose questions that should be examined in depth, but I didn't go into those issues in *Launch Something!* It was a slightly un-science-fictiony choice.

Science fiction writers often think about whether readers will actually enjoy stories that delve deep into certain subjects, almost like research. Some might enjoy such stories, but others might loathe them. It is always tricky to find the right balance, particularly since there is no correct answer. There isn't a single "right balance" in the world, and the balance changes with the medium, reader, or even just the flow of time. Therefore the mission of a science fiction writer in the pioneer era must be to explore as many points of balance as possible.

In that context, the narrative style of *Launch Something!* differs significantly from my other works over the past fifteen years. The narrator is far removed from the events that unfold in the novel, and it took me about two years to develop, polish, and refine this kind of writing style. I am grateful for those who worked on it with me during that time, and I hope that the readers can find more room to breathe, as much as the narrator's distance provides. Because—I notice it sometimes as I write—the narrator of a novel can be rather stifling at times.

For Korean protagonists to take on active roles in space, Korean writers often have to borrow and use foreign institutions such as NASA. Even though it's only for the purpose of writing fiction, I can't help but feel as if I'm trespassing on someone else's territory. But this time, I was able to write with confidence instead of feeling like a trespasser. After all, this is a story about the Republic of Korea Space Force. With the hope that many readers will find comfort in that as I have, I will now take my leave and retreat to a place more distant than the position of this novel's narrator.

Bae Myung-hoon
March 2020